SOUVENIR

Therese Fowler grew up in the American Midwest, where there was lots of room for her imagination to grow alongside the corn. After years of working part-time, writing in her spare time, and almost giving up, Therese stumbled across an idea close to her heart: the untimely loss of her mother, the wish that her mother had left some of her own words behind, and her belief that there is such a thing as true love. Her debut novel *Souvenir* followed, and has been sold worldwide.

Therese now resides in North Carolina with her husband and sons and is working on her second novel. For more information, visit her website at www.theresefowler.com.

Visit www.AuthorTracker.co.uk for exclusive updates on Therese Fowler.

THERESE FOWLER

Souvenir

AVON

This novel is entirely a work of fiction.
The names, characters and incidents portrayed in it are
the work of the author's imagination. Any resemblance to
actual persons, living or dead, events or localities is
entirely coincidental.

AVON

A division of HarperCollins*Publishers*
77–85 Fulham Palace Road,
London W6 8JB

www.harpercollins.co.uk

This production 2011

Copyright © Therese Fowler 2007

'What You Won't Do for Love' Words and Music by Alfons Kettner and
Bobby Caldwell © 1978, EMI Longitude Music, USA. Reproduced by
permission of EMI Music Publishing Ltd, London WC2H 0QY

'Anthem' Lyrics by Leonard Cohen
© Sony/ATV Music Publishing
All Rights Reserved

Therese Fowler asserts the moral right to
be identified as the author of this work

A catalogue record for this book is
available from the British Library

ISBN: 978-0-00789-976-0

Set in Minion by Palimpsest Book Production Limited,
Grangemouth, Stirlingshire

Printed and bound in Great Britain by
Clays Ltd, St Ives plc

This one is for Mom, whom I like to believe was reading over my shoulder.

*Love is a promise, love is a souvenir, once given
never forgotten, never let it disappear.*

John Lennon

Do, for love, what you would not do.

PROLOGUE

August 1989

What she was doing was wrong. But then, everything was wrong, wasn't it?

She was sneaking out to see Carson, even though in thirteen hours she'd be another man's wife. *Brian's* wife. Brian's *wife*. No matter how she phrased the words, they hardly made sense to her, even now. They belonged to someone else's reality. It was as if she, Meg Powell, would cease to exist at the end of the wedding ceremony, becoming some unfamiliar woman called Mrs Brian Hamilton. But maybe it was better that way.

She left her house in the dark and traced the familiar path through the pastures, toward the lake and the groves and Carson's house. The sun would rise before much longer, and her sisters would wake, excited – *Meg's wedding day!* Her parents would find her note saying she'd gone for a walk and wouldn't be concerned. They'd know she'd be back in plenty of time; she was nothing if not reliable and responsible. A model daughter. Their deliverance.

And she was glad to be those things. If only she could shut down the Meg who still longed for the future she'd sacrificed. This visit to Carson was meant to do that, to shut it down. *This* part of her mission was appropriate, at least; this was the part she would explain to him. If she knew Carson – and after sixteen years of best-friendship, she knew only herself better – he would accept the partial truth without suspecting there was anything more to it.

She wanted so much to tell him the truth about the rest, to explain why she was marrying Brian. But besides jeopardizing everything, it would make him want to try to fix things. If that had been possible, there would not now be a breathtaking four-thousand-dollar wedding gown waiting in her bedroom like a fairy tale in progress. The thought of it hanging from her closet door, specter-like, made her shudder; she'd read enough fairy tales to know they didn't always end happily.

Carson lived in a converted shed on his parent's Florida citrus farm. The McKay farm adjoined her family's horse farm, sharing an east–west line of wood posts and barbed wire. The fence kept the horses out of the groves but had never been a serious obstacle for Meg or her three younger sisters or Carson. When she was seven or eight years old, they'd found a wooden ladder and sawed it in half, then propped the halves on opposite sides of a post to make their passage easy. Meg wasn't surprised, now, to see the ladder gone. Climbing the barbed wire, she took care not to get a cut she'd be hard pressed to explain tonight.

Fifteen minutes later she emerged from the shadows of the orange grove and stopped. In the light of the setting moon she could see the shed, its white clapboard siding and dark windows, a hundred yards to the left of the main house. She and Carson had spent most of his senior year working with his father to renovate it, creating two downstairs rooms and an upstairs bedroom loft. They'd called the shed their love nest, not only because they first made love there but also because they meant for it to become their home. Not for always, just for starters. The plan had been to eventually build a new house on the far side of his farm. On the wooded hillside where, as children, they'd hung a tire swing for themselves and her sisters. Where, years later, they had spread an old horse blanket and gone as far as they dared without protection.

This morning, she was purposely – some might say selfishly – no better prepared.

Though the day would grow hot later, the moist air and light breeze chilled her by the time she reached his door. Her feet were wet inside white canvas sneakers, her thighs hardly covered by cut-off denim shorts. She was braless beneath Carson's John Deere T-shirt, could feel her nipples pulled in tight and small. Her gold chain, his gift to her on her nineteenth birthday two years earlier, lay cool against her damp skin.

She hesitated before putting her hand on his doorknob, imagining what Brian would do if he knew she had come here, imagining her parents' disappointment and distress if she spoiled the plan, imagining that she might hate herself even more, later – and then she turned the knob.

The door was unlocked, as she'd known it would be. No need to lock your doors out here; everything of value was kept outside the house – for Carson or for almost anyone who made a living off the land. In the implement shed was a new pair of mortgaged tractors that had cost upward of $80,000 apiece. In the barn was a treasured thoroughbred bay – Carolyn McKay's 'hobby' that helped make up for being unable to have more children after Carson. Meg knew the details of the McKays' lives intimately. But when she left here later this morning, she would do everything possible to forget them.

She stepped inside and eased the door closed, wanting Carson's first awareness of her to be when she slid beneath his covers. She stood and let her eyes adjust to the darkness. The place still smelled slightly of cut pine and stained wood and curry, one of Carson's favorite flavors.

When she could see, she crossed the wide front room to the stairs that divided it from the kitchen. Grabbing the railing, she pushed off her sneakers and began climbing the stairs. A tread creaked underfoot and she paused, waiting, her heart loud in her ears, then went on. By the eighth step she could see into the dark loft. She stopped and listened for the sound of Carson's even breathing. Though they'd spent only a few nights together as adults, they had slept over at each other's homes innumerable times as children. She knew the sound of his sleeping self almost as well as she did her sister Kara's. Before Brian and his unexpected proposal eighteen months earlier, Carson had been the son her parents never had, and she had been Carolyn and Jim's adopted daughter.

Straining to hear Carson, the only sound she could make out was the low hum of his refrigerator, and then the *chirpee-chirpee-chirpee* of a cardinal in a nearby tree, announcing the sun's progress. She climbed the remaining steps, cringing at another creak, then stopped, trying to make out his form on the bed at the far side of the room.

'Does this mean you changed your mind?'

Meg jumped as if stung. There was Carson, sitting in the love seat they'd once hauled away from a bankrupt orange grower's estate sale. She couldn't quite see his expression, but she could hear in his voice that he was wide awake.

With all her heart, she wished she could say yes, her presence meant exactly what he guessed. But softly she said, 'No.'

'Then why are you—?'

'Shh,' she said, going to him and reaching for his hand. 'Come here.'

He stood, and before he could speak again, she kissed him hard, kissed him until she felt dizzy and brave and determined not to chicken out. She put his hands on the hem of her shirt and, with her hands on his, helped him draw it over her head. In another moment, they were undressed and lying on top of his sheets, the pale light painting them moonlit blue.

One last time. She would savor every touch, every

sensation, the fullness of his lips, his squared jaw, the dark stubble as it rubbed her neck and grazed her breasts. She would not forget one moment of this, would always look back and remember how making love with him *transported* her. She would keep the memory like a priceless, irreplaceable jewel. She would remember how he pressed into her as if his life, *their* lives, depended on it, as if he could secure eternity.

Afterward, Carson lay on his side watching her, twisting a strand of her coppery hair. 'What other proof do you need?' he asked. His eyes shone with determination and hope, and she had to look away. Her first loyalty was to her family; how could it be otherwise? She had to marry Brian for their sake, was resigned to it, would do it and would try to never second-guess herself afterward; this she had already vowed.

'I know how it seems,' she said, 'but that's exactly why it can never work. We're too intense. *That's* what this proves.' The lie, same as she'd told him a year and a half before, tasted bitter. Love that had grown from childhood friendship and adolescent curiosity, that had now withstood so many long months of complete separation, could never be a damaging, undesirable thing – and yet that was the story she was selling.

He sat up and looked away. 'I should've made you leave as soon as I heard you open the door.'

'No,' she said, touching his back. 'We needed to do this, so we can put our past to rest.' This much at least was true, she thought.

He looked over his shoulder at her, eyes narrowed. 'You think this, one last quick fuck, is going to do it?'

he spat, making her flinch. 'You thought you could come here and offer something you *knew* I couldn't resist, and then marry Hamilton with a clear conscience? You are unbelievable.' He lunged out of bed and pulled on his jeans, keeping his back to her.

The matter of her guilty conscience – and God knew it *was* guilty – was balanced by the good she was doing her sisters, her parents. What he said was *exactly* what she'd thought, and what she would do. She stood up and pulled on her shirt, absorbing his anger, deserving it. Then she reached up and unhooked her gold chain from her neck.

'I never took this off,' she told him as she draped it around his, hooked it, then smoothed his wavy brown hair, filing away yet another last sense of him.

'Not even when he—'

'Not even then.'

Carson turned and looked down at her. 'Does he know I gave it to you?'

She nodded.

'Then he's as stupid as I am,' he said, moving away from her to the window, to a view of endless rows of orange trees lit emerald by the early sun.

She loved that view, the way the Earth always looked newborn there in the rising mist. But by this evening, the view would be as lost to her as if she'd left the planet. Brian's apartment windows did not look out on this, the kind of life she was born to. She would be a businessman's wife. The man she would see on all her future mornings would not be this rangy one, whose long fingers were equally capable of picking fruit or strumming a guitar – or holding her hand or feeding her pizza or braiding her hair. Once she left here, she would never touch Carson again.

The thought was a gut punch. How, *how* could she have let this happen?

Her longing to take back her bargain with the Hamiltons surged, so strong it threatened to undo her. She could take it all back, reclaim her life as her own . . . If Carson would push her just a *little*, if he tried to persuade her, if he assured her that everything he didn't even know was wrong would somehow turn out all right, she would come back to him.

But he stayed at the window, his heart already closing to her, and the moment passed.

She finished dressing, engulfed by regret but still daring to hope she would take a part of him with her, if God or fate allowed. Then she went to him and touched his arm.

He jerked away. 'You better go,' he said, turning. His face was closed now, too. This shouldn't upset her – she had it coming, all his anger, all his venom, the chill of such a blank look – and yet she was cut through by it.

'Okay.' She would *not* let herself cry.

'But here – let me give you this.' He put his hand on her cheek and leaned in, kissed her with slow deliberation, kissed her with such passion and grace that she could no longer hold back her tears. Then he pushed her away and said, 'Guess I'll see you in hell.'

PART I

God gave us memory so that we might have roses in December.

— *James Barrie*

ONE

Reminders. Meg didn't need more of them, but that's what she got when her father let her into his new apartment at the Horizon Center for Seniors Wednesday evening. He held out a plastic grocery bag.

'What's in there?'

'Notebooks, from your mother's desk,' he said. 'Take 'em now, before I forget.'

He did more and more of that lately, forgetting. *Idiopathic short-term memory loss* was his doctor's name for his condition, which right now was more an irritation than an issue. *Idiopathic*, meaning there was no particular explanation. Idiopathic was an apt term for Spencer Powell, a man who lived entirely according to his whims.

Meg took the bag and set it on the dining table along with her purse. This would be a short visit, coming at the end of her twelve-hour day. Hospital rounds at seven AM, two morning deliveries, a candy-bar lunch, and then four hours of back-to-back patients at her practice – women stressing about episiotomies,

13

C-section pain, stretch marks, unending fetal hiccups, heavy periods, lack of sex drive, fear of labor. And still four hours to go before she was likely to hit the sheets for five. An exhausting grind at times, but she loved her work. The ideal of it, at least.

'So how was today?' she asked, taking the clip out of her shoulder-length hair and shaking it loose. 'Are you finding your way around all right?'

'Colorful place,' he said, leading her to the living room. He sat in his recliner – why did old men seem always to have one, fraying and squeaky, with which they wouldn't part? 'Pair o' guys over in wing C got a great system for winning on the dogs.'

The greyhounds, he meant. 'Is that right?' she asked, looking him over. He looked spry as ever, and his eyes had regained the smile she'd never seen dimmed before last fall. His hair, once the brightest copper, had gone full silver, making him seem more distinguished somehow, silver being more valuable than copper. Distinguished, but no less wild than before – a man whose mind was always a step ahead of his sense. His diabetes was in check, but since her mother had died suddenly seven months earlier, Meg felt compelled to watch him closely. She was looking for signs of failing health, diabetic danger signals: swollen ankles, extra fluid in the face, unusual behaviors. *All* his behaviors were unusual, though, so that part was difficult.

The other difficult thing was how he kept confronting her with random pieces of her mother's life. A pitted chrome teapot. Stiff and faded blue doilies from their old dining hutch. Rose-scented bath powder,

14

in a round cardboard container with a round puff inside. Last week, a paper bag of pinecones dipped in glitter-thick wax. Trivia from a life forever altered by the sudden seizure of Anna Powell's heart, like a car's engine after driving too long without oil.

'Yeah, those boys said they win more'n they lose, so what's not to like about that? Hey – my left kidney's acting up again. Steady pain, kinda dull, mostly. What d'ya s'pose that's about?'

'Call Dr Aimes,' she said, as she always did when he brought up anything relating to his kidneys. 'Tomorrow. Don't wait.' He looked all right – but then, she'd thought her mother had too. What a good doctor *she* was; she should've seen the signs of runaway hypertension, should've known a massive heart attack was pending. She never should have taken her mother's word that she was doing fine on the blood pressure medication, nothing to worry about at all.

Her father frowned in annoyance, as he always did when she wouldn't diagnose him. 'What good are you?'

'If you go into labor, I'll be glad to help out. Otherwise, tell Dr Aimes.' She would remind him again when she called tomorrow.

His apartment was modest – one bedroom, one bath, a combined dining-living area, and a kitchen – but comfortable, furnished mostly with new things. He'd sold the business, Powell's Breeding and Boarding, along with the house and all the property, in order to move here. She didn't know the financial details because he'd insisted on handling that part of things himself. But he assured her he could afford to 'modernize' a little, as he'd put it.

Meg looked around, glad to not see much of her mother here. Memories were like spinning blades: dangerous at close range. Her mother's empty swivel rocker, placed alongside the recliner, would take some getting used to. If her father would just stop regurgitating things from the farm – or send them to her sisters, all of whom wisely lived out of state – she might be able to get comfortable with the new order. Was that his strategy, too? Was he giving things away so that he didn't have to be reminded of his loss every time he opened a closet or a drawer? He certainly wasn't much for facing the past, himself. The past was where all his failures lived.

Well, they had that in common.

He pulled the recliner's lever and stretched out. 'So yeah, I'm doin' fine. Whyn't you bring Savannah over Sunday; we'll have dinner in this establishment's fine dining room. They just put in one of them self-serve ice cream machines, you know what I'm talking about? Toppings, too. Y'oughta see the old farts elbowing each other to get there first! If I'd known this place was so entertaining, I'd've moved Mom here. This would be her kind of place, don't you think? Lots of biddies around to cackle with.'

'Sure, she would've liked it a lot,' Meg said. The farm had overwhelmed her mother perpetually, even after Brian and his father – officially Hamilton Savings and Loan – forgave her parents' mortgage as promised. In the years afterward, Meg liked to take her mother out to lunch for a break and a treat; she offered her spending money (as she secretly did her sisters too), but the reply was always, 'Oh, heavens no, Meggie. You've done so much as it is. Besides, you know your father.'

She did. Though cursed with a black thumb for profits, he was too proud to let her put cash in their hands. He hadn't been too proud, though, to let her – to *encourage* her – to take Brian's offer. That was different; no money changed hands. Meg hadn't had to give up anything – Carson didn't count. It was her choice anyway, that's what he always said.

'Hey – whyn't you bring our girl over here for dinner Sunday?' He said this as if the idea had just occurred to him.

She stood next to his chair, noting how his invitation didn't include Brian – intentionally? 'I'll do that,' she said. 'Right now I need to get going.'

'Okay, fine, go on, Miss Hectic Schedule. I know, you got things to do. Y'oughta enjoy the ride a little more, though. Now that you can. Don't you think? I'm fine here, everything's settled. I don't know why you don't just get on with your life.'

Now that she could? What was he talking about?

He continued, 'You're not happy. I've known that for a long time. Move forward, Meggie, while you're still young.'

She looked at him quizzically – he didn't always make sense, but he hated having it pointed out – and kissed him without pursuing it. 'I'm fine, Dad,' she said. 'It's just been a long day.'

TWO

'The northeast side's where the best waves are,' yelled Valerie Haas, over the sputtering whine of the motorbikes she and Carson McKay had rented for their excursion on St Martin. The West Indies isle, known for its split Dutch and French identity, was one of three islands they were considering for their wedding location, as well as the site of a vacation home. 'And the nude beaches are there, too!'

'Where's a good bar?' Carson yelled back, ready to be done with the noise and the hot wind and the vibration in his crotch, nude beaches or not.

He preferred riding horses to motorcycles by far, and was riding this souped-up scooter only in deference to Val. She would've had him on something much more powerful if it had been available to them – something worthy of a motocross track – and had been disappointed to have to settle for only 100 cc's. She wouldn't even consider the little Suzuki SUVs, insisting that the best views were accessible only with the bikes. He had to admit she was right; the roads up the low mountains deteriorated as they got farther from the small coastal towns, and a few times they'd taken mere trails to different points of interest. Val had wanted to locate a home rumored to have belonged to Brad Pitt and Jennifer Aniston several years back. Though the house wasn't officially on the market, they were told, she thought it might be fun to buy it if possible – a surefire conversation starter, she'd called it, as if their lives weren't already full of those. They found the house this morning, tucked into the hills of the island's French side, but he wasn't wild about its rocky landscape and lack of large shade trees. Val, raised in Malibu, would have gone for it anyway. Carson thought of the lushness of central Florida, the oaks and cedars and palms and twining, flowering vines, and declared that notoriety wasn't enough to persuade him.

Now he pointed to the side of the gravel road, indicating that he was pulling over.

'You're not done already?' Val said when she came to a stop next to him.

The sun pressed heavy on his forehead, forcing sweat down the sides of his neck. He wiped it away. ''Fraid so,' he said.

'We aren't even close to finishing the tour.'

He snorted. They'd been out since seven-thirty, and it was closing in on two o'clock. Lunch had been fried plantains and some fizzy fruit soda at a roadside stand. 'Feel free to go on, but I'm heading back to the villas.' There was a terrific bar there, and, should he happen to consume a drink or two more than made it safe to ride, he'd already be 'home'.

Val pushed her sunglasses up onto her shaggy white-blond hair and squinted at him. 'Okay, I'll go back with you – *if* you make it worth my while,' she said, grinning that same provocative grin she'd used on him the night they'd met, in LA at the launch party for his latest CD. He'd seen thousands of come-hither smiles over the years, but hers was different. Confident – but not threatening, the way some women's were. Some women were so aggressive they scared him. Val, who at twenty-two was already world famous in her own right, had enticed him with a smile that made him feel like he could reciprocate without remorse. He'd had his share of remorse over the years, and a few extra portions for good measure.

He shook his head, admiring her brilliant hair, the long, lean muscles in her thighs and arms that were products of uncountable hours of surfing and training. She'd won her first junior championship at fifteen, had her first endorsement contract a year later. 'You're awfully easy on me, you know.'

'I know,' she agreed.

'It's a real character flaw.'

'I never said I was perfect.' She pushed her sunglasses down and turned her motorbike back toward their resort, a collection of luxury villas on Nettle Bay. 'Catch me if you can!'

THREE

Meg left her father's apartment and stopped to admire how the setting sun glowed through the moss-draped branches of live oak trees. Spring was in full force, honeysuckle snaking its fragrant way into the trees, azaleas of fuchsia and pink and white and lavender lining the sidewalks and underlining windows. Spring was Meg's favorite season, but Brian, with his allergies, hated spring. Messy pollen and drifting seeds, messy flower petals. He'd had their home builder clear a fifty-foot perimeter around their house when it was built. Without trees to shade the house, their electric bill was outrageous. He didn't care; 'That's what money's for,' he'd say.

In the parking lot, as Meg dug out her keys, she noticed a strange weakness in her right arm. She struggled to raise the arm, to aim the remote at her six-year-old Volvo, feeling as though her arm had become weighted with sand. Bizarre.

A very long day, she thought, walking the remaining twenty feet to the car. That awkward twins delivery just before lunch must have strained her arm – and those damn speculums she was trying out, some new model that was supposed to work easily with one hand but was failing to live up to the product rep's promises. Three of them had jammed open this afternoon, causing her patients discomfort and embarrassing her – and, she'd noticed at the time, making her hand ache in the effort to get them to close.

She squeezed her hand around the remote, then tried the button again. Her thumb cooperated, and the odd feeling in her arm began to pass. Once inside the car, she sat back with a heavy sigh and directed the vents so that cold air blew directly onto her face. The prospect of a shower was as enticing as diamonds. No, *more* enticing; diamonds had little practical value on their own, and almost no value to anyone unable to see them. A shower, though, offered universal appeal: wash away your cares, your sins, the evidence, the damage, the residue – whatever it was you needed; she would choose a well-timed shower over a diamond any day.

As she flexed her hand, she looked at the bag of notebooks where she'd set them on the seat beside her. Opening the bag, she saw maybe a dozen blue composition books, a neat stack tied up tightly with the same all-purpose twine she'd seen, and used, everywhere on their farm when she was a kid. Twine was almost as good as duct tape for making what were meant to be temporary repairs, but which inevitably became permanent.

The notebooks looked almost new. Likely her father

had found them in a recently unpacked box – leftover office supplies, unneeded in his full-time 'retirement'. As if he was the one who'd kept the business records to begin with.

The clock on the dash read seven-forty, and Meg's empty stomach growled in response. She would stop by KFC on her way to get her daughter from the library, where Savannah and her best friend Rachel were hanging out. Supposedly. Supposedly they had a biology project to research, but she doubted this. They could research almost anything from the computer at home. Knowing Rachel – a bubbly girl whose exis-tence disproved the theory that blondes were the airheads – there were boys involved, and the library was just a staging ground that the girls imagined would fool their parents.

Who might the boys be? Savannah revealed so little about her life these days. Somewhere between getting her first period and her first cell phone, Savannah had morphed from a curious, somewhat needy, somewhat nerdy little girl into an introverted cipher. She was nothing like Meg had been as a teen, which was a good thing. Savannah was just as reliable, but not as caught up in all that boy–girl business. Not grafted onto the heart of a young man who would later hate her for betraying him. Not, Meg hoped, destined to live with her own heart cleaved in two.

Razor sharp, some memories were.

She pushed the past away and sat another minute in the air-conditioning, stealing just a little more time for herself before moving on to her next work shift.

Food. Kid. Reports. Case studies. Thirty minutes on the Bowflex, if she could dredge up the energy – or maybe she'd just spare her arm, let it have another night off. And now that it was feeling nearly normal again, she put the car in gear and headed for the library.

FOUR

Carson watched the sun easing itself closer to the low mountains, a glass of sangria in front of him on the thatch-covered outdoor bar. Val had gone to work out with Wade, her trainer, leaving him alone with his musings. He was accustomed to being alone with his musings, had produced some of his best work this way. But this afternoon, the musings were neither creative nor as positive as a man who'd just made love with a vibrant younger woman ought to be having.

Though the bar was shaded, he kept his sunglasses on, along with his ball cap – the ineffective disguise of celebrities everywhere. St Martin wasn't as rife with fans as most stateside locales, but he'd been approached for autographs seven times already in the two days they'd been there. This, however, wasn't the reason for his moodiness; in fact, he was having a tough time identifying what the reason was. He had no reason to be moody whatsoever: in addition to having just had sex, he'd recently won two Grammy awards, his Seattle condo was under contract for more than the asking price, his healthy parents were about to celebrate their forty-third wedding anniversary, and he would soon marry a woman who didn't hold his unseemly past against him – a woman who'd done two *Sports Illustrated* features, who could have pretty much any man she wanted. Maybe it was this last part that was hanging him up.

'I know doing this is a cliché,' he said to the bartender, a short-haired buxom brunette, 'but let me get your opinion about something.'

'Of course,' she smiled, her white teeth artificially bright and even. She set a towel aside and leaned onto the bar in front of him, her V-neck blouse straining.

He sat back a little. 'Why would a woman – young, beautiful, appealing – like yourself – what would make a woman like you want to marry a worn-out guy like me?'

'You *are* the rock star, no?'

Rock star. That had been his tag for a dozen years now, and still it sounded strange to him, and wrong. He was a songwriter, a singer, front man for a band that sold out most of its venues – all of that was true. And yes, the music *was* rock music – though broader in scope than most, modeled after Queen and the socially conscious, always-fresh music of Sting, whom he'd met for the first time last year. Still, he didn't see himself as a rock *star*, though he recognized that he lived the life of one. It was a strange disconnection, one he'd been aware of peripherally for a long time, but which had only in the last year or two come into focus. Probably the awareness was a result of his age

– that midlife business his manager, Gene Delaney, said stalked men more relentlessly than band sluts. Gene had a way with words. Whatever it was, Carson felt increasingly dissatisfied with the rock-star label: it sounded shallow, two-dimensional at best. He wanted to be *thicker* than that. He wanted to be substantial in life, had once believed his deeply felt music would make him that way.

'Right,' he told the bartender. 'I'm the rock star. Are you saying that explains it?'

'*Non,*' she said. 'It is good, yes, *mais non pas tout* – it is not everything. You have a handsome face, and very good . . . *qu'est-ce que c'est?*' She gestured to indicate his body. 'And you are not so much an American asshole.'

He raised his eyebrows, and the bartender clarified, 'Not to hit his woman, or make a woman service him. You are *généreux, non?*'

He shrugged. He supposed he was generous – he always tipped well above what was expected, news he assumed had spread to all the staff quickly. He donated to several charities, worked with Habitat for Humanity twice a year – some people might call that generous. To him it all seemed like the least he could do when he had so much money that it seemed to replicate itself.

Money management, now that was a job in itself, and he didn't have time for it. He left that to his mom, who liked to tease him that a wife and half a dozen kids would help him put the money to use. She thought it was a shame Val had so much money of her own.

'She'll be too independent, Carson, mark me on that.' When his parents came to Seattle to meet Val at New Year's, his mom told her about a seven-bedroom Ocala estate she'd heard was for sale: 'Plenty of space for you two and all the kids,' she said, not even attempting to be subtle. 'Kids?' Val said. 'Ocala?'

Carson told the bartender, 'My fiancée is seventeen years younger than me – not that *I* mind, but shouldn't *she*?'

The woman reached over and laid one manicured finger on his arm. 'Must be your motor is good, eh?'

'For now.'

'*Mais oui*. What else is there?'

FIVE

When Meg drove into the parking lot of Ocala's main library, her headlights swept over and past her daughter sitting alone, earbuds in, on a bench near the entrance. Savannah stood, lifting her patch-covered book bag from the bench and swinging it onto her shoulder as Meg pulled to the curb.

'Hi, honey,' she said when Savannah climbed in, loudly enough to be heard over whatever was playing on the iPod. 'Take those out, will you?'

Savannah pulled out the earbuds and hung the cord around her neck. 'Is that better?' She turned and shoved her bag and the notebooks into the backseat, then grabbed the plastic bag with the fried chicken and brought it up to the front.

'It is,' Meg said, making herself not react to Savannah's rudeness. She knew it wasn't intentional, knew from past arguments that the 'tone battle' wasn't a battle worth fighting. 'What are you listening to?' she asked instead.

'Nobody you've heard of.' Savannah began to rifle through the bag.

'Why don't you wait – I thought it'd be nice to eat together with Dad, at home.' For a change. She couldn't recall, right off, the last time they'd done this.

'I'm hungry now,' Savannah said, opening the box inside and taking out a wing. 'You're late.'

Meg pulled away from the curb, ignoring the weakness that remained in her arm and ignoring Savannah's accusatory tone. Ignore whatever doesn't suit: a strategy she'd learned at her father's knee. She asked, 'Where's Rachel?'

'*Her* mom picked her up at eight.' It was now seven minutes past.

Meg sighed. A parenting book she'd read advised fighting only the truly important battles. The challenge was in how to determine, while her buttons were being pushed, just which battles were important. Yesterday morning, both of them tired after the security alarm had gone haywire and awakened them all at two AM, they'd fought over whether the milk was beginning to sour.

Savannah added, 'Thanks for the chicken. It's good.'

There was hope. 'You're welcome. Why don't you hand me a piece? A leg – and a napkin.' They could eat together in the car; Brian probably wasn't home yet anyway.

Savannah rummaged in the box and found a leg. 'Here,' she said, holding it out. Meg intended to reach for it, started to move her hand off the steering wheel, but her arm felt sluggish again. Something wasn't right. She thought back to her anatomy courses, considered the networks and pathways of nerves and signals; something must be pinched, torqued out of place by the

30

difficult entrance of that second twin this morning. Janey, the labor nurse, had been rooting for a C-section, but in Meg's view C-sections were overdone, riskier sometimes than just patiently working with nature. Besides, Corinne, the mother, wanted to do it all naturally as long as the babies weren't at risk. Meg had been very satisfied, as Corinne had, when little Corey and Casey came through unscathed. The only price for taking the harder route, Meg thought, was this nuisance with her arm – which could probably be fixed with a short visit to Brian's orthopedist.

When Meg didn't take the chicken immediately, Savannah said, 'Mom?'

Meg forced a smile. 'You know, I think I'll just wait – keep both hands on the wheel. What sort of example am I setting if I eat while I drive?' *One I've set a hundred times*, she thought. Well, what was parenting if not a series of inconsistencies and the occasional hypocritical action?

She changed the subject. 'So, tell me about this project you're doing.'

'It's no big deal. Cell anatomy and function. Pretty boring.'

Meg remembered taking high school biology, studying those same things with her lab partner, Carson. More often, *not* studying. Savannah, though, was a serious student, curious about everything – or so she'd been, back when her every thought manifested as a question or observation. Presumably she was still the same girl, just quieter. Was she caught up in identity issues? Questioning her sexuality? She hadn't yet

31

had an official boyfriend; maybe she was gay – which would be fine, Meg would love her no matter what. Or maybe Savannah was just picky; she could be awfully judgmental, the 'curse', her fifth-grade teacher once said, of gifted children. In truth, Meg hoped Rachel *had* persuaded Savannah to meet some boys, if only so that Savannah would start getting her feet wet.

'Well, did you find the info you needed?'

'Mostly,' Savannah said, her mouth full.

The traffic signal ahead turned red, and Meg slowed to a stop. She looked at Savannah, really *looked* at her, in a way she rarely remembered to these days. The dangling wood-bead earrings, the thick, hammered-silver wrist cuff, the mascara, the slight sheen of lip gloss – when did she begin wearing that? – the swell of breasts inside a snug green tée; all these signs said her daughter was essentially a woman. When had this maturing taken place? Surely it was just last week that skinny, flat-chested, unadorned Savannah was dressing Barbie dolls and perfecting cartwheels on the pool deck behind their house. Yet *this* week she was a sophomore at a private all-girl high school; a little more exposure to the opposite sex would do her good.

Meg rubbed her shoulder while thinking whether she should ask outright if the girls had been 'researching' with boys. But knowing Savannah, the question would be interpreted as an accusation – and she simply didn't have the energy to defend herself tonight. So instead of asking, she changed the subject again.

'Hey, I just saw Grandpa Spencer. Do you want to go have dinner with him Sunday? He thought you'd get a kick out of using the self-serve ice cream machine they have there.'

Savannah smirked. 'I'm practically *sixteen*. Did he forget the *teen* part or something?'

The signal light changed and Meg turned the car, heading toward their gated community on the north-east side of town. She left her arm resting in her lap. 'Be nice,' she said. 'The important part is that he wants your company.'

'Whatever,' Savannah said.

Meg glanced at her. 'Is that a yes?'

Her daughter shrugged, slim shoulders signaling noncommitment. 'Are you and Dad going?'

'*I* plan to. I don't know about your dad.'

'He never does anything,' Savannah grumbled.

True as it was, Meg felt obliged to defend him. 'He has a business to run.'

'I think I know that.' Savannah opened the glovebox, shuffled through a few CDs, selected one, and slid it into the player.

Meg waited to hear what she'd picked. In a moment, the sounds of acoustic piano and guitar surrounded them, joined, after a few bars, by Carson's voice. She smiled at how Savannah had moved from a grumpy thought about Brian to soothing herself with Carson's music. Meg had done the same thing many, many times herself.

'Good choice,' she said.

'Can I borrow this to upload when we get home?'

'Sure, borrow it – but make sure you put this one back afterward.'

'Duh,' Savannah said as though she'd never forgotten before.

Savannah sang along softly, as invested in the music as if she'd composed it herself. Meg knew why *she* loved Carson's music, but was Savannah's connection inborn? The possibility alternately pleased or worried her, depending on how close the past felt when the thought bubbled up. Tonight, the thought was a bittersweet pleasure – a longing for the simpler life she and Carson and Savannah would have had if things had been different. But sometimes she hoped fervently that Savannah was Brian's – wished for a clean break from Carson, for pure, open space between her past and the truth of her life *now*. The deliberate mystery of Savannah's paternity had turned out to be much more troubling to her than she'd expected.

Probably, she concluded, she'd trained Savannah to love Carson's music. Inadvertently, by example. Probably it meant nothing.

'I *guess* I'll go to Grandpa's,' Savannah said when the song ended. 'Oh, we have our opening ballgame Sunday at one. I told Dad; he said he has a nine-thirty tee time with some client, so you'll have to take me.'

Of course. When Brian wasn't jetting off to some branch or another of the company he'd founded, Hamilton Investments Management, Inc., he was on the golf course. He rarely involved himself in their lives – ironic, considering he'd once been so determined to

34

win her away from Carson that he and his father had spent $387,000 to close the deal.

He just wasn't the sort of man who wanted intimacy, in the fullest sense of the word. What was surface level was uncomplicated and therefore desirable; he saved his energies for work. He was about accomplishments. Results. The successful pursuit of an ever-higher standard. He collected achievements the way other people accrue trophies. She admired his energy but was cowed by it too; he expected the same from everyone around him and, especially lately, she didn't have it to give.

'Well, whether Dad comes with us or not,' Meg said, 'Grandpa will be glad to see you; he wants to show you around – "show her off", that's how he put it.'

'Why?'

'It's his new home, the people there are his new neighbors – he wants them to see his beautiful offspring.'

'Which would be *you*, or Aunt Beth,' Savannah said. 'Not me. *I'm* not beautiful; I got Dad's big nose.'

Perhaps, Meg thought. Savannah's nose did look something like Brian's, and the shape of her face was similar, too; the broad forehead, the wide smile. Meg wouldn't bet her life on a genetic connection, though. She said, '*You* are absolutely gorgeous. I'd give anything for that wavy hair.' She wanted to reach over and touch Savannah's long auburn hair, willed her tired arm to cooperate. Happily, it did, and she pushed some strands behind her daughter's ear, letting her hand linger. Carson's low, soulful voice sang one of his early ballads, a song about a pair of young lovers separated by a washed-out bridge.

'Hey, two hands on the wheel,' Savannah said.

In the darkness, Meg allowed herself a wistful smile.

SIX

Savannah passed the ninety minutes before her on-line 'date' by working on a new song. Her guitar, a fifteenth-birthday gift almost a year ago, made a good diversion most nights, especially now that her grand-parents' horse farm was sold. But last Sunday, while she was chatting online with her friends, she got a message from someone intriguing. A guy – no, a *man* – who wanted to get to know her. And at nine-thirty tonight he would be online to chat with her again . . . she hoped.

She sat on her fuzzy purple stool, trying to improve the final three bars of her song. The purple, the fuzz, annoyed her. Nothing in her bedroom suite felt like 'her' anymore; her *life* didn't feel like 'her' anymore. She'd outgrown the lavender walls and spring-green carpet, the white dressers and desk. Her fuchsia curtains, with their bright appliquéd daisies, annoyed her. A lot of things annoyed her, in fact: most of her classmates, her dad's refusal to let her get a dog even to keep outside, the stares of the creepy lawn-care guys, the way she still wasn't allowed to stay home alone when her parents traveled, as if she couldn't be trusted – just to name a few. It was all so *irritating*, like a cloud of gnats she couldn't shoo away. Even this song, which she'd been so dedicated to at first, was getting on her nerves; she just couldn't seem to get it to end the way she wanted it to.

Finally, at nine-twenty, she gave up trying to concentrate and propped the guitar against the wall, wishing there was some way to fast-forward to a time when she had her own life, her own place. Space that was decorated by her, not by some fussy designer who thought she knew 'just what smart little girls like!' Someplace like a park ranger's cabin along the Chassahowitzka River, where she could do research on manatee populations – that would do her just fine. The gentle mammals were her main interest outside of music. If she could have music and manatees, that was all she needed. Well, music and manatees and a boyfriend who loved those things too. And maybe now she'd found him.

'Ten minutes to Kyle,' she said, nervous. Would he show? Would he be as interested in her as he'd seemed last time? She grabbed her laptop and settled onto her bed with purple velvet pillows propped behind her, facing the door like she always did – so that no parent could stroll in and read over her shoulder. Not that they *would* stroll in. Not that she ever had anything to hide, in particular . . . until this week.

She signed on and scanned her buddy list for Kyle's screen name: still offline. Suppose he didn't show? Suppose he found someone he liked better than her?

Her webpage, where he'd first discovered her, was as appealing as she could make it. She'd fudged a little on the facts, though, including posting photos specially selected to make the case that she was twenty, not a month shy of sixteen. One showed her by the pool, wearing a bikini and holding a highball glass filled with amber liquid meant to look like a cocktail. In reality she didn't drink at all – she was smarter than that. But success in life was all about presentation, that's what her dad always said. So her page presented the Savannah she thought would attract the kind of boyfriend she wanted: an older guy whose interests matched hers. Guys her age – the ones she knew, anyway – seemed to care only about sports or money or, like her friend Jonathan, were more into playing video games than having an actual life.

Her page was her portal to the *real* world. And she hoped – hoped so hard that it made her stomach hurt – that her strategy had worked, that Kyle would become her companion and guide.

She traded IMs with Rachel about the guy they'd met up with earlier at the library. Some senior from North Marion High. She'd gone to the library as moral support, though Rachel, who'd practically licked the guy's ear while whispering to him, seemed to not need any kind of support at all. Now Rachel was saying he'd promised to call her, but she'd forgotten to give him her number before her mom arrived. In typical Rachel fashion she wrote,

OMG!! wat do i do???? i just no i will never c him agn!!!!!!!

chill, Savannah wrote. In her opinion, the guy was too skinny, and he hadn't seemed that into Rachel anyway.

Savannah kept up her end of the conversation mindlessly, waiting, waiting, her heart seeming to stall, until the chime of Kyle messaging her jump-started it again:

hi babe, wassup?

To Rachel she wrote hurriedly, *its him! gtg.*

If what he'd said in their first chat was legitimate, he was twenty-three years old and had a bachelor's degree in marine biology. He loved music, including some of her favorite bands: No Doubt, Evanescence, Nickelback, and Carson McKay. He sounded *perfect.*

Everything she'd posted on her page was accurate – well, except for her age: long wavy red-brown hair, 5′8″ (too tall, she thought, but what could she do?), green eyes, 127 lb. She hadn't revealed her whole name, just first and middle, wise to the risks of giving too much information. *Savannah Rae.* If she ever got into professional songwriting or performing in public, that was the name she planned to use.

i'm studying 4 bio quiz, she replied. She'd told him that first night that she was a student at the University of Florida – but only after making sure he hadn't gone there.

ah, the good old days, he wrote. He was working on his PhD now, doing some kind of research for a professor at Harvard – fieldwork around the western Everglades, only a few hours south of Gainesville, he'd said. Gainesville, where *she* supposedly lived in an apartment with three girlfriends.

Kyle's very first message included a picture of himself standing on some decrepit dock wearing only cargo shorts that hung low on his hips, and hiking boots with socks showing above the tops. He was trim and muscled like the Greek sculptures she studied in art history. She thought his body was amazing, but it was his face that really drew her in: his wide, long-lashed eyes looked kind. Caring. Dedicated to his passions – which would include her, she hoped. His dark, curly hair and café au lait complexion made her think he might be part Latino or black – something her dad wouldn't approve of, but she didn't really care.

wut r u up 2? she asked.

sos. waiting 4 the wkend. i really want 2 meet in person, he wrote, thrilling her. *wut r u doing sat?*

it's my dad's b-day, she wrote, adding a frowning-face icon. Another white lie, but it wouldn't be good to sound too eager. She waited anxiously for his reply.

idea: meet 4 may day in miami?

Savannah perked up. *wut's in miami?*

my bros. we meet every yr 4 beach party. got a bikini?

duh. He'd seen the pictures of her on her webpage.

got a car?

duh, she wrote again, though she wouldn't have one until her birthday in mid-May, a small detail she could work out later. She wiped her damp palms on the bedspread, waiting to see if he was serious.

Kyle wrote, *luv 4 u 2 hang w/us. try?*

sure! she replied, though she didn't have a clue how she could get there without her parents' permission. Not that they paid close attention to what she did with her time, her dad in particular. They believed whatever she told them. If she planned things carefully, she might be able to make it work. 'Holy shit,' she whispered, but played it cool, typing, *will check to see if I'm free.*

hope so, Kyle wrote. *hey babe, gtg – frenz here. Call your cell sat?*

Disappointed to be done so soon, she wrote, *ok. ttyl!* and added a smiley face, to show she was just fine with letting him go. Then she signed off, so that none of her friends could interrupt her glow.

Wow, she thought, snapping her laptop shut: *Kyle. Miami.* She couldn't wait to talk to him about it – it would be only their second conversation, the first having been Monday night. They hadn't talked for long, but long enough for her to determine that he wasn't geeky or weird. Long enough to discover that his voice, a midrange tenor that might complement her alto if he could sing, filled a hole in her heart – or maybe her soul, she wasn't sure – in a way nothing else quite managed to. She stood and stretched and grinned.

As she washed her face, she imagined walking with Kyle on soft white sand, holding hands, kissing … French kissing, like she'd done experimentally a few times with her friend Jonathan, who lived two houses over. She was fascinated with the male body and the way she felt when she thought about getting firsthand knowledge of Kyle's. Now that she'd found a guy worth her time, she was ready to try out a lot of the things she knew most of her friends were doing already. Had been doing since eighth grade, some of them. Her stomach turned a funny little flip when she thought of how it would be to slide her hand inside the waist of his cargo shorts.

She leaned close to the mirror to inspect the few blackheads dotting her forehead and the top of her nose. She'd need to get rid of those before Miami – what twenty-year-old girl would still have blackheads? Getting rid of the freckles banding her nose and cheeks would be nice, too, but that wasn't going to happen. Her height, her freckles, her smile, and the red highlights in her brown hair were gifts from her mother – that's what her Grandma Anna used to say; she tried to appreciate them, but what she wanted was to be petite, with blond hair and spot-free skin. Or that's what she often thought, but now that she'd snagged Kyle's interest, she might concede that she looked okay as is.

With his perspective in mind, she peeled off her T-shirt and looked at her breasts critically. 'Average,' she said, turning sideways, then facing front again. Not like she could do much to improve them, short of getting implants, and she was *not* an implant kind of girl. She knew girls who were, though – girls who'd already had nose jobs, girls who were all about improving their bodies so they could get better guys. Girls who knew how to flirt. Girls who wore those mini-stilettos called kitten heels, and big smiles for their daddies so they could get more money to shop with.

Savannah knew she wasn't especially good at flirting, not with boys and not with her dad, but she *was* a straight-A student, good at figuring things out – which was much more valuable in the long run. Besides, Kyle obviously liked smart women, seeing as how he thought she was a college student with serious career aspirations and all.

She'd just changed into the yellow Earth Day tank top and gray knit shorts she slept in when she heard a tap on her bedroom door.

'Yeah,' she said. 'Come in.'

The door opened. 'Hey, sweetie, you ready for bed?' her mom asked.

'What does it look like?' Savannah said, moving her laptop from her bed to her desk in a show of being finished with it. She knew that once her mom left the room, she could play guitar or make a phone call or open up the computer again without any fear of being interrupted. Her mom was nothing if not predictable; once she said good night, Savannah wouldn't see her again until the next morning. Some kids might take much better advantage of this predictability than she ever had – sneaking out, for example, or sneaking someone in. She never did that kind of thing, never had a reason to, before.

Her mom sat on the side of the bed. 'You're such a wise guy. What does it *look* like? It looks like you're ready to race sled-dogs in the Iditarod. But I think maybe a good night's sleep is in order first.'

Savannah sat down near her pillows and pulled her knees up to her chest. 'Funny,' she said. 'Not.'

'Actually, you look like you might be about to audition for a strip-club job.'

'*Mom*,' Savannah said.

'What? Those shorts are scandalous.'

'You bought them.'

'When you were *twelve*, if I remember right. What is it with teenage girls and short clothing?'

'It's just a style.'

'Hmm. Well, don't wear those in public. Dad would kill you.'

Savannah looked down at the shorts, which she was planning to wear in Miami. 'Don't worry,' she said.

'So . . . do you need anything?' her mom asked, looking around her bedroom in that way Savannah knew parents did when searching for signs that their kids smoked or drank or whatever. This made her feel guilty before she'd even done anything wrong.

She took a bit of her hair and pulled it in front of her face, braiding it quickly. *I need my car*, she thought. She said, 'Shampoo.' And then, seeing an opening, she added, 'Oh, and I have this question: Remember how, when we were in London last fall with Aunt Beth—'

'Wasn't that a great trip? This fall, the conference is going to be in Singapore. Do you think you'd like to go? Dad's been there and he loved it – well, he loved the golf courses, anyway; the food wasn't his thing. But—'

'Mom,' she interrupted, now unbraiding her hair.

'Oh, sorry. What about it?'

'I was thinking it might be cool to fly out to visit her this summer, like, just on my own. Can kids do that, fly alone, I mean?'

Her mom said, 'Sure. Remember, there were three

little boys in matching tie-dye shirts and airline badges on that flight to London?'

'Oh, yeah. So then, you don't have to be eighteen or whatever?' She began braiding again, then caught herself and pushed the hair back behind her ear.

'Nope. As I understand it, the airlines all have special services for unaccompanied children – they have flight attendants assigned to them, and a parent or relative has to meet them at their destination gate.'

'So basically I'd be tracked like a convict.'

Her mom laughed. 'No, you're old enough to go on your own, the program's for younger kids. Do you know, I heard on the radio not long ago that Atlanta has the busiest airport in the world? I always thought it would be New York – but they're not even in the top ten! I think O'Hare was the second busiest, and then Heathrow . . .'

Savannah listened with half attention while thinking of how to buy a ticket to Miami. Her mom was always taking the long way through explanations, which used to delight her but now often felt unnecessary. Sometimes she wanted to say, *Just get to it already.* She never did though, maybe because a small part of her still liked seeing her mom as an all-knowing authority. Maybe because she knew that asking questions was a good way to get and hold her mom's attention – not that she wanted so much of it anymore. She didn't. She wanted her own life, a life where she fit, a life where no gung-ho dads looked down on low-money career aspirations. A life where she was important to the people around her. To Kyle, maybe. With her

Grandma Anna gone now, most of the time she felt invisible. And that was on a good day.

Her mom was still talking. 'Well, I know Aunt Beth would love to have you, no question. She could tour you around Berkeley, introduce you to some of the other professors – you really should apply there, you'd be a shoo-in. I'm so pleased that you want to spend time with her. What a nice idea!'

Savannah nodded. She probably would enjoy going, though she hadn't thought about it one way or the other until this minute. And attending Berkeley for its environmental science program was a possibility, if she wanted to work for the manatees through politics and policy. Right now, though, all she cared about was whether she could hop a plane to Miami with nothing more than a ticket and ID. From the sound of it, she could.

'I'll talk to Beth,' her mom said, 'and if you think you might want to go to Singapore, I should get that arranged before too much longer.'

'I'll think about it.' She was impatient now to be alone so she could get online and look into airline schedules. She gave a smile that was meant to encourage her mom to move alone. 'So . . . good night,' she said.

'Oh. Okay then.' Her mom stood, smiling back in a way that made Savannah fear she'd been too abrupt. Again. She never *meant* to be rude; things just came out that way.

She watched her mom walk to the door, then turn and look at her.

'Honey?'

'Yeah?'

'This weekend, let's have that chat about birth control I'm sure you've been dreading.' Before Savannah could answer, she was gone down the hallway.

Savannah sat as if frozen, though her face was ablaze and her mind was spinning. Did her mom suspect something? An impulse to forget the whole Miami idea swelled inside her, but then she thought of Kyle, brought that image of him on the dock to mind, and the impulse subsided. It had to be the fact of her sixteenth birthday coming up that provoked her mom's suggestion. Knowing her mom, the birth-control chat had been scheduled since the moment she heard 'It's a girl!'

Suppose during this chat she just up and told her mom that she wanted to go on the pill? Suppose she said she had a boyfriend and they were considering having sex. Right – that would go over well. Going from having had no real boyfriend ever, to the announcement of having not only a boyfriend but also a sexual relationship with the guy . . . it just wouldn't work, even if she wanted to tell her about Kyle – which she didn't. Couldn't. He was definitely *not* who her parents would have in mind for her, not by, oh, six or seven years and, in her dad's case, several shades of skin color.

So no birth control pills for her, not just now. But as soon as she got a chance, she'd pop in to Wal-Mart or someplace where she could be anonymous, to buy a box of condoms. It was no big deal; she knew girls at school who did it all the time. She liked to think that if her parents found out she bought condoms, they'd be proud of her for being so responsible and mature.

What would probably happen, though, was that her mom would feel betrayed and her dad would just shrug and head for the club.

SEVEN

When Brian strode into the living room Friday night, Meg saw he had showered before coming home. Comb marks angled through his thinning dark hair. A lightly starched golf shirt – not the same one he would have worn while playing – was tucked into tailored navy shorts. His waistline swelled over his belt like the top of a muffin. She had never thought him unattractive. His style, though, wasn't her preference. She liked a more rugged look. Less refined, more adventurous. Brian was so . . . tidy, she thought. Orderly. Like their home, like their life.

She put aside the stack of blue notebooks, which she'd forgotten in the car until this evening. She'd been trying unsuccessfully to free them from the string, wanting to make sure they weren't anything important before putting them in a box for Goodwill.

'Been at the club?' she asked Brian, to snag his attention. She needed to make an effort more often; in two years, Savannah would be off to college, and then where would they be? Familiar but distant occupants of their six-thousand-square-foot, professionally decorated house. A house with too many unused rooms as it was; how hollow things would be with Savannah away.

Brian stopped and set his gym bag on the polished hardwood floor. 'Yep,' he said, perching on the side of an armchair opposite her. 'Got nine holes in, with those clients from Germany I was telling you about the other day. They're really bad – don't know a wedge from an iron – but good-natured about it. We stopped keeping score.'

Meg nodded, empathetic to the German men's plight; she hardly knew the differences between golf clubs herself. She supposed she *should* know, golf being Brian's life outside of work. It just didn't interest her, and her mind was crowded enough with the things she *had* to know.

Perhaps he understood this; he never bothered to discuss the particulars of his golf games. Their conversations molded around common interests: the house, Savannah, their families, their careers. A movie, if by long odds they'd seen it together – or separately, if one of them was traveling and caught it on the plane or late at night in a hotel.

Sometimes, now that Savannah was watching many of the same movies, she joined the conversation. *If* they had all seen the movie and were all in one room or one vehicle at the same time, an occurrence about as rare as conjoined twins.

Manisha Patel, Meg's partner, assured her that her reality was nothing unusual; Manisha's family's worked the same way, which was like that of most other families they knew and was often the subject of talk shows Meg came across late at night, times when she couldn't sleep. She and Brian and Savannah were planets orbiting a common sun, occasionally swinging into close proximity. Held together by the gravitational pull of a shared address, they had little in common with what had once made the 'traditional' family. She felt guilty about this as regularly as she felt defensive about it and figured she'd come to terms with the whole muddy issue just about the time Savannah was grown and gone.

'You look refreshed,' Meg said. 'I'm going to hit the shower in a minute myself. But it feels so good to just *sit* here.'

Brian smiled in that way he had, slightly condescending and self-affirming. *He* could put in a full, hectic day and still have the energy to entertain clients *and* play nine holes of golf, that's what she imagined him thinking. He was never overtly critical, but still, she *felt* his judgment, *felt* the comparison – it was his nature to think that way. She half expected him to give her a Team Hamilton pep talk.

'Was it a busy day?' he asked – *his* attempt to connect, she supposed, given that he knew all her days were busy.

She sighed and put her feet up on the sofa, taking up the space that he might have filled if he'd tried a little harder. If he had wanted to try. If she had wanted him to.

'Yeah, busy, but also taxing,' she said. 'I had a pre-eclamptic mother with back labor who dealt with it by screaming, and then a transverse baby I practically

52

had to climb inside with to get out.' She rubbed her arm, thinking about that one. 'And two new high-risk patients this afternoon; you probably know the one's husband: McKinney? Joseph, I think his name is.' The surname, when she read it on the chart earlier in the day, had made her think of *McKay*, of Carson, of how she'd learned a week ago that he was planning a May wedding. To a much younger woman, the news website's headline announced – 'Musician McKay Robbing the Cradle for a May Bride?' – and Meg had elected not to click the link to read the details. Since then, even the weakest prompts called him to mind.

'Yeah, I know him, Joe McKinney,' Brian nodded. 'Partner at Decker McKinney Peterson. He's pretty good – at golf, I mean – though judging from that little black Ferrari I saw him in, likely at law, too. What's his wife's trouble?'

'She's forty-three.'

'Ah. It's good, though, you getting all these new high-risk patients – obviously you're building quite a reputation as a specialist. You should raise your rates, take space somewhere a little more . . . upscale, let's say.'

'We like where we are,' Meg said. She and Manisha chose their office location, a modest brick building downtown, precisely because it *wasn't* so upscale that they'd price out women less affluent than the Mrs Joseph McKinneys of the world. Or the Mrs Carson McKays, for that matter, she thought, wondering if pregnancy explained his short-notice announcement. Their wealthy patients came to them because they were good doctors, not because their offices looked like a luxury spa.

'I just don't see why you'd choose not to take advantage of an opportunity when it's practically dropped in your lap,' Brian said, standing up. 'You're savvier than that.'

His criticism, delivered beningly, still stung. 'What does "savvy" have to do with anything? Just because I don't feel like I need to earn more money, I'm not "savvy"?'

Brian pushed his hands into his shorts pockets, relaxed and confident in his opinions. 'Look, ever since I've known you, whenever you've been faced with an opportunity to better yourself or improve your status, you've taken it. I don't see why you'd stop now.'

He was right, and yet his assessment missed seeing her clearly, as though time had made his memory as farsighted as his eyes. Had he forgotten that her first *opportunity* was one he'd constructed so carefully that there was no way she could turn him down? Once he'd set the wheel in motion, then yes, she'd tried in every way to better herself. She was practical. There were limits, though, to her ambition. Maybe he didn't want to believe this about her, or maybe he hadn't noticed. He loved to tell people what a terrific pair they made, how alike they were in temperament and taste, how accomplished she'd become; he had constructed the reality he wanted in their marriage the same way he'd done for his business.

He had her all wrong.

She was not the woman of his tales, would never

be that woman, but was there any value in arguing the point? In part, he didn't know who she really was because she kept pieces of herself hidden from him. Money couldn't buy *everything*.

Before she could frame any sort of response, Brian picked up his gym bag, said, 'I have to make a couple calls,' and left the room. She let him go.

He didn't know, either, that she'd thought of leaving him many times, the way a blond woman might think about coloring her hair black: interested in the possibilities but unwilling to take such a drastic step. What if black hair looked awful? Was black an advantage, or was it just different? If she were the ambitious woman he saw, she would have divorced him as soon as she was earning enough to pay back her parents' mortgage. She'd have moved 'onward and upward', as was Brian's refrain. But no, she had already blasted apart the one bridge she'd want to travel again, and so because she wanted to keep Savannah's life stable and she and Brian were as compatible as she needed them to be, she stayed.

Standing, she reached down for the notebooks and felt her left knee begin to buckle. She caught herself with one hand on the sofa's arm. 'Getting old, girl,' she said, shaking her head.

Brian's voice, persuasive and firm as he talked on the phone, resounded as she passed the kitchen. He was fixing a snack while he talked – warming up brownies, from the smell of it. He'd add vanilla ice cream and chocolate syrup, which illustrated why she'd had to take his suits in for alteration despite his playing some twenty hours of golf a week. That was the other curse of middle age: a slowing metabolism. Keeping in shape was harder all the time – and she'd skipped her workouts more than she wanted to admit, these months since her mother's death. There never seemed to be time for exercise; the number of hours in her day had shriveled like an unpicked orange, and she was just too tired to wedge in anything she could excuse as nonessential.

In the master bathroom, she set down the notebooks and turned on the shower. While it warmed, she rifled through a drawer for the pair of tiny scissors she used to trim her pubic hair. Brian preferred her trimmed, almost hairless, except for the hair on her head, which he liked long, and the coppery down of her arms. How long since she'd bothered to trim herself up? She didn't even shave her legs weekly anymore. They hadn't made love in ... what was this? April? Two months. Not since Valentine's Day, and even then it had been more of an expected gesture, a guilty ought-to rather than an anticipated *finally*, which, honestly, hadn't occurred even in the first months – for her, anyway. As steam drifted around her like unsettled ghosts, she took the scissors and cut the notebooks' binding string, expecting that when she cracked open the first of them, she'd find blank pages filled with nothing more than pale blue preprinted lines.

What she found instead came as such a surprise that she reached into the shower and turned the water off.

A quick perusal showed that each book was filled

with neat pages of her mother's calculations and observations on the status of the farm, the weather, the horses' health – interspersed, it seemed, with similar comments about Meg and her sisters and father, all done in fine blue or black felt-tip ink. Seeing the curves and loops made by her mother's hand weakened Meg; she sank to the thick cotton rug and spread the books around her.

Had her father known he'd given her *these*? These twelve diaries, as in essence they were, spanned close to two decades, ending the day before he woke on a Sunday morning last September and found his wife had slipped away in the night, leaving behind her stilled body . . . and these words. Of gossip? Of wisdom?

If she had known ahead of time that the notebooks were diaries, she never would have opened a single cover. Why *invite* pain? Now, she didn't know what she would do with them. She didn't want to read them. She didn't want not to.

A knock on the door startled her. 'What?'

'Mom, I need you to sign a thing so I can do the end-of-year field trip.'

'Can't Dad do it?'

'He's on the phone.'

Meg piled up the notebooks and stashed them in the vanity cabinet. 'I'll be right out.'

EIGHT

Meg sat in the kitchen Saturday morning, coffee in hand, notebooks stacked on the table before her. Brian had gone for his usual Saturday breakfast with his cronies, first dropping Savannah at Rachel's so they could go ... someplace; Savannah had told her, but Meg, distracted by the diaries and her ambivalence about reading them, had passed Savannah off to Brian and thought no more about her plans.

The house was peaceful now, which made it easier to decide to try reading an entry or two. Just to prove to herself that they were frivolous, that she could throw the whole lot away without regret.

She paged through, sampling the entries, surprisingly compelled to turn the pages. Even the shortest of her mother's comments revealed pieces of her past – their past – she hadn't seen before.

June 8, 1985
   Meggie's been hired on at the bank. We need her here, but we need her there, too. Or somewhere

that pays good. The Lord knows the money will be useful! We had to let our health insurance lapse, so I just pray none of us takes sick. Blessed Mother, watch over us all.

So they'd gone without insurance; the very thought of it was frightening, even long after the fact. She remembered her mother's pinched face from back then, the worry lines ringing her mouth and wrinkling her forehead. It hadn't mattered how early Meg got up in the morning, her mother was always up before her. No matter how late she stayed up, her mother was still up too. Little wonder her mother's blood pressure was high.

'June eighth . . .' she said. The day she met Brian.

Her first day of work at Hamilton Savings and Loan. Her training was set to begin at ten, but first she was required to meet her boss – Brian, who was the owner's son, only six years older than herself. Belinda Cordero, head teller, led her to his office doorway and disappeared, leaving her feeling self-conscious and somehow wrong for this moment in time, as if she'd been dropped into the scene by mistake. Her real life was waiting in the paddocks – horses that needed to be exercised, tack that awaited repair. She wanted to bolt.

Brian was sitting at a desk that looked older and more distinguished than *he* was. He wore an off-white linen jacket and a pastel pink shirt, à la Sonny Crockett from *Miami Vice*. His hair was longish and styled just right, meant to dazzle all the women and show the men he was on top of the trends.

He sat back and waved her in. 'Hi, come on in, Meg. I'm Brian Hamilton.'

She took three small steps and stopped. His office smelled of old leather and young ambition, embodied by an expensive cologne she would forever associate with him. She took one more step and stopped.

Brian folded his hands behind his head. 'Welcome. We're glad to have you as part of the Hamilton team. Eileen tells me you're a rising senior at North Marion High?'

'That's right.'

'Good in math?'

She nodded. She did her best to keep eye contact, the way her father had told her she should, but it was hard. Brian kept smiling at her as if he knew that her black polyester skirt and ruffled brown blouse came from a thrift shop. Her shoes, too – though she hoped he couldn't see them while she stood there in front of his desk. It was the same outfit she'd worn for her interview the week before, and she suspected Ms Guillen had told him everything.

She'd gotten the job out of sympathy, she was sure. Everyone in Ocala seemed to know how tenuous things were for the Powells; her father broadcasted his failures as loudly as his successes, afternoons at the co-op. She had applied for a position with the janitorial staff, the job advertised in the *Ocala Star-Banner*, but during her interview with Eileen Guillen, director of human resources, she'd talked about her plan to study accounting after she graduated. Because of that, instead of cleaning floors and toilets in the historic building that Adair Hamilton had rebuilt right after the 1883 fire, Meg would become a part-time teller. 'We like to give our people the best possible start,' Eileen had told her. "Specially those who need it most.'

Brian said, 'I like math a lot, myself. My degree's in economics, and I'll have my MBA soon. Do you plan to go to college?'

'I hope to.'

'Terrific.' He clapped his hands, an exclamation point. 'We like our people to be motivated beyond all this marble and brass.' He stood and offered his hand. 'It's great to have you here. I know Belinda's waiting for me to turn you back over to her, so I'd better let you go.'

At first Meg thought she'd rather be cleaning toilets; working as a teller meant being visible, presentable, and this was a challenge for a girl whose best clothes were jeans and T-shirts without patches or stains. She and her mother scoured the thrift stores for decent professional wear with some success, but being dressed up in skirts and heels every afternoon was like wearing a costume. A costume that wasn't quite as nice as the ones the other tellers wore. Brian went out of his way, though, to help her feel like she was a valuable part of the Hamilton team – that's how he always talked about the tellers, as a team. If her white blouse was dingy because they'd run out of detergent, he overlooked it. If the fake leather on the heels of her shoes was peeling away, he overlooked that too. Was she good with people? Was she careful with procedures and funds? Those were the things that mattered. By the time school started again, her senior year, she'd been converted to permanent employee status, which Belinda said was 'super high praise'.

Brian made a point to befriend her. He would find her during her breaks, ask the occasional question about their farm or her family, her boyfriend, her aspirations in life. She thought he did this with everyone – they all talked about what a hands-on manager he was, how he was destined to be a big success – and only learned later that he'd singled her out. Sometimes he joined her and a few of the other employees at the Trough, after work – a treat she allowed herself only every other Friday. Carson never went. 'Too many guys with ties,' he joked. She went anyway, wanting to fit in if she could. They all talked about their career goals, and once, she admitted that her dream job wasn't in finance at all, but in medicine. Maybe veterinary, maybe human, she wasn't sure. 'I'm used to doctoring everyone and everything already,' she'd said. 'My sisters, the horses, our cats . . . I've helped with foaling – and I even gave our pony stitches once.'

Brian slapped the tabletop. 'Then do it,' he said, surprising her. 'Figure out what you want and how to make it happen, and do it.'

But surely he knew how impossible that was for her, for any Powell girl. Every paycheck she earned went to her parents, to help pay for groceries. Trying for medical school of either type was as futile as trying to use her arms to fly.

Brian. He'd known so well how to play her, when the time came.

NINE

At their Nettle Bay villa, Carson watched Val and Marie-Louise, the ambitious French real estate agent Val had picked, pore over photos and property fact sheets on the patio's café table. He knew he should be as immersed in the activity as Val, knew by the way she kept looking over at him, sitting on the rattan chair to her right, that she thought the same thing. And he *wanted* to be. He wanted to be fully focused on ideal elevation, proximity to the best surf, amenities such as built-in pools and spas and breeze-catching screened rooms. But his seditious mind kept moseying back in time, to the evenings when he and his father had sat at their square kitchen table and sketched out plans for a very different new residence, one he'd share with a very different girl.

He could see it, as clear as if it happened last week instead of twenty years ago: his dad looking young and capable in the heavy twill pants and cotton button-up shirt he always wore to work in the groves; the kitchen light, a cone-shaped pendant, hanging above the table's center, its circle of golden light on their outspread papers; his mother singing some '60s tune while she updated the books at the desk nearby – the Carpenters, he thought, hearing her contralto in his memory. And Meg, sitting close at his left, pushing her long hair off her shoulders and smiling at him, at the future they were drawing with a wooden ruler and pencils sharpened with a knife.

How different a scene that was from what came later.

He remembered his twenty-second birthday, long after the breakup, months after Meg's wedding in '89. George Pappas, his good friend and would-be guitarist, had taken him out for lunch and a few beers. They were waiting at a red light in George's faded brown Chevelle, Pearl Jam blasting on the aftermarket stereo. He didn't notice the glossy red sports car pulled up alongside the left of them at first. Four or five – or six? – beers since lunch had made him almost oblivious, to his surroundings and to the fact that he was spending another birthday without Meg. It was the first since her marriage, but who was counting?

'Hey,' George said, tapping his window. 'Isn't that Meg?'

Carson turned at the same moment she looked over, her hand pressed to the glass; they stared at each other as if George wasn't seated between them, as if they weren't passengers in two different cars, separated by window glass and harsh words and wedding vows.

George started to roll down his window. What did he think, that they'd all just have a nice little chat?

That she'd wish him a happy birthday and throw a kiss? But then the arrow turned green, and the Porsche pulled out, turning left.

George whistled. 'Nice wheels, eh, bro?' he said, as the car moved farther and farther away from them, disappearing into the Ocala twilight. 'She did pretty well for herself.'

'Fuck you,' Carson said.

He was jarred back to the present when Val elbowed him. 'Carson! I think this is the one!'

He cleared his mind of the memories of Meg so that he could be, instead, with the woman he was reasonably sure *would* marry him. Sitting up straighter, he leaned in to see what Val was looking at. 'Yeah? Let's see.'

Val passed him a fact sheet for a charming blue-roofed house, its stucco exterior and arched doorways reminiscent of South Florida's Caribbean-influenced architecture. Or rather, the Florida homes mimicked the ones here in St Martin, which were influenced by French tastes – which of course was true about many structures in the West Indies. This was, he decided, the architectural circle of life, Caribbean version. It could be a reality show.

Marie-Louise said, 'That one, it's in Terres Basses – "lowlands" *en français*. It is *très exclusif*.'

For three-point-five million US dollars, it ought to be, he thought.

'That's where we were looking yesterday morning,' Val reminded him.

'*Alors*, there is a view of the Caribbean Sea from the

65

stone pool and spa – so nice for romantic soirées, no?' Marie-Louise smiled her ingratiating smile. 'But if you get company – maybe your real estate agent, yes? – you have four guest rooms, three baths – and your kitchen, well, it is *magnifique!*'

He fought to keep from rolling his eyes. Marie-Louise reminded him of the kinds of women he tried hardest to avoid. She would make an ideal host for his imaginary reality show, he decided, viewing Caribbean properties with wealthy couples and booting off the islands anyone whose net worth turned out to be less than ten million dollars.

'Carson *loves* to cook, right, Car?' Val said.

'"Loves" might be a little strong.'

'He's being modest. He's terrific in the kitchen – his Thai food is *killer*. Men should be self-sufficient, don't you think?'

'Oh, *oui*,' Marie-Louise said. 'They must cook and clean and make the money – it's what *we* do, *non*?'

'Equality,' Val said, nodding.

'*L'égalité*,' Marie-Louise agreed, both women looking at Carson.

'I'm all for it. I'll cook, and Val can do the dishes.'

'Not!'

'Spoken like a twenty-first-century princess.' Carson smiled. He'd known how Val would respond – she was useless in the kitchen, capable of little more than pouring cereal and pouring wine. It was part of her charm.

'The Princess *de la Mer*,' Marie-Louise declared.

Val took the fact sheet from him. 'And this house

looks like the perfect princess hideaway. What do you think, Car? Want to go see it?'

He considered what might happen if he said no, if he told her he thought dropping *any* million on a vacation house felt ridiculous and unreal and contrary to what his life was about – not that he could fully define 'about'; he considered how her smile would falter, replaced by confusion over his uncharacteristic – to her – behavior. She'd never seen him pessimistic or witnessed one of his 'philosophical jags', as Gene liked to call the lapses into dark introspection that seemed to sneak up on him now and again. He hadn't had one since hearing that Meg's mother had died so suddenly last September, just before he and Val met. Val wouldn't know what to do with *that* Carson, much as he usually didn't know himself. And maybe it was unfair to marry her without her having witnessed one of the spells – though he'd told her about them. Maybe he should make her see his full range, first.

Or maybe, in marrying her, he would effectively short-circuit his melancholy side and they'd live happily ever after. He stood, reached for Val's hand, and said, 'Let's go.'

A few minutes later he trailed the women down a flagstone path to where the real estate agent had parked her late-model Mercedes. The reality of his surroundings – the ridiculous blue of the Caribbean sky, the palm trees so perfect they hardly looked natural, the sculpted shrubbery, the flash of the $79,000 diamond on Val's left ring finger as she swung her arm – this reality was not the one he had planned for, growing up. It was not the reality he thought he was built for. Yet here he was. He trusted that if he tracked all his life's events or decisions in the long sequence that had led him to this moment, this reality, it would all make sense. It had to: he was getting too jaded, too tired of the rock-star life to maintain its status quo. This vivacious young woman in front of him in her faded denim short-shorts and snug pink tank wanted to marry him. She was, if not exactly the sort of woman he once thought he'd spend his life with, a very appealing alternative. So, barring brain damage or death, in four weeks they'd return to the island with wedding apparel, parents, and friends, and get the deed done.

Maybe then, he thought as he held the car door open for Val, he could put the past behind him for good and all.

TEN

When Kyle called her Saturday night, Savannah pretended to be busy with family – her dad's birthday gathering, she lied. Rachel had taught her by example how to string a guy along at first, to get him more interested. 'But, thanks for calling! Sorry I can only talk for like ten minutes,' she said.

'Nah, that's cool. Nice that they still like having you around.'

'Yeah,' she said, wishing they truly did. This morning it seemed like her mom wanted anything *but* her company, and her dad spent the whole drive to Rachel's on the phone. 'So what are you doing?'

'Thinkin' of you.'

'Seriously,' she said, turning on her stereo, low, so he'd hear background noise.

'Way seriously. I think about you all the time. I feel like we . . . you know, like maybe we belong together.' He laughed. 'You think I'm a dork, right? But it's just . . . you have this amazing effect on me. I can't wait to see you in person.'

She tried not to give away how flattered she was, though from the sound of it, he didn't need more stringing along. From the sound of it, he was hooked. What a relief; she wasn't good at all the boy–girl game-playing that came so naturally to other girls.

'Yeah, well, I'm really looking forward to seeing you, too,' she said. 'Where should I get a room?'

They talked about hotels, and then he asked if she was getting a rental car from the airport.

'Oh – well . . . do I have to? Because, um, it's kind of a hassle driving in Miami, right?' Especially without a license to allow a person to rent a car in the first place.

'True,' Kyle said. 'I usually let one of my brothers do the driving. So whatever – we can pick you up.'

'Or there might be a shuttle.'

'Or you can, you know, bunk with us at my brother's place, right? If you wanted to save some bucks, I mean.'

'I can afford a hotel,' she said. She knew enough to not plan to stay in an unfamiliar city with someone she'd met over the Internet, no matter how great he seemed so far. 'Thanks, though.'

She asked him about his brothers (he had two, both older and both 'making the parents proud'), and then they talked about what sorts of things they could do in Miami, including topless tanning, if that was her thing. Not that he was expecting it, not at all. And no, it wasn't exactly *legal*. But girls did it. 'If something like that appeals,' he said, 'well, you're so gorgeous you could fit right in with the other babes on the beach.'

Gorgeous. No one ever called her gorgeous before.

She was savoring the compliment when Kyle said, 'So, I want to make sure you really do have the bucks for the trip.'

'Yeah, definitely,' she assured him, wanting to sound independent, mature. 'I've got tons of money in savings – 'cause my parents, they're paying for school.' This wasn't a lie, they *were* paying for her private high school. And they'd be paying for college when the time came. 'So yeah, money's no trouble. What about you? If you needed, I could help you out.'

'What, me? Hey, no, I'm good.'

'Are you sure?' she asked. He sounded like he was trying to cover.

'I don't want to take your money. Anyway, I'll be bunking with my brothers and all, so it's cheap for me.'

'Okay. But I'm definitely paying for my own food and stuff.'

He laughed. 'One of those liberated girls, right? Hey, I'm good with that. I admire independence – which is why I'm not taking money from my parents anymore.' He and his parents didn't quite see things the same way, he said, and so he'd broken ties with them. 'Good that *you* didn't have to go to that extreme.'

Savannah was impressed by his strength of conviction. She said, 'So far. My parents don't really get me either, though, you know? Luckily, if things get bad there's always my trust fund to live off of.' Part of her dad's obsessive financial-planning strategy, not accessible until she was eighteen – but of course she didn't say that part.

'That *is* lucky,' Kyle agreed.

They talked a minute or two longer, during which he told her again how he couldn't wait to see her, and how he already felt like they were so *right* for each other. 'I've never felt this way about a girl so soon, you know?'

'Never?' she asked, skeptical but wanting to believe.

He said, 'Trust me, you aren't like everybody else. You're special, and I dig that, I see it – bet every other guy does, too.'

When she got off the phone she was *glowing* – she went to her mirror and checked.

ELEVEN

Sunday morning wasn't going well. Forty-one-year-old Cristina Lang's labor had slowed to a crawl after fifteen trying hours, and Meg watched the fetal monitor with narrowed eyes, her mouth a grim line on her pale face. The baby's heart rate had been fluctuating for the last hour, and was now in a steady downward trend. In a voice low enough that only Susan, the labor nurse, could hear, Meg said, 'You're right: I don't think we have any choice. Get her prepped.'

To the sweat-covered mother-to-be she said, 'Cristina, you've worked awfully hard, but I think we're going to have to take over. Your cervix doesn't want to finish dilating, and I'm not sure why yet, but your little guy's getting stressed. We don't want to see him suffer any long-term effects, okay?'

Cristina's husband Martin, a stocky man whose landscape company did Meg's yard maintenance and many of her neighbors', looked alarmed. 'Take over? You mean she can't have a natural birth?'

'I'm sorry,' Meg told him. 'It was worth trying, but

her failure to progress and the slowing fetal heart rate suggest that the baby's having trouble.' She turned to Cristina. 'Sometimes even the most prepared moms have to go with plan B. Susan is going to get you all set up, and I'll see you in the OR in just a few minutes.'

Cristina reached for Meg's hand. 'He's okay? My baby, he's going to be all right?'

'He should be fine, as long as we get him out soon. Try not to worry.'

'Okay,' the woman nodded, and Meg read the relief in her eyes. 'Okay, good.'

Meg squeezed her hand, then gave Martin's shoulder a pat as she moved past him and out of the room to head to the OR. Her mind was focused on the task ahead as she walked down the hallway and around the corner. When she stumbled just before reaching the door to the OR suite, she recovered her balance quickly and went on to get herself ready to deliver the baby.

She ran the hottest water she could stand and scrubbed all along the ridges of her nails and the creases in her hands. Having to use a scalpel to finish Cristina's job was regrettable but necessary, and she looked forward to the moment when she would lift the slippery infant out and hand him over to the nurse, a fresh miracle hot and pulsing with the force of all life. The regular opportunity to witness a child's first shocked breath was why she chose obstetrics; nothing was more wondrous, more startling or fantastic. Every healthy child was a symbol of *possibility*. All these new tiny people she helped enter the world reminded her that her own life was not terribly significant – and made it easier for her to forget her own disappointments.

Keith, the portly scrub nurse whose own wife was due to deliver their first any day, pushed open the door. 'We're just about set. You ready, Doc?' he asked.

She turned off the water with her elbows. 'Be right there.'

He nodded and stepped back into the operating suite. Meg glanced through the window as she dried off, considering the baby's position, previous scar tissue on Cristina's uterus, how much time had passed since she'd made the decision to operate. Emergency C-sections were her least favorite part of her occupation, the riskiest of all procedures just by their nature. The mothers required general anesthesia, the babies were always in distress – these surgeries felt like crapshoots *despite* her expertise, despite her absolute dedication to her patients. She only ever had to do them when what was supposed to be predictable and routine became a cascading flow of everything opposite.

She backed into the suite, keeping her hands sterile, and stood still while a tech assisted her with gown and gloves. Her right arm, the one that was giving her trouble, felt a little stiff, sluggish as she held it out for the glove. As soon as the tech stepped away, Meg lifted both arms above her head and stretched.

'Need a nap?' asked Clay Williams, the new surgeon who would be assisting. 'Susan said you all have been at it all night with this one.'

'We have,' Meg agreed as she approached the

table, where he stood facing her from the far side. 'But I think I'll wait on the nap until after we finish.'

'Well, I s'pose that *is* the better protocol,' Clay joked, his mouth hidden behind the light green mask but his smile apparent in his eyes – as was a kind of interested regard that surprised her. Was he flirting? He added, 'You pros know best.'

He had to be several years her junior, and they'd worked together only a few times, socialized at a couple of conferences, chatted before or after staff meetings now and then; even so, she had the distinct feeling he was attracted to her. Her response was friendly but circumspect: 'I tried that napping-during-surgery approach and, well, somehow the results weren't up to American Medical Association standards.'

'Bah, rules are made to be broken,' Clay said – alluding to marital rules, perhaps? Or was she just imagining that sparkle of interest, that suggestive tone?

The anesthetist, a serious, middle-aged man named Leo, spoke up then, bringing Meg's attention back to the job at hand. 'She's all set.'

Meg looked closely at her now-unconscious patient, at the draping around Cristina's iodine-orange belly, at the tray of instruments nearby, checking that everything was in place. 'What was the last fetal bpm?' she asked, referring to the baby's heart rate.

'Eighty-one, right before we unhooked her.'

Very low, but not absolutely critical. Meg nodded at the assembled team of nurses, technicians, and a pair of neonatologists, and said, 'Okay then, let's make a birthday.'

At first, everything seemed to be fine. She reached for the scalpel, grasped it with no trouble, aligned the blade with Cristina's skin just above the pubic bone. Then it was as if all the strength simply leached out of her arm. The scalpel dropped from her fingers, tumbled onto the edge of the operating table and down to the floor, landing with a clatter. Meg looked up, embarrassed and concerned. There was a baby in distress here; her arm could *not* refuse to cooperate.

'Butterfingers,' she joked, sweat breaking out on her forehead, dampening her armpits and her palms, inside her gloves.

'Mmm, a candy bar does sound good, but I think another scalpel's the better choice,' Clay said.

'Right, a *scalpel*,' Meg nodded, trying to play along. She looked down at her hand. It rested, yet, on Cristina's belly, on the mound of a baby who was almost certainly fading fast. It took all her concentration to lift her arm and pull it in, close to her chest.

'Here you go,' the tech said, holding out a second scalpel. Meg looked at it, its steel blade glinting under the lights, taunting her. The moment stretched out in long, agonizing delay as Meg willed her arm to extend normally. It felt leaden.

Clutching her wrist with her left hand, she stepped back abruptly.

'Dr Williams, would you proceed?' she said, feeling the eyes of everyone there watching her with concern. 'I have a . . . a cramp. In my hand.'

'I – sure,' Clay said. He hurried around to her side

and reached for the scalpel. 'Thanks for the opportunity,' he added, making it seem like she was staging this as a favor to him.

Marshalling her focus away from her arm and onto the crucial matter of delivering Cristina's baby, she guided Clay through the relatively unfamiliar-to-him procedure. He worked quickly and with steady assurance, but when he pulled the baby out, it was clear that something had gone very wrong. The tiny boy was well formed but gray, motionless as Clay put him in the hands of the neonatal specialist. Clay glanced at her, his eyes full of dread.

Her own heart had plummeted, but she tried to reassure him. 'You did everything right.' Behind them, the specialist and his team worked to revive the baby. 'Let's finish up here,' she nodded toward her patient, who, as difficult as it was for any obstetrician to remember when there was trouble with the baby, remained her priority.

'Right,' Clay said. 'Do you want *me* to—'

'Yes,' she said, her voice low. 'My arm ...' She frowned behind her mask.

'No problem.'

'Thank you.'

She stood by, feeling helpless in every sense. What had gone wrong? She reviewed Cristina's labor in her mind, recalled the events and procedures of the surgery, thought again about the baby's heart rate troubles – but as soon as Clay delivered the rest of the umbilical cord and the placenta, the culprit became obvious: a knot in the cord.

'Shit,' she said, reaching for it with her left hand. 'It must've gotten looped early in her pregnancy.' Rarely, but once in a while, a very active fetus with a longer-than-usual cord could manage to loop through it. Rarely, but once in a while, an ultrasound would fail to show it. Then, at some point in the labor, the knot, which had been loose enough not to be a problem, tightened up or got compressed, cutting off the baby's blood and oxygen supply. In the minutes – literally *minutes* – between when the monitor had been removed and Clay had reached in to pull the baby out, the baby had crashed. Silently, fading away without a struggle. There was no way for them to know, or to do anything differently even if they *had* known. Except . . . except for those forty-five or so seconds after she'd dropped the scalpel: it was possible that those seconds made the difference. Clay nudged her with his elbow, and when she looked at him, he shook his head as if he were reading her thoughts, as if to say, *Don't go there.*

She looked behind them, at the slumped shoulders of the group surrounding the warming table, and swallowed hard.

Alone in an elevator two hours later, Clay and Meg rode in silence until he reached forward and pushed the Stop button.

Startled, she said, 'What are you doing?'

Clay touched her chin, to get her to look up at him. 'It's not your fault.'

She looked away. 'You don't know that. If I hadn't screwed up my arm—'

'You didn't know it was going to cramp up just then.'

'I knew it *could*. It happened once last week.'

'Once. Last *week*.'

She appreciated his support, but the truth was that she'd had a hint while getting suited up, and she'd ignored it. And now a baby was dead.

Clay continued, 'Look, suppose we could have that minute back. The baby *might* have survived – I double-emphasize "might" – in which case he almost certainly would've been severely brain-damaged from what had already occurred, and dependent on his poor parents for the rest of their lives. A vegetable, if you'll forgive the crassness of the term.'

'Maybe,' she acknowledged, imagining Cristina and Mark trying to manage the needs of such a child along with their chubby, charming two-year-old daughter Chloe, whom she had also delivered by emergency C-section, without a hitch. She saw their baby boy with vacant eyes, a permanent feeding tube, a ventilator, no future – and couldn't wish such a life on anyone.

Clay took her right hand with both of his, massaging it gently, and looked into her eyes. 'We can't save them all, you know. Hell, we can hardly save ourselves.'

She knew without asking that he was referring to his attraction to her, a married woman. Saying they had no control, not over death and not over what-ever strange forces brought people together, not over love. She let his eyes hold her that way for a long moment, a moment when the comfort and support and affection of someone who truly understood was exactly the salve she needed.

Unfortunately, it couldn't last. 'I have to get going,' she said, the rest of the day's obligations intruding, reminding her that her world existed outside this tender gesture, that she was wrong to welcome it.

Clay said, 'Me too.' But still he held her hand, and she didn't pull it away. 'Meg . . .'

'Clay.'

He sighed quietly, then let go and leaned over to start the elevator again. It gave a small lurch and began the rest of its journey to the main floor.

He said, 'You're a damn fine doctor. Everyone says so.'

'You did a good job today,' she told him.

The chime sounded and the doors slid open. She stepped out first, into a crowd of lunchtime visitors. 'Try to enjoy the rest of your weekend,' she said.

He nodded, his eyes unreadable. 'You too.'

She walked away from him then, and away from the hospital, the paperwork, away from the grieving parents who had so graciously already absolved her of wrongdoing – for now anyway. Her other responsibilities were calling: she needed to phone her father and cancel their dinner date, Savannah needed to be picked up from the game Meg had missed, Brian text-messaged her from the golf course, asking her to buy a bottle of Moët for a friend of his who'd just gotten engaged. Self-indulgence, especially with Clay Williams, was a luxury she could not afford.

TWELVE

Savannah and Rachel soaked in the poolside spa while Meg stood at her black granite kitchen counter making a turkey sandwich. The counter was so glossy that she could see her reflection, a tired woman with a deep crease between her brows; she reached up and pressed the crease, stretched her cheeks to erase the scowl. That was better, but she thought she might have the granite changed for something matte; the glossy stuff was obviously meant for Suzy Homemaker types who whistled pleasantly while they mixed and kneaded and dolloped and minced and sautéed, nothing more taxing than making a tasty meal on their minds. A kitchen counter should not remind a woman of her stresses and faults; it was bad enough just to have such a beautiful kitchen in the first place, its underuse a vague but ever-present guilt.

Through the open patio doors she could hear the girls laughing, hear their cell phones ringing every few minutes, while she concentrated on smoothing mayonnaise onto cracked-wheat bread with her right hand.

She dipped her knife into the jar, scooped little globs of mayo, spread it easily with the knife's tip, over and over again without even a hint of weakness. 'Son of a bitch,' she said.

When her own cell phone began vibrating in the pocket of her white linen pants, it startled her and she dropped the knife onto the floor. She took the phone from her pocket, saw it was her sister Kara, and answered, her eyes on the knife.

'Hello, sis,' she answered, making her voice normal, as she'd done for the girls when she picked them up. How accomplished she was at pretending.

'Did you see it?' Kara asked.

'Did I see what?'

'The official announcement – Carson's engagement, what else?'

Kara *would* be all a-tizz about that. She'd followed Carson's career and life like a groupie, just as she'd once trailed Meg and Carson over the hills and fields of their farms. 'I saw something about it on the CNN website,' Meg said, bending down to get the knife. 'Is that what you mean?'

'No, no, not that. The Ocala paper's got the real official thing.'

'How do you know?' Meg asked, picking up the knife. Kara lived in Northern California now, near Travis Air Force Base where her husband Todd, a master sergeant three years away from retirement, was finishing out his enlistment.

'I read it online – how do you think I keep up with what's going on back home?' For Kara, who'd had four homes since leaving Florida in 1992, only Ocala would ever be the real thing. She'd told Meg she was trying to talk Todd into going back there when he got out of the service; she wanted to start a plant nursery. She had it all planned out and was certain it would be a hit. Of all the Powell girls, Kara was the most like their father.

'I assumed you were psychic, obviously,' Meg said.

'Oh, I wish! Then I wouldn't have to ferret out every detail of the kids' lives. God knows they don't tell me anything! Well, at least I can read the news – and you really need to see this. You get the paper, right?'

'We do – but I haven't read it yet.'

'You haven't read it? Jesus, it's four-thirty out there – what've you been doing all day?'

Kara's innocent question was an ice pick in Meg's gut, but she made herself stay calm. 'I had a mom in labor all last night and this morning, then Savannah had a softball game this afternoon. I'm just getting a chance to make a sandwich and sit down for five minutes.'

'Well, don't sit yet – get the paper so you can see this.'

While Meg tracked the paper to the den, where Brian had left it after his cursory glances at the front section and sports, Kara asked how their father was doing.

'Haven't you talked to him?' Meg said.

'Not in about two weeks. He's being pissy about us not being able to visit this summer. Screening his calls, I assume. But I know he's fine or you'd have told me.'

Of course she would think that; gatekeeper of information was Meg's role, had always been her role. Her parents had left her to mind her sisters, and now her sisters had left her to mind their parents – parent, now – and always, she was to keep everyone informed. 'He's doing okay. Settling in. His left kidney's acting up.'

'Is he eating right? I swear, he's so stubborn! What's the deal with the kidney?'

Meg pulled out the newspaper's lifestyles section, where the engagement and wedding announcements appeared each weekend. 'I'm not sure; I told him to call his nephrologist.'

'There you go with the big words,' Kara teased. She was bright, but not college-educated, having married Todd at nineteen, three years after meeting him at Meg's wedding, where he'd parked cars for a few extra bucks before starting basic training. Four kids – all boys – had followed. Meg hoped Kara would prevail with her desire to come back to Florida; she missed her sister, who had been her closest friend besides Carson. She and Beth were close now too, and she could visit any of her sisters by plane if she could just find the time. Time, however, hid from her as well as Savannah had done in department stores when she was little. Any more time stubbornly refused to be found.

Returning to the kitchen, Meg said, 'Okay, so I have the paper – lifestyle section, I presume.'

'Open it to page two.'

Meg did, and there was the announcement. 'Grammy winner Carson McKay to wed Miss Valerie Haas of

Malibu, CA,' read the caption beneath a photographer's picture of the betrothed couple. Meg closed the paper.

'Well?' Kara said. 'Isn't she just as cute as you can imagine?'

'Cuter,' Meg said. She finished constructing her sandwich, grasping the knife again and cutting the sandwich smoothly.

'I never would've pictured him with a professional *surfer*. Have you ever heard of her? My god, it says she's twenty-two! And he's, what? Forty?'

A professional surfer? Meg hardly knew there *was* such a career, particularly for women. 'Not yet – he's thirty-nine until November.' Her own thirty-ninth was coming up in late June.

'Wonder what they'll do for his fortieth. Probably rent an island for a party and invite their hundred closest friends.'

As Kara was saying this, an image of Carson on the old tire swing came to Meg; he was sitting with his legs through it, holding on to the thick rope they'd used to suspend it from a high branch of the oak near the swimming lake. He leaned back and, with bare feet, pushed himself in a lazy circle, while she watched from the shady base of the tree. 'For your fortieth birthday,' he said, 'I'm taking you to Africa on safari.'

'Are you, now?' she asked, more interested in watching his naked back than in considering anything that might happen more than twenty years in the future.

He said, 'Yep. Count on it.'

'What about for *your* fortieth?' she said.

'Thailand,' he answered, 'for lemongrass shrimp.' He let the tire sway then, peering into the oak leaves like their future was painted there, episodes of their life-to-be displayed for preview on each toothy leaf.

Kara laughed. 'God. Seventeen years.'

For a second Meg thought Kara was talking about how long it had been since that day. Not seventeen years, she thought. Twenty – no, twenty-one. And then she realized Kara was calculating the age difference between Carson and his fiancée. No wonder they were calling him a cradle robber; his bride-to-be was probably just learning to walk when he'd made his safari promise.

'Whatever makes him happy,' Meg said, wanting to be done with the topic. 'Now tell me, how go your plans for the plant nursery?'

'Do I detect a change-of-subject attempt here? I mean, c'mon Meggie, you had your shot and you let him go.'

'True,' Meg said. Neither she nor her parents had ever told Kara or Beth or the youngest, Julianne, the whole truth about why she and Carson broke up.

Kara sighed. 'Jesus, if I'd known he was going to get famous, *I* would have snagged him, for God's sake. Nothing against Todd.'

'Of course.'

'Well, I guess we both fucked up where old Car's concerned – gotta live with it. But life is good, right? I mean, I have Todd and the boys, you have Brian and

Savannah – you wouldn't trade her for the world, even to have a kid of Carson's.'

'Nope,' Meg agreed, though of course it was fully possible that the two children Kara was referencing – Savannah and a theoretical child of Carson's – were in fact one in the same. But Kara had no clue that Savannah might not be Brian's. No clue that Meg had seen Carson the day of her wedding and that she had not been nearly as successful at closing the door behind her as she thought she'd be.

'Are you doing okay? You sound cranky. Maybe get a nap in. God, I wish I could steal time for a nap! You should see my kitchen counters – do you think Keiffer and Evan could get their lunch plates past the clay mockup of Mt Doom and into the *sink*? Anyhow, I better go; I hear Tony screaming about something, and Todd's out in the garage.'

Meg smiled at the happy disorder of her sister's home. 'I'm glad you called.'

'Tell Dad to call me. Kisses to all,' Kara said, and they hung up.

Meg simply stood there holding her phone for a minute afterward, wistfulness and loss washing over her. She missed Kara and Beth and Julianne, but they, at least, were still walking the Earth. They, at least, were accessible by a half-day's airplane journey. But their mother, snatched away so suddenly that Meg still sometimes picked up the phone to call her before remembering, was lost to her, to them, forever. How was a girl – all right, a woman – supposed to manage without her mother? The notebook diaries gave her windows through which to view her mother in their past, but what of today, when she needed a supportive arm around her shoulders?

'Oh Mom,' she sighed. 'Is this as good as it gets?'

The dark quiet of the screened porch, late that night, soothed Meg only a little as she sat on a chaise and sipped gin, straight. Brian and Savannah both had been asleep for hours, but she had yet to even feel like closing her eyes. She *was* tired – so tired she couldn't even calculate how many hours it had been since she'd slept. But her thoughts swirled and tumbled like river rapids, making sleep impossible.

Her mother, she knew, had lived with turmoil most of her life – she was the youngest of eight kids whose father died in Normandy. Then she married into it; Meg's father was always launching some half-planned scheme that inevitably failed. The first was a citrus farm like the McKays', with thousands of young trees that were killed in the second year by some blight he hadn't known to look for. Next he bought the land that would later become their horse farm and built a huge greenhouse, for the supposedly easier job of growing rare orchids to sell to collectors. Yet neither he nor her mother, who by then was also tending *her*, could master the expensive, sensitive plants, which died off steadily while the debt blossomed.

Just after Kara's birth, when Meg was five, he gave up that particular dream; they sold off all the orchid paraphernalia at a loss and built stables, with the goal of not just boarding thoroughbreds but also breeding them. Her father was sure his powers of persuasion wouldn't be lost on the horses *or* the people who liked to buy them. He succeeded just often enough to encourage him to sink more money into the venture, and by the time Julianne was born, nine years after Meg, the family was firmly shackled to what would become her father's most enduring obsession.

She remembered many times – whole seasons, in fact, when all she and her sisters ate for lunch was bread and jam, or eggs from the noisy, skittish chickens they raised. They wore shoes from the thrift store and clothes bought at Saturday-morning yard sales. They learned early how to answer the phone and politely tell the bill collectors that their parents were busy but could they please take a message? She had coached her sisters, the three of them standing in front of her looking like uneven stair steps, each taking a practice turn with the phone. She'd been twelve, maybe thirteen. 'Show them all,' her mother had directed. 'You know how Julianne likes to run for the phone.' Julianne, at three, was easiest to train – she was happy to imitate, to earn Meg's praise, while Beth and Kara had asked questions Meg couldn't answer and knew better than to forward to their parents:

'Why do the people keep calling, Meggie?'

'Why won't Mommy or Daddy answer the phone?'

Only when some large man or another showed up – always in an ill-fitting suit – did her father deal with matters himself. From her bedroom window she would watch the men leave, her father putting them into their nondescript sedans with a smile and a handshake.

Making dubious promises that had, a few years later, led to one of her own.

Her affluent adult life could hardly compare with the craziness her mother endured for so many years, but she liked that they shared a steady temperament. For as far back as she could remember, she too had weathered what crises came by trusting that solutions would present themselves – always with the help of the Blessed Virgin, of course, or so her mother wanted her to believe. Meg endured, too busy minding her sisters, or feeding the chickens, or currying the succession of horses her father always insisted were Triple-Crown winners in the making, to do anything else.

Tonight the low chirping of crickets outside the porch spoke of good luck, something she felt sorely short of just now. Yet as quickly as this self-pity reared up, she pushed it down; she had no right to feel sorry for herself, *none*, and she buried the urge by remembering that, short of the unstoppable medical crises she'd faced now and then as a doctor, she was responsible for everything in her life, good *and* bad.

Responsible, *that* was the trait that made her rescue her parents from looming foreclosure and allow her sisters to finish growing up there on the farm, instead of crammed into some tiny, roach-infested apartment. That was the trait that kept her from seeking out a definitive answer to Savannah's paternity. The trait made her a popular, respected doctor – and tempered her guilt when things went wrong even after she'd done everything right. She was always careful, responsible, even when she didn't want to be. Almost always.

But in the same way her mother could not, despite valiant efforts, save the family from the ruin that seemed sure until Meg married Brian, Meg's effort had not been able to save the Langs' baby. Nor had it secured the satisfying life she'd rationalized would follow her marriage in due time. You could work hard, stick to all the rules, and still fail.

Which made her wonder why, then, she bothered to be so damn careful.

The sweet, musky smell of aging honeysuckle blooms drifted to Meg on the warm night's breeze. She closed her eyes and inhaled deeply, putting aside the heavy thoughts, her worry about her arm, the guilt she felt over losing the Langs' baby, and the odd lack of guilt she felt for having encouraged Clay's attentions, putting them aside and simply filling herself with nature's sensual buffet. A warm spring night. Sweetly scented flowers. Damp soil. The smell of wild mint and freshly mowed grass.

The grass brought her back, for a moment, to something Brian said earlier. She'd told him about the stillbirth, and he was, of course, sympathetic. 'Jesus, Meg, how awful for them,' he said. But then he added, 'I don't mean to sound insensitive, but do you think Lang will still do our lawn?'

Ever practical.

A mockingbird, apparently confused about the hour, began its litany of calls someplace off on the east side of their property, a three-acre estate in a community of similar ones. Meg turned in the direction of the sound, as if it was possible to see the bird at three AM.

She saw the silhouettes of towering pines and oaks and magnolias and wondered if maybe the bird, too, was trying to shake off a bad day: some offense by its mate, or a wound inflicted by too zealous a flight. She thought maybe *she* ought to sing too, despite the hour; singing worked for Savannah. It worked, she supposed, for Carson.

She drew her bare legs up and wrapped her arms around them – both arms behaving just the way they should, go figure. Resting her chin on her knees, she let herself be distracted by thoughts of Carson and the news that he was about to be married.

Probably she should just satisfy her curiosity and go read the details – maybe even plan to send them a gift. Whoever Valerie Haas was, she would have to be very impressive, considering how long Carson had been single, and how eligible he was.

Probably she should get the details about his wedding and his bride so that she wouldn't be distracted any further, so that she could close that chapter of her life – hadn't it been open for far too long as it was?

Carson, married. In love – a *good* thing, even if the thought of it gave her a pang of possessiveness that hurt. Even if imagining him permanently joined to anyone else brought pain like a sharp stone being pressed into her heart.

THIRTEEN

Meg took one of the notebook diaries with her to work Monday, reading it in her office during her lunch break.

December 5, 1987

Carolyn and I were talking about the kids today, over at the co-op. Carson's thinking of buying Meggie a ring for Christmas. He hasn't told Meggie. Nothing could be more natural than the two of them married. Caro thinks he means to have an April wedding, since Meggie loves springtime. To be purely honest, the timing couldn't be better for her moving in with Carson, because if things keep up like they are, we'll lose the whole farm by May.

But of course it hadn't gone like that. It was Brian who proposed – in a sense – two weeks before Christmas, a time when she couldn't fail to see the romance in his gesture.

He hadn't been her supervisor for several months,

but she saw him often. Back in early fall he'd told her that the reason he'd moved himself out of front-end management and into Investments was because he hoped to date her. He wasn't pushy about it, and he assured her that her job was in no way affected by her firm refusals to do anything more than have a platonic lunch with him now and then. She never let him pay.

This lunch, though, was unlike any that had come before.

They went to Margot's, a café she couldn't afford to eat at on her own, by way, he said, of a 'Christmas bonus – my treat'. The place was done up for the holidays, with swags of fresh holly and twinkling white lights and deep red velvet ribbon hanging above every doorway. Brian sat across from her at an intimate, white-draped table and told her he had an outrageous proposition. Would she just listen and promise to give it some thought?

'Meg,' he said, 'I heard something impressive a while back, one Friday when you weren't at the Trough. I usually don't listen much to gossip, but – well, here's what I heard: Vicki was telling Mark how you give your whole paycheck to your parents to help pay their bills, that you've been doing it since you started with us.'

Her cheeks burned; Vicky wasn't supposed to tell anyone about that – and *especially* not when someone like Brian could overhear. Her family's difficulties embarrassed her, made her look bad by association. She said, 'Yeah, well, they've had some money problems. One of the stallions fractured a leg, and—'

'Oh, don't get me wrong – I think you're amazing.

That's so generous. So loyal. What kid is willing to sacrifice their own agenda to help their parents these days?'

Meg shrugged. 'I have to help if I can.' The choice was simple to her, automatic as breathing.

'And, you've been loyal to the bank, working here, what? – over two years now? Then there's your loyalty to your boyfriend – which I'm *not* so crazy about.' He laughed.

She shrugged again, embarrassed but flattered, too, which she feared was *dis*loyal, and her face grew even hotter.

He reached over and took her hand in his cool, smooth ones, white-collar hands. 'I admire you, and you know I really like you, Meg. You work hard, you take care of your family – and Jesus, you're *so* pretty. We've known each other for a while, right? We worked well together, we get along – and, I know this sounds crazy, but, I . . . I want to help you out. You have to give me a shot, Meg; you owe it to yourself to see if you think we're as compatible as I already know we are. And if you do, I want you to consider marrying me.'

She was sure she heard him wrong. 'You want *what*?'

'If you agreed to marry me, well, Dad and I would be in a position to help your parents with their mortgage.' He held up one hand to stop her protest. 'I know, it sounds like a bribe, but think of it as an incentive. A bonus.'

'How do you know about their mortgage?' Even she knew little about the details of her parents' finances.

'We hold it,' Brian said. 'They refinanced with us a couple years ago. I've had Dad delay the foreclosure proceedings until after I talked to you today.' He leaned closer, looked into her eyes. 'Look, Meg, I'm not a crazy person; I'm just a man who knows his mind. We could be really good together, I'm sure of it. Maybe you think you love Carson, and maybe you do love him, in a way. But what is that? *Adolescent* love, which never lasts. He's been your escape from a stressful, crazy life, but you won't need that – him – anymore; you'll be able to solve your family's problems. You'll be the hero.'

Then he kissed her, and she was too astonished to object. 'Say you'll think about it.'

She hated to, but how could she not?

She couldn't tell Carson, Brian said; no one could know, because of the 'creative financing' that would take place if things worked out. She didn't exactly want to tell Carson anyway; the whole situation felt outrageous, unseemly – and yet, it could be a lightning strike of good fortune for her family. Maybe even fate.

She had to save her family if she could. It was the right choice. The moral choice. By choosing Brian, she could save her sisters from a family reputation even lower than it was already. She could lift them up to a higher social plateau, where they'd have a chance to be popular at school and never have to give up their free time just to keep the family in bread and milk. Without the overwhelming debt, her parents would have money for extras: Kara wanted to go with the high school's Spanish Club to Mexico City; Beth wanted to take piano lessons; Julianne wanted riding boots and an English saddle and regulation jump bars to practice with so that she might compete. The girls could *dress* better.

As much as any of those things, Meg wanted her mother to be able to sleep nights instead of wandering the house like a restless spirit. So how could she self-ishly hold on to Carson and watch the rest of them spiral into misery, deprived of the land that gave them, if nothing else, room to own a piece of sky, a shaggy oak, a footpath to a shallow pond where beautiful, if mostly barren, horses stood in the morning to drink?

So she'd gone along with it, meaning to give Brian a fair try. There was truth in what he said about adolescent love, she couldn't argue with this even now, on its theoretical basis. But in her nontheoretical life, the answer that had seemed so clean and obvious to her at the time of Brian's proposal became murkier as time passed. She liked Brian, liked the new work schedule that allowed her to commute to Gainesville three days a week for school, liked the places she got to go with him: New York, Puerto Rico, Washington, DC. But she missed Carson like she'd miss her right hand if she woke up to find it suddenly gone. Though there was no real choice but to marry Brian, she felt so guilty about her decision that she literally ached, as though her heart had weakened but was forced to keep beating. She just could not understand why what was supposed to be right felt so wrong.

Well, she understood better now.

Leaving her sandwich untouched, she read her mother's entry from the day she married Brian.

August 20, 1989

I'm exhausted, but what a beautiful day we had for a wedding! Thank God the country club's air-conditioning didn't wear itself out, or none of us would've lasted until midnight the way we did. Spencer was in his element with all those horse people . . .

Creamy white orchids and red roses and white satin ribbon everywhere, but Meggie was the loveliest of all. Four thousand dollars for just her dress! Heavens, it was beautiful, that strapless style that's in all the magazines, smooth satin on top, seed pearls and tiny crystals on every inch of the skirt. And the train! I can't get over it. It was a gift from Nancy Hamilton, Brian's grandmother, so how could we say no? They are all treating our girl like royalty. Spencer insisted we pay for the girls' dresses, and they were princesses too. Beth and Julianne were asleep in the car five minutes after we left the reception, and I'll bet Kara won't last much longer. She's been on the phone with some boy she met there since we got home half an hour ago. I'm still too wound up to settle into bed, but when I do, well! I plan to sleep until eight! The horses won't starve if their breakfast's a little late.

She looked happy. Well, a little dazed, but what bride isn't? We raised her right, I have to say. She has plenty of poise. I couldn't stand being the center of that much attention, I know that.

My biggest fear, I admit it, was that people would look at us and know how little we had to do with putting on the wedding. If not for that famous Preakness trainer buying Spencer's baby, Earned Luck, last week, we wouldn't have seemed anywhere close to successful enough to pay for such a party. It made it easy to sound like our fortunes had turned around.

Well, they have, haven't they? She went through with it after all. Bruce took Spencer aside just before the reception, told him it'll all be taken care of Monday. That's almost three thousand dollars a month it'll save us. Three thousand! I hardly know how to sit here and write happy thoughts, when usually I'm just trying to figure out a new way to rob Peter. What good luck Meggie has had.

I remember when she first came to Spencer and me to ask about the mortgage. Was it true, she wanted to know, that we'd been late for seven or eight months in a row? Was it true we'd heard from the bank that they were starting foreclosure proceedings? That we could lose the whole business and the house, too, in just a few months' time? I felt so ashamed. Spencer hedged, not wanting to worry her with all that mess, but then she told us why she was asking. Told us that Brian wanted to help us out – depending. I was against it at first, but not Spencer. He washed the doubt right out of Meggie's eyes and mine with his enthusiasm for the idea. It was up to

her, of course, but since she was asking, well, we
had to say it was a terrific bit of luck that Brian
had taken a shine to her. An amazing opportunity
for her, if she wanted to take it.

She did look happy today. The more I think
about it, the more I'm sure of it. And I'm sure
she never saw Carson's truck parked down the
street from the church. He'll find someone else
before too long, now that he's seen she isn't ever
coming back to him. My heart ached for him,
but he's young, he'll be fine. They're all so young.
They can make their lives be whatever they
want. Isn't that how it works?

'Sure. Whatever we want,' Meg whispered.

Her nurse, Laurie, knocked once and opened the
door. 'Your one o'clock's here.'

'Thanks. Give me three minutes.'

She closed the notebook and stuffed it back into
her satchel, certain that this foray into the past wasn't
doing her any good. The spinning blades were uncom-
fortably close right now.

FOURTEEN

On Tuesday, their last morning on the island, Carson woke before Val and lay watching the fan turn lazily above him. Hung over from the night before, he tried to sort out the remains of a dream. Something about Spencer sending him out on one of the mares – to check that she'd been shoed right? Something crazy like that, and as he rode off, he saw Meg standing in Brian's arms. He tried to turn the horse, but it kept running, and when he looked behind him, he couldn't even see Meg anymore.

A stupid dream; as it happened, she'd been the one to run.

Val slept soundly next to him, a pillow covering her head, smooth browned arms flung out toward the headboard as if she was surfing in her sleep. He lifted the pillow and looked at her, thinking again how young she was; she looked especially youthful when sleeping, long blond eyelashes against her tan face, no lines around her eyes, lips chapped from salt and sun, just as she must have looked as a teen. Her age – the difference in their ages – didn't concern him too much, but he did wonder how long it would be before she was ready to slow down some, do the family thing. He wanted kids eventually, would have had them already if not for Meg's about-face.

He didn't especially *like* thinking about Meg, but obviously, with his wedding to Val approaching fast, he could see why all these memories were being triggered. Unfortunately you couldn't just dump your past to clear the way for your future – although Meg sure seemed to have succeeded at doing just that.

Leaving Val in bed, Carson pulled on shorts and left the villa. After stopping at the outdoor breakfast buffet to grab some coffee and a couple of chocolate croissants, he meandered down to the beach, marveling at the multi-toned clear blue water and the benevolence of morning sunshine – something he had too little of at home in Seattle. He wished his mind felt as peaceful as the scene before him looked. Maybe if he could spend the whole day lying here on a chaise, he'd feel like he was actually having a vacation. That, however, wasn't in the cards.

Val wanted to stop in Philipsburg to look at wedding bands before their early afternoon flight. Dutch St Martin, or St *Maarten*, as it was when you crossed the French–Dutch border, was known for having great jewelry at low prices. Already they'd browsed some shops, Val buying platinum-and-diamond tennis bracelets for each of her bridesmaids. He wasn't eager to have to cram in yet another activity before they headed to Florida for more wedding planning with his parents, but he wanted Val to be happy.

He was a sucker that way, when it came to people he cared about. The last time he'd ventured so far – almost as far as he'd come now with Val – he'd gotten pretty badly singed. Okay, burned; why minimize it?

Though he was looking at the calm water of the bay, he was seeing the past.

It was almost Christmas, '87. He'd been working for a friend of his dad's, warehousing fruit for extra money to buy Meg an engagement ring. Later on the day he'd been in town to get the ring – a simple solitaire, less than a third of a carat, set in gold – she called him and asked him to meet her at the tree.

'Just come over here,' he told her. By then he'd been living in the shed for two years; they spent most of their free time there.

'No, I . . . I'd rather be outside, okay?'

'Sure.' Distracted by his excitement about the ring, he missed the tension in her voice. Instead, he thought of how he could give her the ring there at the tree; that was a better plan than the elaborate fancy-dinner-bended-knee thing he'd been thinking of doing. Outdoors, at their spot – a much better plan.

The sun was low, the temperature dropping with it. He threw on his denim jacket, tucked the ring box into one pocket, and hurried through the groves, past the lake, rehearsing his proposal in his head. When he got to the tree, hands in pockets, the box square and promising in his right hand, he saw Meg's expression and pulled his hands out, empty.

'What's the matter?'

She was sitting at the base of their oak tree, arms

wrapped around her knees. 'I've been thinking,' she said.

'Waste of time,' he joked, nervous without knowing why. She shrugged and looked past him, biting her lip. He squatted in front of her. 'Just spit it out.' Whatever it was couldn't be so bad, not for the two of them anyway. Must be it had to do with money and the Powells' farm – the talk was that Spencer was about to go bankrupt.

'It's over, Car,' she said, looking down at her sneakers. She was about to wear a hole in the left one, at the big toe.

'I heard. What are they planning to do?'

She looked up sharply. 'Who?'

'Your parents. Are they filing for bankruptcy or what?'

She shook her head and stood up. 'No, I mean *us*. I . . . I'm . . . Did you ever think how we might actually be bad for each other?'

'What, are you nuts?'

She looked it, wild-eyed and flushed. 'No, I'm serious. You . . . you need to experience other . . . you know, date other people. We – we're too close. It's unhealthy. I mean, you've never had any other serious girlfriend.'

'You like it that way,' he said, mentally scrambling to catch up to what she was saying. 'What do you mean, too close? We're just right, we're perfect.' The box in his pocket was the proof that he firmly believed his words. Why didn't she? Why all of a sudden?

'No, we're just . . . you know – *kids*. We need to get

some space between us and ... and ... and see what else there is in the world. *Who* else,' she added, her voice hoarse.

'We're not kids. I just turned twenty, you're nineteen – both legally adults.' It was a weak response, he knew. The force of her insistence emanated from her like a magnetic field. Already he could feel the futility in arguing.

She looked around them, as though enemies might be hiding in the brush. 'I can't see you anymore,' she said. 'It's for both our good.' He grabbed her wrist, but she was already in motion, already running away before even taking a step. 'I love you, but I have to go.'

She broke free, and he watched her run, the copper hair he loved so much streaming out behind her like a wild mare's mane. He would let her run; she wouldn't go far, he was sure of it.

Carson couldn't commit to any of the wedding bands on display in the Philipsburg jewelry shop. Each silky platinum or diamond-encrusted gold band looked good, but he couldn't quite see himself wearing any of them. Too plain, too elaborate, too gaudy, too wide, too narrow; Val and the salesman, whose English was approximately as good as Carson's Dutch, frowned at him as he pondered.

He pushed the navy blue velvet tray away. 'You know, our flight's in ninety minutes ... There's this nice store in Ocala; why don't we look there when we get in? I guess I'm just not in the mood for this right now.'

'But the prices are so much better here,' Val said.

Carson smirked. 'You can afford the difference. Come on.' He stood.

'Okay, fine.' But she didn't look fine. She looked disappointed. 'If you're sure none of these work.'

She must have an attachment to one, one that he was supposed to also prefer, that maybe she'd been trying to signal him about and he hadn't caught on. Well, he was still tired, still hung over; every night here was a party and his middle-aged body was feeling the effects.

Wherever Val went, she collected friends. Young, energetic friends, most of whom surfed. He swam pretty well, thanks to years of racing Meg across the lake, but didn't surf worth a damn, so what he did most during these parties was observe and drink. Oh, people were intrigued with him, sure, but once they'd declared their love of his music and admiration for his ability to create it, they had little else to say. The conversations, when they lasted, usually turned to Val and her career, a subject of common interest.

Val. No one was more charismatic. He often joked that she'd been given an extra dose of personality, maybe the one his bass player Ron seemed to be missing. She was good to everyone around her, and he hated that he'd missed whatever signal she was trying to send about the wedding bands. So he sat down and took another look.

He supposed she wanted him to choose something in platinum, to match her engagement ring and the band she'd wear with it. When they discussed a ring for him, they agreed his didn't need to match – that it was most important for it to suit him personally, the way hers was such a perfect match for her. The truth was, he'd made such a 'perfect' selection simply because when he described Val to the Tiffany clerk, the woman proclaimed he needed the Schlumberger ring – a very large, round diamond encircled by smaller diamonds and, as a modification, some exceptional aquamarines, set only in platinum – and he went along with it.

Glancing at Val's ring, he pointed to the band that looked like the closest complement, a wide polished band with an inset sweep of nine small diamonds. 'How about this one?'

She nodded eagerly. 'You should try it on.'

He did, and she grinned, and when he gave the consent she'd been hoping for, she kicked him out of the shop to make the purchase, insisting that it was bad luck for him to know the price.

He waited on the sidewalk outside, glad to have satisfied her. *That* was the more important thing. He could wear the ring, flashy as it was. He'd get used to it. A man could get used to just about anything if he set his mind to it. He'd gotten used to being angry at Meg, gotten used to being without her after all their years growing up together. He'd gotten used to feeling incomplete and had even turned that feeling, and the associated ones, into an incredibly lucrative career. He'd gotten used to living on the road for huge chunks of time, to the sharp smell of sweat and exhaustion that filled his tour bus after a concert, to relying on Gene to tell him where to be and when and for how long. He'd gotten used to the idea of never finding a woman worth marrying.

And while he wasn't so young and romantic as to believe that Val was his *soul mate*, the one woman he was *meant to be with*, the woman he'd *waited his whole life for*, etcetera, he thought they made a pretty good couple. She kept him distracted and entertained. She was sweet and affectionate, and fun in bed. She was beautiful, in a tomboyish way. And she loved him. It was enough; it had to be.

That evening, Carson and his father, James, walked the fence line of the McKay citrus farm, checking for rotted posts. James, a sturdy, upright sixty-five-year-old with still-dark hair, was gradually replacing the old wooden posts with steel in the steady, conservative manner with which he did everything. The McKays' was one of the fortunate Ocala-area farms that by luck of diligent grove management and the two small, warm lakes within their groves, lost only a few trees when the freeze of '89 put so many growers out of business. If it had gone otherwise – if the groves were lost and had to be replanted, as so many had – Carson never would've left to pursue his music. Instead, he'd have stayed to replant, rebuild the business. It was funny how things turned out, how you couldn't predict where luck would land or which kind it would be when it did.

Post-checking was only an excuse, he knew, for his dad to get him alone. As an only child, he'd forged a strong, close bond with both his parents, one that had helped see him through what they all referred to as 'those years', and which told him, now, that something other than fence posts was on his dad's mind. But he knew not to rush the matter, and so he ambled along at his dad's side through the calf-high grass, appreciating the peace layered all around him: rosy sky, soft breeze stirring the nearby lemon-tree leaves, a trio of horses gamboling across the way on pasture land that had until recently belonged to Spencer and Anna Powell.

'I see the new people have things up and running over there,' he said, pointing toward the horses.

His dad stopped walking and looked that way. 'They do. Kind of strange to see the place active again, after so long.'

'How long has it been?'

'What? Since there were thoroughbreds over there?'

'Yeah,' Carson nodded. He couldn't remember, having lived away from here for more than fifteen years, now.

'Oh, maybe a decade, maybe more. Around the time Julianne married that Canadian fella and moved up to Quebec.'

Carson recalled hearing about it. Meg's youngest sister, only seventeen at the time, got pregnant just before her senior year and married the father, a college student from Quebec who'd been visiting relatives for the summer. He got the news by phone while he was touring with his first band and wondered, then, how different things might've gone for him if he'd accidentally gotten Meg pregnant. She would've had to stick with him and try to make a life together, would've seen that there was nothing to fear about being so much in love – *if* that was her real reason for breaking up.

He never did quite buy that excuse, though. He figured she'd fallen for Hamilton, was seduced by the money and just didn't want to admit it. And that morning before her wedding, all she wanted was a fling for old time's sake. One last toss with the guy she'd thought was such a good lover but wasn't worth marrying – he didn't have money, after all, didn't have what looked like a life of luxury ahead of him, not then. He'd been nothing but a shit-kicker, a grower's kid who intended to be a grower himself. He couldn't compete with Brian Hamilton, couldn't give her the life she apparently wanted.

'Carson?'

'Oh, sorry, just lost in thought.' *Well, whatever,* he thought; water under the bridge.

His dad went on, 'After the youngest left, Spencer sold off the last of his stock and stuck to just boarding. I never did know why.'

'Maybe he just got tired of failing. God knows he couldn't seem to make any money breeding.'

'That's the truth,' his dad said. 'And I wondered about that, about just what *was* working for Spencer. Because time was when all the talk was on him sliding into bankruptcy and foreclosure – he was overextended everyplace around.'

'I remember,' Carson said.

'But *something* turned around for him, and I found out just what when I was over to the co-op last week,' his dad said, turning to continue their walk. 'Dave Zimmerman pulls me aside. He says, "Hey, what do you know about Spencer Powell?" And I say, "Well, we been neighbors for thirty-some years, till about two weeks ago." And Dave says, "Then you probably know all about the business with the money."'

'What business?' Carson asked, more to be polite than because he cared.

'Well, that's what I said. 'Cause I never heard anything – but you know, I don't, always; Spencer never let on about the details of things, and I got better things to do than hang around the co-op and gossip like them retired guys. So Dave tells me, "This is all in confidence – I trust you, Jim, not to get me in trouble," and he starts telling me about the sale of the farm there. Seems that Dave's wife – you remember Linda, she's the real estate lawyer – made out a pretty sizeable check when she was putting together all the paperwork – $387,000, which was a little more'n a third of what Spencer got for the place.'

'So I guess he found some way to borrow against the farm, and that solved his problems.'

'You'd think. But that's the funny thing. He didn't have any sort of mortgage. Hadn't, according to the title record, since '89.'

'Okay . . . he owed for something else,' Carson said, curbing his impatience.

'Nope. No record on his credit of *any* debt that size – or so says Dave. But get this: the check was made out to Bruce Hamilton personally.'

So, Carson thought, *this* was what their walk was

all about. Something was going on between Meg's father and father-in-law, and his dad hadn't wanted to bring it up around Val, believing that anything Meg-related might yet be a touchy subject. It felt a little ridiculous, his dad still trying to protect his feelings about that long-ago trouble; he was done with it, moving past, moving on. To prove it, he would talk about Meg plainly, show that the topic wasn't worth tip-toeing around.

'This money stuff's not so hard to figure – do you think?' he said. 'After Meg married Brian, they must've lent Spencer the money to pay the mortgage off the books, you know? A friendly loan between in-laws.'

His dad nodded, one eyebrow raised slightly in what Carson knew was silent acknowledgement of this shift in Meg-related communication. 'Sure, maybe, but it's hard to imagine that kind of generosity – Hamilton giving over the title of the land and no guarantee Spencer'd ever pay it back. I mean, we're talking *Spencer Powell* here.'

Carson pushed his hand through his hair. Why did they have to keep at this, anyway? Not that he'd admit it after his show of bravado, but all this talk was raising his hackles in a way he couldn't explain. He said, 'I bet it just amounts to some shady bookwork on Hamilton's part – wouldn't surprise me any.'

His dad nodded. 'Maybe so. But if that's the case, I wonder why Spencer paid it back like he did, in a regular check made out to Hamilton personally. That's a big chunk of income to get all at once – Hamilton'll get hit hard on his taxes, and it might flag an IRS audit.'

'Maybe Spencer wasn't thinking about that, or figured it's not his problem,' Carson said.

'Maybe. I can't help wondering, though, why Spencer'd pay it back at all, if he didn't *have* to.' His dad scratched his cheek and looked over at the horses, still puzzled by the behavior of a man who'd once been a close friend.

Carson tried to ignore the prod that said there was more to this money thing than what he and his dad could suss out. He was ready to be done with the subject for good.

He said, 'You know, I always figured Meg married Hamilton for his money, and now it's obvious Spencer got good mileage out of it, too. I don't know what's up with all that, but none of it really matters, does it? I mean, what any of them did or do hasn't been our business for a long time. And we have better stuff to think about, don't we?' He put his hands on his dad's shoulders and smiled. 'For example, getting you fitted for a tux.'

FIFTEEN

'Good job,' Ms Henry said Wednesday, handing Savannah her graded world history test. The score, in purple ink at the top right corner, read *104* – an A+, short only one of the possible five extra-credit points.

Savannah looked over at Rachel's test. 'Eighty-two,' Rachel said, holding up the paper. 'Your fault, for not letting me come over and study with you.'

'*Your* fault, for not studying enough on your own.'

Rachel, dressed today in a tight yellow shirt that made her look chubby – which she was, a little – scooted her chair closer to the aisle and leaned toward Savannah to whisper, 'When are you going to tell me who was keeping you so busy last night that I couldn't even bribe you with peanut-butter cup ice cream?'

It had been a good offer; Savannah was usually glad to hang out with Rachel, and she loved that flavor of ice cream, one of many foods they never kept in her own house because her dad was severely allergic to peanuts in addition to dogs. But she had something else more important to do: finalizing her plans for

Miami. 'It's not just a "who",' she whispered back. 'It's a "what" too. And I can't tell you yet – but I will, I promise.' At the very last minute, so there'd be no chance of Rachel leaking the plan and screwing things up. Well-meaning as Rachel might be, she was too close to her sister, Angela. While Angela could usually be trusted on small stuff, something like this might bring out her righteous-older-sister side. Savannah couldn't take that risk.

'Okay, fine,' Rachel said, leaning back. 'Whatever.'

Caitlin Janecke, the most spoiled of all the spoiled girls Savannah knew, said from the desk at Savannah's left, 'What's her problem? Is she pissed about her grade?'

Savannah looked at Caitlin's pink cashmere-blend shirt and belted khaki Hollister shorts, the matching pink ribbon in her perfect blond hair; Caitlin was perfect down to her slim tanned legs and calfskin boaters. *No*, Savannah wanted to say, *she didn't want to believe you gave blow jobs to three different guys last weekend* – a story that had come from a reliable source: Caitlin's sister Riley, a freshman in Savannah's gym class. Riley, by contrast, had been at the same party but done it to only *one* guy, she said, and 'Ohmigod, it was the most awful, bizarre thing you could imagine!' As slutty as the sisters' actions seemed, Savannah wished Riley had elaborated just a little more.

Now was not the time to get into any of it, so she just nodded and said, 'She didn't study.'

'Did you?'

Savannah lifted one shoulder. 'Not really.'

'*God*. My parents make me study *every* night, and I only got a ninety-one. Must be nice to be so brainy.' The compliment, even delivered so grudgingly, surprised Savannah.

'I guess,' she said, suddenly chagrined. Maybe Caitlin wasn't *so* bad . . . and having someone so popular envy her out loud pleased her. Brainy was okay, brainy was good – better than her usual tag of 'hippie girl', usually delivered with a sneer as though she was smelly and unwashed. This school, filled by girls whose parents had too much money, was made for Caitlin clones. As great a prep school as the place was, originality, unless it was in the pursuit of the finer arts like painting or classical composition, was not so welcome here.

And she still had two more years to endure. If she could somehow make things work out with Kyle – eventually she'd have to confess her true age and hope he'd stick with her – the time would be much more enjoyable.

She liked to think that in addition to being brainy, she was also strong on organization and determination. When she came up to a roadblock, she didn't turn back; she found a way around it. Ever since she was a toddler, this had been true about her. One of the stories her Grandma Shelly liked to tell all her rich friends was of how Savannah once escaped from her parlor, which was gated off to adjoining rooms, while she, Shelly, had gone to the bathroom. 'I came back – not two minutes later, you understand – and Savannah was *gone*. Just disappeared from the room! I looked under the furniture, behind it, all around the house, thinking she could've climbed over one of the gates. But no! The child had pushed out a screen and gone out through the window! I finally saw her on the patio, where she had a chair pulled up to the fountain so she could reach the water – she was soaking wet and giggling, pleased as punch!' Her grandma used this story to show how much Savannah was like her dad, and maybe in some ways she was: results-oriented, single-minded – but she would use her powers for good, not evil, that was how she thought of it.

She packed up her world history textbook and her binder, wondering what her grandma, and the rest of the family, would think if they knew how she was making the Miami trip work; her mom should do a better job of hiding her credit cards. By the time the bill came, she'd have a good excuse to give if she got caught – but more importantly, even if she was caught, she'd have already been to Miami with Kyle.

After class, she and Rachel walked together to the locker room to change for softball practice. Rachel was back to her chatty self before they were dressed, talking about a guy named Hunter, whose brother went out with Rachel's sister a few times, and one of Hunter's friends.

'He's hot – they both are. I think Hunter likes me, and you could maybe go out with R.J. He graduated last year, but he goes to State. Do you think a college freshman's too old?'

'Not even,' Savannah said. 'However,' she added, thinking, as she laced up her cleats, that she could tell

Rachel a *little* about Kyle, 'I met somebody – he's around that age, and I want to see how it goes with him before I check out other guys.'

'*You* met somebody? Who? Where? God, you think you'd tell your best friend!'

'I *am* telling you.'

They left the locker room and headed for the practice field, their cleats thrumming over the hallway's tile floor. As they walked, Savannah told her about Kyle in the most general, and not completely honest, terms. But telling Rachel even in this abbreviated way felt good, as if in sharing Kyle with her best friend he became more real. There were times this past week when, if she hadn't heard his voice, hadn't stayed up until three AM Sunday talking about ways they might be together in the future, she wouldn't believe in him at all.

She thought again of his voice, how it had seemed to permeate her as she'd lain in the dark, phone to ear.

What d'you plan to do, you know, after getting your bachelor's?

I'm thinking something in conservancy. My dad, he wants to push me into business, but that's just not happening.

Hey, how 'bout this: You and me, we buy some land, get our own nature preserve started. Right? Get your dad to front the money – he would, don't you think? I mean, since that's a business. I'd ask mine but, you know, we aren't exactly talking.

Yeah, what's that all about?

I don't really, you know, want to get into it. That's

history. Me and you, though – we're the future. I mean, we could be. It'd be killer, you and me and the great outdoors . . .

She loved that he would do this, dream with her, put himself in her future.

'He sounds fab, and I bet he's even cuter in person,' Rachel was saying. 'And nineteen isn't that old.'

'That's what I thought,' Savannah agreed, mentally excusing her lie about his age. She reminded herself she'd tell Rachel the whole truth soon, and even if she had to tell a hundred lies before her weekend with Kyle was over, the experience, the adventure would be worth all the guilt, and then some.

They went outside and down the wide concrete steps, then onto the clover-covered field that stretched between the main school building and the softball diamonds. A few bees buzzed around their ankles, angry to have their important work disturbed.

Savannah repeatedly tossed and caught a ball as they went. 'Kyle and me, we made plans to get together on May Day,' she said, not revealing, of course, that this first date would be in Miami.

'Seriously? How are you going to get your mom to let you go out on a Monday?'

'Monday?' Savannah stopped, letting the ball fall into the clover.

'Uh, *yeah*,' Rachel laughed. 'Smart girl, May Day is like next *Monday*. When did you think it was?'

'Next *Friday* – May fifth. Cinco de Mayo – oh, Jesus,' she said as realization dawned. 'That's *not* the same as May Day, is it?'

Rachel laughed even louder. 'Oh my God, that is so funny! You thought—? *Everybody* knows—'

Savannah punched her arm. 'Shut up! I just got it mixed up.'

'Yeah you did,' Rachel said. 'But oh well, so you can see him that Friday.'

'Maybe,' Savannah muttered.

'Oh, c'mon, don't be like that. Everybody does stupid shit sometimes. He won't hold it against you – he's probably, like, panting over getting to meet you in the first place. I mean, what guy wouldn't?'

She prayed Rachel was right. Maybe it was crazy, but she'd gotten really attached to Kyle. He offered a kind of attention and reassurance no one else did. In a way, he was taking her grandma's place.

'Thanks,' she told Rachel.

'Sure. And hey, maybe you can hook me up with one of his friends.'

SIXTEEN

Meg was just finishing up with her third pharmaceutical rep of the day, a severe-looking, ambitious young blonde dressed in all black, when Manisha knocked on her office door.

'Oh good,' Meg said, 'I was hoping you'd finish before Ms Trumbull left; I want you to take a look at this IUD coil she's pitching. The data look all right, but I don't want to decide until you've seen it.'

Manisha, as petite and dark as Meg was tall and fair, came into the office and said, 'Sure. And I'm reminding you to call the orthopedist.'

'Right. Jesus,' Meg said, jumping up. All week she'd been meaning to call him and had put it off, forgotten, remembered, put it off again. 'I'll use your phone and be right back.'

The orthopedist, Cameron Lowenstein, was another golfing acquaintance of Brian's – though not a friend, owing to what Brian called the man's 'bizarre' attitudes. 'He does this Zen golf thing – not my kind of guy,' Brian said once. 'But he's good. I know a bunch of guys who go to him. He gets the kink out of my shoulder every time.' A golf-related kink, resolved weekly so that he could keep playing golf.

Lowenstein took her call directly, which surprised her, and was willing to see her at the end of his schedule, in about an hour. 'I'm sure it's something simple,' she said, after describing her symptoms. 'I hope it won't take much of your time.'

'Glad to help,' Dr Lowenstein assured her. 'Your husband is one of my favorite patients.'

After Meg hung up and returned to her office, she found Manisha sitting on the edge of the desk, swinging one leg and talking about her new shar-pei puppy. 'You have never seen so many wrinkles, worse than my great-grandmother – though their faces, they are about the same with fur. The puppy is much prettier, but neither has to worry about dating, yes? So it's all good.'

Meg smiled. 'And the IUDs? Are they "all good" too?'

'In fact,' Manisha told her, 'Laurie here, she is not fully convinced of their efficacy because her sister became pregnant while using one. But that is to me just fate. I think we can try them.'

That Manisha had managed to turn what for Meg had been an aggressive sales call into a girlfriends' candid chat surprised her not at all. Manisha was the warmest, most outgoing person she knew. And Meg admired how firmly convinced in the concept of fate her friend was. Manisha's motto for all of life was, in effect, *Acknowledge, Accept, Appreciate*. If Meg could learn to follow that motto, then maybe she, like

Manisha, would be able to look at the loose affiliation that defined her family life as a matter of course. Maybe she would sleep more soundly, act more decisively, let life's troubles wash over her like a gentle stream over a pebble.

'So,' Manisha said, when Laurie Trumbull had gone, 'you are to see the doctor?'

'In about an hour.'

'Ah, good. And how is the arm today?'

'Today it's fine, just a little tired,' Meg said. 'It's been fine all week, pretty much. I'm probably wasting my time.' She had none to waste. Just fitting the exam into this afternoon meant she needed to persuade Brian to get Savannah from softball and meet her at Horizon for dinner with her father, neither of which he would be happy to do. The two men had not, in all these years, found a common ground on which they could stand comfortably, so Brian avoided seeing her father whenever he could get away with it. And having to leave work early for any reason other than his own agenda always irritated him.

Manisha folded her arms and gave Meg what Meg called her 'mom' look. 'Maybe it wastes your time, but go anyway. Okay? You will not want another time like Sunday.'

'I know,' Meg said, the image of the lost baby vivid in her mind. Maybe it wasn't her fault, but still ... 'That's why I'm going; that's why I called him.'

'After I am reminding you,' Manisha scolded.

'Guilty as charged.'

'And me, I am thinking you are due for vacation –

a week on a quiet island, no pager, no cell phone, no laboring women. You still like to swim, yes?'

Meg nodded. 'But I hardly ever do. I think our pool is mostly for looks. Did I ever tell you I set the one-hundred-meter freestyle record at my high school?'

'I recall, yes. So I prescribe a swimsuit and sunscreen, taken with one charter sailboat, daily, for seven days.'

'Thank you, Doctor.' Meg smiled. 'I'm cured!'

Manisha moved to the doorway. 'In six years together, I see you work hard, try to please everyone, and this I admire. But remember, you must care also for yourself – one empty pot cannot refill another.'

Meg sat in Dr Cameron Lowenstein's office, listening to his assessment: her X-rays were clear, no signs of compression in her spine or joints, nothing out of place. 'I can't see anything that needs work,' he conceded with a shrug.

'Nothing,' Meg said.

'Nope. You're structurally sound. Which means the culprit is invisible, at least to X-ray technology. My primary recommendation at this point is, wait and see if you have any further problems, and if you do, give this a try . . .' He handed her a business card printed with an unpronounceable name and the declaration 'acupuncturist and psychic'.

She looked up at him, trying to ignore his violet-and-brown-patterned tie, which looked to her like a baby had puked the pattern onto it. What odd taste he had, in clothes and in referrals. She could understand his suggesting acupuncture, *maybe*. But *psychic* therapy?

'You don't think a neurologist's my next stop?' she asked, looking above the tie at dark eyes set deep beneath bushy black eyebrows.

'You would be astonished at what acupuncture can accomplish. I'm surprised you don't already support it,' he said, eyebrows raised in disapproval. He reminded her of Groucho Marx. 'However,' he added, 'loathe though I am to bring it up—'

'Yes?' she said, not imagining what his next words would be, though later she would reflect on them at far more length than she wished.

'The symptoms you've experienced: repeated periods of weakness in arm and hand, possibly in the leg, the stumbling—'

'That was just the one time. Maybe twice.' Maybe a third time, she realized, recalling how she'd caught her toes on the edge of a step just yesterday evening.

'The symptoms, when seen with an absence of pain or malaise, no sign of spinal compression, and no mental process malfunction, are *suggestive* of ALS.'

The import of the three initials slid past her at first, a silvery fish through a cupped hand in the surf. *Al's*, she thought, and then, *A-L-S*? And then, when she finally understood which disease it was that he was referring to – no, *suggesting*, she sat very still and blinked several times, quickly.

Amyotrophic lateral sclerosis; the motor neuron disorder. 'Lou Gehrig's disease,' she said.

'A *very* remote possibility.'

'Sure.'

'There are a hundred more plausible scenarios,' he added, and she thought, *Then why did you bring it up?*

He went on, 'If your symptoms persist, you *will* want to talk to a neurologist, but try the acupuncture too. It can't hurt. That's a joke – get it? It can't hurt? Acupuncture *can't hurt?*'

She smiled wanly and leaned down to collect her purse. 'Maybe I will.' She stood. 'Thanks so much for seeing me on short notice.'

He waved away her gratitude. 'Not at all. Glad to help a fellow doctor.'

'If ever you're pregnant . . .' she said, pushing herself past the nightmarish image of his suggested diagnosis and into the much more comfortable space of humor. 'Or just need a last-minute Pap smear—'

'I'll call,' he agreed, extending his hand. 'Take care.'

Outside his office building, the air was thick, steamy from a just-ended shower. Meg crossed the hot asphalt parking lot, her sense of humor evaporating like the rainwater in the returning sun's heat. Under scrutiny, every fumble, every misstep, every dropped item or awkward movement she'd experienced recently became suspect. She might well have had symptoms for months and not paid them any attention. As if to prove Lowenstein wrong, she took measured, steady steps, keys held easily in one hand, her purse in the other.

She knew enough about ALS to know her chances of having it were very slim; she also knew that her symptoms did, in fact, correspond with those of the rare disease. Reaching her car, she paused, trying to recall what the other possibilities might be ... and couldn't come up with them, her mind distracted by her knowledge of what ALS patients suffered: the steady loss of ability to move arms and legs and head and lips and lungs. A progression from cane to walker to wheelchair to bed. To being fed by some overworked health aide or dutiful family member, and then by a tube. Extending life through use of a ventilator, if the victim was willing to bother – because there was no reversal, no cure, not even, she was pretty sure, much in the way of medication to slow the onset of each symptom.

She stood at her car and looked up at the palm trees bordering the road – a sight as normal and familiar to her as her own face – then past the tree trunks, at the passing motorists, all looking ordinary and content with their place on the planet. Certainly *she* was just as ordinary, just as content; certainly she was *just like them*, not afflicted with ALS – or anything else so grim and unfortunate. Certainly all the sacrifices she'd made for her parents and sisters, for Savannah's happiness and Brian's, for her patients throughout the years, had earned her better karma than Cameron Lowenstein's stab-in-the-dark diagnosis.

Hadn't they?

The frightened woman in her wanted to believe she'd earned good fortune, but she couldn't silence the informed doctor in her, that part of her with extensive knowledge – and experience – with life's unavoidable truth: bad things happened to good people every minute of every day, just as surely as the sun was always rising, and setting, somewhere.

SEVENTEEN

Savannah was surprised to see her dad's new car pull into the ball field parking lot after practice. She couldn't think of the last time she'd seen him on a weeknight before, say, seven o'clock. She watched him inch the new black BMW through the gravel so that it wouldn't raise any dust.

When he stopped, she walked up to his window, resisting the urge to scuff her feet. 'Where's Mom?'

'She couldn't get here in time. Come on, get in – you need to get showered and changed for dinner with Spencer.'

She didn't have time for dinner at the old folks' home; she needed to talk to Kyle about Miami ASAP. 'That's *today*?'

'So I'm told.'

'Why didn't Mom pick me up? Is someone in labor? She's coming, right?' She couldn't imagine trying to have dinner with only her dad and Grandpa Spencer. They were like a pair of repelling magnets.

'Yes, she's coming. Get in,' he urged. 'She had an appointment.'

Savannah rounded the car, trailing her aluminum bat in the gravel. Kyle was going to be pissed ... For the entire two-hour practice, she'd tried to think of a way to get to Miami on Monday but couldn't make anything work.

Inside, the brand-new 740 her dad ordered custom from one of his clients smelled of supple leather and new carpet and something like clean laundry – from an air freshener mounted discreetly near his knee. She buckled her seatbelt and ran her hands over the hand-stitched seat. Her own new car would have leather too, but not like this. Her car, a two-door Honda Accord, would have what her dad considered practical features – including ordinary leather, because it wiped clean so easily, and a GPS system for when she traveled – and was meant to last her until she was out of college. When she graduated, he said, she could choose whatever car she wanted as a reward, a lesson meant to teach her the benefits of working toward long-term goals.

She hardly cared what she drove, now or later. As long as she had wheels, as long as she could set her own agenda, not rely on her mom or her dad or anyone for rides, take a day off school and drive down to see Kyle in Naples if she wanted, she'd be satisfied. Her friends chattered about getting better cars: Caitlin had gotten a custom-painted pink Mini for her sixteenth; Holly Showalter, a senior, had been promised a convertible Saab for graduation; Lydia Patel, whose mom was Dr

Manisha, was looking forward to 'inheriting' her dad's three-year-old Mercedes when she turned sixteen in August. They were a privileged crowd, a fact which her Grandpa Spencer never tired of reminding her. Even she, with a brand-new Honda on the way, was far better off than the average kid. She *should* feel lucky. She should feel *grateful*. Her mom sure hadn't grown up privileged – she'd worked hard to get where she was, something her Grandma Anna said repeatedly. But mostly she felt . . . stifled. Impatient to get out of the lap of luxury and into the lap of . . . well, of her own life, whatever it would be – an interesting, *useful* existence that included people who, like her, created and explored and questioned things. Luxury was dull and clean and overrated.

'How was practice?' her dad asked, bringing her out of her reverie.

'Fine.'

'What position do they have you in now?'

'Same as always.'

'Which is . . . ?'

She looked at him, amazed he didn't remember – though she shouldn't be surprised, considering how he hadn't seen her play since she was in sixth grade. 'Are you serious?'

'What?'

'I know you're way too busy to, like, come to a game, but you don't even know my position?'

He sighed. 'I have a lot on my mind, Savannah.'

'Right field,' she lied, choosing what everyone knew was the worst position on the field. Right fielders saw the least action and were usually the weakest players on a team, a fact her dad would know too; after golf, he was a big fan of baseball, having played both sports in high school and college. Was there anything he didn't do well?

He said, 'Oh. Right, sure . . .' and she took satisfaction in how puzzled he sounded, like he thought *this* was something he would recall, and felt bad that he didn't. Then he said, 'I was thinking, we should get you into a clinic, work on skills – what are you batting so far?'

'.145,' she lied, again, just to get him going. He was as predictable as her mom, though in a different way. Her mom didn't care whether she was the best student or softball player or singer or composer. Her mom didn't care if she made a C in geometry or sang like a caterwauling animal – which never happened, but Savannah knew it wouldn't freak her out if she did. In fact, she wasn't sure her mom would even notice, as busy as she always was. Her dad, by contrast, cared about how everything *appeared*, even if the appearance didn't match reality. If his kid was stuck in right field and was only batting .145, he looked bad by association and was compelled to *do something* about it, show what a good father he was, so *concerned*. So *involved*. If she weren't already self-motivated, the pressure of his expectations, his 'help', would weigh her down like wet cement.

'You'll need to raise your average in a hurry,' he said. 'Hey, I know one of the batting coaches for the Florida Marlins – why don't I give him a call and set up some Saturday practices?'

'What's the big deal?' she snapped. 'Why don't you ever think I'm good enough just like I am?'

Her vehemence surprised him, she could tell. Well, too bad. He never accepted her for *her*, and she was tired of it.

He said, 'I just want to encourage you to be your personal best.'

'What if .145 is already as good as I am?'

'But it's not. Look, it's like I've told you about choosing your profession: make the most of the abilities you were born with. You're a gifted child—'

'I'm not a *child*.'

'You're a gifted *young woman*,' he said, 'and to do less with your gifts – to go into biology, for example – is to shortchange yourself. But about your batting—'

'Why?' she interrupted him. 'I'm shortchanging myself just because I want to keep manatees from becoming extinct? What's wrong with that, besides it not paying as much as *you* think I should make?'

'You could help *people – and* be well paid. Let me set you up to intern with me this summer; you'll see how fulfilling it is to help people keep their money instead of forking it all over to the government.'

Savannah glared at him. He didn't have a *clue*.

They rode the rest of the way home without talking.

As soon as she got into her bedroom, she tried Kyle's cell phone but got voice mail. Though it took a lot of effort to shake off her bad mood, she left a short, upbeat message saying she was *so* sorry, but she couldn't make it to Miami Monday after all, and asking him to either call her later or chat with her online at nine.

'Maybe we can work something out for the weekend after,' she said, sounding deliberately suggestive. *Please, God,* she thought, *don't let him decide I'm not worth his time.*

Savannah, her parents, and her Grandpa Spencer sat at a table for four in Horizon's dining room, a place that reminded her of the dining room on a cruise ship they'd been on when she was small. Everyone on the ship had seemed ancient, just like everyone here, and the décor in both places was what her grandpa called the 'timeless senility' style: pale pastel wallpaper, table-cloths, floor tile. 'Nothing to excite the senses,' he said, 'which, in a place like this, is a wise choice.'

He was one of the younger residents – only in his early seventies – and seemed to be having a good time making fun of some of his older neighbors. But Savannah noticed her mom wasn't paying much atten-tion, leaving the rest of them to hold up the conver-sation in whatever ways they could. Her dad had barely spoken to anyone except the people who kept calling his cell; he left to take calls three times before they'd even finished touring Horizon's apartment wing. Which meant she was carrying most of the load; so far, she'd talked about softball and school and how to upload songs onto her iPod, a system that fascinated her grandpa. 'Damn, I wish I'd had a knack for all that computer jazz. Those Apple boys'll get Bill Gates yet!' he said.

He was now in the midst of describing a trio of men who stalked the nurses and the old women by following them in their wheelchairs and whispering to one another in the hallways. 'Now you do realize, Vannah, that none of these geezers I'm talking about is in my section. They house 'em over there,' he pointed toward the far side of the dining room, 'in the assisted-living wing. I go over there sometimes just for the entertainment. And across the parking lot's the nursing home, for the ones who're as good as dead.'

'*Grandpa.*'

He waved his hand and said, 'Don't "Grandpa" me. When you're as old as I am, you'll see how it is. Life is for the living; the rest're just a waste of money and oxygen someone else could be using. Isn't that right, Meggie?'

When her mom didn't answer, Savannah nudged her with her foot.

'Hmm?'

'Grandpa's talking to you,' she said.

'What's that, Dad? I'm sorry, I was thinking about something else.'

'Don't we all know it. I said, there's no use in people hanging around when they got no life left, like most of them over in the nursing home. It's pitiful. Don't you think?'

'What *I* think is that we should all have dessert.'

Though Savannah wanted to watch her weight so that when Kyle saw her – whenever that might be – she was as thin as possible, she jumped at the chance to liven things up. 'Oh yeah, ice cream for dessert. Where's that self-serve machine, Grandpa?'

'There, by the doors to the kitchen – see it?'

Two bent old men were jostling each other to use it first. She said, 'Yep. C'mon, Mom, let's try it out.'

'How about you get some for me? It's been a long day.'

'I had a long day too,' she said, standing. 'You don't hear me whining about it.'

'Girl's got a point,' her grandpa said.

'Really, Dad, I'd rather stay put.' Her mom's sharp voice cut into Savannah's conscience. What was making her so edgy?

Just then, her dad's cell phone began to buzz again. He checked the display and started to stand in order to take the call outside.

'For God's sake, Brian!' her mom said. 'Why can't you turn that thing off?'

Everyone froze. Savannah looked from her mom's angry face to her dad's startled one as he silenced the call and sat down. His brows knitted and he said, very quietly, 'Let's act like civilized people, why don't we?'

'*Civilized people* don't answer their phone during dinner with their family, which you would know if you ever had dinner with yours.'

'That's enough, Meg.'

'How do you know what's "enough"? As far as I can tell, *nothing* is ever enough for you.'

Savannah couldn't believe her mom was making a scene. Her parents *never* fought.

Her dad stood up and said, 'I don't know what your problem is tonight, but I don't need this grief. We can talk about it later, when you can act like an adult.'

'Sure, leave, *that's* mature,' her mom said, though her dad was still standing there. He looked unsure, a look Savannah couldn't ever recall seeing on his face.

Her grandpa reached over and put his hand on her mom's. 'Let him go, Meggie – I didn't give Bruce all that money for nothing. You don't have to take any crap from Mr Big Shot here anymore.'

'*What* are you talking about?'

'The money. *You* know.' He cocked his head toward Savannah, making her frown. What money, and what did it have to do with her?

Her mom looked confused too, but then understanding replaced the confusion and she said, 'You gave Bruce money *when*?'

'Now I'm sure I told you—'

'No, Dad, I'd remember . . . Brian?'

'I am *not* talking about this in front of Savannah.' He glanced at her, then turned his back on all of them and left.

'God damn it,' her mom said. Then she rubbed her face and said, 'I'm sorry, both of you. I'm in a rotten mood tonight – we should have rescheduled.'

Savannah shrugged. She wanted to know what they were all talking about, and what it was that put her mom in the rotten mood to begin with, but she was reluctant to ask and bring the wrath down on herself too. All she needed was to get in trouble and be grounded from her computer or phone – grounded, in effect, from Kyle.

Her mom said, 'You know, Dad, I think we're going to call it a night. I'll check in with you tomorrow, okay?

Here, Savannah.' She handed over her keys. 'Why don't you drive us home.'

They said good-bye and left without having tried the ice cream machine, a fact that oddly saddened Savannah, even though she hadn't much cared about it in the first place.

Kyle wasn't online when she logged on at nine, and not at five after or ten after or nine-fifteen, which troubled her more than anything her parents had going on. She sat on her bed, ignoring the IMs from Rachel, wondering if Kyle had heard her message and changed his mind. A guy his age, looking like he did, could have his pick of willing women. He didn't have to settle for someone who couldn't even remember when May Day was.

She put her earbuds in and pulled up the songs she'd uploaded from her mom's old Carson McKay CD. Sometimes the old ballads – his and other bands' – really spoke to her. The melodic songs, with lyrics that often shared her worries and sorrows, helped her feel better at times when it seemed like nothing was going to come out right in her life. Leaning back against her stupid purple pillows, she closed her eyes and listened to Carson singing about a guy lost in a snowstorm, who thought he might freeze to death and never again see the woman he loved. *Buried Alive* was the title; she remembered hearing it at their old house in Gainesville, where they lived until her mom finished her medical residency. The memory was just a flash: she was maybe four years old, being held up on her mom's hip while they waltzed around the living room. This rare recollection of a shared afternoon pleased her; there had been so few of those.

She hadn't known, way back then, that her mom and Carson were neighbors growing up, and went to the same schools. She remembered learning it a few years after they'd moved back to Ocala – maybe when she was twelve? It was something her Grandma Anna said when Savannah and her mom were visiting the farm, about how the McKays next door were adding on to their house with money from Carson's career. 'You mean Carson McKay, the rock star?' she asked her grandma, who confirmed this and then said, 'Sorry, Meggie – I assumed she knew.' Savannah didn't know why her grandma apologized, and didn't much care; she was excited about the possibility of meeting the famous Carson McKay someday. She said, 'Next time he has a concert here, we have to go! Maybe he'll let us backstage!' Even at that age she'd admired his music, the way he could play piano like another of her mom's favorites, Freddie Mercury.

She felt her cell phone buzzing in her shorts pocket. Quickly she dug it out, pulled off her earbuds, and flipped open the phone before it stopped.

She glanced at the caller's number but didn't recognize it. 'Hello?'

'Hey, babe.' *Kyle.*

'Hey! Where are you calling from?'

'Dude who's a good buddy of mine, 'cause my phone is, like, dead – and I just had to call my favorite girl.'

His favorite girl! Then he wasn't pissed off by her

changing plans. Or . . . he hadn't heard her message. 'Well, I'm really glad you called!'

'I'm really glad you're glad. Do you think you'd be, like, glad to meet up this weekend, like Friday night?'

'What, this weekend, seriously?'

'I don't want to wait till Monday to see your sweet face in person. So I thought, I'll take a little road trip, go see my favorite girl – my car's crap, but we can drive down to Miami in yours, save your ticket for another time.'

Shit, he definitely hadn't heard the message.

She heard laughter in the background. 'Sounds like a party there.'

'Oh, yeah – just a few friends hanging out, indulging a little. You know.'

'Are you drunk?'

'Me? No. No, no, I'm not drunk. Booze is not my thing.' More laughter.

With the weekend only two days away, she'd have to do some quick planning. 'I'm supposed to go home again this weekend. Let me see how I can work this out, okay? And I'll call you back at this same number.'

'Hey, yeah, I'll be waiting.'

She hung up and sat scanning her room, pulse pounding. How to work this? How was she going to meet him without anyone knowing? And where would he stay? Could she scam her parents into thinking she was at Rachel's . . . and maybe stay in a hotel with him? She could tell him her car was in the shop—

'Get a grip, girl,' she said aloud, though she was almost bouncing with joy. She took a deep breath, made herself think of a sensible plan, and then she pressed her speed-dial for Rachel.

EIGHTEEN

After returning from dinner with her father, Meg fell into uneasy sleep in the den, dreaming of Bride, the mare they'd had when she was young . . . shutting the hugely pregnant Bride into her special pen, night falling, the stable so dark she couldn't see her own feet . . . Then somehow, the curry comb was in her hand and she was standing on a wooden box to reach Bride's forelock, murmuring soothing words. Bride jerked and stumbled sideways, knocking Meg backward, pinning her to the wall, then lurched down to the straw, pulling Meg with her. Meg's legs folded, her back scraping as she went down. There was no pain in the dream; her unconscious mind spared her that part of what she'd experienced as a ten-year-old. But the darkness, the panic of being trapped there, the futility of yelling until she was hoarse – all of that was here in the dream.

Bride groaned and panted, the noises harsh and threatening in the blackness. They would both die there, Meg was sure of it as minutes passed like desperate, heaving hours. She couldn't budge the 1,200-pound mare, couldn't help pull the foal – which would later emerge stillborn. She knew this in the dream, but there was no comfort in recognizing that if she knew it, she must have survived this horror; in the dream, she couldn't breathe. Bride pressed her down until she was flattened, invisible. Doomed.

The garage door rumbled closed, waking her. Damp with sweat, she checked the time: two-fifteen. Her pulse slowed as she waited for Brian to come inside, to stop in and explain himself. But he weaved his way past, shoes off and shirttails out, never even looking into the room. She sat up, relieved to have escaped Bride once again, and reoriented herself with the life she was living now, tonight. With the issue of Brian having left Horizon and gone drinking, apparently, rather than coming home and discussing the subject raised at dinner.

She heard a thump and a crash and Brian saying, 'Shit!'

A more dedicated wife, she thought, would get up and check if he was hurt. A more dedicated wife would confront him with a demand that he explain where he'd been for the past six hours. A bar? A friend's? A woman's? A more dedicated wife would not now be reaching for the phone to wake her father-in-law in the middle of the night in order to get the answer to another question, the one Brian wouldn't answer earlier and obviously decided he wasn't going to answer now, either.

Bruce and Shelly's phone rang five times before Bruce answered. 'Hello?'

'It's Meg. I apologize for the hour.'

'Is Brian okay?' He sounded panicked. 'What's the matter?'

Of course he'd be panicked about his precious oldest child, his heir. As Shelly herself would admit, they'd sheltered Brian – maybe too much, she'd say, smiling indulgently – from the day of his first allergy emergency. Peanut-butter toast, when he was two. He'd nearly died because the housekeeper of the time, Esmeralda, thought he was choking and kept trying to help by smacking him on the back. Fortunately, Shelly returned from her oil painting lesson in time to call for an ambulance; a hefty dose of epinephrine saved his life. Since then, his parents lived in perpetual dread of his accidental ingestion of peanuts, peanut dust, peanut oil; the stuff was everywhere. Shelly devoted a whole week to educating Meg, when she first began seeing Brian, including trips to the market and a three-night 'allergy-free' cooking class.

Meg said, 'Brian is fine – well, I think he's fine. He just stumbled in, drunk.'

'Have *you* been drinking?' Bruce asked, his voice shifting from fearful to cautious.

'No, actually I've been sleeping. But never mind that. I'll be brief: did my father give you money recently?'

Bruce coughed. 'That's between Spencer and me.' She could hear Shelly asking who was on the phone and Bruce telling her, 'Meg – everything's fine.'

'Bruce, look, I'm not twenty-one years old anymore. It's late, I'm cranky, and my father mentioned something that I want to confirm. Did he pay you back?'

'I told him not to. Damn stubborn man wouldn't take no for an answer.'

So it was true. 'The whole amount?' she asked.

'That's right.'

'And you took it.'

'He insisted. Look, I'm putting it into a trust for our girl, all right? And if Spencer gets into any more hot water – not that he should, if you're watching his spending – but if he does, well, I'm sure we can help him out.'

'I appreciate that, but I'll handle it if need be. Brian knew about the payment?'

'I think that's for the two of you to discuss.'

Which meant yes. 'I'm sure we will,' she said.

Bruce sounded weary when he asked, 'Now is Brian around?'

'No, I imagine he's passed out on the bed. Call him in the morning, okay? I'm sorry I woke you.'

Now the pieces fit. Her father's words at dinner – *I didn't give Bruce all that money for nothing. You don't have to take that crap from Mr Big Shot here anymore* – made sense.

Brian's behavior tonight did not. Why hadn't he told her?

She padded down the hallway into the kitchen, which was quiet and empty again. Standing at the French doors, she looked out at the shifting and folding light thrown off by the pool's illuminated water. At this time of night the lights were supposed to be off, controlled by an automated system that also told the sprinklers when to run and kept the back boundary of their yard electrified by a mild current meant to repel alligators and deer. The light was ethereal and lovely, an unexpected late-night gift. But obviously there was a glitch in the control – perhaps a glitch like the one she feared was in her brain.

For sure, there was a glitch in her *life*, she thought, watching the light dance on the portico ceiling and the wide terrazzo floor tiles, imported from Spain. She wanted *that* glitch fixed ASAP. The person Cameron Lowenstein recommended, the acupuncturist psychic, might be a life-fixer. Could a set of long, ultra-sharp needles and some prescient knowledge be the tools needed to get hers back on track?

Unwilling to join Brian in bed, Meg sat down at the kitchen counter with the last of her mother's notebooks, to read an entry she'd only skimmed before:

August 10, 2005
 Low: 71°; high: 87°, good storm this afternoon.
 I spent most of tonight on the phone with Julianne, calming her down. Allan broke his wrist and needs surgery. She's just no good in a crisis, never has been, probably because she had so many sisters to buffer her all those years growing up.
 Speaking of a crisis, Spencer's had kidney pain all day, but won't do anything about it. Men are stubborn like that. I tried to get Meggie earlier, to ask her about it, but she's in the middle of handling somebody's premature labor. I hope

*that won't result in another one of those fragile,
one-pound babies stuck with all those needles
and tubes and everything – I saw a feature
about it just last week. Small enough to hold in
one hand, nothing but transparent skin stretched
over bones as fragile as a bird's. Poor things! I've
always believed in letting nature say which ones
live. A baby born before it can even breathe is a
baby called back to the Blessed Mother, and us
keeping it here is cruelty. That's my view. And I
can talk, losing my tiny boy the year after
Meggie came; I know how it feels.*

*My, how grim I am tonight. Enough of that.
I've never been one to look backward too much,
which probably accounts for how I've managed
to survive Spencer all these years! Oh sure, I
wish I could've kept Julianne home longer and I
wish Beth would stick to one man for more than
three weeks – she was just saying, though, that
she's got no good examples of marriage to make
her want to. I said, 'Look at Kara and Jules and
Meggie. Look at Daddy and me!' And she laid it
out like a row of ducks: Kara and Julie are
nothing but baby factories (!!), Meg's depressed
and lonely, and their dad's been nothing but a
financial wildfire his whole life – she'd never live
with any man like that. Then she said, 'I don't
mean to insult you, Mom,' which of course I
know. Spencer is an acquired taste to be sure,
but I love him. How can you explain the force of
true love? I told her, true love doesn't go around*

*looking at a situation from every angle, it strikes
at its whimsy, and we are all helpless to defend
ourselves. I said, 'It just hasn't happened to you
yet. But it will.'*

*Beth is right about Meggie, though, and I said
to Spencer just a few minutes ago how I wish we
had never let her take up with Brian. 'She was
an adult,' he said. 'Not like we could've stopped
her.' 'Oh, we could've,' I said, and I told him, if I
could go to the flea market and find some
magical lamp with a genie inside, the only thing
I'd wish right now is to have the money to pay
Bruce back. What a yoke that debt must be to
her. How could we have failed to see?*

But I know that answer.

Meg closed the notebook and slid her hand over its
cover, a caress.

Her father thought he'd already told her about the
money, but there was no way he could have. Was there?
In the commotion of her getting his house packed and
cleaned, of coordinating all his appointments with the
real estate agents and the inspectors and the lawyer, the
disconnections of power and gas and phone, the noti-
fications to post office, relatives, friends, doctors – in
all of that, might he have told her he was writing a check
to Bruce, satisfying what turned out to be one of her
mother's last wishes, and she'd forgotten? It sounded
possible, but she was certain she would remember something so significant. She would have reacted as she was
reacting now: with growing indignation.

Because for all that returning Bruce's cash was a respectable thing to do, her father had not, in almost seventeen years, even obliquely referred to the favor *she'd* done him, except to say, at her wedding reception – a lavish, four-tent affair he knew he was supposed to have paid for – that her marriage would be a terrific thing for all of them. If he had only *thanked* her, even, she might not feel so angry now.

She poured some milk, grabbed a stack of Oreos, and went out into the muggy night to sit beside the pool. The sharp croak of a tree frog greeted her as she passed the portico columns. She sat and put her feet into the water, shivering a little and then relaxing as she grew accustomed to the temperature, a constant eighty degrees. Then she dunked one cookie halfway, waited for it to be saturated, and quickly bit off the soggy half, the same way she'd done each of the rare times they'd had Oreos in their house when she was a kid.

Someone – on a talk show, maybe, or perhaps she'd read it – said that American adults were obsessed with addressing their unresolved childhood issues. Meg supposed that explained why her shopping list always included Oreos. It also included whatever peanut-free sugary cereal Savannah was in the mood for when the list got made, and ice cream and real cheese and orange soda. Everything Meg coveted as a child filled her refrigerator and cupboards now. Everything she didn't have back then, she gave her daughter now. Things like a big, cheerful bedroom suite – a *suite*, whereas she and Kara had shared a room so narrow that they could hold hands while lying in their beds. When Carson slept over, they would wedge an old army surplus cot up against the ends of the beds, leaving maybe six inches between the cot and their dresser. Jules and Beth *shared* a bed in their tiny room. The house had a single bathroom for the six of them.

Savannah had her own, with a clawfoot tub and dual sinks so that her sleepover guests didn't have to share with her. She had guitar and music theory lessons, summer camp stays that rivaled most people's best vacations. All the stuffed animals, dolls, clothes, shoes, jewelry she wanted ... More recently Savannah'd gotten the cell phone and computer and iPod, and soon she'd have a brand-new car. When Meg listed all these things in her mind, and then pictured their lifestyle – this pool, the million-dollar French-inspired villa that was their house, the trips they'd taken, their membership in an exclusive country club, to name the obvious – the picture of what she'd provided for Savannah by marrying Brian, by becoming an obstetrician, by choosing the material path as if the wrongs it righted were the important ones, brightened to a blurry glare of excess.

'I suck,' Meg said as she dunked the rest of the cookie. Her fingers held it in the cold milk with no trouble, suggesting there was nothing wrong with her at all, nothing more than what she'd assumed in the first place: a strain, perhaps a pinched nerve, which had worked itself out in the week that had passed since the first problem. The relief contained in this thought pleased her as much as the cold, wet chocolate in her mouth; she took a second cookie from her lap and dunked it as easily as she'd done the first.

If only a week and a handful of cookies could improve everything else.

The water beckoned, its shimmer a visual siren's call she didn't even try to resist. After shedding her blouse and slacks, she stood poised at the pool's edge in her panties and bra, then dove in. As she'd done as a child swimming in the McKays' clear, largest lake, she let herself drift down to the bottom, eyes open, studying the soft swirls of light that covered her now, too. She was a water nymph, weightless, ageless; she was as one with the molecules of hydrogen and oxygen, no more than they and no less.

When her lungs began to ache, proving the folly of her fantasy, she put her feet against the bottom of the pool and pushed off. Breaking the surface, she filled her lungs and broke into freestyle, pulling herself across the water's surface with the same sure motion that had won her so many races so long ago. For a few sweet strokes she was fifteen again, racing Carson and Kara across the lake. But then her rhythm faltered, the weak arm struggling to match the other, and she paddled to the steps and climbed out. She simply needed to get back into the routine, that was all. 'Use it or lose it,' she sighed, taking an oversize towel from a teak storage bin and wrapping it around her shoulders. Lowenstein was way off base.

After picking up her clothes, she walked back into the house, her feet leaving damp prints behind her. Inside, she locked up and turned off the interior lights, then went to the bedroom she and Brian had been sharing for eight years now, since they'd built the house. He was asleep on top of the covers, shirt half unbuttoned, pants off but light tan dress socks still on. In the low light of the bedside lamp, the socks looked skin-colored and made it seem that the dark hair of his legs ended abruptly three inches above his ankles. He looked ridiculous, and worse, he was snoring with his mouth hanging open, the way he always did when he slept on his back. *Mr Big Shot*, her father had called him. Right.

As she stood in the bathroom drying off, she thought, what was it that her father had said when she was leaving his apartment last week? Something like, why didn't she just get on with her life? Ah, another reference to repaying Bruce ... he'd been trying that day and again tonight to show her that her debt was cleared. And the diaries – might they, like the repayment, be his gift to her, a gesture toward an apology he couldn't quite make with words? He wanted her to see that he'd freed her of the shackles she had incurred on his behalf. That must be it.

Now she understood. He believed he had bought back the property title to her life – something far more valuable than what he'd given Bruce. What she would do with it, though, was not as simple a matter as her father might think.

She put on her nightshirt, then slid under the sheets next to her snoring husband, looking at him closely before turning off the light. His jaw and chin were peppered with black and silver whiskers, grown in since the morning. He had a pleasing enough face – handsome, in the slightly effeminate way of many Southern boys she'd known whose families had run plantations or luxury hotels – or banks. It was as if privilege had softened their features over the course of too many unchallenged generations.

Brian was a man who expected to succeed; he had expected to win her, and it was this confidence, more than his looks, that she'd found appealing. He'd been friendly, self-assured, amusing – once she'd gotten to know him she'd liked him a lot. But not in a way that turned her head, not at all. She had been in love with Carson right up to – and past – the day Brian came to her with his surprise proposal.

Proof that love didn't conquer all.

Weariness infused her every muscle as she lay there; using her left arm, she reached over and shut off the light. Brian turned onto his side facing her, liquor sour on his breath. She turned away, toward the windows, where the silvery light from the pool bobbed and dipped on the sheer curtains. She watched it, her eyes growing heavy under its hypnotic dance.

She wished she could say her life with Brian was awful and she would be delighted to take her father's advice and run away from it, shackles dropping from her ankles like an emancipated slave's. But for all that their relationship had begun with a spoiled young man's ambition to win a girl away from a supposedly lesser man, she couldn't say her decision to let him win made her a martyr. She couldn't say she had suffered, not in any tangible way. As she concluded every time the thought of leaving came to mind, Brian was a supportive spouse, a reasonably good parent. They were a family, albeit a less-than-ideal one. 'It's not so easy, Dad,' she whispered.

Her ankles might now be unbound, but here she stood.

PART II

There is a crack, a crack in everything. That's how the light gets in.

– Leonard Cohen

NINETEEN

'So are you going to show it to me?' Val asked Carson at breakfast in his parents' kitchen Thursday morning. James and Carolyn were already up and out of the house to work on hedging the lemon trees with their regular crew of migrant grove workers.

'Insatiable girl,' Carson said, passing Val a pitcher of orange juice. 'I showed it to you just last night.'

She grinned. 'Not *that*. Your little house, the one you and your dad built.'

'Oh, the *shed*.'

'The shed, right. You said I could see it today.'

He vaguely remembered saying as much, but sharply regretted it now. The rum and Cokes had loosened his tongue the previous evening as they'd all sat outside around the firepit, his folks and him reminiscing, inspired, he supposed, by his impending wedding. The shed renovation had come up – though Meg's name had not – and Val predictably declared her interest in checking it out. She was fascinated with everything about his early years as a farm kid; his history was so different from her own upbringing that they might have been raised on different planets.

'I'll give you the tour if we have time,' he said. 'Lots to do – we need to go see those florists, and we have to be at the tailor's at twelve-thirty.'

Val smirked. 'It's right over there.' She pointed to the shed, visible through one of the tall casement windows that had been added in recent years, one of many improvements his parents had made as a result of his success. 'I think we can fit it into the schedule. I can't believe you haven't been in there since you first moved away.'

'You know, I keep meaning to go in and sort through stuff . . . I stay here in the house whenever I'm back because to tell you the truth it's a lot more comfortable. Central air, stocked fridge. I like the creature comforts.' That sounded plausible.

'Your mom said she might turn it into an art studio, right? So I want to see it before it's different.'

He wanted to put her off further but couldn't think of any more excuses for delay. And he didn't want to make her suspicious; that would only provoke questions he didn't feel like answering. In the seven months since they first met, he'd managed to gloss over his relationship with Meg so smoothly that Val wouldn't think to differentiate her from the myriad other women in his past. Underplaying that relationship – the only one that had mattered before Val – was a sort of sin of omission, and he did plan to tell her more about it at some point, but not yet. For no good reason that he could figure, he felt protective of his history with Meg. Or maybe he just hated looking weak for having been a heartsick fool for so long. Whatever it was, the thought of taking Val into the shed and showing her around hung him up inside. The place was so permeated with Meg that he was afraid even Val would be able to see and smell her there, the way he knew he still would.

His phone began ringing. He looked at the display; 'It's Gene. I better take it.' He answered the call. 'Gene-o, how's it going?'

'Like usual, I'm working like a dog while you're off someplace playing with Surfer Girl.'

'So take a vacation.'

'Are you kidding? Your career would collapse like a prostitute on a Sunday morning. No, listen, what are you doing tomorrow night? No plans? Good, 'cause I need you to do an old friend of mine a favor.'

Carson said, 'Whoa there, I do have plans. We're going to a play with my folks.'

'Nah, that play sucks. Send Surfer Girl if you want, but you, my friend, have a date with a piano, two guitars, some drums, and my best old friend from the neighborhood, Johnny Simmons.'

'Her name is Val,' Carson said patiently, 'and you don't know if the play sucks, because I didn't name it.'

'Yeah, and anyway, Johnny's got this great club over in Orlando, and the band who was supposed to play tomorrow night canceled on him. And he just happens to mention this to me and I just happen to know that you, my star pitcher, just happen to be an hour away and could fill in and make Johnny owe me for life.'

'In other words,' Carson laughed, 'it's all about you.'

'When is it not? So you'll do it? Great! He'll pay you whatever they were gonna get, and I won't even take my percentage.' Gene filled in the details, and after they hung up Carson thought of how a date like this, unpromoted, in a smallish club where a good crowd was practically guaranteed, would be a pleasure after so many gigs at stadiums packed with thousands of faceless fans. It would be like when he was starting out, except now nobody would be asking, 'What was your name again?' and he wouldn't be sweating the question of whether he'd find another place to play the next weekend.

'I'm going to play a club tomorrow night,' he told Val as he stacked the breakfast dishes and carried them to the sink. Shep, his mom's mottled mixed-breed dog, clicked across the tile floor and nudged his leg, so Carson set the plates, with their scrambled egg scraps, on the floor. He patted Shep's back and added, 'I hope you don't mind. Gene needed a favor.'

'Won't your mom have a fit? She really wants to see the play.'

'And she will see it. You should go too.'

'Are you serious? She'll eat me alive if you leave me alone with her and your dad.'

'Mom? She *loves* you. What are you talking about?'

Val shook her head. 'No, she loves *you* – and she was expecting you to pick somebody . . . else. She's just tolerating me.'

Val was right, but he was surprised she'd noticed the subtle vibes; his mom was doing a good job of

162

supporting his decision to get married even though it was just as Val said: she'd expected him to choose someone older, for starters, and more like him – or, to be precise, someone more like *her*. A woman who had her roots in the land, not the waves. A woman who wanted to raise kids, not act like one. Not that Val was childish, but she was very youthful. She played it down around his folks, but her energy was irrepressible.

'Mom and Dad both think you're spectacular – but if you want to come down to Orlando with me tomorrow, that'd be great. Then I won't have to pick up any groupies to help me pass the time.'

'Oh, I have nothing against groupies,' Val said, matching his straight face. 'Let's find us a few. The more, the merrier.'

'Girl,' he said, 'don't get me hoping like that.'

'As if you could handle more than just me.' She wrapped her arms around his neck and then hopped up to wrap her bare legs around his waist. He put his arms around her hips and snugged her against him.

It would be bad form, just now, to confess what he knew from actual past experiences he was capable of handling. Cocaine was a powerful aphrodisiac in the new user, and he wasn't particularly proud of the stories he could tell of his earlier 'rock star' days. She'd heard some of them, and not only from him; his old reputation was documented on plenty of websites and in a lot of photo albums, he was sure. But now that he and Val were serious about their relationship, engaged to be married in about three more weeks, the proper response to her challenge was a diplomatic one. So he said, 'As if I would *want* more than just you.'

She pressed her nose and forehead to his. 'Right answer,' she said, then kissed him. 'Take me to the shed?' she asked in a husky voice.

Ah, the shed. He was not about to take her there for *that*. 'No,' he said, easing his arms down so that she dropped to her feet. 'We need to move up our timetable if I'm gonna play tomorrow night. I need to work up a playlist, get it to the other musicians, and get some practice in this afternoon, so we'd better hit the road.'

Val made a show of looking pouty, so he added, 'Well, we could forget all this grand wedding business and just elope.'

'God no, my mom would kill me! She's already mad that we're choosing florists without her.' Val's mother was also mad that the wedding would be in St Martin instead of Malibu, and the resort manager in St Martin was mad that they weren't using a local florist because Carolyn insisted they support her fellow agriculturists there in the Ocala area – and if Carson thought further, he was sure he could add many more names to the list of people whose idea of what or where their wedding 'should' be was not being fully addressed. Weddings were too much aggravation by far.

'All right, then.' He gave Val a playful push. 'Get your stuff and let's go.'

TWENTY

After meeting back home for lunch, Carson drove Val and his dad into town, where the men would be measured for custom-made tuxes. The other men in the wedding party had faxed their measurements to the tailor of Carson's choice, a Thai transplant who went by the name Penguin Pete. Pete was one of Carson's favorite people; despite the inconvenience of Pete being located here in Ocala, he went to him for all his suits – the few he owned. Carson just wasn't a suit kind of guy. 'Dressing up' usually meant jeans without holes and a shirt with a collar.

Pete's name had been one of the few things he was able to remember on returning from his first visit to Thailand – a Bangkok concert in 2000. The whole time he was there, he fought to forget his declaration that his first trip to the country would be for his fortieth birthday, and that Meg would be with him. Fought the memory with cocaine supplied by the local concert organizer, a fast-talking Chinese man named Jinn. It worked famously. Not only didn't Carson preoccupy himself with thoughts of his Meg-less future but he kept busy, the two nights he wasn't performing and afterward on the one night he did, with a string of lovely but interchangeable dark-haired women – the ones he elected not to mention to Val earlier today.

Pete, who was related to Jinn by some convoluted marital connections, had already made him one tux, which he'd worn to the Oscars two years earlier. That one, in forest green velvet with black silk lapels, was a huge hit and won him spots in every celebrity news rag he could think of. Pete had even clipped some from Thai papers, and taped the clippings to the edge of one of the big mirrors inside the shop.

The shop itself defied celebrity expectations; at best, the front room was fifteen feet square and looked like Pete had lifted it directly from some Bangkok back-street. It came complete with intriguing spicy smells and a patina of age and dust and humidity that he imagined made Pete feel right at home. As for the customer, well, who could argue with superb tailoring?

'Look here, Miss,' Pete said to Val, pointing at the pictures on the mirror in the back left corner of the room. 'He gets red carpet with my suit.'

'Everybody gets the red carpet,' Carson explained, adding, 'Nothing against the suit.'

Pete, who was shorter than Carson by almost a foot and wore what looked a lot like a toreador's outfit, looked up at him and frowned. 'No, no, you wearing that suit make you *look* celebrity. Otherwise they not recognize you, make you stand behind fence like mortal.'

'If you say so. Anyway, it's a great tux. But not what

Miss Val here has in mind for our nuptials. Tell him what we're going for, Val.'

'Yes, yes, come on; we have some tea, you tell me all your ideas, and Doreen, she measure your men,' Pete said, waving Val into the back room, whose doorway was separated from the shop's front room by long strings of wooden beads. Val looked back at Carson as if hoping for rescue, but he just smiled and moved toward the small dais in the corner, where Pete's Cuban wife Doreen waited with her measuring tape and a tiny spiral notebook. Doreen, a curvy, florid woman of about fifty, wore a ruffled low-cut blouse of turquoise and ten or more thin silver bracelets on each of her wrists. Carson glanced at his dad, who was eyeing Doreen's cleavage with trepidation.

'Dad, why don't you go first,' he said.

'Okay then,' his dad replied. This was the first time he had seen the shop too, and Carson could tell he was a little disconcerted by both the place and the proprietors. His dad was not a worldly man; it had taken a lot of arm-twisting to get him to come out to Seattle four months earlier. He didn't like to leave the groves, claimed the trees would miss him and bear sour fruit the next season.

'Jou step up right here,' Doreen said in her thick Cuban accent, bracelets jangling. 'No slouching, no twitching – hokay?' she added, her round face fixed in a strict scowl. 'We make *hwun* measure, get it right, and jour suit *fits*.'

'Better do as she says,' Carson warned. 'She was schooled by some no-nonsense nuns.'

As she began stretching the tape across his dad's shoulders, then down each of his tanned arms, Doreen said, 'So, Mister Music, who is to be jour best man?'

'Dad here.'

'Oh, jou are so *sweet*. He is a good son,' she pronounced, pushing the tape into his dad's crotch.

'He is,' his dad said, flinching just a little. 'Can't complain.' He smiled at Carson, a genuine smile that said he no longer held any grudges about his son's defection. In the beginning of Carson's music career, the smile wasn't so genuine; they'd burned up the phone lines quite a few Sunday afternoons and weekday evenings, Carson defending his absence and his choices and his dad arguing that working as a singer and songwriter was like asking to be miserable and poor. And even if success was in the cards, he said, Carson needed to know what hepatitis looked like, and herpes and drug addiction and AIDS. 'All those things you don't want to think about, I'm here to tell you, that's what's out there.'

But what Carson didn't want to think about was a different sort of disease, one that was endemic in his family's orange and grapefruit and lemon groves, where, if he was not moving from town to town and club to club, he would have to spend every day. Where he had spent practically his whole life with Meg at his side, catching fireflies and chasing adolescent dreams on hazy summer nights. If he were living there, he would be so much more susceptible – or so he'd thought. The fact of it was that his heartache went with him to Jacksonville and Durham and Pittsburgh and Cleveland; it hopped the Mississippi when he did, in Minneapolis; it tagged along to Denver and Vegas and San Diego. It grew smaller, though, and hid in the shaded coves of his heart, places where the light of his daily routines didn't often reach. He wondered, now, if he'd *protected* it by escaping, wondered whether, if he had stayed and made his life on the farm, overexposure might have erased the pain of his heartache entirely.

Doreen finished with his dad and nudged him off the dais. 'Now jou,' she commanded Carson.

'Guess I'll see how Val's getting along,' his dad said.

'Good idea. Have some tea – Pete makes great tea.' Carson stepped onto the wooden platform and held his arms out from his sides while his dad passed through the beads into the back room, where Val's higher tones took turns with Pete's lower ones in what sounded like a pleasant discussion so far.

He told Doreen, 'Don't expect I've changed size much. Val's got me learning the surf – trying to learn, I should say.'

'Oh, surfing, hoo!' Doreen said. 'I hwatched that movie, *jou* know, with that hunkie Swayze man. Oh, Dios!' she fanned herself in mock passion. 'And the other sexy one – Matrix Man?'

'Keanu Reeves,' Carson said. 'Yeah, I saw that movie too. Val's a world-class competitor – a pro.'

'No!' Doreen said, sitting back on her heels. 'That little girl? The waves will eat her up. Do not joke with me, Music Man.'

'I wouldn't,' he said. 'Ask her yourself. She has a competition next week in Bali.'

'Bali, oh, rough life,' Doreen said, finishing up with his inner and outer pants seams. 'Jou're going, I suppose?'

'Nope, I have to miss it. I'm doing a benefit concert next Wednesday in New Orleans.'

Doreen shook her head. 'So busy. How she is going to cook for you when you are not even in the same country, huh? I want to know *hwat* jou are thinking, to marry a woman who is not always *there*. Huh!' she snorted. He knew better than to answer; the last time, her rant had been about his going to the Oscars with an actress who had portrayed a character Doreen hated. She'd named half a dozen 'better' actresses then – women who he was sure also weren't home cooking dinner every night. She was capricious, but kind and honest and great with detail work. He liked her a lot.

He had his back to the door when he heard the bell above it ring, announcing entry. He saw the customer in the mirror, though, saw her before her eyes had a chance to adjust from the bright midday sunshine to the much dimmer store interior.

'Hola, Missus Hamilton!' Doreen called out. 'Be right with jou,' she said, words that came out sounding like 'bright weeju' to Carson's ears, which were equally as stunned as his eyes.

Nowhere to hide. His lungs felt suddenly shallow and inadequate, his mind incapable of forming something coherent to say. Should he announce himself or wait for her to see him?

'Take your time,' Meg said, still unaware of his identity. He was, in this moment, an anonymous tallish man in dark shorts and a T-shirt with his back to her. He watched her walk over to the counter while she took her sunglasses, which had dangled from her left hand, and lodged them in her hair.

'Done,' Doreen said, nudging him off the dais. He stepped to the left side, near the corner, and saw it, saw his escape if he wanted it: he could move quickly to the beaded doorway right now, just slide past the mirrors before she turned her attention away from the business cards displayed along the counter. His heart thundered with indecision.

But Doreen had her own agenda, and before he could act, she took his arm and said to Meg, 'Your husband's suits are just done, and good thing! We will be *so* busy making wedding tuxes for Ocala's big star—' She pulled him toward Meg as if she were showing off a prized stallion, and he watched Meg turn toward him. Doreen finished, 'Jou know, Carson McKay!'

Meg stared, and her lips parted as if to speak, but it took a beat for her to make any sound; her eyes locked on his for just that second and then slid away, to Doreen. 'Well, good timing then,' she said. She glanced back at him and added, 'Congratulations.' Her hazel eyes were wide and appeared sincere.

He started to speak, had to clear his throat, then said, 'Thanks, Meg.'

'Oh, jou know each other?'

Neither of them responded right away, both waiting for the other to delineate that answer. Then Meg laughed, a small, nervous laugh, and said, 'Well, it was a long time ago.'

Doreen, oblivious to the tension that felt, to him, as palpable as a cloudburst, beamed up at him. 'His bride is a professional surfing champion.' She said the words slowly, stressing each syllable.

'I've heard,' Meg said politely.

'One minute. I get Mr. H's suits, hokay?' Then Doreen disappeared through the beads, leaving him alone with Meg for the first time since he'd promised he would see her in hell.

It was inevitable they would run into each other, sooner or later. He didn't come back home to visit all that often, but every time he carried the expectation in the back of his mind that she could turn up at the grocery store or a restaurant, next to him at a stop-light again, with her parents at the co-op – until she lost her mom and Spencer sold the farm. He'd never made a plan for what he'd do when they did meet up, and even if he had, he was sure, now, that he'd have botched it.

The words he'd spoken with such passionate certainly the morning of her wedding had troubled him in recent years. Why had he been so ugly to her? Why couldn't he have just taken her rejection like a man? So she didn't love him enough to choose him; so she'd come over for a quick fuck, crass as it sounded; he *should* have just sent her off to Hamilton with good wishes instead of that moody proclamation. But then, he was young and stubborn and hurt . . . and he really had believed that seeing her again would be hellish.

It wasn't, though. Jesus, seeing her made his fingers tingle and his heart pound.

She looked tired but luminous still, like the copper in her hair and the pale pink of her skin were lighted by something inside her, some energy that even a stressful day couldn't eclipse entirely. He knew she was an obstetrician, that she had a practice across town – his mother mentioned these kinds of things over the years, as if to periodically test the waters. He knew she had a teenage daughter whose name he had known she would choose, if she ever had a girl. And he knew that she'd wasted no time getting pregnant, as if trying to cement herself to the Hamiltons as rapidly as possible – probably to secure an inheritance, in case something happened to Brian. He hadn't ever thought of her as shrewd, but he hadn't thought of her as any other man's wife, either, and he'd been dead wrong about that. Well, whatever she was, she was still beautiful to him. Having her there, ten feet in front of him, was purely, unexpectedly, a pleasure.

TWENTY-ONE

Meg could not have been more surprised to find Carson at the tailor's. He was the last thing on her mind this afternoon, while she squeezed in yet another errand for Brian before heading over to her one-fifteen appointment with an old med school colleague, neurologist Brianna Davidson – Manisha had insisted she call Brianna and ask to be seen right away. 'Answers are always better than questions,' she'd said.

The start of the day had been tense, Brian waking up hung over and unwilling to talk about the money and his coming home drunk. But then he'd called her at ten-fifteen and sweetly asked if she could get his suits and drop the gray one by his office; he was leaving for Boston right after work.

She heard Doreen in the back room asking Pete, 'I am getting Mr Hamilton's suits – where jou have put them?' and prayed they'd be found, fast. She knew she should say something more to Carson, but what? Where to even begin?

'How do you know about this place?' Carson said,

and she was hugely relieved that he was able to dredge up a casual remark, because she was tongue-tied, awkward in his presence in a way she'd never been before.

'Oh. He – Brian – heard about it from somebody, God knows. Pete's very good.'

'Yeah, I've been coming to him for a long time.'

'Oh, terrific.'

'Yeah.'

He looked so good in person. She'd seen his face on CD covers and magazine covers and, thanks to Kara, in the newspaper, and always he looked appealing – well, wasn't that the job of those photographers and stylists? In person, though, he had a presence now, a kind of vibrant energy that resonated around him. His hair was longish and rumpled, much like it'd been when they were teens, and a flock of light brown whiskers grew from his chin, no fuller than when he was twenty. He rubbed them.

'So . . .' she said, taking her turn, 'is your mom well?'

'She's great! Yeah. She's, um, keeping busy . . .'

The beads swished. Meg looked over, expecting Doreen, but seeing James McKay instead. How funny she and Carson must look to him, her standing there clutching her purse to her like a life vest, Carson with one hand at his chin and the other jingling loose change in his pocket. Awkward kids, struggling for words.

James came over to her. 'How are you, Meg?' he said, leaning in to kiss her cheek.

'All right, all things considered. Dad's getting used

to retirement over there at Horizon.' How much easier it was to talk to James!

'Good, good,' James said. 'Give him our best.'

'I will, thanks. You look well.' She'd seen him several times since her split from Carson, most recently at her mother's funeral. He and Carolyn both attended. James had been warm and sympathetic, Carolyn sympathetic but also aloof, as she always was when their paths crossed. Meg had never taken it personally; she understood Carolyn's protectiveness, understood what she must think of a woman who would just casually rip out her son's heart and stomp on it, as Meg had seemed to do.

Carson had sent her father a card, or so she'd heard.

James moved to Carson and put his arm around his shoulders. 'I'm plugging along,' he said. 'Making sure Carson keeps the wedding plans on schedule.'

She saw the sideways look Carson gave his dad, who she could tell was playing the protective parent himself just now. Did James see her as a threat? Some instincts died hard, clearly – her own included, because she hadn't been able to help her first reaction to Carson, the sudden tightness in her chest, the immediate urge to press herself against him, her shoulders fitted into his armpits when he wrapped his arms around her. He had held her so many times, for comfort, for support, for protectiveness, for desire ... she'd lived in his arms, grown up there.

She made herself smile, her professional smile of assurance that everything was under control. 'So when's the big day?' she asked.

Carson said, 'Next month – Mother's Day weekend, in St Martin. Sounds weird, I know, but her mom – Val's mom, she liked the idea of combining the two things.'

'Sure,' Meg nodded, recalling too well how her own mother-in-law had steered so many of *her* wedding plans, taking the helm as if the fact of the Hamiltons paying for the wedding granted Shelly the right to plan it all. Her mother accepted the role-reversal gracefully – gratefully, in fact, which irritated Meg at the time. She wanted to tell her to have some pride; she, Meg, was also doing *them* a favor, by allowing Brian to marry the girl he wanted most. The money being thrown around, the Hamiltons' wealth, that was a *tool*, not a scepter, and she wanted her mother to recognize this. But with her own limited ability to see the bigger picture at that age, she hadn't understood the dynamics of the situation. Her parents were, in essence, selling her off, just as some families in other cultures sold *their* daughters, as a way to improve their own circumstances. The seller might be able to fetch a high price because of some desirable quality in the daughter, but it was the buyer who could afford that price who truly held the power.

In the case of Carson and his bride-to-be, the situation surrounding their wedding was, of course, much more usual. Valerie Haas might not have quite the wealth Carson likely did, but there was no 'sale' taking place. Envy prickled the back of Meg's neck as she thought how it must feel to Valerie to be marrying a man for no other reason except that you loved him.

Oh, she'd been *fond* of Brian when they got married – had told herself she would never have married him otherwise; that would be a fool's bargain. She forgave his main defect: that he wasn't Carson. She hadn't *loved* him, though. Love, she'd told her mother, would come in due time – no different than with arranged marriages, she'd said. 'Of course it will,' her mother agreed. 'Why shouldn't it?'

Doreen reappeared, carrying Brian's altered suits, and passed them to her.

'On jour account?' Doreen asked.

'Yes, thanks,' Meg nodded. She was just about to tell the men she had to run when the beads parted again and a trim, white-blond young woman appeared.

'I think we got it!'

Carson jerked around like a kid caught reaching for a cookie right before dinner. 'Oh, good,' he said. He looked at the woman – Valerie, obviously, for not only did she look like the bride-to-be in their engagement photo, she had the lithe body of an athlete in her prime: smooth, long leg muscles bared by shorts like the ones Savannah slept in, curved biceps displayed under the same type of meager sleeves Savannah's form-fitting tees had. Carson looked at Valerie as if unsure of his next move.

James saved him. 'Val, this is Meg Hamilton, an old friend. Her folks used to own the farm next to ours.'

'Hey,' Val said, raising her hand up in a quick wave. Her friendly look told Meg that Carson had spared her the details of his young adulthood – or one particular detail anyway.

Meg said, 'Glad to meet you,' as warmly as she could – which was lukewarm. Not bad.

Val, obviously distracted by whatever it was they *got*, didn't notice either way. She turned to Carson. 'Pete and me, we're simpatico on the tux design. You guys are going to look *fab*.' She held both hands out in a thumbs-up gesture for emphasis.

Fab, Meg thought, watching Val snake her arm around Carson's waist. The bride-to-be looked smaller next to him, no more than five feet three inches and two thirds his width; she was *fab* herself, with that gleaming hair and golden tanned skin. Well, what else would she be?

Meg remembered suddenly to check the time, and saw she really did have to run if she was to make her appointment with Brianna. 'Sorry, but I have to go. I'm on my lunch break.'

'Of course,' Carson said.

End it quick. 'It was good to see you – and congrats again.' She shifted the suit hangers from her right arm, which was feeling very tired, to her left, then turned for the exit. James hurried ahead of her to hold the door.

'Thanks,' she told him, stepping out into the blazing sunlight. She tried to raise her hand up for her sunglasses, but it had become leaden, just like before.

James didn't notice anything. 'Take care,' he said, and let the door close as he returned inside.

Meg squinted as she went to the curb, then waited for traffic before crossing to her car on the opposite side of the street. Something clicked in her mind: the wedding was set for Mother's Day weekend, Carson said – not Mother's Day itself, then, but the day before. Savannah's birthday. That was a coincidence she didn't want to think about.

She tried making her right hand into a fist, and it cooperated, but only weakly. 'Son of a bitch,' she said under her breath.

When the road was clear, she crossed, making each step careful and deliberate; this thing with her arm spooked her, made her feel she needed to be doubly cautious not to stumble or get off balance in her low heels. She reached her car without incident and laid the plastic-draped suits across the hood, followed by her purse, which she slid off her left shoulder. With her left hand, she rummaged for the keys and found them, pressing the unlock button. Then she hoisted her purse, hoisted the suits, and tried to drape them over her right arm so that she could use her left hand to open the car door. But even that minor task was too much for the arm, which collapsed with the weight. Everything spilled onto the asphalt, landing at her feet.

'God damn it!' It was all too much, just too much at once. The stupid errand for the stupid suits – why couldn't Brian pick up his own damn clothes? And Carson, and his pert little fiancée and their wedding plans, and the heat, and this stupid, terrifying, weak arm . . . She stood there in the street, facing the car door, awash with tears.

'Hey, Meg—' Carson's voice came behind her, and, not knowing how long he'd been standing there, she quickly squatted down to pick up the mess.

'Let me help you with those,' he said, bending down. She felt his gaze on her face, knew he would ask what was wrong – which he did. And what could she tell him?

She moved aside so he could open the back door and hang the suits, letting the silence drag out, indecision gripping her. She couldn't tell him the truth; she didn't quite know what was true herself. How to explain the weakness in her arm and the emotions that had pushed her over the edge? What excuse would release him from his feelings of chivalrous, at best habitual, concern?

Carson prompted her. 'Meg?'

'I—' she started. 'Nothing. I'm okay. Just a dizzy spell – the heat, you know?' The lie sounded lame even to her.

'Dizzy? Come on; you're *crying.*'

'Not on your account,' she said, wanting to dispel that suspicion right away.

He said, 'No, of course – I didn't think—' He stopped and took an audible breath. Then he said, 'From in there, you looked like you were having trouble with your arm.'

'I was – I had a cramp. It's happened a couple times; I'll be fine. It goes away.' She was in a hurry now to leave, not only to get to her appointment – which until a few moments ago she was sure would be medically pointless and instead a good excuse to see an old friend – but also because she couldn't bear having him so close to her, acting so much like his old self that she was frightened by the comfort of his presence, the sensation of time having been erased.

TWENTY-TWO

One benefit of being a doctor was the connections to other doctors who would gladly work a friend or colleague into an already overscheduled day. Brianna Davidson had no time for new patients on the kind of short notice Meg gave her, and still, she was working her in. Today's visit was supposed to be a consultation – a chat, really, about what might be going on, and a determination about what tests, if any, might be needed.

Meg carried her X-rays from the orthopedist in an enormous manila envelope, tucked beneath her left arm as she stood at the check-in desk of Central Florida Neurological Associates.

'Dr Meghan Powell,' she told the receptionist.

The woman found her name on the computer monitor, then looked down at a note. 'One moment – let me tell her you're here.'

The waiting room, austere but soothing in its grays and blues, held three other patients, all of whom studiously ignored one another and her. The scene differed dramatically from her clinic, where comparisons and commiserations about pregnancies and birth experiences always had to be interrupted when a patient was called. These three souls – two gray-haired women and a man of perhaps forty-five – looked as if the last thing they would do was compare notes on what had brought them in. Obstetrics was, usually, a business of hope and renewal, whereas neurology suggested lost ships chugging through dark, ice-laden seas.

'All right, Dr Hamilton, come on back.' A nurse in deep blue scrubs held the door to the exam hallway. She waited for Meg to come through, then said, 'Dr Davidson's just down here.'

Meg followed down the hall and into a room on the right. Brianna, a thin, dark-haired, serious-looking woman who had aced every exam the university could throw at her during their med-school days, waited behind a glossy cherrywood desk so uncrowded that it seemed the practice had opened just that morning. Meg's own desk was a cluttered collection of folders and samples and Post-it notes, and photos of Savannah, primarily, though she also had one of Brian and Savannah together, circa 1994.

Brianna stood, reaching out to Meg with a long-fingered hand. 'Meg, you're looking terrific.'

Meg reached with her right hand and shook Brianna's. 'Thanks. You too. You wouldn't know it, but ten minutes ago I was ready to cut this damn arm off.' *To say the least.*

'Pain?' Brianna asked as Meg sat down across from her.

'No, no pain – just the same thing I described to

you over the phone: overall weakness. It comes and goes.'

They talked a little about each of their practices and their overfull lives. Brianna had nine-month-old twin boys, served on two research committees, and was leading a research trial of her own, plus her husband had just been laid off from an engineering firm and was trying to find new work. 'Seeing patients here is the slow part of my day,' she said.

'I know how you feel. Thanks again for seeing me so soon; I really need to solve this mystery – I don't have time to be laid up!'

Brianna put on frameless reading glasses. 'Do you need these things yet? Every passing year I feel more and more like my mother.'

Meg felt the sting of loss. How long before the sting turned duller? How long before her first reaction was fond remembrance rather than sorrow? 'No,' she said, 'my vision's still in good shape.'

'Lucky you. With all the reading we have to do . . . Let me have a look at the orthopedist's report.'

Meg passed her the giant envelope. 'He recommended a psychic,' she said, then waited, picking a hangnail, while Brianna read over Cameron Lowenstein's write-up.

Brianna took the X-rays and slid them onto the light box to Meg's right. 'A psychic, huh? Funny, his report is so professional.'

'He's eccentric. But I guess he knows his way around medicine.'

'Hmm.' Brianna studied the X-rays carefully, then

switched off the light and went back to her chair. 'I think a psychic might shortcut things for us, because I don't see anything on the films.'

'No,' Meg agreed, 'I didn't either.'

'His official opinion is "inconclusive", but you said he brought up ALS.'

'Right. And so I looked over some of the literature,' Meg said, working to keep her voice steady, professional, though what she read had only confirmed what she remembered about the disease, 'and until just before I came here, nothing more had happened. I was fairly convinced he was just casting in the dark.'

'ALS *is* a tough fish to hook – a lot of things look similar.'

Meg heard a pause in her voice. 'So?' she said.

'So . . . his report notes no symptoms that *rule out* ALS . . . There's whole lot of nothing here,' she mused. 'No pain, in particular, but also you report no numbness, there's no swelling, no spinal or joint compressions, no extreme fatigue or physical malaise. How long would you say you've been experiencing muscle weakness?'

'I really don't know. I mean, I've felt *tired* a lot – not sleepy, you know, but like I just want to sit down and do nothing. I'm on my feet full time, and I use my hands and arms all day long.'

Brianna nodded, empathetic.

Meg said, 'If I had to make an outside guess, though? A few months. Maybe since late last fall, after my mom died and I added my father to my workload.'

'Understandable,' Brianna said. 'So . . . why don't

you get into a gown, and then we'll repeat the reflexes check, see if Lowenstein's on the ball.' She sounded almost cheerful, a detective eager to track the clues. This, Meg thought, was one of the qualities that sent them down different medical paths: Brianna loved the hunt, the investigation, while she, Meg, preferred being a kind of creation assistant. An obstetrician was very often a bystander – a coach or a guide for one of the most basic of life's processes. A big sister, passing on wisdom and supervising outcomes – like she'd done all her life.

In the exam room, Brianna put her through the same round of basic arm and leg reflex tests Lowenstein had, using a small, heavy hammer on her arms, knees, and ankles. Then she told her to clench her teeth while she pressed her fingers along Meg's jaw and neck.

'Relax your fingers,' Brianna told her next, taking her right hand. She held Meg's middle finger pinched between her own thumb and index finger, pressing the nail and sliding her thumb down it until her thumb clicked off the end of it. When it clicked, Meg's other fingers flexed.

'Huh, that's cool,' Meg said. Brianna didn't reply but repeated the move twice more, then did the same to Meg's left hand. The click-flex response was less on the left.

Meg said, 'I don't remember that test.' It had been years since she'd done a reflexes exam on anyone – back in her residency, she thought.

'I'm checking for what's called the Hoffman response. It's basic neurological protocol, but you might not have learned it in general medicine. Honestly, I don't remember when I learned what. Med school is all a caffeine haze in my memory, you know? Now, put your legs up here,' she directed, and Meg shifted so that she was lying on the exam table. Brianna grasped her right foot and flexed it back, holding it there. She repeated it, then did her left foot.

'Now I'm going to run a key up from your heel to the ball of the foot and across the metatarsal pad – the Babinski test.' She took the key from the pocket of her white lab coat. 'Isn't it fascinating how these things get named for whoever was bright enough to figure out the significance of the thing? Joseph Jules François Félix Babinski – his parents had trouble making choices, I guess. Now just relax your leg.' Meg lay as relaxed and still as she could, trying not to guess what Brianna was or wasn't noticing as she stroked the sharp metal against each of the soles of her feet. Being the patient instead of the doctor was discomfiting to say the least.

'Okay, last one: just lie there and relax all your muscles.' She opened the front of Meg's gown. 'I'm going to stroke the key across your belly a few times.'

Afterward, Brianna had Meg sit up, then wrote extensive notes while Meg made herself wait without speaking. Finally, Brianna said, 'Okay, why don't you get dressed and meet me back in my office?'

'Why don't you just say what you're thinking right now? I know the drill about delivering bad news to the undressed patient.'

Brianna looked at her, lips compressed. 'All right.

This is *not* conclusive,' she said. 'But okay. Yes. I see why Lowenstein was suspicious. He noted spasticity in his general exam ... And as I see it, the Hoffman response is troubling, in particular – your fingers shouldn't flex at all. Taken by itself, I'd be concerned about a cervical lesion, but in conjunction with the clonic reflex of your left calf and low reflex response on your abdomen ...'

She said some other things, but Meg was no longer focused on the words or even the tone of her old class-mate's voice. Her mind leapt ahead to what she'd read, to how no single one of those irregularities indicated ALS itself, but the combination of abdomen, foot, and hand signs and symptoms equaled what would be called a 'clinically probable' diagnosis.

'... an EMG needle exam and an MRI too,' Brianna was saying, 'to rule out other possibilities. Why don't you go straight to the lab for blood and urine tests, and I'll have Heidi get you appointments for the others.'

'Right,' Meg said numbly.

'And even if we don't unearth anything more opti-mistic, we'll want to keep close tabs on your symp-toms over the next several months before we can make a definitive diagnosis.'

Brianna's voice was flat and factual, delivering the information like she might in a lecture or panel discus-sion. Meg understood; it was only the rarest of physi-cians who could put an arm around a patient and tell him or her, in a warm, concerned voice, that a horrible, torturous slide toward certain death was on their horizon.

'How many have you had?' Meg said, interrupting

Brianna's suggestion that she get a more expert opinion from an ALS specialist she knew in Orlando.

'How many what? ALS patients?'

'Yeah. How many have you diagnosed since you started?'

'Three, in ... what? Ten years? It's almost always something else.'

Meg nodded. 'And when the patient presents with pretty definitive symptoms like mine, what, in your opinion, are the odds that it's not,' she looked Brianna in the eye, '... that it's *not* ALS?'

'Meg, listen, there's always hope—'

'And there's acupuncture and psychics and herbal remedies, and the chance that I'll find a beatific healer wandering the streets of Ocala in a robe and sandals. Be straight with me, okay?'

Brianna looked down, as though her shoes had become suddenly fascinating. 'There are several other, less serious conditions we need to consider. But if it *is* ALS ... the standard prognosis is progressive debilitating physical – but not mental – decline, resulting in complete respiratory paralysis, and death,' she said. Then she looked up, eyes full of sympathy. 'But I cannot stress enough that we might be looking at some other neuromuscular situation here.'

'Oh, joy.'

'Have the tests, and let me see if Andre Bolin can make time for you tomorrow.'

'Sure,' Meg said. 'That'd be – gosh, that'd be great.'

TWENTY-THREE

Carson approached the door to the shed solemnly, glad that Val and Wade had planned a two-hour endurance run for her workout. He wanted time alone here before he let Val see the place – and he'd have to let her see it. They were going to be married, which meant letting her into every part of his life, or so he believed marriage was supposed to require. Whether he could allow her to tour the darker, less concrete places remained to be seen. After that strange, awkward meeting with Meg earlier this afternoon, he was starkly reminded of just how much there was to him that Val didn't know. Nothing about Meg, or how long he'd waited without hope before moving on.

Two years. He didn't know any other guy who, once he'd lost his virginity, had remained celibate for so long. But he just hadn't been . . . willing. Even his first encounter after Meg, with Lisa Kline, a high school classmate of theirs, wasn't something he'd sought out.

She'd bought him a beer after a set one Saturday

night when the band, newly assembled, played a dive bar in Jacksonville.

'I *thought* that was you!' Lisa said. Her hair was blonder and her breasts bigger, but she looked otherwise the same as she had when they'd all been in Lou Davis's trigonometry class together.

'It's me, all right,' he said. He'd thrown down a few Jack and Cokes already; he wasn't his most articulate.

She smiled, that big, friendly, I-screw-the-band smile he would become too familiar with in the months and years to come. 'You guys are just *so* great. I mean, way better than I usually see here.' She swigged from her own long-necked bottle and wiped her mouth. 'What are you doing after?'

He'd thought he was going back to the roadside motel with George, but instead he went out back with Lisa. They'd kissed, sloppily, both of them glassy-eyed, and then Lisa pulled her denim skirt up around her waist and leaned over, putting her hands on the edge of the wooden landing.

He just stood there, looking at her tanned ass with its thin, white Y of a tan line.

'Come *on*, baby; you know what to do,' she said.

He did. He moved behind her and dropped his jeans.

As soon as she'd gone, he curled up on the steps and passed out. That was the start of his post-Meg love life, the first of many indignities dulled by binges of alcohol or drugs. Thank God he was done with all that.

The broad arms of an ancient cypress tree stretched

overhead, filtering late-afternoon sun that dappled the scrubby path beneath his bare feet – dappled his feet, too, and arms and shoulders ... he stood still and watched the play of shadow and light on his forearms, the motion provoking a new melody in his mind, distant and faint but worth paying attention to. Songs came to him in all sorts of ways; once he'd been entranced by the low drone of a prop jet's engines, which had translated into a song one critic described as 'hypnotizing and erotic'. Another time the germ of a tune came from the shush of rain pelting the canvas patio awning at his Seattle condo, which he'd be vacating permanently next week.

The melodies would whisper to him for days or weeks or even months, sometimes, and build on themselves, become fuller and more dynamic, and then the lyrics would begin to come, as if in response to whatever the music had stirred in him. He'd been writing music long enough to recognize the process, to understand how the songs were reflections of his psyche; any musician who claimed to be able to make music on a lark was either bullshitting or creating soulless pop music as disposable as tissues.

Humming, he put his hand on the shed's doorknob, turned it, and pushed. Humidity had swelled the wooden frame and the door stuck stubbornly at first, then gave way, opening into the dim, musty-smelling front room. First he simply peered inside, leaning in with his hand on the doorframe. If anyone had been in there since 1990, he couldn't tell. The room appeared exactly as he'd left it, as if he'd stepped out to take a turn driving the tree shaker, or go pick up a pizza. He and Meg had gone for pizza scores of times, the two of them hopping into his Ranger pickup, its door panels rusting out, and getting an extra-large pepperoni and mushroom takeout from a little pizza shack at the corner of the highway, inexplicably named Vladimir's.

God, she was beautiful at eighteen . . . she'd hated her freckles, wished for curly hair and bigger breasts – women were never satisfied with their looks – but he wouldn't have changed one spot or strand, had no desire for her to be anything other than who she was. They would take the pizza upstairs, feed each other, and he would get distracted by her bottom lip as he brushed it with his thumb, or the way she licked sauce from the corners of her mouth. She'd laugh at him, tease that he was a sex fiend – and at nineteen he was, of course. But he'd believed with every cell that his lust and love for her were inseparable, inspired by the perfection of their physical, mental, and emotional fit.

Closing the door behind him, Carson stood on the multicolored rag rug and let the memories wash over him: Meg at the table in only his T-shirt, eating scrambled eggs he'd cooked for a late dinner, telling him all about her first day of college – junior college, before Brian, before she'd transferred to University of Florida; Meg up on a ladder with hammer in hand and nails in her mouth, nailing window trim; Meg asleep on his bed, her accounting textbook – the epitome of boredom, she'd said – facedown on her chest; Meg coming upstairs the morning of her wedding, renewing, then dashing, his last remaining hope – he'd felt at first that he'd willed her there that morning, a specter conjured from his longing and frustration and anger. And maybe he had. Now he thought maybe if he'd just gotten over her right away instead of carrying a torch for those eighteen months, she'd have had no power over him that morning, or any time since.

This cascade of history, this waterfall of plans made and futures imagined then destroyed, was exactly what he'd feared would come if he went into the shed – and was why he'd avoided the place every time he visited before. He knew his mom was waiting for him to clear it out when he was ready – and he hadn't been ready. Plunging into the past today was healthy, though. Necessary. It was only right that he go to Val whole.

If he could.

He moved through the front room and then the kitchen, touching the surfaces, recalling the textures of the four years he'd lived there before leaving for good. The kitchen table, made from a door salvaged from some other farm, sanded and painted by Meg, later witnessed many long nights of coffee and bourbon and his pitiful beginnings at writing the songs that had begun lodging in his soul. He'd started on guitar, which he'd been playing somewhat poorly for years. When he began to see his potential, he brought in a piano that had belonged to the widow who lived up the road, past the Powells'.

That piano was the only thing he'd moved from here, having it sent first to his tiny Los Angeles apartment, then to the San José house, and finally to his Seattle condo – where it would soon be crated and moved to the house he and Val were buying in Malibu. He thought of how, in his escape from Florida, he'd gone as far away as he possibly could go and still pursue the music. As if three thousand miles were enough to buffer his awareness of Meg's presence, of her promise to love another man till death did them part.

He opened each of the six cupboard doors, all of them painted a robin's egg blue that she'd said would contrast well with the honey-stained pine of the floors and walls. Though the cupboards were mostly empty, vestiges of his bachelorhood still remained: a box of Frosted Flakes, three cans of baked beans, spice tins of curry and red pepper flakes and saffron. His Seattle kitchen, outfitted with every gourmet ingredient and gadget, would sneer at this humble assortment of foods and the three aluminum pots that had served every culinary need at the time.

He would miss his condo, the murky but soothing light of the damp afternoons, gray-blue with a shimmery wash of orange as the sun dropped toward Puget Sound. The sunny Malibu house, fabulous in its linearity, its glass expanses overlooking the ocean, was so exposed, so energized. It suited Val perfectly.

She loved those edge-of-the-land spaces. They were in her blood, part of her character. She loved the kinetic vibe, the daringness of a house perched on a cliffside – like her at the crest of a towering wave. Val was a woman always ready for adventure, and he admired this in her beyond all. Admittedly, he was more vibrant in her company; he'd found the experience of running with her and her gang a real charge, in the beginning.

It wasn't sustainable for him, though, and he'd told her as much. 'So you'll just, like, join in when you're in the mood,' she'd said, unperturbed. That was another thing he admired: her independence. She didn't cling – which was good, but he had to admit that a *little* bit of clinginess might be nice, just every now and then, just enough to make him feel . . . essential.

Catching himself staring into the cupboards, Carson checked his watch, startled to see he'd lost the better part of an hour here, musing. He shut the doors and turned toward the stairway, looked up into the loft. Might as well get it over with.

Up he trod, the fifth and tenth steps creaking like always. At the top of the stairs, he paused, taking in the bed, dresser, love seat, armoire – furniture all scarred and worn but so familiar. More familiar, somehow, than the far more expensive, more stylish furnishings that populated his condo now, furniture he'd been living with for twice as long as he had these pieces in front of him.

Though he couldn't fail to recall Meg in his bed, he was most concerned right now with the small box on top of the low, four-drawer dresser. Made of layers of heavy paper and painted a delicate pattern of black, red, blue, and yellow by an uncredited Asian artist, the box was a Christmas present from Meg. He went to it, ran his fingers over the top, then looked up, out the window in front of him, the brilliant green treetops of his heritage all he could see.

Drawing a deep breath – more resignation than dread – he opened the box. Only one object waited there, one small piece of his past, of their past, which until today he'd thought of as coiled and waiting like a rattler: her gold chain. He drew it out, impulsively wanting to run downstairs, jump in the Land Rover, and track Meg down to return it to her. *Here, I'm done with this*, he might say. Or, *I think you should keep this now*. Or, *I wanted you to have this souvenir of our past, no hard feelings*. He was sure she hadn't saved anything from then.

But it was clear from her skittishness earlier that a second encounter wouldn't be welcomed – probably she wouldn't welcome his gesture, either. She had undone one circle of gold in favor of a different, smaller one, one which he'd noticed still encircled her finger today. She was done with the past – and he should be too. Maybe he'd mail her the chain, let her decide what to do with it. For now, he enclosed it in his hand and then dropped it into his pocket so that when Val came in later for her tour, the whole place would be safe for her curious, loyal, and devoted eyes.

TWENTY-FOUR

Meg stood at the maternity floor's nurses' station early Thursday evening, replacing a chart, when Clay came to the counter. 'Triplets,' he said.

'What?'

'John Bachman and I just delivered triplets, two girls and a boy. You should see them.' He was beaming.

Melanie Harmon, a brilliant, organized Haitian immigrant who was the nursing supervisor, said, 'That's the second set this month. What's in the water?'

Meg wondered that too, only not about the increase in multiple births; that, she knew, had more to do with fertility treatments. But the disease that might be manifesting inside her muscle fibers, where did *it* come from? And why was there no way to get rid of it?

Clay reached into his pocket and took out his prescription pad. He stood at the end of the counter, writing, while she forced her attention back to the subject of one of her patients who had just checked in. She told Melanie, 'She's a ways out, yet – but she's very eager, and every member of her family is here, I swear it. Her brother was just trying to interview me on video.'

'First baby?' Melanie asked.

'How'd you guess? First for her, first grandchild for the grandparents, etcetera.' She wanted to share in their excitement, but it was failing to reach her through her fog of dread. Brianna's words would not leave her head; for the last two hours, whenever her attention was not focused on a task, she heard the refrain *respiratory paralysis, and death.*

'So you're sticking around?' Clay asked, moving to stand next to her.

Maybe not. 'Yes – but I'm hoping she'll progress quickly.' Quick delivery or slow, she would miss yet another of Savannah's softball games and had arranged with Rachel's mother for Savannah to ride home with them.

She felt Clay's arm brush hers, then the pressure of him pushing something into her left jacket pocket. 'I'm stuck here too,' he said. 'Serving on that hurricane preparedness committee. We're meeting at seven.'

Unless, Meg thought, *we end up in surgery.* She sent up another prayer for her patient to have a medically uneventful delivery, thinking of the infant girl who would join them soon, slippery and pink and outraged. The father, an Emergency Medical Technician, would 'catch' her – a plan long arranged, and one for which Meg was thankful. If all went well, she'd have little to do besides supervise.

Melanie told Clay, 'Make sure somebody knows to stock up on *chocolate.*'

'Got it,' Clay laughed. 'I'll put it on the list, right after morphine and bottled water.' He put his hand on Meg's shoulder. 'See you ladies later.'

'See you,' she said as he left them. She felt in her pocket, found a folded square of paper. So now he was passing her notes. On any other day, she would have been flattered at the very least, maybe even pleased. Brian was not a note-writer, unless e-mail and text-message reminders to do or buy or find something counted as notes. She held the paper with the tips of her fingers and wondered how long it might be until her left hand began acting like her right.

'Mmm,' Melanie said, watching Clay go. 'That is one fine man.'

Meg looked too. He *was* fine – more tennis player in his looks than surgeon, his sandy hair worn long around his ears and neck, strong forearms exposed by rolled-up sleeves. His surgical skills were admirable, as well; he was going to be very successful, with his good looks and sociability and genuine concern for the patient. Too bad she wouldn't be around to see him reach his prime – nor to follow him, if she should ever want to, along the path he was cutting into the dark forest of her feelings. If what Brianna and Lowenstein suspected – what she, too, suspected now was true – it would not be long before she wouldn't be able to hold any man's hand, kiss any man's lips . . . or reach out to move a strand of Savannah's hair from her face. With this last thought, panic grabbed her stomach and squeezed it hard, her protest – *No!* – pressing for escape behind clenched teeth.

Meg grasped for a normal moment as if it could save her, saying, 'Melanie, do I need to remind you that you're already married – and to a doctor?'

The nurse said, 'Sure, today. But who knows what'll happen tomorrow?'

Meg didn't want to know. 'I'm going to the lounge. Page me when my services are required.'

On her way, she stopped in the neonatal intensive care nursery. The triplets were tiny but looked healthy and strong, odds-beaters. Too often, they started out on life support, one or more of them at a clear disadvantage, competitive for their mother's resources even before they were born. These three, though, looked like they stood a good chance to fend for themselves. The girl, in her pink knit cap, waved a fist and pursed her lips, already demanding service. *Go, girl*, Meg thought. The boys – likely identical twins, lay alert, taking in their surroundings with their fuzzy newborn vision. She touched the girl's tiny rosebud fist, thought of her own daughter and of the babies she might have had after, if she'd stuck with Carson. Brian hadn't been sure he wanted *any* children; after Savannah, he said they were done – and Meg had no desire to change his mind.

She remembered how she and Carson used to laze in the lake, floating on their backs with the washed blue sky above, and talk about what they'd name their kids. She liked Savannah for a girl's name, Austin for a boy; Carson had teased, 'Sure, and then we'll have Denver and Cheyenne and Sacramento.' She dunked him then, holding him down until he started to untie her swimsuit. He came up laughing as she hurried to retie it, saying, 'What? I thought you wanted to get started now.'

The memory felt as close as yesterday, yet as unreachable as the stars.

When she was alone in the tiny closet of a room used for the doctors' lounge, she reached into her pocket and drew out the folded paper Clay had put there. The note, written on his prescription pad, read, 'Western courtyard, 5:30? Strong coffee and tuna salad, my treat.'

He was a sweet man ... but what was he getting out of this interest in her, an older, married woman? Not that it mattered; whatever he thought she offered, she wouldn't have it much longer. 'Rain check,' she said, refolding the note and putting it in her pocket.

She'd just put her feet up when her pager began to beep. 'That baby is *not* here already,' she groaned. But no, it was Savannah. She reached for the phone on the table beside her and dialed Savannah's cell number.

'Hi, honey. What's going on? I got your page.'

'We *have* to go to Orlando tomorrow – I just got a fan club email saying Carson McKay's doing a one-night-only show at a *club*!'

'Sweetheart, it's been a really stressful week—'

'Mom! You said the next time he was in the area we'd go. You *promised*.'

There, the classic guilt-wringing move every child was somehow born knowing how to execute. She had promised, but that was when she thought attending

202

one of his concerts would be a safe, distant experience, where they would be two anonymous fans in the midst of thousands. 'I know, but—'

'Come on, just think how cool it would be. A *club*, not one of the big arenas; we could sit up close. He might recognize you – maybe you could get us backstage, since you know him.'

'*Knew* him,' Meg said.

'Whatever. We wouldn't have to meet him. But it would be *so* cool to go. Please? Please please please *please*? If I had my car already, I'd drive myself—'

'Not to Orlando, you wouldn't.'

'Okay, then you have to take me. Come on, it'll be fun.'

Meg thought of how little they did together, how little they'd done together over the course of sixteen rapidly passing years. There had seemed to be so much time back when Savannah was tiny. She'd believed she could balance school, then career, with her duties as mother and wife, believed in the have-it-all myth promoted by print ads and television shows. The money, hers and Brian's, made it easy to solve problems. A good nanny, housecleaning and yard crews, repair services, private schools – all these things were supposed to allow her time to focus on family life when work was done.

Funny how things were never as simple as they appeared they'd be.

She hadn't intended to choose obstetrics, knowing it was one of the more demanding fields in terms of family-time interruptions, but once she'd done her

203

rotation she found that it intrigued her beyond any other option. She thought she could make it work. But coordinating all the household help took a lot more time and effort than she expected.

Then there were professional obligations – meetings, conferences – and extended-family obligations – to the Hamiltons in particular, who weren't content unless they came for dinner often. And then she had to fit in the social invitations Brian insisted they accept. Savannah was always her first priority, but how often did that manifest as making sure someone else was tending her daughter? If ALS *was* now destroying the neurons that allowed her to walk and eat and breathe, how long before she simply wasn't able to do anything with Savannah?

'Okay, okay. We'll go.' *And stay way in the back, in the darkest possible spot.*

'Really? Seriously?'

'Really seriously. Can you buy the tickets? My purse is locked up right now, but go to the desk in the den, and in the middle left-hand drawer is a file folder with my other credit cards – just use any one of them.'

'You are the best mom!'

'I'll remember you said that. Oh, is Rachel coming?'

'No, she has etiquette class and her mom won't spring her.'

'But you're still planning to sleep over there Saturday, right?'

'Yeah – but I meant to tell you: Her parents won't be home until after like eleven. They have some snob party to go to. Is it still okay?'

'Will Angela be home?'

'I think so. She just broke up with her boyfriend, so she's being all antisocial.'

'All right then,' Meg said. 'I suppose you all are old enough to be trusted for a few hours.'

'That's what I've been trying to tell you for*ever*.'

'I know; all I can say is, wait until *you* have a teenage daughter, and then talk to me about trust.'

How easily those words slipped out, as though her future as a grandmother of a teen – a teen girl, no less – was guaranteed. What a swell habit that future-speak was, so optimistic, so reassuring – and how false, considering how no one could peer ahead in time and discover the date to be inscribed on their headstone. She might be killed by lightning tomorrow night; the forecast was for strong storms, after all. Or Savannah might go off in her new Honda next month, or next year, and slam herself into tree or a truck, God forbid. There was no telling. How funny it was that everyone gave so much thought to their unknown, unknowable futures, and so little thought to each real and tangible moment of *now*.

'So when will you be home?' Savannah asked, words Meg had heard from her daughter too many times.

'By ten, I hope. I have a new mom in labor; first babies often take a while.'

'How long did I take?'

Meg smiled. Savannah always loved to hear the story of her own birth, as though it allowed her to differentiate hers from the hundreds of births Meg attended. As though she feared Meg could somehow lose her details in the crowd of so many others.

'Oh, days,' she said, choking back a sudden urge to cry. 'You were the slowest baby ever.'

'But once you were in the hospital, after your water broke?'

'Twenty-and-a-half hours. I was seriously considering contacting the post office to change my official address.' A tear leaked out in spite of her joke.

'*Mom*. Okay, well, I'm gonna go buy our tickets. And we need a hotel, right?'

'You know how to do that?'

'Duh. Expedia, Travelocity – I'll find us someplace luxurious and relaxing. You can get a massage or whatever.'

'That,' Meg said, admiring her daughter's take-charge capability, 'would be lovely.'

Barely three minutes after she'd hung up with Savannah, her pager buzzed again, this time with a message to call Brianna. She dialed the number stoically. In a brief, brisk voice Brianna's nurse assistant began to lay out Meg's Friday schedule with Andre Bolin, the Orlando-based specialist.

'In Orlando, tomorrow?' Meg interrupted.

'Yes, Dr Davidson was able to pull some heavy strings for you.'

There's fate for you, Meg thought. 'All right; I have to be there tomorrow anyway.'

She'd have a battery of tests beginning at nine AM, after which time she was to meet with Dr Bolin, who would do yet another reflexes exam and review whatever test results they would have by that time. 'You are so lucky,' the nurse said. 'Anybody without these

connections would have to wait *months* to see him.'
Meg wrote down the places and times and said, in a
voice thick with sarcasm, 'I am lucky, aren't I?' She
knew the nurse meant well – and was right, in the
limited context of her statement. Yet she couldn't bring
herself to swallow her self-pity this time; no matter
how deliberately she tried, this time it would not go
down.

Before Meg left the hospital at 9:15, she called
Savannah. 'Did you get us a room?'

'Yep, we're all set.'

'See if they have space available tonight – it turns
out I need to be in Orlando tomorrow morning.'

'Cool – I'll miss my math quiz. Oh, Mom – you're
on your way home?' Meg said she was. 'Did Dad call
you yet?'

'No. Why?'

'Nothing. Just park in the driveway instead of the
garage, okay?'

'. . . Okay.'

Fifteen minutes later, she understood why. The
moment she climbed out of her car, the far left of
their three garage doors began to roll open, and Brian
stood in the doorway. His expression was the cat's
who'd just swallowed the canary; behind him was a
glossy champagne-colored SUV. A Lexus, facing out,
its cat's eye headlamps and chrome grille glinting at
her.

Her first thought was to blurt, 'You're supposed to
be in Boston.'

'I detoured for an early birthday present,' he said, as Savannah joined them.

More like a belated apology, Meg thought. It was a bit much, and hardly the kind of thing she cared about, especially now. She tried to look pleased, though, and managed a falsely hearty, 'Wow.'

Savannah ran her hand over the hood. 'Usually I don't like these gas-guzzlers . . . but I guess they can be practical; half my team could ride in there at once, which would save someone else from driving.'

'They could watch movies in there too,' Brian said. He came and took Meg's hand. 'Well? Do you like it?'

'Of course.' What was there to not like? 'But really, my car's perfectly fine.'

'It's six years old. I have a new car, Savannah's about to get one – I didn't want you to feel left out.' Team Hamilton. 'Besides,' he added, 'this gives us practical options we didn't have before. I could borrow it if, say, I have a big group of clients in.'

Savannah opened the driver's door. 'Can we take it tonight? Please? It's so spacious – and I *was* gonna watch a DVD tonight, before I had to pack. This way I don't have to miss it.'

Brian put the keys in Meg's hand and said, 'By the way, the color? It's called "Savannah Metallic". Perfect, huh?'

Perfect.

TWENTY-FIVE

Savannah turned over onto her belly and untied the red strings of her bikini top, aware that a pair of balding men whose hairy guts overhung their swim trunks kept looking at her. Their stares made her uncomfortable in one way, pleased her in another; men liked the way she looked, a truth that surprised and flattered her. She didn't look at the men directly, preferring to leave a safe distance between herself and any man who wasn't Kyle. Kyle, who she would see in twenty-four hours. Her anticipation grew with each sweep of the minute hand on her World Wildlife Federation watch, making her too anxious to eat. That was fine; she could lose another pound before tomorrow afternoon, when it would be Kyle's eyes devouring her instead.

The pool deck was filling with hotel guests now, at four o'clock. She watched groups of overdressed old ladies in wide hats and pants and long sleeves; perky moms with toddlers in swim diapers; loud, mouthy school-age kids screaming 'Marco!' 'Polo!' 'Marco!' 'Polo!' in the pool's shallow end.

Her mom had called an hour earlier to say she'd be back by six. Her voice was as weary as Savannah had ever heard it, so as soon as they ended the call she booked her a massage appointment for six-thirty. Hopefully that would revive her, destress her from whatever was making the day so rough. And if the massage didn't do it, the concert definitely would.

Closing her eyes, she let the tilting afternoon sunshine color her vision bright orange, the color of zinnias, marigolds, oranges – obviously oranges; she thought about how Carson McKay's parents grew oranges and grapefruit and lemons, and how her mom and aunts had been able to run over to the orchards any time they wanted, just pick fruit from the trees and eat it on the spot. The last time she visited her grandparents' house, just after her grandma died, she'd walked across the pasture to the fence edge, where the bushy fruit trees were visible, lining the land like stalwart soldiers ready to fight colds and scurvy – did anyone even get scurvy anymore? She'd wanted to hide herself in the rows, the thick green canopy like a blanket protecting her from the world, from her loss. She half believed she might find her grandma there, waiting with an understanding smile and supportive hug. It was funny how her grandma had always seemed to have time for her – not just *found* time, but *made* time. Went out of her way to call or come over just to go to the park or wander the mall together. Awful as it sounded, she wished it was her grandpa who'd died, if someone had to. Death was so unfair.

The song she'd been trying to compose was dedicated

to her Grandma Anna, and she was trying to tread a line between edgy melancholy and gratitude. It wasn't coming out right because she was still angrier to have lost her than she was grateful to have had her – that was what her music theory teacher said at her lesson Tuesday. Lying here, the bright orange of her vision shifting to wild geometrics of dark orange and red, she played the tune over in her mind again, thinking of how she might push the sound away from angry. Fewer chord changes, or maybe space them farther apart? What if she layered in an upbeat melody line, something Sheryl Crow-like? Tuning out the noise of the yelling, splashing kids, she mentally ran through some possibilities, wishing she'd thought to bring her guitar. Not only could she have tried out some of her ideas during her downtime, she could've taken the guitar with them tonight, gotten it autographed.

Another tune distracted her, and it took a third ring for her to realize it was her phone, stored inside her green canvas purse. Forgetting that she'd untied her top, she propped herself on her elbows and leaned over to reach the phone. She realized she was half naked at the same moment a preschool boy yelled, 'Boobies!'

She dropped onto her towel, mortified, and dug out the phone.

'Hello?'

'Babe!'

'Kyle, hi!' she said, the horror of her mistake lessened by the sound of his voice. 'Can you hold on two seconds?' She set the phone down and tied her top securely, then sat up and wrapped her towel around her. No more free shows today, she thought, not brave enough to even glance the way of her earlier admirers.

Phone to her ear, she said, 'Sorry – I, um, I'm laying out at the pool, and I had to put my bikini back on.' Why not use the truth to keep his interest at full steam? Sure, she wanted him to like her for more substantial reasons than her looks, than sex, but wasn't her body and her sexuality also an important part of who she was? He should love all of her.

Kyle whistled. 'I'm real sorry to be stuck here in the swamp, man, I'll tell you that!'

'Yeah . . . well, tomorrow's not so long to wait, right?'

'Five minutes is too long to wait, if you ask me.'

His sultry voice sent a thrill from the pit of her stomach straight south. She shifted on the deck chair and decided she should turn the conversation in a safer direction, at least while she was in public. She said cheerfully, 'So, what's up?'

'Well, I had the afternoon off, so I took a nap, right? And I had this dream about you.'

'You did? What was it?'

'You want me to tell you?' he said. ''Cause it's kind of . . . personal, if you know what I mean. Kinda sexy, you know?'

This wasn't turning out to be safer at all. She liked it, though. 'That's, um, that's cool.'

'Oh, no no no, not *cool*. *Hot*. It was definitely hot.'

Embarrassed, Savannah stared at her toenails, painted a deep plum to match the shirt she was going to wear to the concert. Kyle's suggestive responses made her feel the way the stares of the overweight men had – uncomfortable and intrigued at the same time. She wished she had more experience with this stuff. What if, when they were face-to-face, he'd be able to tell she wasn't even close to sexually experienced – let alone twenty years old? What if he got mad, or demanded to see her driver's license? She would just have to force herself to be bolder, not give him any reason to doubt her story – now or tomorrow.

'Yeah, okay,' she said, glancing around to make sure no one was listening in. 'Tell me.'

'So we were at some beach – it looked like Gulf side, right, like Tampa. And you were wearing that little flowered bikini, the one from your webpage.'

She could picture them together, Kyle shirtless, the calm water lapping at the sand. 'Okay. Go on.'

'Is that the suit you're wearing right now?'

'No, this one's red with tiny white stars on it.'

'Huh, bet that's real pretty too. Anyway, so you were telling me about some manatee that you'd named . . . I don't know, Melanie or something, and okay, I was trying to listen, but what can I say? I'm a guy.' He laughed. 'I was getting distracted by your body, so I was, well, hard, you know? So I pulled you against me and said, "I can't wait one more minute. I need you *now*."'

Savannah gulped, eyes wide. Two little girls of about six ran past her, their bare feet slapping the wet concrete, a younger little boy chasing them, carrying a squirt gun almost as big as himself.

'You there?' Kyle said.

'Yeah. Wow. That's . . . that's a good dream.'

'There's more. You want to hear it?'

She wasn't sure; she felt so far out into uncharted waters that she had no idea where the line was – or if there was a line. Would a twenty-year-old encourage him to spell out all the details? She thought of the ads she'd seen for that video about wild girls on spring break. *Those* girls would ask for all the details – and probably add a bunch of their own.

Kyle didn't wait for her to answer. Instead he said, 'I'll just tell you this: It was, like, beautiful. Really romantic.'

Savannah sighed, charmed and relieved at the same time.

'Oh, there you are.' Her mom appeared from behind her. 'No wonder I couldn't get through.' She sat down on the end of the deck chair.

'Mom, hi!' Savannah said, trying to look innocent. 'You're early.' Into the phone she said, 'I have to go, okay? I'm sorry – I'll call you later.' She flipped the phone closed fast.

'I didn't mean to interrupt your fun.'

Savannah felt as if her face would catch flame any second. Her fun? Could her mom somehow sense what she'd been talking about? 'Oh, no, it's fine. I was just, um, talking to Rachel. She was . . . saying how we should buy her a souvenir tee-shirt tonight.'

'Okay,' her mom said, with no trace of suspicion. 'But I wouldn't expect there to be any McKay band tees, since this was a last-minute thing.'

Savannah nodded, studiedly gathering up her sunscreen and book and phone and stuffing it all into her purse. 'Yeah, well, maybe the club will have cool ones.'

'Maybe. So, how about some dinner?' her mom asked, and Savannah noticed a too-bright edge to her voice, something forced and tight that was different from her usual long-day sound.

'I'm not hungry yet. Are you okay?'

'Oh, sure, I'm fine. Tired. Those meetings today just wouldn't seem to end. The sessions are like that sometimes.' She stood up, and Savannah stood too. 'And you know, I'm not hungry either.'

'Okay, well, I made you an appointment with the masseuse for six-thirty. Is that cool?'

Her mom's eyebrows rose above the top of her sunglasses. 'No kidding? That was thoughtful of you. But, I'm not sure—'

'You don't have to. I mean, I just thought maybe, you know, after a busy day—'

'Thank you, sweetheart.' She kissed Savannah, a quick peck near her ear. 'No, I *do* want to go – what about you? Did you want one too, or . . .'

'I got a pedicure already,' Savannah said, sticking out her foot, now clad in her dyed-red hemp flip-flops. 'I'll just take a shower and watch TV or something till you get back.'

She followed her mom into the hotel, noticing, first, the sloppiness of her mom's hair – coiled hurriedly into a loose bun and secured by a crooked gold clip. And was she limping a little? Just the slightest bit?

Letting the space between them widen as they walked through the pool lobby and to the elevators, Savannah looked more closely. It was something in the uneven rise of her mom's left shoulder, accentuated by the rise and fall of the cream linen jacket at the shoulder, and lower, at the hip.

'Did you hurt your leg or something?' she asked at the elevator.

'What? Oh, no. Well, yes – that is, I have a blister. New shoes.'

That sounded plausible, but Savannah sensed that something else was going on. The messy hair was so abnormal – it made her wonder, suddenly, if her mom had spent the day in bed with some man. But no, that was *crazy*, just her Kyle-influenced mind talking. She couldn't imagine her mom having sex with anyone, not even her dad. What she could imagine – not about her mom – was what Kyle had been describing just before her mom showed up. He wanted her, dreamed about her – was there a bigger thrill than knowing that?

When her mom was gone to have the massage, Savannah called Kyle and apologized.

'My mom showed up – I am *so* sorry I hung up on you.'

He laughed. 'Keeping me a secret, huh?'

'No! I mean, why would I? I just haven't gotten a chance to talk about you, that's all. My mom's been tired and stressed out so—'

'Don't sweat it, babe. There's time for all that, plenty of time. Now listen, make sure you don't, you know, hook up with anybody at the show tonight. I want you to save yourself for me.'

She had saved herself for him, all right. The thing about sex, as far as she'd heard, was that teenage guys weren't so great at it. A guy Kyle's age, on the other hand, should know what he was doing. She didn't want to be anybody's guinea pig. Didn't her dad always say, 'If you're going to bother to do something, do it right'?

'The only guy I want to talk to tonight is Carson McKay,' Savannah said.

'Who would jump on you in a hot second, from what I hear – dude's marrying a chick barely older than you!'

'Please! He's my mom's age – and anyway, they used to know each other, remember? I told you that last night.'

'Yeah, but still.'

'Anyway, she hasn't seen him in a long time, but we might get backstage when she tells whoever that they're old friends.'

'Pretty awesome. You should, like, ask if you can join his band. You're really good.'

Savannah grinned. She'd played for him over the phone and he had seemed truly impressed. 'He's got a full-time guitarist, but thanks. Listen, I need to get ready to go. I'll call you tomorrow, okay?'

'Be thinkin' of you,' he said suggestively.

'Me too.' This time it was easier to flirt – it was just a matter of practice, like anything else.

After hanging up, she pressed the phone to her chest.

Finally, life was *happening* – to her! She couldn't explain it, but she had the strongest feeling that she had come to the crest of a hill, and in no time at all everything in her life was going to change.

TWENTY-SIX

Johnny Simmons's nightclub took up nearly an entire block of prime Orlando real estate, not far from some of the area's biggest attractions. The club boasted three dance floors, each in its own soundproof room, each room featuring a different kind of music. At the center of everything was the main stage, where live acts performed five nights a week. Johnny made every effort to book performers on the rise, and was building a good reputation for choosing quality acts who went on to break into entertainment's major leagues. Carson listened to Johnny, a swaggering, jovial New Jersey transplant with pure silver hair and a build like a professional wrestler, talk up the place as he toured him around early Friday morning. He was sure the guy could sell ice to Inuits, sand to desert nomads, water to whales – probably all in a single meeting over cocktails. It was easy to see why Johnny and Gene were friends.

'We got bouncers at every entrance and exit, see, and nobody gets in tonight without a ticket. You ain't gonna be surprised when I tell you they sold out in three hours last night. But me, I'm impressed! Holy Mary in a bathtub, that's the fastest of any act we've had!' Johnny put his arm around Carson's shoulders. 'I'm gonna make a pile of money off of you, you know that, right? And I feel kinda bad about it, 'cause I got pretty much nothin' to offer *you*. I mean, what's money to a guy who's swimming in it, right? So I was thinkin', you haven't tied the proverbial knot yet, and I got a daughter, twenty-nine, who's your biggest fan – whaddya think, huh?'

'You're offering me your daughter in trade, is that it?' Carson laughed. 'Good thing my fiancée's out shopping!'

Johnny wrapped his arm around Carson's throat in a mock headlock. 'No, wise guy, I'm just saying she's a pretty girl and nice company and you would be privileged to enjoy that company with my blessing, if you thought you might still wanna look around. And when I say "enjoy", I don't mean "*enjoy*", got it?'

'That's kind of you, man. I appreciate it.' He eased out of the headlock and went up the three steps to the stage. 'But I'm going to have to just settle for the regular fee.' He wasn't in it for the money anyway. Never had been – and not for the easy access to women (as well as access to easy women) either. He wrote songs and played music because it kept the demons at bay, and because he loved creating things that came to mean something to others. If anything, he wished his career had not rocketed into the stratosphere of corporate labels and corporate expectations. He wished he'd been able to keep a tighter hold on his integrity, but God, how hard it was to concentrate on something so ephemeral back then, when they were coming to him with wheelbarrows full of cash, and feel-good substances, and inhibition-free women . . .

He walked the stage, its surface painted matte black to help prevent glare, and looked out into the club. The room was bright right now, as a small crew of employees buzzed about, getting tables and chairs positioned, checking oil levels in the tabletop lights; some of them paused to look his way as he went to the piano and pulled back the bench. He'd asked for a standard grand, plus a bass player, a rhythm guitarist, and a drummer. He hadn't tried to bring in his band members, all of them either home in Seattle or spending their time off in sunnier locales, as he was. For tonight's show he would make do with some quality local musicians who were meeting him in a few minutes for a first run-through.

After seeing Meg yesterday, he'd been haunted by the way she'd looked so frustrated and upset, and his first draft of tonight's song list was filled with early songs he'd written with her in mind. Then Val had come back from her workout, limp from the exertion and humidity – pitiful, really, compared with her usual peppy self – and he turned his attention back where it should be. The revised song list was more crowd-pleasing, and less bogged down with the distant past. He included his Grammy winners and his 2003 hit 'Redheads', a category that did, of course, include Meg, but only coincidentally. He couldn't say he'd thought very much about her at all while writing it – though, if forced, he *might* admit to her being the original inspiration.

'How's about a preview?' Johnny called from the bar.

Carson pushed the cover off the keys and ran his fingers over them in a quick rising scale, limbering up. 'Okay, see if you know this one.' He started with the low opening bars of Beethoven's *Fifth*, then segued into his breakout hit, 'Facedown', a song teens liked to think was about a woman's sexual position, but which in fact examined his unsavory habit, in those earliest years, of indulging too heavily and waking up sprawled facedown on floors, lawns – the hood of somebody's blue '69 Camaro, once.

Without the microphone turned on, his voice carried only to the first row or two of tables; the staff began to migrate there, leaving tasks half done as they were drawn in.

He had always loved this part of performing, the times when it was just him and the piano and a small, appreciative audience. Making music was therapy for him, but giving it to others was like giving a gift that pleased or invigorated or inspired or soothed; he felt humbled doing it, and useful.

To prolong the pleasure a little longer, he ended that song and moved right into another, 'Buried Alive', a favorite ballad he'd left off the program because it focused so much on Meg, and to sing it well meant bloodying his wounds again. Now, though, with this safe, anonymous audience listening, he felt like it was the right time to bring the song out and hopefully exorcise one more demon.

The piano resounded with the sweet, mournful chords of the intro, and he let the notes hang suspended in the now fully quiet room. He felt his stomach clench as he began singing the first verse, felt the resistance of his heart trying not to let go. Like the snowbound hiker in the song, it wanted to hold out hope even when hope was unreachable, denied. He closed his eyes and let the song rise up and out of him, wanting it to wrench free his futile wish for a past that had never been and a future that would never be.

The lyrics came to his lips easily, as though the song was always playing somewhere inside him, quiet but steadfast, waiting – for him to do what? Notice and take action? Like a wild creature, it needed to be either soothed or set free. As he sang the final chorus, though, he knew he'd failed to release it. His love for Meg, established so long ago that he barely recalled a time when he didn't love her, could not be forced out. Not by drinking, not by drugs, not by recreational sex, not by willful effort, and not even by his genuine, if qualitatively different, love for another woman. He was stuck with it. He tipped his head back as the piano's final notes drifted upward to the sound of enthused applause.

Johnny joined him at the piano. 'Jesus, man! You about have me bawling like a baby!' He wiped his eyes, which Carson saw were truly wet. 'You perform like that tonight, we'll have to hand out fuckin' tissues with every admission!'

TWENTY-SEVEN

Meg brought one of her mother's notebooks to read in between appointments Friday, drawn into discovering more of her mother's thoughts despite herself, despite the knot that lodged in her stomach each time she read. Each word made her miss her mother that much more, and each discovery or reminder of the past did more to heighten her regrets than soothe them. Still, reading was like taking a dose of horrible-tasting medicine with the belief that it would, eventually, make her feel better.

November 30, 2001
   Low: 55°, high: 82°. Tied the record! No rain.
   I saw in the paper how Carson's gone and made himself into one of the most popular singers on the radio today. They interviewed him by phone; he's living way out on the West Coast. How hard that must be for James and Carolyn.
   But they must be proud of him – another platinum album! And a song included on that

September 11 CD, raising money for families of the victims. Merciful Mother, it's so hard to understand the world today . . .

Still unmarried, and living the wild rock-star life, that's what the article says. Guess that's nothing to be proud of! But probably they exaggerate, to sell more papers. I mentioned the article to Meggie when she called after dinner, but she didn't want to talk about it. 'It's his business,' she said, then changed the subject to one of her patients who's got ovarian cancer. The poor woman, it's so far gone that she asked Meggie to help her kill herself when the pain gets too terrible. Why can't our doctors help people this way? What a crazy system we have in this country! The very people who won't support merciful assisted suicide are willing to see healthy, innocent bystanders killed in the name of war.

My, I'm feeling scattered tonight. I should add that Beth called to say she met someone new, a man who edits some magazine I've never heard of. She meets all sorts of people like this nowadays, who have strange jobs and talk about things like world politics and philosophy. I have a philosophy for her: find a good man and settle down! She's twenty-six, not getting any younger. But she's set on getting that Ph.D. in Asian history first. I wonder sometimes whose child she is, because I can't even pronounce the names of the places she's studied!

Meggie says just let Beth be; she'll find her place in life like we all do. Can I help it if I want to see all my girls happy? Or settled, anyway. Meggie, she's so serious now, and she works such long hours. She's good at what she does, but I swear, it's like her smile has disappeared entirely.

I suppose it didn't help any to bring up Carson; I'm not sure she ever forgave herself for breaking his heart. Guilt has a big appetite, don't I know it – I'm the one that let her turn her back on him – so sweet, so devoted to her! That was the surest love she was ever going to find, and there I was, trying to make it out as puppy love. I let her talk herself into dating Brian because I really wanted to believe he was better for her. So much good would come of it, that's what we all said! But the Blessed Virgin above knows as well as I do that Spencer spends all the money he gets; we are truly no better off today than we were in '89.

So where is the good? Carson's rambling all over the world, going from woman to woman, drinking and all that mess; Meggie's shut up inside an office building or hospital eighteen hours a day. Well, I suppose the good is that we have Savannah – you can always find a cloud's silver lining if you look for it!

I'm going to include Carson in my prayers tonight, and James and Carolyn too. And a special prayer for Meggie, that she find her way out of regret and into happiness. Mother Most Beloved, help her – and all of us, really – find the way to the light.

TWENTY-EIGHT

On Friday night, Meg let Savannah tow her into the nightclub and up to the second row of square tables where small placards declared *VIP*, each with a number. Behind the two rows was a section of narrow folding chairs, and beyond that, open space, for standing. The room smelled of stale cigarettes and fresh anticipation, the sweaty excitement of eager fans. The table they stopped at, VIP 12, was so close to the stage and the piano that Meg suspected they'd be able to count the hairs on Carson's chin, if he hadn't shaved since yesterday.

'This is us,' Savannah said. 'Oh my god, this will be so great.' She stood there, staring up at the stage, enchanted by the display of microphones and amplifiers and guitars, the glossy grand piano, so aptly named.

Meg sat in the chair she judged to be most peripheral to Carson's view and hoped, feebly, that the footlights and spotlights would prevent him from identifying anyone in the audience at all, even the ones seated almost directly in front of him. After her day today, feeble hope for a solution to a relatively minor problem was the most she could muster.

Beginning with the MRI at 8:15 AM, she'd spent all day being scanned and prodded and stabbed by a series of effusive technicians, their treatment so deferential that she'd wanted to throttle each of them. No one was ever so friendly or kind when she'd gone for her prenatal tests, years ago, or when she'd spent seven hours waiting in the ER last summer after spraining her ankle dismounting a horse. That day, with that ordinary injury, she'd been as faceless as any other patient to those overworked medical professionals. Only when you were truly marked did you get the kind of treatment she'd had today. She'd been that effusive person herself more than once, and as recently as two weeks ago, when she had to tell a thirty-four-year-old patient that her enlarged abdomen wasn't a pregnancy but rather a malignancy – endometrial, and so far gone that the woman's odds of survival were about as good as for a Florida snowfall in August. At least, though, that woman *could* pull through. *Might* pull through, if the hyper-aggressive chemo, radiation, and surgical regimen in front of her succeeded. Modern medicine held a pinhole ray of hope for that woman. For Meg, it held only the blackness of being buried alive.

She watched Savannah, in her plum tank top and low-rise faded jeans, decorated with a prismatic array of rhinestones falling along each thigh. The stones caught the light as Savannah stood there, hair loose on her shoulders, taking in the scene of her first official rock concert. Meg saw how bright her eyes looked, how grown up her face was, with the careful rim of green eyeliner and darkened, lengthened lashes. She was such a pretty girl, unique in her beauty, and so smart, too. What would she make of her life in ten years? In twenty? When she was Meg's age, thirty-eight, how would she feel about being motherless? Because motherless she would be – Dr Andre Bolin, the ALS expert, hadn't been able to say otherwise.

He'd come into the exam room, where she waited in a patterned cotton wrap, and socks, because her feet were freezing. How long had she sat there, legs dangling over the table's edge? Five minutes? Fifty? She didn't have any idea by that time, her appointment with Bolin coming at the end of a long day of waiting, coming at the end of the line.

The end of the line. That's how she already saw it, sitting there, waiting for him. She didn't need an expert to interpret the down-turned corners of the EMG tech's mouth, the skittish eyes of the nurse who'd ushered her into the exam room. She could have scripted Bolin's words – though she wanted desperately to be wrong. He put her through an extensive exam, testing every large muscle, testing her neck, face, hands . . . he'd asked her to speak and to swallow and to laugh (a rueful laugh is what she managed) and to cough and nod . . . Then she dressed and went and sat beside him in his spacious office, its bookshelves filled with medical tomes but also novels – for what purpose? He couldn't possibly find time to read during the day. Were they there to lend to patients who, like her, would very soon be unable to clasp the book, let alone turn the pages? Save them the precious time of making a separate trip to the library or bookstore? She'd left with that curiosity unanswered. What she did have was Bolin's 'unfortunate concurrence' with Brianna's finding, plus two informational booklets (*Resources for the Newly Diagnosed* and *Living with ALS*, how droll), and a note on Bolin's stationery with the names of ALS patients she might want to meet.

Her only question for Bolin was to inquire about the status of drug trials. He said, 'There's nothing significant, nothing that'll impress you as a patient. The only drug shown to have appreciable effect is riluzole – if we start you on it right now, it may extend your life.'

'How long?' she asked.

He sighed, then said, 'Studies find that some patients gain as many as sixty days.'

She laughed when he said this, actually laughed. '*Sixty extra days* of full-body paralysis, with a feeding tube, maybe a respirator – wow. Write out that prescription for me, doc!'

Bolin had let her rant, let her refuse the prescription, and now . . . now, no matter how shell-shocked she felt, she had to be a mom; now she had to act normally so that her child wouldn't be affected, wouldn't be alarmed. She wouldn't tell Savannah, not so soon, not when the mortal wound was still so raw. She had to tell her eventually, of course she did, but she had no idea when 'eventually' would be. How could you ever tell your child you were dying? How could you not?

'These are such great seats,' Savannah said, taking

the chair to Meg's right. 'I hope you don't mind I got VIP tickets.'

'I'm glad you did,' Meg lied. If she had her way, she'd rather be just about anywhere else than seated thirty feet from where Carson would be performing songs she knew were, in many cases, written with her crimes in mind.

As a buyer of his music, as a fan, she'd been able to keep Carson at a safe distance. She'd been able to hear, in his lyrics, their history commemorated, romanticized, and she'd felt sort of special knowing she was the inspiration for some of the songs. The distance between their past and Carson's voice reproduced on a plastic silver disc was broad and forgiving; it let her taste the bittersweetness of that past without very much of the guilt. It let her have a part of Carson even Brian could not take issue with – and he didn't listen to the music anyway. First of all, she didn't play it around him. And second, Brian's CD library was made up entirely of audio books on investing, management, global economics, and golf.

Once Meg was his, Brian had ceased being jealous of Carson; why wouldn't he? He was a man who believed in *results*. She'd chosen him, she'd remained faithful – the fact of Carson's success and notoriety was hardly more to him than an amusing party anecdote. When Carson was charged, in 1998, with some throwback North Carolina law against having sexual relations with another man's wife, Brian enjoyed relating the news to friends and saying how lucky it was he'd rescued Meg from a life of infamy. As if Carson would have led that life if she had stayed with him. She never said this; she only smiled and shrugged – *How true!* – sharing the derision-laced humor like a faithful spouse would. To defend Carson would only raise suspicion, draw attention to her stubborn, deceitful heart – and make Brian look bad. No, she knew very well not to stray outside the safety of the wagons she'd circled around her life.

The night club's tables filled with lucky fans; Meg overheard a pair of twenty-something women behind them comparing notes with a trio of young men close by: who'd seen the website announcement, who'd gotten the e-mail, how fast they'd acted in order to get tickets . . . Savannah, also listening, turned around and chimed in.

'It's so great my dad gave me a BlackBerry last Christmas, or I never would've known in time! Whenever I have an e-mail I get an alert, and so I checked right away and was like, oh my god, I have to get tickets! My mom knows him,' she added.

'No way!' one of the women said, a dyed redhead whose body-hugging tee-shirt stretched Carson's face over braless A-cup breasts.

The other woman, her matching tee revealing rolls of pudge, declared, 'You should have backstage passes!'

Savannah nodded. 'Yeah, I know, but she didn't want to, like, presume on their past friendship. But probably we'll see him after the concert. Right, Mom?'

Meg observed this new, animated version of Savannah with interest, but she didn't contradict her.

A waiter stopped at their table to deliver pretzels and take their drink orders, additional perks of the VIP admission. 'Gin, rocks, lime twist,' Meg said. Savannah ordered a Diet Coke.

'I brought all the CDs,' Savannah told Meg, patting her bag slung over the back of her chair. 'So Carson can sign 'em for us. And don't let me forget to buy Rachel a T-shirt. They have some at the front, did you see? Maybe the waiter could get one for us? Maybe I'll get one too – and Carson could sign those, too, do you think?'

'I don't know, honey . . .'

Savannah frowned. 'Can't we at least *try*?'

Meg opened her mouth, ready to deliver another momism like, *We need to respect people's privacy* or *It's not polite to impose for your own gain*, but she held her tongue. How many more opportunities would she get to be Savannah's hero? She truly did not want to impose on Carson – she wanted to see him perform, yes, but otherwise avoid him entirely. For her daughter, though, she could make this effort.

And to be honest, a part of her, the part that still clung to a foolish wish indulged on her wedding morning, thought how interesting it would be to see Carson and Savannah together, side by side. Savannah looked so much like *her* that she had never been able to settle on which of the two men she made love with that day was the more probable father. In person, together, she might find between Savannah and Carson some new glimmer of resemblance.

The comparison game was one she'd been playing

for a very long time, from back when she'd accidentally discovered Carson's first CD while shopping at
the Gainesville Target. Savannah, who was four, was
strapped into the cart, occupied with a tiny Tigger
in one chubby hand and Piglet in the other. The
characters were 'conversing' in high and low sing-
song voices, deep in discussion over whether they
should cook macaroni and cheese or grilled cheese
for dinner that night. It was a week when Savannah
would only eat things with cheese. The next phase
would be blue foods; she'd eat a lot of raspberry
popsicles that week. Meg indulged her so much, that
last summer before she began her medical intern-
ship; it eased the guilt.

The CD cover was a close-up of Carson's face, scruffy
and shadowed but wearing an enigmatic smile. His
eyes were dark green and a little sad. He had a small
silver hoop in his left earlobe, and she wondered how
his dad had reacted to *that*. Feeling like a kid sneaking
a nudie magazine, Meg grabbed the CD from the shelf
and stuffed it into the red cart – *This cart's not cheese
colored!* Savannah had complained – beneath a package
of paper towels and new summer clothes for Savannah,
who was outgrowing everything. Meg looked around
to see if anyone had seen her take the CD, as though
they might also see her duplicitous heart. She was not
supposed to be thinking about Carson, should not have
stood there transfixed by the way Savannah's ears
looked so much like his.

If she'd listened to her mother-in-law and her
husband, she wouldn't have been there at all. Brian

and Shelly always fussed at her for shopping at Target; they could afford better, and didn't she want to show it? But she couldn't get used to having so much money available to her. The checking account balance was intimidating, even after her med-school bills got paid. She could afford the expensive department stores, was expected to shop in those places, but she felt like a trespasser in them. Target was safer. Usually. Before they started stocking Carson McKay CDs.

She'd put it in her new Volvo's CD player as soon as she got in. Her stomach was tight, hard as glass as she sat there, hearing Carson's voice for the first time in nearly five years. She knew before the end of the chorus that the song was about her; she let the music pelt her, let his voice fill the space, enveloping her in his melancholy. Only when the stuffed Tigger sailed over her head and landed on the dash did she reach out and snap the stereo off.

'Mommy, Tigger's hungry. Can we go home now, please? He wants Cheetos and a side of cheese grits, pronto!'

Before Meg complied with Tigger's request, she took the CD and tossed it into the garbage can in front of the store.

At the end of the blue-food week, she snuck back to Target on her own and bought his CD again.

Tonight, if she saw Carson and her daughter side by side, she might find new evidence of Savannah's paternity. Or she might not. If not, that wouldn't prove anything for certain, just as Savannah having what seemed to be Brian's nose and face shape didn't prove

236

she was Brian's – because how, then, to explain Savannah's musical abilities? Were her eyes, green like fresh-cut lime, her small-lobed ears, the wave in her hair all merely coincidental? Nothing but expressed genes from the extensive Powell and Hamilton pools?

'I'll try to get us backstage,' Meg said.

Savannah reached over and kissed her cheek. 'Thank you, Mommy!' She grinned, her smile a match to Meg's own – though Savannah's crooked right eyetooth had been corrected with braces.

How lucky it was that Savannah looked primarily like her. Suppose she had turned out to be the spitting image of Carson? Meg had overlooked that possibility before she'd gone to him, proving just how idiotic she was back then. Ruled by her emotions – a dangerous state she'd tried to avoid ever since.

If Carson *was* Savannah's father, then very little had been accomplished by marrying Brian. Because as her mother's diary pointed out, her father simply wasn't capable of being lifted out of the hole he'd dug – or, once lifted out, he dug another. Yes, her marriage allowed them to hold on to the business and the land, and that was no small thing. But how much had that benefited her mom or her sisters in the end?

Well, no point in second-guessing everything now – it took too much energy, and nothing could be changed by it. As Manisha was always saying, your fate finds you no matter where you put yourself.

The house lights dimmed, and with them the cacophony of eager voices. Just as the waiter reappeared with their drinks, a spotlight lit up center stage, directed there from narrow balconies high up on the walls. In a moment, the empty disc of light was filled by a large, silver-haired man with a full mustache.

'Greetings!' he said into the microphone.

The crowd cheered and whistled.

'I'm Johnny Simmons' – more whistles – 'and you all are in for one *hell* of a treat!'

The crowd erupted, Savannah included. Meg, to her confusion and chagrin, found herself fighting back sudden tears.

'Now, some of you know we *had* planned to bring a new band out tonight, a great little indie group called Frito Bandito – and they are *hot*, let me tell you! Mr Bandito, though, has been waylaid by some ugly thing – and I don't mean a woman *or* a gator, I mean a bad head cold. So, by my God-given powers of persuasion, or maybe the dumb luck of his being in town to plan his *wedding*' – boos filled the hall – 'to world-class surfer Valerie Haas, who . . .' – Johnny shaded his eyes and looked down at a table in the front row, hardly fifteen feet away from Savannah and Meg – 'who is right here to watch her man do his thing' – a spotlight from the right side swung down and illuminated Val, who squinted and waved – 'I am proud and pleased to bring onstage, here at Johnny Simmons's Orlando music hotspot, Mr Carson McKay!'

The spotlights swung to the left and Carson jogged onstage, made a brief bow, then went to the piano. Behind him, the stage lit up in brilliant blue, illuminating the other musicians.

He adjusted the microphone. 'Thanks, Johnny, and thank you all for bothering to come see us on such short notice.'

Whistles and applause rang out again. How fascinating, Meg thought, to see him onstage. He wore black jeans and white dress shirt – cuffs rolled to expose some sort of vining tattoo on his left forearm, the shirt open at the neck, long tab collar reminding her of a shirt he'd worn to homecoming her freshman year. There he was, suddenly larger than life. Was this how Val always saw him? Meg looked at Val, whose back was to her, and wondered what it was like to know *this* Carson.

He tickled the keys a little, and the cheers died down again. 'Thanks. Thanks *so* much. Now, before we get the show started, let me also say thanks and introduce you to the band. These fine musicians have had to put up with me all day, rehearsing songs they don't have lots of experience with, wondering why the hell they said they'd fill in for the madmen I usually tour with – who are, I should add, a bunch of slackers compared to these guys.'

Carson introduced them, praising each musician and letting each one tell a bit about himself – or herself, in the case of the guitar player, a lanky woman in knee-high boots. Savannah nudged Meg and pointed. 'That could be me!'

Meg studied Carson: his easy onstage persona, the generosity of spirit that led him to share the limelight. Val Haas was a lucky woman.

'Okay, we're going to open tonight with a song I

wrote, oh, five or so years ago when I was coming back from Bangkok, jetlagged and a little . . . worn out, let's say. You may have heard it; it's called "Altitude".'

He cued the band, and the song began. Instantly Meg felt locked into the energy of the crowd and the drowsy, seductive sound of the music, enough to be able to ignore, for a few sweet moments, the perceptible weakness in her hand when she grasped her glass of gin and brought it to her mouth. For a few sweet moments, she was just one of Carson's many fans.

TWENTY-NINE

Vince, the oldest of Johnny's three sons, found Carson backstage a few minutes after the second encore ended. Carson was chatting with Alex, the drummer, his arm draped over Val's shoulders.

'Mr McKay? Sorry to interrupt, but someone who says she's an old friend is out there hoping she can talk to you a minute.'

Not another groupie, Carson thought. They always tried this, as if he hadn't heard the 'old friend' bit ten thousand times before.

'What's her cup size?' Alex asked. 'Maybe she's an "old friend" of mine, too!'

Vince grinned and shook his head. 'Nah, it's not like that. Here, she wrote down her name.' He handed Carson a gum wrapper. 'Guess it's all she had.'

Meg and Savannah Hamilton, Carson read with surprise. Val read it too. She obviously didn't remember the name of the woman she'd seen so briefly the day before, because she said, 'So, is it legit?'

He considered how he might say, 'Nope, never

heard of them,' and just go on with the night. He'd hoped to get out of Florida without seeing Meg again. What was she doing here? Why had she brought her daughter? It hadn't ever occurred to him before that she – or they – could be fans. He could blow them off and, in another day, be on his plane to New Orleans unscathed. Sure, and then he'd feel awful about it ad infinitum – for disappointing the kid, if nothing else.

'Bring 'em on back,' he told Vince. 'They're legit.' To Val he said, 'You remember, you met Meg yesterday, at Penguin Pete's.'

'Oh! God, what a bright light I am. I totally didn't pay attention to her name.'

No, he thought, *why would you?*

Alex left to look for 'a livelier scene', he said, and then Vince was back, leading a very eager-looking, very appealing teen, followed by a not-as-eager-looking woman. Still, after how miserable Meg had looked yesterday, this was an improvement.

When they reached him, Savannah hung back – suddenly shy? Meg moved ahead of her just a little and extended her hand. 'Carson, it's good to see you again – God, it's been *years*. The show was great!'

Years? Quick as the question came, so did the answer: she didn't want Savannah to know about yesterday's meeting. He shook Meg's hand. Light grip, clammy; she was nervous. He looked at Val and said, 'Yeah, *years*. And thanks. Hey, this is my fiancée.' The title, once very nearly Meg's, stuck a little in his throat.

Val, it seemed from her silence, had understood the cues and was playing along. Carson said, 'Val Haas, Meg Hamilton and her daughter – Savannah, right?'

Savannah nodded, then moved forward a little, to stand shoulder to shoulder with Meg.

'You two could be sisters,' he said, not to flatter them but because it was true. Savannah looked older than the sixteen she must be, or nearly, and Meg, in jeans and a slim-fitting tee, showed little evidence of her own age save for the dark circles under her eyes, translucent half-moons of stress.

Val shook hands with both of them and said, 'Like sisters. Definitely.'

'You're too kind,' Meg said. 'I hope you'll forgive our imposition, but Savannah was hoping—'

'I would be so honored if you'd sign these tee-shirts.' She pulled two from where they were draped over the crook of her arm and held them out. He took them. 'And these, too,' she added, digging into a canvas bag – Val had a yellow one – and pulling out a mess of CDs, which she also handed over. 'And, I have this,' she said, brandishing a permanent marker like an exclamation point.

'Well, when you put it like that,' he laughed, glancing at Meg. She was smiling that crooked, embarrassed smile so familiar to his heart. The smile that debuted, if memory served, after the first time he kissed her bare nipples. She would've been . . . around Savannah's age, Jesus.

He piled everything on top of an amplifier and took the marker. 'Tell me how to spell your name.'

Savannah did. 'Just on the red shirt, okay? The pink one is for my best friend Rachel, so, could you put *her* name on that one?'

'Is she here?'

'Oh, huh-uh, she couldn't come. Her mom is this totally evil person and wouldn't let her skip her etiquette class.'

'Etiquette class?' He looked over at Meg.

She shrugged defensively and said, 'They learn how to waltz, which utensils to use at formal dinners, how to write thank-you notes . . .'

'It's *so* lame, holy crap,' Savannah said. 'I did it last year.'

He smiled at Meg as he started on the CDs. 'Amazing we made it so far without the right training.'

Val said, 'I would never put my kid through that. No offense, Meg, but, it's so, like, archaic.'

'It didn't hurt her any,' Meg said.

Carson signed the last of the CDs and handed the stack to Savannah, but he was watching Meg. 'Bet it made the in-laws happy too,' he said, unable to resist the small dig. The Hamiltons, by his recollection, were all about proper social etiquette, making sure their best feet were always forward, so to speak. Their sons went to private schools, played golf at an exclusive club – it was a wonder they let Brian marry someone like Meg. But then, if his reputation was accurate, Brian always got whatever he wanted. He and his brother Jeffrey both. Meg wasn't a *bad* choice; she was no skanky cocktail waitress or overtanned aerobics instructor looking for a sugar daddy. She was an intelligent, hardworking young woman who just happened to be from a family of lower social standing. He was sure it had been easy for her to win over Brian's folks. And seeing how Jeffrey had married Deirdre Smith-Harvey, a woman whose father had just won a seat as a state superior court judge, the Hamiltons were probably plenty content with how things had gone. And how things were going.

Meg looked at him closely as he signed the tee-shirts and gave those back too. She said, 'Yes, well, thanks so much for letting us come backstage. This is a real treat.'

Such good manners. She might as well have done the etiquette thing herself, as Hamilton-like as she'd obviously become. Not, of course, that she would ever address any of their old business in front of Val or Savannah … How pissy of him; he shouldn't have challenged her that way in the first place.

Val's cell phone rang. She checked the display. 'My mom. I'll be back – nice seeing you, if I don't see you later,' she said, waving at Meg and Savannah as she left to take the call in private.

'She's … vibrant,' Meg said, watching Val go.

'Keeps me young,' he nodded. 'And she's incredible on a surf board.'

'Oh, I can imagine,' Meg said – with innuendo? Or was that just his imagination?

Savannah finished repacking the CDs in her bag. 'What a cool sport, surfing. Is she on TV?'

'Sometimes. Her next thing's in Bali, starting Monday. Check the listings.'

'Rachel is going to be so jealous that I met you *and* Val!'

'I'm really pleased to meet *you*,' he said, and meant it. 'And it was great to see your mom again.' He meant this too, sort of. 'Such a surprise! I had no idea she'd let you waste your money on my CDs.'

'Oh my god, it's not a waste!' Savannah said. 'The first real song I ever played on guitar was one of yours – and anyway, they're hers.'

'What's hers?'

'The CDs. All the CDs are hers, and I just upload—'

'Well, we *share*,' Meg said.

'So you play guitar?' he interrupted, startled by the revelation that Meg bought all his music – but, like Meg, wanting to steer away from the topic.

Savannah nodded. 'Mm. But I suck pretty bad.'

'*Savannah.*'

'Sorry – Ah am not terribly accomplished,' she drawled.

He laughed. 'I started on guitar, too. What song was it?' She was a charming kid. Like mother, like daughter; except for her hair, she could just about be Meg at sixteen.

'What? The first one I played, you mean?'

He nodded.

'"Tunnel Vision". I like the opening melody – it's not as hard as some of the others.'

Another of the Meg songs. He made himself not look at her. If she owned the CDs, if she knew the songs, then surely she had been able to see herself in them, had seen him with his soul cracked open. Well, that was the danger of it, wasn't it? He'd known every time he sat in the recording studio that she might one day hear the songs. But he felt sure she wouldn't ever *own* them – wouldn't want pieces of him around, wouldn't hear a song enough times to catch the lyrics, would change the station if one of them came on. He was sure she had no further interest in anything Carson McKay-related – wasn't that what her marriage to Brian said, unequivocally and with emphasis?

Maybe not. *Obviously* not.

What other mistakes of judgment had he made?

Possibilities whispered to him, but he couldn't pay attention while Meg was making a show of checking her watch and saying, 'Wow, it's getting so late – we really have to go.'

'Oh wait,' Savannah said, digging in her bag and pulling out a camera. 'Can we do a picture?'

Meg took the camera. 'Fine – stand over there.' When they were posed, she stood looking into the camera's display screen for a long moment, then took the picture.

'Now one of us,' Carson said, surprising himself and Meg, both. 'Savannah, would you do the honors?' Before Meg could speak the refusal he saw in her eyes, he'd moved beside her and Savannah had the camera in hand.

'Smile,' Savannah said.

When she was through, Carson told her, 'Send me copies, okay?'

'We will,' Savannah said, extending her hand toward

him. 'Thank you *so* much for your autograph – er, auto*graphs*. Everyone's gonna freak when I wear that T-shirt to school on Monday!'

Carson took her hand, then impulsively pulled her in for a quick hug. 'Anything else you want me to sign, you just send it to the address on my website, okay? Have you been on the site?'

''Course,' she said, grinning.

'There's a fan club address – that's the surest thing. Never know where I'll be!'

Meg held her purse in both hands. No parting hug or even a handshake from her. He met her eyes, deep and secret. Things were not exactly how they seemed, he was sure of it. 'Take care, all right?'

She bit her lip and nodded, then looked away quickly. 'You, too.'

And then she was gone.

THIRTY

'Rachel and Angela are here – I gotta go,' Savannah told Meg the following afternoon, passing through the kitchen on her way to the door. They'd been home from Orlando for maybe two hours. Meg was staring into the refrigerator as though she might discover a cure for ALS there, a formula written on the back of the ketchup bottle or growing like mold on the onion rolls.

'Oh. All right.' She turned, leaving the refrigerator door standing open, and the phone rang.

Savannah glanced at the ID display as she passed it and said, 'It's for you.'

'Who is it?'

'I don't know. See you tomorrow!' Savannah kept going, leaving Meg to grab the phone.

'Hello?'

'Hi, Meg? It's Clay Williams.'

Calling her at home on a Saturday? 'Well, this is a surprise.' She pushed the door closed with her foot.

'I hope it's all right to call; I'd heard you were out

sick all week and wanted to make sure things were all right.'

Hopeful, maybe, that her 'illness' was her marriage? 'That's so thoughtful,' she said, opening the patio doors. The sharp, sweet scent of magnolia blossoms came in on the breeze. 'I guess I owe you an apology for not joining you in the courtyard the other day.'

'But the delivery went all right, I gather.'

'Textbook,' she said. The baby girl had come easily, slipping out into her father's waiting hands. Meg cried right along with the new parents, overcome with wonder and joy when the baby took her first shocked gulp of air and began to squall. Life's most profound moments were, paradoxically, its most common ones: first breaths, and last.

'So you're feeling all right?' Clay asked. 'You *sound* good.'

'Do I? I'm still having some issues with my hand and arm, and I might as well tell you, I'm taking a leave of absence.' That would suffice, for now.

'Oh, hell, I hate that for you,' he said. 'When are you coming back?'

The question cut through her protective fog and made her wince. 'I'm not sure. I'm referring out all my patients.'

'What's the trouble – if you don't mind my asking. I . . . I'm concerned about you, you know?'

She thought of how good it had felt to hold his hand, to be enveloped in his warm, caring gaze. To feel understood. How long it had been since she'd had that. 'I know. Thanks. It's some kind of nerve damage,' she said.

'You seeing a good neurologist?'

'I am.' As if it made a difference.

He said, 'Listen, I s'pose you must think I'm a little . . . well . . . I mean, I know you're married, and still I . . . Oh hell. What are you doing for lunch today?'

'What are my options?' she asked, surprising herself. The breeze seemed to be whispering past her ears, saying, *Why not?*

'I make a mean garden omelet, *and* I can offer you outdoor seating on my backyard verandah.'

'Your verandah . . .' She drew out the word. 'It sounds lovely.'

'It's a great little escape, out back – been working with my landscaper for a month or so, and I would love to show it off. The rain's stopped, it's not ungodly hot . . .'

An escape, he said. She liked the notion of escaping, an hour or two's diversion from her life, which vibrated now with a strange, uncomfortable energy, as though the MRI and EMG machines had infected her entire existence. Brian, golfing as always, would never even know she'd gone out.

'All right, I'll come. What's the address?'

He gave it to her. 'I'm out of rotation today, so come by as soon as you want. I'm told my etchings are worth a look.'

'I expect they are,' she said.

Still feeling somehow *outside* herself, she changed her clothes – shorts instead of slacks, a baby blue linen shirt in place of the rose-colored polo, simple flat sandals – and, after two tries, changed her earrings, too, then left the house. She had trouble getting the key in the ignition and starting the car but refused to let it frustrate her, reined her mind in from its gallop toward the day when even stubborn effort would no longer allow her to escape.

Forty minutes after his call, she parked behind Clay's old convertible Jaguar, a reconditioned classic. He came out to meet her, opening her door with a smile that made it easy for her to feel welcome. In his sporty white shorts and colorful madras shirt, he was even more attractive than usual. She could smell his cologne, a mild, spicy scent that made her think, somehow, of a hotel she'd stayed at in Caracas.

'I like a woman who doesn't waste time,' he said as she got out of the car.

'I like a man who doesn't wear shoes,' she said, noting his bare feet.

He shut her door and kissed her on her cheek. 'Soon as we get inside, I'm throwing all my shoes away.'

He showed her around the remodeled low-country house, much larger than the one she'd grown up in, and much nicer, of course. It was airy and cool and, as he pointed out, far more in every sense than a bachelor needed, but he loved the space, and what else did he have to do with his money? At thirty-three, he'd outgrown the free-and-easy single life and wanted to feel more settled, he said. 'All I need now is the right woman.'

'So what's the holdup?' Meg asked as they entered the kitchen.

Clay opened the refrigerator and began taking out

small bowls of chopped onion, peppers, mushrooms, tomatoes, broccoli. 'The best ones are already married.'

'I find that hard to believe.'

He stopped and went to her, stood very close. She noticed the dark gray ring that surrounded the blue of his eyes as if to highlight his feelings. He said, 'The best *one* is already married.'

Any other day of her life, she would have backed away and made light of his comment, knowing better than to encourage this sort of interest. Where did affairs get people, besides entangled in something likely to become a joyless burden for one of them, if not for both? Today, though, she needed to be *alive*, to be a woman alone in a house with an attractive man who desired her. Was that so bad? So wrong?

'Not so happily married,' she said with a small shrug.

Clay came even closer then, moving his hands to her waist and kissing her tentatively, a test. His lips were warm and soft, but their unfamiliarity reminded her of who she *wasn't* kissing. And she knew, then, that he was only a stand-in for the man she wanted to be with but couldn't.

He kissed her again, pressing his body to hers, and she willed herself to go with the moment, to close off her sense of duplicity. What difference did it make if she thought of Carson more than Clay – and nothing at all of Brian? None of them would know. She could let Clay make love to her and imagine they were *both* different people: he would be Carson and she would be herself before her body had begun to fail.

Clay leaned away and began to unbutton her shirt,

careful surgeon's fingers making what was now a trial for her look effortless. She watched his hands and then glanced at his face, those gray-ringed eyes.

'Clay.'

'Am I moving too fast? I'm sorry.' He began to do up the buttons again. 'Overeager.'

'How about the bedroom,' she said.

He led her there, and she closed her eyes as he finished undoing her buttons, stripped her shirt away, unclasped her bra and moved his hands over her bare skin. She let his murmured compliments, his kisses, his lips on her neck be Carson's. False though it was, all of it – him touching her, her being there – it was better than the truth.

'Tell me if I'm going too far,' he said, taking off his shirt. 'We don't have to—'

'It's okay,' she said, shaking her head. 'I want to.'

He drew her down to the bed with him, smiled as he leaned above her and stroked her belly. 'I won't say I haven't thought about this a few hundred times. Don't worry, though; I know better than to think this means forever.'

Like an animal caught by headlights, Meg froze. Something in the soft drawl of his *forever* set off a panic in her. Her pulse raced, and not with passion.

'I have to go,' she said, struggling out from under him, looking for her bra, her shirt.

'What? Wait – what's the matter?'

She found the clothes, put them on as she moved for the door. 'It's not you,' she said without looking back. 'It's – I'm sorry. It's me. I *wanted* to –' She stopped at the doorway, closed her eyes, then opened them again and turned. 'I am so fond of you. But I can't stay.'

He stood up, bewildered. 'Don't go; I really did mean to feed you, not seduce you. Please, stay. Outdoor seating . . . ?'

'I'm sorry,' she said again.

As she backed the car out of the driveway, he watched from his porch – perhaps thinking there might be another time for them. She drove away without looking in the rearview mirror, not blaming him if he hoped he'd get a second chance, a third. She'd wished for the same thing herself. But she wouldn't have that wish granted, nor any of her other more basic ones, wishes she should be entitled to the same as everyone else. To see her daughter find a career, marry, have a family – whatever Savannah chose. To *be* there.

And because she could not face this wishless future, she began to try to outrun it.

THIRTY-ONE

For her first in-person date with Kyle, Savannah wore her genuine 'Carson @ Johnny's' tee, as Carson had written over the front left shoulder. Then he'd signed his name, big and obvious, on the left sleeve. Rachel, who was riding with her and Angela to the hotel where Angela would drop Savannah off, wore her tee-shirt too. 'I love love love it,' Rachel was saying from the front seat, 'but aren't you worried Kyle will get, like, possessive or jealous?'

'He's not like that,' Savannah said, picking at a third broken fingernail. 'He's not the jealous type.' As if she knew for sure. She wasn't worried about it anyway; mostly she just wanted Rachel to shut up.

'Have you told him about Monday?'

'I left him a message about it, but he never got it.'

'If he, like, gets really mad, just call us, okay? I mean it. We'll come get you, won't we, Angela?'

Angela shrugged. 'Sure, whatever.'

'He won't be mad,' Savannah said. 'He's really sweet and, you know, understanding.' As far as she knew.

What if he wasn't? What did she *really* know about him? If she got there and saw he wasn't who he was supposed to be – if he was, like, forty and fat, or worse, she wouldn't bother to call Rachel. She'd just bail right there on the spot, just call a cab or something.

Angela drove up into the hotel's circle drive. 'Have fun,' she said. 'Don't do anything I wouldn't do!'

'Which leaves, like, *nothing*,' Rachel said, turning around to face the backseat. Savannah reached for the door latch, but Rachel grabbed her arm. 'Do you want me to come in and wait with you?'

'No – I'm good.'

'Be careful, then, okay? I mean, like, use protection and all that. God! I can't believe you're going to, you know, do all this stuff before me! I never would've believed it.'

'It's fate I guess,' Savannah said, sounding braver than she felt as she opened the door. 'Don't worry, you'll find the right guy soon.'

She got out and shut the door. Rachel leaned out the window. 'Call me tomorrow, you swear?'

'I will. And remember: if my mom calls your mom for any reason, I just left your house and am walking home – and then you call me that second, no matter what time it is.'

Rachel nodded dutifully. 'You can count on me. On us.'

'But don't call otherwise. Okay – see you. Thanks, Angela.' Now that they'd helped her scam her parents, they'd protect her – or it would be their asses too.

She turned and walked inside with faked confidence,

inhabiting twenty as best she could in case Kyle was there already, watching for her. The walk was unnecessary, though; she knew the moment the doors slid closed behind her that the guy standing at the check-in desk was him. His back was to her, but she *knew*. Something about his clothes – a rumpled white T-shirt and caramel cargo shorts, black flip-flops – and the canvas bag dropped at his feet, along with his mop of curly black hair, assured her this was the guy she'd been growing to know – maybe even to love? – these past few weeks.

She stopped and studied him. He sure wasn't forty and fat. His skin was like coffee-milk, his calves muscular and hairy, but not *too* hairy, and his broad shoulders angled down to small hips. He looked a little shorter than she expected, but still very good – from the back, at least. And if his back matched his picture and description, his front would too; it only made sense. She flashed again to that photo of him, thought of the lean slope of his belly, the trail of hair . . . it made her palms itch.

He picked up his bag, turned, and saw her. She began walking toward him, the same walk she'd used coming in, that she'd practiced in private all week.

'Whoa,' he said. 'I am definitely in the right place!'

The urge to turn tail and run almost overwhelmed her – not because she was scared, though she was a little, but because she felt like an imposter. Kyle didn't just look like his picture; he looked like *more*. More . . . genuine, more male, more . . . adult. She just hadn't realized what twenty-three *looked* like – who did she know that age? Nobody. It had been a number not so far ahead of her fictitious twenty, but she had no real, no *true* idea of how it would look on a man. He looked like everything he was supposed to be. Whereas she felt more like twelve than twenty just now, and was sure it had to show.

She was here, though, and he was here, and . . . and so she had to *try*, anyway.

'Hi,' she said. 'Yep – if you're Kyle, you're in the right place.'

'The envy of every man – *that's* me, as of this moment.'

'Um, thanks,' she said. She could feel her face getting hot, knew it must be red. She reached for some poise, came up with, 'You're very sweet to say so.' The etiquette training hadn't been for nothing after all.

He stepped closer to her and they stood there, in the middle of the lobby, close enough for her to smell the slight salty scent of him, mingled with a musky perfumelike scent she assumed was deodorant. Was his heart beating as hard, as quickly as hers? He looked very calm.

'I got us checked in.'

'Oh . . . good.'

'They asked me if I wanted to leave the charges on Ms *Hamilton's* credit card.'

Oh *shit*. 'Yeah, um—'

'No sweat,' he said, reaching out and tugging a bit of her hair. 'I already knew your last name wasn't "Rae". I just didn't know what it was. It's all good. I don't blame you for keeping it back, right?'

'I'm sorry – I hated to lie. But yeah, I didn't want to just have it out there for anybody to see.'

'Makes sense – I like a smart woman.'

Smart, right. Not smart enough to know they'd ask him about the credit card.

He said, 'My other question is – and don't freak because I'm asking – do you really go to the university?'

Oh God, she'd really screwed up. What made him think she might not go there? She felt trapped by his question, by his proximity, standing so close that she could see his pulse in the side of his neck. To buy some time and space she asked, 'Could we like, sit down?'

'Yeah, of course!'

She was relieved he didn't insist they go to their room instead; she wasn't ready to be alone with him. They moved to a grouping of sofas and she stopped, unsure which seat to choose, unsure what she would tell him, unsure that she could handle this whole scene. She'd thought it would be *easy*, as easy as chatting online, as easy as talking on the phone. Until she saw him, she'd felt she knew him; now, she felt awkward and stupid.

Kyle took her hand and sat down, pulling her with him. 'So?' he said. He let her hand go.

She set her purse, the green canvas one that, in addition to holding her usual stuff now held her bikini, a pair of panties, a tank top, and a small bottle of a lemon juice solution, on the seat next to her. She kept the strap in her hand as if it were a security blanket, and prepared to confess. If he was going to reject her because of the lies, now was the best time to find that out.

She shrugged. 'So . . . okay. I don't go there.'

He nodded amiably. 'Yeah, I didn't think so. I checked their directory at first, in case, you know, Savannah Rae was your real name. No match, right? So I asked around, e-mailed your picture to some dudes I know there – nobody knew you. Not that they *would*, right? Necessarily? But I figured, a babe like you gets noticed. So I decided, hey, just ask her!'

He didn't sound angry at all. 'You must think I'm awful, but really I'm not! You know how it is with Internet stuff – girls have to be super careful. I planned to tell you today; you just, you know, beat me to it.'

'I totally understand,' he said, and she could see in his dark brown eyes that he did. He smiled and a dimple appeared on his left cheek. 'But your name, it *is* Savannah, right?'

She nodded vigorously. 'Yes! Savannah Hamilton. And . . . I actually live here, in Ocala.'

'I appreciate the honesty,' he said, taking her hand again. 'Look, it works both ways, right? People have to be careful. Now I gotta tell you: I'm not really a grad student.'

'You're *not*?'

'Nah – truth is, my parents cut me off before I even finished my bachelor's – some stupid-ass lie the dean told them . . . so I'm a few credits short. I just didn't want you to, you know, think I'm some loser. I'm serious about marine biology, right, and I really want to go back to school.'

Savannah gaped at him. 'Okay, well . . . do you really live in Naples?'

He shook his head. 'Me and a friend rent a place down by Summerfield.'

'Oh my god! We're, like, just a couple of liars,' she laughed. 'I don't feel so bad, now!'

He reached over and ran his fingers over her lips, sending an electric thrill straight to her groin. Leaning close, he said, 'You don't look so bad, either. So how about we check out our room, now that we've set the record straight?'

The record wasn't straight; he still thought she was driving to Miami with him on Monday, and he still thought she was twenty. Those clarifications could wait. Obviously he was an easygoing person, just as warm and sweet as he'd seemed to be – probably he wouldn't care about her other lies either. But just to be safe, she would confess them later – or tomorrow, maybe. Yeah, tomorrow would be just fine.

THIRTY-TWO

After four hours of driving away from the fiasco with Clay, Meg was thick into south-central Florida under a sky whitewashed by heat. Colorless grassland flanked the pale gray highway for as far as she could see. Here, long miles away from anything that would attract a tourist's dollar, the landscape looked desolate. She hadn't seen another car – except abandoned ones wearing rust like barnacles – in an hour or more.

There was a numbing simplicity to the view and the hum of her tires on the road. She was nowhere, she was no one, she was contained, she was safe.

She was lost.

The road came to a T-junction and she slowed the car, then stopped, unable to decide which way to go next. She needed some road signs – sticks with placards nailed to them if nothing else, signs with arrows pointing the way to 'Salvation' or 'Cure' or 'Do-Over'. What she saw, though, was tall grasses and shocked, barren, limbless trees reaching skyward. A toppled jug that once held radiator fluid. The carcass of a washing

263

machine, a few yards away. She turned off the Lexus and got out.

Heat like a blast furnace enveloped her; this part of the state was its own special hell, it seemed, with its roads to nowhere and its heat and its dust. She began to sweat immediately, tilted her face upward to the blank sky so that the sweat streamed into her hair and ears. There was a fetid smell, as of small fish and crustaceans decomposing in the hidden swamp, and the only noise was the sound of grass against grass, a slight hiss in the barest of breezes.

She wanted to yell something, to say, 'Why, God?' To make promises, barter her way back to good health. She would welcome the devil, even, if he was the one to offer her a commutation of her sentence. Anything, anything but the failure of her body and of her efforts to do right, to be right.

'Please,' she whispered.

Nothing.

THIRTY-THREE

'Model the bikini for me,' Kyle said, as soon as he and Savannah were inside the hotel room. 'You brought the flowered one, right?'

'What? Like, now?'

'Yeah, now.' He put his arms around her shoulders and pushed her playfully backward, against the wall. With his full body pressed against her, he kissed her – first just lips, then tongue, too. This felt fabulous; this felt right. He drew back. 'I just want to see you in it; been thinkin' about it all day.' He pushed his hips in tighter, and she felt the hard length of him, bulkier, she thought, than her friend Jonathan. Because Kyle was older, maybe?

She liked this, what they were doing; the thought of changing into her bikini and modeling it for him, though, the thought of being scrutinized, embarrassed her. 'You can see me in it when we go to the pool.'

'No, no,' he kissed her neck. 'It's not the same in public. C'mon, please?' He kissed her mouth again. 'Do it for me?'

'I'm shy,' she protested.

'Oh, shy, huh?' He stepped back a little and looked into her eyes. 'Well, you don't look shy – but okay. Okay, I think I know what to do about that.'

He took her hand and led her to the bed. 'Have a seat,' he said, stripping off his T-shirt and dropping it onto the top of the low bureau. 'I know just what you need.'

His skin was darker in the room's dim light, his nipples tiny and hard. She wanted to slide her hands over him, palms wide open, every nerve connecting with his trim muscles and solid shoulders . . .

'Here we go,' he said, pulling a baggie from his pocket. 'Inside this little bag is the recipe for relaxation.'

It took Savannah a second to understand just what exactly was in there. 'Oh – I don't – I mean, I've never—'

'No? Well, there's always a first time, right?'

Not for her. She wasn't stupid. Drugs screwed up your brain, and she happened to like hers the way it was. But . . . to be fair, pot wasn't as bad as a lot of the other stuff. Supposedly it wasn't addictive at all – and, she recalled, they'd legalized it in Canada. Maybe she should just try it *once*, and then she'd know firsthand if it was something she wanted to avoid in the future.

She said, 'Okay, yeah – first time for everything.' If it helped her relax, that would be a good thing. She wouldn't *need* to do it again, after they were . . . more familiar.

Kyle took a thin white joint from the bag and lit it up, then he sat down next to her. 'The trick is to start small, right? Put it to your mouth like this,' he showed her, 'then pull in just a little toke. Here, try it.'

She imitated his actions, feeling foolish, but adventurous too.

'Just breathe it in and hold it as long as you can,' Kyle said. When she managed to do it just as he said, not coughing or anything, she felt pleased with herself.

Letting out her breath, she laughed. 'That isn't so hard. And I actually like the smell.'

'Sweet Mary Jane,' he said. 'Okay, try it again, but take a bigger toke.'

This time she coughed a little as she inhaled, but did it once more and succeeded. Kyle slid his hand along her bare thigh, pushing her gypsy skirt up until she was sure her panties must be showing. She held the smoke in as long as she could, then blew it out. Piece of cake. 'Again,' Kyle said, and this time she felt like a pro. The smoke was hot and harsh in her throat, but strangely smooth, too. And she didn't feel different at all.

'I don't think it's doing anything,' she said.

'Give it a minute, virgin girl; it's good shit, I promise you that.'

Virgin girl, he'd called her. If this stuff worked like he said, if it relaxed her, she thought she could pull off acting experienced; then he'd never know she was a sexual virgin as well.

When Kyle took his turn, she put her left hand on his back, experimentally, then ran it upward, over his shoulder to his neck, caressing the spot just below his right ear. She'd heard guys liked to be touched here – who told her that? She couldn't remember, and she wasn't sure if Kyle liked it or not, but she liked doing it.

He grabbed her right hand and pulled it over to his chest, then pushed it onward, down his belly – he had other ideas, better ones. She let him guide it to the trail of hair she'd thought of so often that she felt she already knew it intimately.

'Your turn.' He handed her the joint and leaned back on the bed, creating a gap between his belly and the waistband of his shorts. Savannah took the joint with her left hand, put it to her lips and inhaled, her eyes all the while watching her right hand with fascination. She could do it, she could slide it right down into that gap anytime she wanted . . .

'Careful now,' Kyle said, and she thought at first that he meant her hand, but he was talking about the joint, which had gotten very short. He took it from her, took one more hit, then got up quickly to go put it out. When he sat down again, he reached for her shirt and tugged it up. She lifted her arms reflexively and the shirt came right off.

'Now go change,' he said. 'I'll wait right here.'

She hardly knew that she was on her feet and in the bathroom pulling her bikini out of her purse, but suddenly she was. The surprise of it made her laugh. In the mirror she looked the same as always, but she felt giddy and light. 'It works,' she called out. The rest of her clothes came off fast, and she was in the bikini without a second thought. He was going to love what he saw, she decided, smiling at her reflection. Who knew pot gave you such confidence? She glanced at her purse, at the bottle of lemon-juice solution meant to prevent pregnancy if you rinsed with it just before sex, and decided it was too awkward to bother with. She'd ask if he brought condoms – and if he hadn't, it wasn't that big a deal. Nobody got pregnant the first time; half of her mom's patients were women who couldn't seem to get pregnant no matter how hard they tried.

'Okay, babe, here I am,' she said as she left the bath-room and strode back into the room. She stopped in surprise. Kyle was still there on the bed, but he was sitting against the headboard, naked.

He said, 'Oh, wow – stand right there.'

Savannah stood still; she felt that's all she *could* do.

'Now untie the top – that's it.' He stared, then looked up at her face and smiled. 'Check me out,' he pointed to his lap. 'Didn't I tell you? This is what you do to me. Now just, like, slide your hand into the bottoms.'

One part of her felt as turned on as he clearly was, but she also felt strangely disconnected from the whole thing; part of her mind seemed to be outside her, wondering if this was how foreplay was supposed to go. She was excited but a little confused.

'Kyle, I don't—'

'Come on over here,' Kyle said. 'Am I freaking you out? Sorry.'

Savannah went eagerly, ready for the passionate kissing and stroking, the body-to-body contact that was *her* idea of foreplay. Kyle pulled her down beside him, and for a minute – or it might have been longer, it was hard for her to pay attention to time – they kissed and he stroked her back, then her breasts, then lower.

'You like it, don't you?' he said, his voice a rough whisper.

His touch was a little rough too, and she wasn't sure if she liked it or not, but she said, 'Oh, yeah.'

'You are *so* hot – I knew you would be. I knew it'd be just like this. Now let me feel that sweet mouth.'

He shifted and reached for her head, pulling her down so that she had to catch herself with her hands to keep her balance. And then she was staring right at him, at the erection she'd been so curious about; well, she was seeing it now! But she had no good idea how to do what he wanted; she felt muddled and a little intimidated and a little ridiculous – but fine, she thought, how hard can it be? And the question set her to giggling. How *hard* can it be? She pushed away from him and sat back on her heels, hands over her mouth, unable to stop laughing.

Kyle got onto his knees too. 'Chicks don't usually laugh at it,' he said, then he pushed her a little. 'Lay down.'

When she started to turn over onto her back, he said, 'No, on your stomach.'

She did it, still giggling a little. He peeled off her bikini bottoms and then pushed her legs open. 'That's such a great view ...' She felt his hand between her legs again, then suddenly his whole weight was on her, pressing down and in with such abruptness that she stopped laughing and gasped in pain.

'Not a laughing matter, is it?' he whispered, his mouth against her ear. She could tell he was teasing, that he meant this to feel good – it was supposed to feel good, that's what it was all about, right? – but it didn't, it stung badly at first, and then it hurt every time he thrust.

'You on the pill?' Kyle asked after a while, she had no idea how long.

'No,' she gasped, trying to just endure. It would feel better next time, she was positive; she should have told him she was a virgin so he'd take it slower.

'Bad girl,' he said, pulling out and off of her, and then he let out a series of short groans. She felt hot fluid on her lower back – better there than inside.

He plopped down beside her. 'Man, you make me crazy,' he said, and she watched how his dimple deepened when he grinned. 'I got carried away. Now, how old are you really?'

'Twenty, remember?'

'Give me a little credit.'

How did he *know*? 'Eighteen, okay? I'm eighteen.'

'You're sure?' He trailed a finger across her belly.

She started to laugh again – something about the way he raised his one dark eyebrow and gave her that dimpled smirk. 'Okay, fine – I'll be sixteen in a couple weeks.' There, she'd said it. Now he knew the truth.

'You're *fifteen*?' he said. 'Fifteen? You're not shitting me?'

She shook her head.

'Oh, man. Fifteen.' His face clouded, and she was scared, suddenly, that she'd gone too far with her deception. 'Was this your first time?' he said. 'For, you know, the deed?'

'I'm sorry, I should've said—'

'No, babe, it's cool.' His smile returned. 'You just can't tell anyone, right?'

'But Rachel and her sister already know. They brought me here.'

'Do they know how old I am?'

'Huh-uh.'

He pulled her against him so that their hips were pressed together. 'So then,' he kissed her neck, 'life is good.'

As stupid as the thought seemed to her, Savannah expected that when she got home Sunday afternoon her mom would look at her and *know*. She had so little experience with outright deception; guilt of this measure felt strong enough to be smelled, if not seen. She knew before she walked in, though, that she had extra time to disguise any traces: both of her parents' cars were gone.

As she was supposed to do, the minute she was in the house she called her mom; she got voice mail, and left a message to say she was home. For all anyone knew, she could be calling from Iceland and making the claim. They were so irritatingly *sure* she'd be responsible and honest ... which was her own fault, for having been that way all along. Yet, taking advantage of their trust made her feel almost as weird as she felt about having just spent a whole night with a guy, smoking pot and having sex. Deception wasn't her style any more than drugs and sex were. Who had she become, in the short space of twenty hours?

She flopped down on her bed and stared up at the ceiling. Her thigh muscles ached, she was surprisingly sore between her legs, and her brain felt sluggish. Her heart, though, seemed fuller than it ever had before. Yes, she'd deceived her parents and she'd smoked pot and she'd tried out most every sexual thing Kyle wanted, and maybe all that was out of character for her – but that was the old Savannah. The new Savannah had a sexy, funny, older boyfriend who thought she was *scorching*, who said, when he dropped her off a couple blocks from the house, that he was afraid he would never be able to get her out of his mind. The way he'd looked at her – as if she was the best, most important thing in his life – gave her butterflies even now, just remembering it.

The new Savannah was smart enough to use whatever she needed to get what she wanted, just like the old one; only the stakes had changed. Laying there on her flowered bedspread, she vowed not to lie any more than she had to, vowed to stay clearheaded and drug free in the future (if only so she'd remember all the details better), and vowed to be the best girlfriend Kyle ever had. With this happy thought in mind, she closed her eyes and caught up on a few badly needed hours of sleep.

THIRTY-FOUR

Meg arrived home Sunday night feeling as if she'd spent her days mildly overdosed with Valium. She could not recall whole chunks of time from the night before, just that she'd ended up parked in the lot of a seedy motel off I-75 after almost causing a head-on collision in the middle of the night. She'd slept curled up in the back of the Lexus, waking to the sound of eighteen-wheelers chugging to life around her. Today was lost to her too, just a haze of images and road noise. She hardly knew how she found her way back home.

When she came inside, she was glad to find Savannah preoccupied and closed off in her bedroom, talking on the phone. She was glad when Brian gave no more than passing interest in her vague story about a long, difficult delivery keeping her at the hospital for the past day and a half. Or she *thought* she was glad – no: she *was*, because she wouldn't have had an answer for him if he'd looked at her closely and offered a concerned *What's wrong?* She was glad not to have to try to ad-lib, even if his noticing might have brought her a small measure of comfort. He did manage to notice her limp, but she explained it away with her blister excuse. After telling her there was leftover pizza in the fridge, Brian went to his office to play poker online. Meg drank a tall glass of water and then went to their room and dropped into bed.

At first, sleep refused to come. She kept thinking of how little she seemed to matter to these two people who were supposed to be closer to her than anyone, ever. Here she was, facing the biggest crisis of her life, and they went about their business as they always did. Unless they needed her to *do* something for them, she was inconsequential. A fixture. A convenience. For all they knew, she could have spent last night turning tricks or running small arms to Key Largo. It shouldn't matter that she didn't invite their attention, didn't know how she would have dealt with it. They were her *family*, they should be able to smell her distress. Everything was all wrong.

After a while she tired of her self-pity and lay listening to the steady shush of cool air through the vents. Finally, she fell into a heavy, blank sleep. All night she was dreamless, as if the knowledge of having ALS had paralyzed her brain.

Monday morning she woke disoriented – forgot, at first, that fate had drawn a bead on her like an assassin's rifle. The sound of the shower running, the energized chirping of a wren outside the bedroom window, the golden glow of morning sunlight, all proclaimed an ordinary weekday. Her amnesia didn't last, though;

memory returned like a slap in the face. She had to force herself to get up and get dressed.

Behaving as normally as she could manage, she saw Savannah and Brian off, drank two cups of strong black coffee, and slowly, slowly her focus returned. The cloud was lifting. Not completely, but high enough for her to see that she would not escape her bad news by running to any man, or any place.

She might hope for a miracle, but she didn't expect one. And so, if she was going to *live* the rest of her life, she had better get started.

She made some calls to set up her day, then went to the bookstore, returning with a blank book covered in rugged leather. Durable, because she needed it to be able to last. Durable, the way she was not.

When she got back, she tucked herself into her favorite seat on the screened porch and began to write.

Monday, May 1, 2006

Savannah, this is for you. This morning my doctor called, confirming his diagnosis: I have something called ALS, or Lou Gehrig's disease. I'll tell you about it – not sure when; before you read this, though. This is for you to have when I'm gone. We'll talk a lot before then, but the words, they won't stay with you for long. You'll lose them; they'll disintegrate over time. I know because that's how it's been for me since Grandma Anna died. A few weeks ago, Grandpa gave me some notebooks she'd written in, like diaries, and they're helping me get hold of

*important things from my past. You'll need
something like that, as much or maybe more
than I need to provide it for you – so I'm
writing this journal for both of us.*

*What is ALS? A neurodegenerative muscular
disease. It's irreversible, and fatal. When I think
of saying those two words to you, it makes me
cry . . .*

She paused, and when the welling of tears
subsided, she continued.

*No child should ever have to hear such news.
I don't know why I got ALS; you can't 'catch' it
and it's not inherited (except in really rare cases,
but not mine, so don't fear for yourself). It just
. . . happens. I've learned, in the years since I
started studying medicine, that there aren't
always answers to 'Why?' especially when it
comes to unexpected illness and death. I hope
you won't spend your time battling that
question, and hope this journal helps you accept
what is. Manisha can give you good advice about
how to do this. I wish I'd taken more of her
advice over the years.*

*Anyway, ALS paralyzes all the muscles in the
body, even, eventually, the ones that make you
breathe, but it doesn't affect the mind at all.
What gets set down here in this journal will be
written with a clear head, or as clear a head as
I've ever had, anyway.*

*I suppose I want, with this journal, to pass on
some of my wisdom to you . . . give you advice
on how to grow into a confident woman who
makes good decisions, who doesn't let anyone
determine the course of her life. I made mistakes,
big ones. I know this now, but it's too late for me
to do very much about them. I want to share the
lessons, though, and just . . . tell you things . . .
And yes, it makes me rest a little easier knowing
you'll have a part of me to . . . visit, I guess you
could say, from time to time. Maybe share with
your own children someday.*

She set the pen down, her hand fatigued already. Dr
Bolin told her this might be her luck – that her initial
onset of symptoms had been gradual, but now it
appeared she was in an 'acceleration period'. The disease
was as variable as the people who contracted it: male
and female, every skin color, almost any age, though the
very young weren't usually afflicted. Her symptoms could
worsen quickly, then stabilize again – even hit a long-
term holding pattern. Or not. Because ALS was not one
precise disease but rather a tight spectrum of clinically
similar conditions, and a very few ALS patients had
versions, as Bolin put it, that defied the usual prognoses.
He knew of a rare few who'd lived a decade or more
after diagnosis. Most, though – seventy-five percent –
were dead inside of five years, some dropping like flies
from within weeks of a late diagnosis, to a few dragging
themselves to the five-year finish. If her symptoms
accelerated even faster than they appeared to be doing

now, she could be in a wheelchair in a matter of weeks. She could lose the use of her hand at any time.

She picked up the pen and continued, stubbornly.

I'm meeting Manisha later today to tell her my bad news. I'll have to quit practicing medicine pretty much right away. There's too much risk for the patients, for the babies. My right hand and arm are the main problems at the moment, and if I let myself admit it – and I might as well, here – my right leg too. Now that I know what to blame, I can't make any more excuses about why I dropped something or caught my toe going up a curb or stumbled or what have you. Now the knowledge lives with me full time, like a nagging mother-in-law.

Should she say that? *Nagging mother-in-law?* Savannah might think she intended to paint Shelly with that brush. Well, it was written, and she didn't want to start over. The best journal would be an honest, uncensored one. Mostly uncensored. She wouldn't write anything about her issues with Brian, for example, nothing that could embarrass him or embarrass Savannah. She liked Shelly just fine, and would make sure to say so; Savannah would realize the expression was just a figure of speech. Journaling wasn't so easy when you were writing for others – she was determined, though, to give Savannah this gift, imperfect though it might be. She had little else of real value to leave behind.

*I don't know how I'm going to handle leaving
my practice, leaving the job that has been so
much a part of who I am – the career I worked
so hard for. If I had known it was going to end
so abruptly, I never would have bothered; I
would have spent the time that I gave to classes
and homework and training and patients with
you, instead.*

*Except that makes it sound like I'm sorry to
be a doctor, and I'm not. I only wish I could
have the time back, knowing what I know now. I
wish I could have had both: my career and more
time with you. Well, as long as I'm wishing, I
wish I didn't have ALS and had a future to
share with you, like I was counting on. It just
goes to show that the future doesn't exist. All we
truly have is now.*

Her fingers were so weakened from her effort that
she couldn't hold the pen up straight; she put it aside
and tucked the journal underneath her, beneath the
cushion, where she could access it often without anyone
noticing. As if they paid attention.

She went to her room and put her hair back with
a clip her tired hand could barely work. She was
meeting Manisha for lunch, then driving over to Silver
Springs to meet one of Bolin's other patients, a woman
named Lana Mathews. Lana was thirty-five and the
mother of four kids, all under age nine. It broke Meg's
heart just thinking about the poor woman. When she
called this morning, to see if they might meet in order

to help her begin dealing with her own diagnosis – a call that had taken nothing short of five tries before she made herself go through with it – all she'd known was the woman's name. Lana's sister Penny, who volunteered as caretaker, had answered the phone; she filled in the details and invited Meg over. 'Come on over and meet her. It ain't so bad as you might think,' Penny said.

THIRTY-FIVE

'Get another opinion,' Manisha told Meg over their Asian chicken salads.

'I *did* – three doctors now, one who specializes in neuromuscular diseases.'

Manisha waved her fork. 'See more! And don't stop there. There are other things – Lyme disease! You are just having Lyme disease! I will put you on that anti-biotic, do a three-month trial, check your symptoms after—'

'Manisha.'

'What? Don't lie down for this diagnosis!'

'First off, I have none of the other Lyme symptoms. Second, I've had every test – it's "clinically definite". Bolin called right before I left the house to say they did not find *Borrelia burgdorferi* in my blood. I don't have Lyme, and I don't have some other thing; I have ALS.'

Manisha picked at the mandarin oranges in front of her, and Meg could tell she was trying to come up with a more convincing argument; that was Manisha, stubborn like her, but in a practical, caring way. In their years together as partners, Manisha had looked out for her the way Meg had always looked out for her sisters.

Manisha narrowed her eyes and said, 'Tell me this: How do they know already? It can be many months, making this diagnosis.'

It was a good question, one Meg was sorry she could answer so easily. She said, 'I was a lab rat for Bolin. Besides the usual tests, he did a new spinal fluid assay, looking for some just-discovered ALS biomarkers. And found them,' she added. 'A good friend of mine would say it's my fate to know already.'

'What friend? She is not knowing of what she speaks.'

Meg reached for her hand. 'She is. I think there's a reason I'm not a hard case to crack. Or maybe I'm just lucky in that way; less drama, less stress in dealing with "maybes". I hate being in limbo, so luckily I'm not.' She tried to keep her voice steady, but it wavered, and Manisha heard it.

Manisha bowed her head to hide her tears. 'Oh Meg . . . no.' She sniffled, wiped her nose with her napkin. 'What . . . what does Brian say?'

'I haven't told him yet.'

'When?'

'Soon . . . Honestly, I just don't know. I can't hide it for long, obviously. Not that he notices anything,' she added.

Manisha didn't chide her for criticizing Brian, the way she would have any other time – as she had the few times when Meg, in a fit of annoyance or irritation, voiced a feeling instead of keeping it to herself, instead of wearing it like a hairshirt meant to remind her of her privileged life. *You married him for a reason*, Manisha might have said. *He is loving you in his own way*, she'd likely have added. Manisha, whose own marriage had been arranged, was long accustomed to such rationalizations. This time all she said was, 'And Savannah?'

'I'll tell them. Soon.'

Manisha sat up straighter and sighed. 'You will hire someone to care for you? Or maybe your sister Beth? She could come stay? I will do all I can. Please, Meg, you will just tell me what I can be doing to help.'

Meg had no answers. She didn't know yet what she wanted to do, who she might hire or conscript. This kind of planning was beyond her just now, the reality of what her diagnosis meant still unforeseeable, like mist hiding the far banks of the River Styx. She still felt stunned, as if she'd been walking along a street and was sideswiped by a speeding truck. The disease was so variable, its timeline so fickle. The best she could do just now was put one foot in front of the other and trust she would get where she needed to go.

'I will tell you, Manisha. Thanks. Meantime, who do we know who might be ready to join the practice? I can be out of my office in a week or so.'

Lana Mathews's Silver Springs home was not what Meg expected. She'd imagined a darkened sick-room atmosphere where the fully disabled Lana passed the hours watching TV or sleeping while her younger sister, thirty-three-year-old Penny, managed the household and the kids, taking time now and then to change the channel or the bedpan. What she found instead was the fully disabled Lana at dead center of chaotic everyday life with four young children.

'This here's Colleen,' Penny said, introducing Meg to a skinny blond girl of about five, sitting cross-legged on the end of a hospital bed that had been parked near the living room windows. The view was of tiny houses just like the one she was in: three-bedroom, bath-and-a-half vinyl-sided tracts, all tan or cream or pale yellow or white. Newish pear and maple trees reached pitifully out of the scrubby soil, some of them surrounded by white plastic picket fencing, others by colorful plastic children's toys – as Lana's maple was. Two faded subcompact cars were parked in Lana's narrow drive.

'Melissa and Ashleigh are the little ones you passed with Nicole, the tall one, on your way in. And this, of course, is Lana.'

Meg looked down at the woman in the bed and took her hand, glad to have years of medical training to fall back on. 'Hi, Lana. I'm Meg Hamilton.' Lana's hand was chilly and limp, despite the sunshine coming in through the windows, despite the day being warm enough for the girls to all be dressed in sleeveless shirts and shorts.

Lana, a blond woman with bright blue eyes who would have been very pretty not so long before, turned her head, perhaps a quarter of an inch, and made a barely perceptible nod. Her face was a mask of slack muscles, and her mouth hung open a bit, drool pooling at the corners.

'She don't talk anymore,' Penny said, 'but she listens just fine. Colleen was just reading her mama a story, wasn't you?'

'*Hop on Pop*,' Colleen declared, holding up the book. 'Then I'm gonna read *Goodnight Moon* – it's Mama's favorite, she use t' read it t' me every night.'

'Colleen reads real good – it's the homeschooling, I swear it. And she's right good company, and helpful too! Even helps with the messy jobs, if you catch my meaning.'

'Mama's got t' wear a diaper,' Colleen said cheerfully, 'but it ain't her fault. She got that famous baseball man's disease.'

'Whyn't you go round up your sisters for snack time, hmmm?' Penny shooed Colleen off the bed.

'Four girls,' Meg said, watching Colleen skip to the doorway, above which was a plaque that read *Got Jesus?* in white letters on a black background, and four shiny brass oval frames, each displaying a little girl's face. 'We had four in my family too – I have three sisters.'

'All blessings, these girls are,' Penny said. She smiled, and Meg had an idea of what Lana's face would look like animated. 'Colleen hangs around all the time, but it's Nicole who does the most – she's eight, and she watches the little ones for me right regular – she is an angel.'

'Where's their dad?'

Penny took Meg's elbow and steered her into the kitchen, telling Lana, 'Be right back, hon; just gonna get juice for the girls.' In the kitchen, a narrow space remarkably free of clutter, save for the crayon drawings littering the refrigerator and cupboard doors, Penny said, 'Rob, he was killed in a truck wreck right after little Melissa was born. You've never seen anybody keep things going like Lana did, even in her grief – right up till this thing got her last fall. It kills me how she can't hold that baby girl anymore, I tell you!' Penny wiped her eyes. 'But she will be free to hold other babies in heaven, 'fore too long. Don't you think it's like that, in heaven? Them lost babies, they gotta have somebody to care for 'em – so I think Jesus brings some of the most special mothers up for the job.'

Sure, Meg thought, and leaves their own children motherless on Earth. It wasn't an especially comforting theory, in her view. She supposed, though, that Penny imagined herself the capable understudy – which she obviously was. Maybe they all had a mission in life – and in death, unknowable though it might be ahead of time.

'You got kids?' Penny asked, setting four plastic cups on the counter, each a different, bright color.

'One daughter; she'll be sixteen in two weeks.'

'Bless you, it's an awful tough sentence y'all got – but look at Lana, she don't never complain. Well, she cain't now, of course, not with her voice, but you'd know it if she wasn't content. I've seen her cry a time or two since she got to this state, never in front of the girls, 'course. Even before, though, she mostly just thanked Jesus for the time she's got left.'

'What about you?' Meg asked. 'How do you manage all this?'

Penny paused, the pitcher of juice tipped above the red cup. 'It wears you down, I won't say it don't. I got no life of my own – my husband, Lee, he took up with a coworker since I been gone so long.' She poured the juice and went on, 'But I figure this is just what I gotta do for my sister. It ain't forever,' she said matter-of-factly. 'And ladies from the home health service and the church, plus Rob's mom, once, they come spell me from time to time.'

'And your mother?'

'Bless her, she left us when we was kids.'

'She died?'

'No, left us – went off with some man from Los Angeles. Used t' be Lana watched over me, so now I'm taking a turn.'

Meg looked in at Lana, who was close enough to them, in this tiny house, that she had to be hearing everything. What must she be thinking? How sad, but how understandable it was that Penny talked with such apparent disregard for Lana's feelings. How easily she might come to regard a fully immobile person as a sort of fixture; Lana just lay there, propped up at an incline, her arms and legs limp and lifeless like a rag doll's. The red plastic end of a feeding tube snaked casually out of the edge of her pink shirt. Lana might *want* to interact with them, tell her own story, say whether she was glad to be here with her sister and her girls, or if she wished mightily to spare them all the indignities of injecting liquid into her belly, of seeing her diaper changed like little Melissa's – a grown woman, a beautiful, recently lively woman, needing her legs lifted so someone could wipe her ass. She might want to correct or add to the things Penny was saying, but if she did, no one could tell.

The girls trooped in and seemed happy to tell Meg all about what they liked – jump rope and chalking and riding scooters and playing house – and how they helped Aunt Penny take care of their mommy, who they all knew was being called home to heaven 'to live with Jesus and Daddy' before much longer. Meg wanted to ask them if they thought they would miss their mother, if they felt cheated by God, but of course they wouldn't know the answers. And she wouldn't utter those things with Lana twelve feet away. She asked Penny a few practical questions about Lana's care, accepted a cup of juice from Colleen, then, as soon as was polite, escaped the sunny little house with the dying woman trapped inside.

The drive back to Ocala seemed interminable to Meg. Did she imagine that driving was more difficult now? That she had to press harder to keep her acceleration steady, that she had to *think* about keeping the car centered in her lane? When would it no longer be safe for her to get behind the wheel? The sight of her house when she drove up was a weight lifted off her chest. Dying on the highway would be an untimely irony, and anyway, she had things she needed to do before returning to Jesus or whoever might be in charge.

Inside the house, she made a glass of chocolate milk – which felt like more work than it should be, too – and took it with her out onto the patio, where she would write some more. The image of Lana Mathews was stark in her mind. She wrote:

I visited the home of an ALS patient younger than me, whose status now is near-complete paralysis. She has a hospital bed in the living room, where she spends literally all her time. Her children are there, and her sister, but it's no life for that woman, just lying there waiting for the next failure of her body – her breathing is just about all she has left.

She paused, remembering again being trapped in the stable with Bride that night . . . in a sense, she knew exactly how Lana must feel. How awful, and how sad! She saw herself in Lana's place but tucked away in a less cheerful setting – Brian wouldn't be able to stand having her in plain sight – and Savannah . . . Savannah would need to have a life, not be trapped too. How long the days would be, how *boring*. Would Savannah read to her when she visited? No, she'd sing. Well, those would be good moments, at least.

It's astonishing to me that Lana wants to live this way – which I assume she does. (Not like she could say either way.) I understand the religious argument against suicide, and I do respect it for those who believe. Jesus is very much present in the Mathews house, which explains a lot. As I was leaving, Penny, the sister, said, 'Lord Jesus watches over you, never forget.'

She stopped writing and looked out over the shimmer of the pool, into the shaded vale of long-needle pines. She had wanted to ask Penny, 'How do you know?' but she hadn't. It was faith, after all, that provoked people to say such things – they didn't *know*. They *believed*.

Well, she believed some things too. She believed in the mysterious power of life and the universe – call it God, if you liked; she believed there was some place the spirit lived before inhabiting a fetus and again after leaving a body of any age. She believed there was a realm of knowledge and beauty and peace that existed around everyone, all the time, but that few people understood how to access it. She wasn't afraid to die.

It was the living in futility and helplessness that terrified her.

She would not do it.

She wrote that down.

THIRTY-SIX

It was raining Tuesday, leaving Meg feeling closed off and gloomy in the silent house. As the thunder rumbled, her mind pulled her backward into the past – maybe that was the way it always was when you knew your time was nearly up. She was thinking about what she'd been like at sixteen, about her life compared with Savannah's. Taking the journal with her, she went outside to a lounge chair under the back portico, sat down, and closed her eyes. There it was, the past, come to her with such compelling clarity that, though revisiting it might make new wounds, she couldn't resist.

The night of her birthday. Her party, her sweet sixteen, had been the usual simple family affair: a chocolate cake with white icing, and chocolate chips on top spelling out her name and age; a case of Orange Crush and no restrictions on how many she could drink; green plastic plates (her favorite color, because of Carson's eyes); homemade presents from her sisters wrapped up in old newspaper, stacked on the counter so there'd be room at the table for the whole family plus Carson and her friends Libby and Christine. She'd envied Libby's braces, so conscious, then, of her crooked eyetooth. There was no money for braces for her, of course, and she hadn't even asked. All she'd wanted that year was an album, the Police's *Synchronicity*. Carson bought it for her; her parents gave her cultured pearl earrings and a Jane Austen novel, *Persuasion*, which her mom had heard girls liked.

After the cake and presents and the playing of the album multiple times, her girlfriends left and she and Carson played Scrabble, Kara looking on and offering suggestions to both, which of course skewed the game. They gave it up and went outside into the sultry June evening, walking through damp pasture rife with croaking toads and the loud love songs of cicadas, to their usual spot. When she thought, now, of how much freedom she'd had with Carson, how her parents never followed her or asked where she went, what they did, she wondered how they could have been so uncon-cerned. She knew Savannah's every movement, could reach her by cell phone anytime; she couldn't imagine allowing such freedom – and with a boyfriend, no less! Her parents had put such faith in her . . . too much, it turned out, but she was trying not to blame them – they'd been as well intentioned as she.

That evening, her birthday, she'd felt so certain of her life, of her future with Carson. He was seventeen then, his body a man's body, sculpted by the hard, respectable work of farming. They'd taken everything off, there in the deep shadows of the wooded hillside, and explored each other's bodies with the unabashed joy of being young and together and free. She had tasted all of him, as he had her, and they'd talked in husky low voices about when they would make love for real. They wanted it to be special, believed *they* were special, that their love was rare and real. He had said, that evening, that they should plan on building their house on that very spot some day, so that they would always be a part of the lives their parents led, always close by and ready to help out.

She'd ruined everything by marrying Brian. She didn't see it that way at the time; she'd seen an essential good being done, believed that making such a sacrifice for the love of her family was an act that could not be wrong. That the outcome must, by virtue of the power of moral correctness, be positive for everyone involved. That Carson would recover and eventually find the woman truly meant for him. And maybe now he had. She wondered if he thought so – then she thought, of course he did. He was delighted with Val; why wouldn't he be?

Even so, the outcome hadn't been as good as she'd hoped for the people who were supposed to have benefited: the farm continued hemorrhaging money, Julianne got pregnant in high school, Beth was turned off from marriage and domestic life, and Kara – well, Kara was fine, Kara was happy, but she would've been regardless. She'd gotten the best of their parents' attributes, all the wheat and none of the chaff. And Meg got Brian, and this life of cool privilege. She also got Savannah – but she might have gotten her anyway. Seeing her and Carson together had not resolved a thing.

Carson, though . . . lucky for him, he was about to be married to a young, healthy, beautiful woman who clearly adored him. And his parents, they'd continued to do all right even with him away. Maybe she shouldn't feel guilty; she'd unknowingly protected him from what Brian was about to have to handle: a terminally ill wife whose pre-death care would be laborious and expensive, if she waited until after she was wheelchair-bound to end things; a spouse who would take her own life – though how she'd do it she didn't know. She knew very well what she *didn't* want; figuring out what she did want, however, was no simple thing.

In the journal, she wrote:

It's Tuesday, and raining. Should I take the rain as a sign? No softball practice for you this afternoon, no golf for Dad. I could make us a good family dinner, feed you well, then tell you both what's happening with me. I might do that, after we get back from seeing Grandpa Spencer. Or I might not. Right now I feel like a fugitive, keeping my truth hidden behind a façade of normal life – our life, where we are all so busy that none of us really sees what's true about the others around us.

She stopped to consider that last sentence. My, how the subconscious flows from the pen. What might she be missing about her husband or her daughter while peering so intently inward? What might she have missed all along? It was impossible to know, especially in Brian's case. She didn't bother to look too closely there, unwilling to raise in herself what would be the required reaction to, say, his having an affair.

She thought, too, of the secrets she'd been keeping over the years. Secrets from Brian about the question of Savannah's paternity, secrets from Savannah about how well she knew Carson, secrets from Carson and from her sisters about why she'd taken up with Brian – it was a muddy spiral of revisionist history, and it no longer sat well with her.

What to do about it? She had no idea.

For a long time she sat and watched the raindrops dimple the surface of the pool, stream off the potted palms; for all the gloom, she did love the smell of a rainy day, mist thickening the air with divine perfume. Her mother had liked to say that rain was the Virgin Mother weeping in joy and replenishing the Earth for all her children. Meg hadn't been as attached to her mother's sainted idol, hadn't ever been able to see such benevolence in the hardscrabble life they'd lived. Maybe if they'd gone to church as their mother had as a girl – but her father said church was more likely to ruin them. She wondered now if his real issue was in facing all those judgmental eyes, in having his girls scrutinized and pitied . . . She wrote:

> Be brave in your life, Savannah, but not foolish. Regrets are inevitable, and pile up like the stones of a cairn – but be careful not to let them rise so high that you can't see over the top.

Like a song whose words had been too quiet to decipher until now, she heard her own advice echoing in the pattering rain. Had she let her stones pile up too high? She saw the poor choices she'd made as boulders, her good intentions buried and gasping under the weight of unforeseen consequences. But maybe it wasn't too late to redeem herself, at least in part.

She went inside to get the phone.

THIRTY-SEVEN

It was a rare day when Carson wasn't with Val or Gene or any of his friends and also had no professional event on his immediate horizon. The promoter of his New Orleans concert had canceled the date at the last minute, citing reconstruction foul-ups; they'd try again for late summer. So he'd returned to Seattle and let Val go on to Bali without him; he could use the time to get his condo cleaned up before the movers came. In his experience, they'd pack everything in the place, even the garbage, if you didn't tell them otherwise.

He'd just poured himself a tall glass of Japanese beer when his phone rang. He glanced at the display but without his reading glasses he couldn't see who was calling.

'McKay here,' he answered.

A short silence, then, 'It's Meg. Is it raining there?'

'Meg who?' he asked, never imagining *his* Meg would ever call, let alone start such an exceptional event so casually.

'Powell. Hamilton. Powell-Hamilton.'

'*Meg?*'

'Yes. Have I called at a bad time?'

'No! I'm – no! And it *is* raining here. Why do you ask?'

'It's raining here,' she said. 'Has been all day. But it's warm and really sort of pleasant.'

She sounded so odd; was she drunk? He looked at the clock, an antique circle of distressed wood hung high up his painted brick wall, between twelve-foot-tall windows. Eleven-twenty-five, which meant three hours later in Florida. A bit early for her to be drinking. Him too, now that he thought of it, but he'd been up sorting and discarding since six.

'Not so warm here but not bad. I mean, I'm inside, so . . .'

'Your mother said I'd be lucky to find you home. You're hard to reach, she said.'

'Mom gave you my number, then.'

'I hope that was okay. I told her . . .' she sighed, 'I told her I needed to tell you something very important – and she relented, even though I refused to tell her what it was. Is. It's – well, you know, I probably should've thought about this a little more before I called. I'm sorry . . .'

He sat on a bar stool, baffled and intrigued by the calm yet eerie quality of her voice. 'Don't be. It's fine. I mean . . . I'm, well, I'm glad to hear from you.' He was, strangely.

'I don't know . . . I feel like I might be burdening you, when what I want is to *un*burden *me*. Well, and you, too. I *think* it's something you'll be glad to know . . .'

'Spit it out,' he said, and in saying it remembered hearing the same hesitancy the day they broke up, remembered telling her to just spit out whatever it was. So little had changed.

'If this were a movie, I'd make a dramatic pause here, then say, "Carson, I'm dying."'

'Good thing it's not a movie, then,' he said, taking a sip of beer.

'. . . Carson?'

At the sound of her voice, his whole body went cold.

'No one knows yet,' she went on. 'No one except the specialist I saw last week and my partner Manisha – I had to tell her because, well, I can't go back to work. But nobody else . . . just you.'

He stood and looked around the room as if searching for her; he needed to *see* her. This couldn't be real. The once-upon-a-time love of your life did not just call and say she was dying. It was unreal; it was crazy. Maybe that was it – maybe she was crazy.

'Just wait,' he said, looking out the window at Puget Sound but not seeing it. 'What do you mean, dying?'

'I know . . . I'm sorry. I mean, it's a rotten thing to drop on you, but I have to tell you because that way you'll understand why I'm saying what I'm about to say.'

'Dying how? Dying – dying when?' He couldn't seem to move past this single point.

'I don't know when – or how, for sure; that's a problem I'm still struggling with. It's ALS. Lou Gehrig's disease?'

'No.' He refused to believe her. 'Come on. Nobody

gets that anymore – they found a cure after all those Jerry Lewis telethon things.'

'Carson, that's for muscular dystrophy – a different disease, which, I should add, also has no cure. But that one's not always fatal, thank God.'

'Okay, well – wait, what do you mean, you're struggling with *how*?'

'That's . . . never mind, all right? I . . . I misspoke. The important thing is, I need to tell you something, explain something, just to . . . I suppose just so I can die knowing you that know the truth. About what happened – about why I married Brian.'

So. She wanted to unburden herself, confess that it had been all about what Hamilton could give her that he, Carson, couldn't – not then. She'd say something like she was sorry for rejecting him and if she'd known he had such high aspirations, she would've hung onto him – something lame like that. Well, he'd figured that out a long time ago. 'Yeah? Okay, I'm listening.'

'You sound angry.'

'Well, it's not such a mystery, is it?'

'You know already? How do you know? Nobody knew – I mean, I thought it was kept quiet.'

'It was obvious, Meg. He had money. I didn't.'

She didn't speak. Then, 'Oh. Well, okay, I can see how you'd come to that conclusion. And, well, if you boil it down to its simplest common denominator, as they say, I might even agree. But it isn't quite – that's not how I looked at it, at the time.'

And so she told him how it was. How it wasn't the

fact of Hamilton's wealth that drew her in, but what he'd proposed to do with some of it. She told how desperate things had gotten for her folks.

'Remember how there was talk of the bank foreclosing in late '87? It didn't seem to matter that I was helping with the bills – my parents, they were buried in debt, and, well, Brian knew it because Hamilton had the mortgage and it was paid late, or sometimes only in part, pretty much every month.

'I never told you, but he'd been pursuing me . . . and I always turned him down. This time, well, if I agreed to give him a shot, they'd forgive the late payments, and if I married him, they'd wipe the mortgage off the books. If not . . . well, it was pretty sure we'd lose the farm, at the very least. I couldn't just . . . I mean, I really thought . . . Oh, Carson,' she sighed, 'They were saying, how generous for me to even *think* about it, what a huge burden I'd be lifting from their shoulders – I mean, they never said to do it, but I knew how it was. And I made myself believe we'd get over it, you and me. You, especially. I figured you'd hate me and that would be it.'

'I did hate you,' he said.

He thought about what she was telling him, about how Hamilton was able to wipe out almost four hundred grand of debt for them. How could he blame her for considering it? Sure, it would be easy to take her to task for selling out, compromising her integrity – he could say she sold herself, and he wouldn't exactly be wrong. He wouldn't exactly be right, either.

He said, 'So let me get this straight: Hamilton waited until they were about to foreclose, then set you up as the savior? That dirty son of a bitch.'

'Car—'

'What? That *sucks*, Meg – what he did . . . Christ, you never even had a choice!'

'Look, I didn't call to get you pissed off at Brian; he's not a criminal . . . he just, well, he took advantage of an opportunity. If my parents had been keeping up with the payments, he wouldn't have had that leverage. So it isn't all his doing.'

'Hmmm,' Carson said, not willing to excuse Hamilton at all. He had to admit, though, that her parents did share the blame. Meg, however, bore the least responsibility. What wonderful relief to know that she hadn't rejected him. She hadn't been seduced by the money, she'd been a lamb led to slaughter.

'I hated you for about ten minutes,' he said, 'and then I was just a sorry mess for those eighteen months before you got married. It wasn't until after we . . . well, once you were married, I decided I needed to put a compass on my life and get on with things.'

'I wish I could've told you . . . It was unconscionable, Carson. Ridiculous. I can hardly believe that's what I did, that's what I chose – I should have looked for some other solution. I can only say how sorry I am to have put you through what I did. It . . . things . . .' She sighed again. 'It was a bad choice, I was wrong to make it, and I apologize from, from the bottom of my heart.' The last was almost a whisper.

'Ah, Meg . . .'

He was caught up in the past, in revising his assessment of what went on and why, all those years ago. Suppose she had refused Hamilton's offer and then gone on to marry *him* while her parents were drowning in debt, losing their business and their land? It never would've worked, that seemed pretty clear.

And then, like a buoy that had been pushed under by a wave, Meg's other news resurfaced in his brain. She was *dying*. Or was she?

'Hey – hold on. Wait. Is it – I mean, you aren't planning to *kill* yourself?' Maybe she wasn't ill at all, maybe only depressed and reaching out for help. Or if not help, just trying to make her peace before she did herself in.

She said, 'I really do have ALS. At best, I have a couple months before I'm bedridden ... It's ... it's not a pretty picture, Car ... And ... and ... I just can't see how I can put Savannah through—'

She was crying now, quietly, but he could hear it, hear the pain she was feeling on her daughter's behalf, the helplessness. He wanted desperately to be there, wherever she was. She hadn't even told Brian; she was just handling it, alone, the same way she'd managed everything when she was growing up. Spencer and Anna, they'd counted on their good, responsible, mature little Meggie to see that dinner was ready or the girls' homework was done right or the paddocks were closed off for the night. Counted on her to work at the bank, give them her earnings, and then to rescue them from their incompetence, from Spencer's willful irresponsibility.

But who had ever taken care of *her*? He'd wanted to, he'd tried to . . . Jesus, they'd been so *young*. He was there for her then, but it wasn't quite enough – he hadn't been able to keep the wolves at bay. He hadn't known how to even think about solving her folks' problems. Wasn't that their job? Still, he felt he'd failed her, too.

'Meg . . . hey, you're going to tell your sisters, right? Can they help, or . . .'

'I'll tell them. I'll tell everybody soon. I'm still just – Friday, before your concert? That's when I found out.'

He remembered how she'd looked, the brittleness of her – and what an ass he'd been, all snide about the Hamiltons and their social standing. She must think so little of him.

She went on, 'Listen, I'm sure we could talk about all this longer, but, well, I have to go. I'm picking Savannah up from school, so . . . But thanks for letting me get this off my chest. I – well, I always wanted to tell you, but at first I was kind of trapped – I couldn't risk Bruce reinstating the debt. And then later, when I could've paid it back myself, I figured, "*Carson hates me, so what's the point?*"' She laughed, a self-conscious sound. 'Dad did repay Bruce, by the way, when he sold the farm.'

'So Bruce called in the debt, huh?' This was the only conclusion that made sense – not that any of it did, not really.

'No – believe it or not, Dad just decided it was the right thing to do.' Her voice, still thick from her crying, softened a little.

So Spencer *volunteered* the money. Imagine that. He'd *undone* the deal – in a fit of long-overdue guilt, maybe. Nice for Hamilton to finally get his money back, and Spencer's conscience might be eased, but where did that leave Meg? Freed from chains she didn't bother to break because she believed that he, Carson, hated her . . .

But then, if that was the only reason, why didn't she leave Brian and live on her own?

For Savannah's sake, he supposed. Whatever her reasons, he couldn't blame her – staying with Brian was no more reprehensible than what *he'd* done, whoring around for a dozen years.

She went on, 'I have to run now. I'm glad we talked – and I'm glad I saw you and . . . and met Val. I wish all the best for you, Carson. For both of you.'

He wanted to say something equally kind, something hopeful, supportive, but before he thought of just what that would be, she hung up, without saying good-bye.

THIRTY-EIGHT

Savannah ran to her mom's car from the school's front overhang Tuesday after school, but she was still soaked when she climbed in. She shoved her book bag in back and reached up to twist her wet hair into a ponytail.

Her mom said, 'I have to stop by and see Grandpa, all right?'

'Not Grandpa's *again*. Drop me off first.' She'd promised Kyle she'd call at six.

'I would, but you know, I just don't want to have to drive in this mess any longer than absolutely necessary. We won't stay long, okay?'

She looked at her mom then, saw the bags under her eyes, her furrowed forehead. 'Is Grandpa okay?'

'As far as I know. Why?'

'You look sort of worried.'

They took their turn leaving the parking lot, the car splashing out into traffic, wipers at full speed. 'I'm tired,' her mom said. 'I didn't sleep well, and I had to review and finalize the report about that baby we lost last Sunday – it's very sad, you know?'

'How can you do it?' Savannah asked. 'I mean, babies that die when you deliver them – that must be horrible.'

'It is. I thought I'd give up obstetrics after the first time it happened. But what you learn is that *somebody* needs to be there for pregnant women – you can't just quit because you've failed or nature is working against you. I can't imagine a more satisfying career than the one I had.'

'"Have," you mean.'

'That's what I said.'

'No, you said "had".'

'I didn't.'

'Yes, you did; I heard you.'

'Maybe your iPod has messed up your hearing.'

'Whatever.'

They each took an umbrella for the walk to Grandpa's building, but the umbrellas did nothing to keep their feet dry. Savannah, in her red flip-flops, splashed right on through the puddles, but her mom went slowly in the new leather loafers she'd worn Friday, still favoring her right foot a little. From the entrance door, Savannah watched her walk and said, 'If those shoes hurt so much, why are you wearing them again?'

Her mom shook out her umbrella. 'They don't – oh.' She looked up and smiled, said, 'I, um, I forgot. How stupid, huh?'

Savannah wasn't buying it. 'Come on,' she said.

'What?' her mom asked, sounding innocent but looking guilty. 'All right,' she conceded. 'All right. I haven't even told your dad this yet, but I may as well tell you now: I have some kind of nerve trouble going on – I aggravated something during a difficult delivery, and . . . well, I'm seeing a specialist about it, but, you know, it's making my arm and leg . . . making them spasm, sort of. Weakness. It's—'

'Oh,' Savannah said, sobered. 'Well, that sucks. I mean, so do you have to have surgery, or—?'

'No, no. Physical therapy might help, and I have to go on leave from work for a while.'

'Why haven't you told Dad?'

'Oh, you know how he is. Busy,' she said.

Judgmental, Savannah thought, nodding. 'Okay. So, you know, just tell me if you need help or whatever.'

'Thanks, sweetheart. I will.'

The door opened then. 'Hello, my girls! I thought I heard voices out here. I'm just back from seeing my doctor friend Clifford Aimes – who's got nothing but bad news, nothing but bad news.' He ushered them inside and continued, 'There's those frappacinos you like so much in the fridge, Vannah – help yourself.'

She did, expecting her mom to interfere, or at least caution her about spoiling her appetite, but there was no comment about the drink.

Her mom said, 'What bad news?'

'Well, Meggie, your mother's laughing at me from heaven right now, I just know it – Aimes says it's two huge kidney stones causing my pain; and your mother, she kept saying I needed to go have it checked . . . 'course I was too busy to take her advice.' He sighed as he took a wineglass down from a suspended rack and a bottle from the countertop.

Savannah stood by while her mom sat down at the dining table and asked, 'So what do they want to do?'

'A little surgery – it's got a queer name; I wrote it down someplace . . .' He searched his shirt pocket, then his pants, finally pulling a scrap of paper from his back pocket. 'Percutaneous nephrolithotomy. How many letters is that, d'you suppose?' He paused to count. 'Twenty-seven – longer than the goddamn alphabet! Leave it to the medical profession to make every damn thing overcomplicated. Anyway, I'll be back on my feet in two days. 'Course I'll need you to pick up my mail, water the plants, bring me a shot or two of that Scotch whisky I like.'

'Maybe. Dad, you are going to have to be hypervigilant about your health from now on. You can't just let things go until they reach a crisis point. Your diabetes complicates everything.'

'That's what I got *you* for,' he said, moving past the dining table to the living room to his recliner, the same one he'd used for Savannah's whole life, or for as long as she could recall, anyway. Her grandma's favorite chair sat nearby, on the other side of the end table. She didn't like seeing it empty; it was so . . . forlorn.

Her mom was shaking her head. 'No, you can't count on me to watch out for you – you're going to have to be a grown-up and either manage things independently or let the staff here help. You just can't – I mean, it's *your* job, don't you think?'

'My, you're cranky today! Is it that husband of yours, or has the weather got you down? They say the rain's not going to quit till the weekend. Guess that'll mess up softball, eh, Vannah?'

'I guess,' she said, wondering why her mom didn't explain about her nerve problem. She went and sat in her grandma's chair, pulling a bit of hair from her ponytail, to braid. 'I don't mind the rain, though. I'm pretty tired of playing softball anyway.' Now that she had Kyle, she didn't have time for ball. Everything in her old life seemed pointless; she wanted to move on, *do* something with her life besides regurgitate facts for exams and waste hours on a ball diamond with a bunch of overprivileged teenagers. She wanted to help Kyle get back on his feet, maybe back into school.

To that end, she'd cut class yesterday afternoon, gone to the bank, and wired him five hundred dollars from her savings. He'd asked her to send it to him through his brother's bank in Miami, just to be sure it didn't get lost while he was away from home. He called as soon as he got it and said, 'Babe, you are like truly incredible. This means *so* much. I will love you forever!'

Love! Forever! 'Not for your money,' he'd added. 'It's, like, your generous spirit. Beautiful.'

She pulled her mind back to the present, to catch the details on her grandpa's surgery. He'd scheduled it for two days from now, on Thursday.

'Why don't you call the girls, let 'em know I'll be laid up?' he said as he took a prescription bottle from the end table.

'What's in there?' her mom asked.

'Something for pain.'

'When did you last take one?' She got up and went over to him.

'I haven't taken any just yet.'

Her mom took the bottle, read the label, and poured the pills into her hand. She counted them, then poured them back. 'Okay, now you have to choose: the wine or the pills.'

He grabbed the pills. 'Oh come on, you sound like a goddamn doctor!'

Taking the wineglass, her mom went toward the kitchen, her limp more apparent than it had been earlier. 'I wonder why that is? Now I mean it – no alcohol with the pain pills. And write down the time you take them so you don't forget.'

'What's with the leg?' he asked.

'Never mind – did you hear what I said?'

'I heard, I heard. Bring me some water, then, for chrissake, so I can take one of these horse pills.'

Savannah jumped up. 'I'll get it.' She wanted to save her mom from having to limp back and forth.

'Thanks, honey. Okay, Dad, listen, I'll call you later. Stay out of trouble, all right? Because I'm done for the day.'

He got up, hand to his left side, and said, 'Grab that box there on the counter, Meggie. That's pictures of you girls when you were small. It's a hodgepodge; found 'em in the old hall closet. No idea why she stuck 'em there.'

Savannah watched her mom peer into the box. 'She must've meant to organize them sometime.'

'I s'pect. Oh, hold on – I got something else for you to take.' He went into his bedroom and came back out with a white plastic shopping bag, which he gave to Savannah.

'What's this?' she asked.

'Coupla romance novels, some socks.'

'Oh, okay, well, thanks.'

He followed them to the door as they left, saying, 'Don't say I never gave you nothin'.'

Savannah smiled. He wasn't so bad. Kind of funny, in fact. She hadn't much noticed before, when her grandma was still alive. And it was nice of him to buy the drinks she liked, that her grandma had always kept around just for her. Especially the heavily caffeinated ones; she'd been up so late talking to Kyle these past couple nights that she needed the energy boost. Caffeine had gotten her through last Sunday evening too, after her dad woke her from her nap and reminded her to get her homework done.

Outside, the rain had eased up, so her mom let her drive them home. They rode in silence; she figured her mom was preoccupied with her grandpa's surgery and all that nerve-damage stuff, or whatever it was. Hopefully that would heal fast. Didn't it figure, though, that just when her mom was going to have some extra time to maybe *do* something with her, she, Savannah, wanted anything *but* that? Now that she had Kyle, she had everything she needed.

How *good* it felt to be fully appreciated by someone. To be loved for *who she was*, not just because of blood ties or obligations. She smiled to herself and thought, *I could get used to this.*

PART III

Everyone should carefully observe which way his heart draws him, and then choose that way with all his strength.

— Hasidic saying

THIRTY-NINE

Meg intended to tell Brian about her diagnosis Tuesday night while Savannah was at her music lesson, but spent most of the time on the phone with her sisters instead, giving all the details on their father's condition.

'The stones aren't anything serious,' she told Beth. 'They'll do laser surgery, and he'll be out in a couple of days.'

Beth sighed. 'That's a relief. I think I'll come out anyway – we can have some girl time. I need a change of scenery after the semester I just had.'

It was just what Meg hoped she'd say. She wanted to see her sisters – all of them, if possible, without telling them up front about her condition. She wanted to socialize, for at least a little while, without the suffocating blanket of their pity.

When Julianne heard Beth was coming, she felt like she should come too. But she and Chad were strapped for money, she said. 'Even with bereavement airfares, we spent a fortune coming for Mom's funeral. He'll never let me spend the money.'

'I'll buy your ticket,' Meg offered. 'And Kara's too. And Beth's.' To be fair. 'Think of it as a mini vacation from the kids.'

'And from Chad!' Julianne said. 'This new job of his keeps him home way too much.'

After talking to Julianne, Meg reached Kara, who was glad to come to see them all and glad to accept Meg's offer to pay. 'Thanks, sis. That'll make it harder for Todd to complain about me going! And I can look at real estate while I'm there,' she said. 'I saw an ad in Sunday's paper I want to check out – just for future reference.'

Then Meg called Beth back and said she wanted to pay her way, as long as she was paying for the others. Beth said, 'Thanks, but you know, you don't still have to do everything for us.'

No, Meg thought, but it was nice to do something that mattered, one last time.

By the time she'd finished booking the tickets and e-mailing itineraries, and then confirming it all with yet another phone call to each sister, Brian was gone to pick up Savannah. So she waited until later, when he came to bed, intending to talk to him there. But the long day caught up with her and she fell asleep, waiting for him to brush his teeth.

The next morning, Meg stopped at the bathroom door while Brian was shaving to tell him they needed to talk. If she didn't do it now, she didn't know when she'd get another chance: Beth was due in at the airport at five, Kara at six, and Julianne at eight-fifteen.

She watched him in the mirror. He used a tradi-tional razor and shaving cream, pulling the razor from the top of his cheek to his jaw in practiced confidence, even with one eye on the small plasma TV he'd had installed last year. Good thing *she* didn't have to shave (let alone follow the stock reports while she did it); with her hand like it was now, her face would end up a mess of bloody nicks.

She said, 'Can you stick around a little while after Savannah leaves?'

'What for?' Brian asked, moving the razor past his jaw and under his chin.

She looked over at the shower. She'd had to use her left hand to turn it on this morning, which had depressed her at first, then angered her. *Everything* was getting to be a chore. 'I have something to tell you.'

'Can't you tell me now?' he said, not at all attuned to the tremor in her voice.

'No,' she said, then left the room so that he couldn't debate it with her.

Savannah was mixing sugar and cream into a travel mug of coffee, her iPod blasting already, at 6:45. How did she do that? Meg liked quiet in the mornings; she drove to the hospital with the car radio off, and took as much time in the lounge as she could before launching into her rounds. She never minded, though, the wails of the newborns that sometimes met her when she entered the birth center floor. Those cries welcomed her, made her feel alive and purposeful.

Well, there would be no more of that.

She was dressed as if for work, as she had been every day she hadn't gone in. Brian had no idea she didn't send him off and leave the house right after, as was their routine. Some of her colleagues did afternoon rounds, and she'd considered, briefly, staying in her pajamas these past mornings with a ready lie about switching her schedule, starting her day with office hours at 8:30. That idea was trashed quickly, along with other possible lies – about why she was still limping, for example, and why she needed the sling she meant to buy for her arm, to disguise her hand's impending uselessness. There was no telling when, or if, the slide of decline would slow; lying was pointless. She owed both Brian and Savannah the truth.

Brian first. By rights, he should've known before *anyone* – before she even went to her appointment with Brianna. She should have told him her fears and her plans. Instead, she had left him out of the loop, let him go off to Boston Friday morning thinking she was still irritated about the money business despite his Lexus apology. She hadn't called him Friday after seeing Bolin. Or Saturday, from deep in South Florida. That she had picked up the phone and dumped her news on Carson before telling her own husband was wrong, she supposed, but the truth was, she found it hard to dredge up very much concern.

Outside, a car horn sounded. She tapped Savannah on the shoulder, took one earbud from her ear. 'Angela's here. Don't forget, your aunts will all be here tonight – don't make other plans.'

'I *know*.' Savannah grabbed a bagel from the bread-box, popped a top on her mug, slung her book bag over one shoulder, and hurried out the front door.

Talk about cranky . . . Savannah looked more tired than usual. Had she been up late studying? What had become of the biology project? With all the commotion in her own life, she'd been paying little attention to Savannah's everyday stuff. Exams were coming up, and Savannah's birthday party – oh Christ, she couldn't lay her bad news on Savannah before her birthday . . .

Brian came to the kitchen dressed in his light gray suit, a patterned red silk tie gleaming against his white shirt – the Sonny Crockett days were long gone. He went to pour himself a little more coffee and said, 'It's about Spencer, right? The money?' Looking at her intently, he said, 'Listen, Meg, the thing is – I went out after our argument and got drunk, figuring that it was all over for us. These few weeks since Spencer paid Dad back, I've just been waiting for you to find out and tell me it's over, that you want a divorce.'

That was why he didn't tell her? 'You're joking,' she said.

He shook his head. 'I swear. When it seemed like maybe Spencer wasn't saying anything, I should have told you, but . . .'

'Yes, you should have!'

'I'm sorry.' He looked contrite, though she couldn't help but wonder how deep it went. Brian, for all his surface charm, kept his truest feelings out of sight, even from her.

He added, 'I just . . . look at you: successful, attractive – hell, you practice medicine *and* run our household like the best manager I've got – so I kept thinking, why do you need me? Spencer made it clear that *he* thinks you should be eager to bail—'

'That's not it, Brian. If it was about the money, I could've left a long time ago.'

'So then you weren't going to ask for a divorce?' His voice wavered and she knew he'd been scared.

'No,' she said, sympathy welling in her chest because what he'd feared was nothing compared to what she had to say.

Brian turned and leaned against the counter, more relaxed now, confident, the very image of the high-powered businessman. He looked impermeable. It was good to know that he wasn't, but it made her sad for him, too. He didn't know what to do with real-life troubles. When had anything ever gone wrong for him? He'd been protected, catered to, deferred to, coddled his entire life – by his parents, by his employees, and yes, even by her.

She flexed her hand and said, 'No, the thing is, well, I've been having some trouble lately—'

'What, with the practice?'

'No, not that. That's fine. That is, it *was* fine . . . I don't know if it will *stay* fine . . .' She was hedging.

'Why? Is Manisha leaving?'

'No . . . I am.'

'Okay! That's what I like to hear. Onward and upward.' He turned and set his coffee mug in the sink, as he always did; when he needed it again it would be waiting in the cupboard, as it always was. This was how Brian's life worked. She hated that she was about to disrupt it – calculating as he sometimes was, he didn't deserve the burden of her shitty luck.

She looked at him, at his face in this last moment of innocence, and said, 'It's not what you think. I have a disease called ALS. It's fatal.'

He blinked and stepped back as if someone had pushed him. 'Come again?'

'You'll know it as Lou Gehrig's disease,' she said.

'*Meg . . .*' he said, hands raised as if in supplication, as if saying, *How could you let this happen?*

'I know.' She shrugged, feeling as if she was a lousy actor reciting her lines. They'd feel truer if she sang them in operatic alto, soprano, perhaps; then the music would fit the tragedy playing out in their life.

He said, 'Lou Gehrig's? I don't remember . . . What . . . what does this mean exactly?'

What *did* it mean, *exactly*? She still didn't know. She stuck to the script. 'It's a debilitating neuromuscular disease. I was diagnosed Friday by a specialist in Orlando – I didn't have meetings, I had tests.'

Brian rubbed his face with both hands, then dropped his hands at his sides. 'Jesus, Meg . . . Are you sure? I mean, you look *fine*.' He squinted at her as if the signs must be present but were just out of focus for him.

She felt herself shrinking, guilty for hiding things so well. In her doctor voice, she said, 'I know, but already my right arm's hardly functional, the hand is weak. I'm having trouble with my leg. It's just a matter of time before you'll hear it when I speak. How much time? *That*, I can't tell you. Right now seems to be what's called an acceleration period; things are ... they're going downhill pretty fast right now. An accurate prognosis is difficult – every case is a little different.'

She was tired of hearing the words as she spoke them, the same ones she'd read and heard and told too many times already. The thought of saying them again to her sisters, and again to her father, and again to her daughter – God, it exhausted her, the burden of just *thinking* about repeating this litany.

Brian studied the polished tips of his black oxfords. She felt sorry for him; ever after he would be associated with her story. People would whisper it to one another at parties and picnics, *He's the one whose wife, the doctor, had Lou Gehrig's.* Worse, he would have to figure out how to manage all the details of his life and Savannah's – though her guess was that he would shift that duty to his mother, who would probably be delighted to have him depending on her again.

He looked up and shook his head. 'I don't know what to say.'

'We'll talk more later, all right? Go to work, try not to dwell. I know, it's impossible, but *try*. I'll tell my sisters . . . before they leave. Not tonight, okay? So don't bring it up. But once we know Dad's through the surgery fine, then I'll tell them.'

'Savannah?'

'I told her I have a nerve problem. She can't know it's incurable. Not yet. I just ... I need to get her through her birthday at least.'

'What about treatment? They must have something.'

'Nope,' she said, and he flinched a little.

'Are you going to have to be in the hospital, or . . . ?'

'No.' She shook her head. 'Most people handle it with home care, and hospice.' She thought of Lana Mathews, all but motionless. Waiting.

'I know you can't say exactly, but . . . how long do you think?' He wouldn't look at her.

She went to him, took his chilled hands in hers. 'No idea,' she said. 'But probably not more than a few months.' The knot of his tie was slightly crooked; she left it.

'I don't believe this.'

'Go to work,' she said, releasing him. 'Nothing's going to happen today.'

After Brian left, Meg made a pot of tea and took it to the den. She opened the windows to let in the moist morning air, bring the outside in to her, then began calling her patients to inform them personally that, due to health reasons, she was referring them to other physicians. She left messages for most, spoke to a few without divulging details, and in about an hour had reached everyone whose records were active. Others would learn of the changes the next time they called for appointments. After the last call, she hung up the phone and said, 'Well, okay. That's done.'

How surprising it was to feel so little about this particular ending, to be able to let go of Allison Ramsey and Candace Banner and Jill Jabronski, for example, without feeling traumatized. She cared for these pregnant women, for all her patients, and yet, when it came down to determining priorities, cutting the string was astonishingly easy.

She took up her journal and wrote:

May 3, 2006

Let me tell you a little something about dying in middle age. First, I feel cheated for one main reason: because I owe you more than I've given you so far. Not the material things – my time. I owe you more time, and it makes me sick when I look back and think of all the days I worked late when I could've been home with you watching the Discovery channel or hearing you practice a new song. The weekends when I delivered babies instead of baking your favorite pumpkin-raisin cookies or riding with you at Grandma and Grandpa's. I always imagined we'd have more time when you were older, done with school. I'd cut back my practice and we'd travel together. Or maybe you'd join the Peace Corps and I'd come visit you at your posts, donate some of my skills too. You'd entertain us all by playing songs and singing; everyone would sing along; we'd teach the local children the words, leave them with something that could endure famine or disease or heartache.

If only I had a song for you.

FORTY

Although Meg had to work hard to hide the evidence of her illness for now, Wednesday night felt better to her than old times. She and all three of her sisters sat together on the patio, drinking wine and laughing about the trials of motherhood. Beth couldn't relate fully, but she had her own tales to tell, of college students and their transparent attempts to lie their way out of assignments or low test grades. 'They think I was never nineteen and that I don't understand the Internet and all the electronic gadgets. Do I look that ancient?'

'At thirty?' Kara laughed. 'You're just a baby yourself! The ink on your last diploma is hardly dry!'

'I do have tiny lines around my eyes – see?' She leaned forward, but Meg, sitting at her left, saw only smooth skin. No lines, and no freckles either; Beth looked more like their mother, like the Jansens, creamy-skinned Southerners whose way-back ancestors were Scandinavian. Her hair was dark like Savannah's, but straight, and cut in an engaging chin-length bob that made her brown eyes stand out.

'I don't see any lines,' Meg said. 'It's all those letters after your name that make you seem so different from your students – *Doctor* Powell.'

'Perhaps, *Doctor* Hamilton.' Beth laughed. 'If only *my* letters meant I could do some good, like you. I feel like all I do is grade bad essays and sit through excruciatingly long faculty arguments – I mean, meetings.'

'Can you spell that?' Kara teased.

'What, *meetings*?' Beth asked.

'*Excruciatingly*.'

'*I* can't even say it,' Julianne said. 'Is it a real word?'

Kara said, 'And I thought *my* vocabulary was limited.' She poked Julianne, who sat at her left. 'If you'd finished school, you might know the big words.'

Julianne tossed her long hair, red-gold like Meg's, and said, 'I got my diploma. Anyway, what difference? I'm raising children, not correcting essays.'

Kara, the only one of them who'd gotten the full red of their father's hair, held up her hand, four fingers extended. 'Can you count? This is how many kids I have, but I don't use that as an excuse for being uneducated. Pick up a book once in a while, why don't you?'

'If you weren't sitting around reading so much, maybe you'd be a size six like me,' Julianne said, grinning her Cheshire Cat grin. She'd always deviled Kara, who didn't have Meg's oldest-sister authority and wasn't close enough to her in age to be a pal.

'Marilyn Monroe was my size,' Kara said. She stuck out her tongue.

'Now, children,' Meg said, interceding as she'd always done. 'Play nicely. Jules, grab that box, behind you there.

Dad gave me some old photos of us. I thought you guys might want to divide them up.'

'You've already taken out the ones you want?' Beth asked, and Meg realized she'd nearly slipped up, dropped a clue about her illness before she was ready to tell them.

'Right, I did. Only a few, though, of just me.'

Julianne opened the box and pulled out a messy stack of photographs, various sizes, some with thick paper backing, some with rounded corners, most of them cloudy or faded or creased. 'Is there any system to these?'

'No,' Meg said. 'Apparently Mom just stuffed them in.'

The women all leaned in and began sorting through the photos.

Beth held one up to Meg. 'How about this? You and Carson . . .' – she read the date on the back – 'in '84.'

'His high school graduation,' Meg said, taking it with her left hand. Her right thumb, she found, was twitching and wouldn't quit; she pressed it under her leg to keep her sisters from noticing. 'They had that big picnic out by their lake.'

'I remember that,' Kara said, looking over Meg's shoulder. 'Look at your hair! Definitely an '80s 'do.'

Meg remembered the effort she'd put into getting her straight hair to stay in the upswept, ratted style. 'It took a whole can of hair spray for just the bangs.'

'Yeah, and then you ruined it by swimming.'

Beth said, 'Carson looks so pleased with himself.'

'We'd just finished getting him moved into that shed

we redid.' His smile was in anticipation of their plans for later that night: she would sneak out of her house and join him in his new place, to make love for the first time. She was smiling in the photo too, though with less obvious anticipation – because her mother was taking the picture and she didn't want to look overeager. Carson had an excuse, it being his graduation day.

Beth leaned back. 'So what happened with you two anyway? You seemed like such a sure thing, and then it was just *over*. I felt like he'd moved away or died or something. I never saw him anymore. It was weird.'

'You know what happened,' Julianne said. 'She dumped him for Brian.'

'Obviously,' Beth said. 'But I'm asking why. Until then, Carson was like part of the family. I don't remember you guys fighting or anything.'

Meg put the photo down. She *could* tell them the truth, now that none of it mattered, but why bother? She didn't want them feeling responsible in any way, or guilty. She didn't want them to think less of their parents. Always the protective oldest child – that wasn't going to change.

'We didn't fight,' she said. 'We just … went in different directions.'

'Because he wanted to be a musician,' Julianne offered, 'and you wanted to stick close to home and be a doctor. Right?'

'Something like that,' Meg said, drawing sharp looks from Kara and Beth. Kara would remember that neither her career choice nor Carson's would come until later.

Beth just seemed able to smell a lie. Her sisters didn't call her out on it, though, and she was grateful. There was no other lie should could tell with more conviction. For Beth's sake, she added, 'Brian had a lot to offer, and back then I thought that made a difference.'

'Money,' Beth said, shaking her head. 'Sometimes you're better off without it.'

'How can you say that?' Julianne protested. 'Look around! Wouldn't you love to live like this?' Her place in Quebec was a late-sixties split-level with only one bathroom.

Beth shrugged. 'Only if it came incidentally. I'd rather be happy.'

'Oh, happy,' Julianne said. 'Which is why you're still single. You ideals are too high. Nobody stays truly happy.'

Kara said, 'Not so! I'm happy – Todd too. Wouldn't change a thing about our life – except to move back here.'

'*You* married for love,' Beth said. 'You're the only one who did it right. So far.'

'Are you saying I don't love Chad?' Julianne protested, fickle as she'd always been. She hated to be wrong, hated to lose ground to any of them.

Beth smirked. 'You married him because you were knocked up. You knew him for what? Three months before the wedding?'

'Four,' Julianne corrected.

Meg pulled out another photo, one of the four of them all lined up and dressed for Easter in flouncy dresses and tights and white patent-leather shoes.

Julianne was hardly old enough to stand up on her own. 'Here,' Meg said, passing the photo to Beth in an effort to get them all onto a new tack. 'Remember this? Grandma Alice was still alive; she came down and took us shopping for these outfits and made us go to church.'

Beth gave her a look that said she knew exactly what Meg was doing, then looked at the photo. 'No, I don't remember this at all. Look at us, so clean and pretty – an alternate reality. Nice if that could've been real, huh?'

Meg nodded. She understood the appeal of an alternate reality all too well.

FORTY-ONE

Thursday night, after being at the hospital with their father most of the day, Meg and her sisters sat out on the patio again, drinking wine and telling stories as they'd done the night before. It was as if their combined memories, the energy of them together in one place, created a time machine. One moment they were giving Julianne, at a year old, her first riding lesson on their crabby Shetland, Guinevere. Another moment they were riding the spinning Mad Hatter ride at Disney World, screaming when Kara threw up her blue cotton candy. All anyone had to do was say, 'Remember when . . .' and off they'd go. Meg soaked up the cameraderie and marveled at how their memories didn't always match. Beth, for instance, couldn't recall them ever owning a mare named Bride, while Kara not only recalled the mare but could remember in vivid detail watching their mother pick splinters out of Meg's back and painting the whole raw site with iodine.

Brian came out to the patio to say he was taking

Savannah and Rachel for ice cream – the plan they'd arranged, so Meg would be alone with her sisters. Meg poured more wine then, and when they were all relaxed – for what better time was there? – she edged into the subject of her illness by asking if any of them thought they might be coming to Florida to live anytime soon. Writing to Savannah in the journal was helping to lessen her anxieties about how Savannah would manage – not to mention helping her feel like she had more control over things in general – but ideally, one of her sisters would be able to move back and help look out for both Savannah and their father.

Meg knew already that Kara wanted to return, but in the way she'd always done when they were girls, she set up the question so as not to exclude anyone's possibly secret or remote interest in moving. Then there would be no protests of 'Why did you just assume only *Kara* wanted to move? I've been thinking of it for ages.' Julianne in particular always insisted on a level playing field, forever needing to be considered equal to the rest of them.

Kara spoke up first, saying that Todd was agreeable to the move, but it wouldn't be before he had his twenty years in – three more to go. That led to a discussion of how disruptive it might be to move Keiffer and Evan from the high school they'd be in, and Kara's reluctant conclusion that they might have to wait until all the boys were graduated, to be fair. Julianne, though her kids were younger, was in a similar predicament – not that Chad had any interest in moving to the States. Beth's answer was the one that surprised her:

Beth said she was looking for a change after a dozen years of California living.

'I'm tired of fog.' Beth laughed. 'Besides, one of us should give Meg a hand with Dad. I can find work just about anywhere . . . and I miss Florida, and who knows how long Dad'll be around?'

That was the segue Meg needed. She said, 'Right. Life is so unpredictable. His health – or any of ours – could decline without much warning. Take me, for instance,' she said, and then spit out the bitter words once again: *ALS. Fatal. Unpredictable. Paralysis. Life support.*

They were dumbstruck.

She held her breath, watching her sisters' shocked faces while they tried to make sense of what she'd just said. Then Julianne began to wail, breaking the tension in her characteristic melodramatic way.

Kara vowed to move to Florida immediately with or without Todd, and Beth came and wrapped her arms around Meg. For the first time since Lowenstein had released the ALS worm into her mind, she gave herself over to grief. She put her head against Beth's shoulder and cried.

After they'd all wiped their eyes and noses, Beth asked what she meant to do with the time she had left; leave it to Beth to be straightforward.

'Clean out my office,' Meg said, 'see my lawyer – get things in order, I guess.'

Kara frowned and shook her head. 'No, come on – what are you going to *do*? Like, "I've always wanted to . . ." you know, fill in the blank: See Niagara Falls. Skydive. Sleep with Antonio Banderas. Like that.'

Meg looked at them, their expectant faces, without knowing how to answer. She'd done so much in her life, been so many places, shared so many joys. There was little she lacked. Finally she said, 'I'm going to talk with my daughter, every day.' Her only other wish was beyond her reach.

She repeated the scene in miniature with her father Friday morning while her sisters waited outside his room, ready to offer post-announcement support. He stared at her, then coughed in a futile effort to keep back tears. 'Don't waste any time, Meggie,' he said.

Too late. She bit her lip hard to keep the words back. 'That's good advice, Dad, thanks,' she managed.

She left the room recalling a placard posted in the coffee shop near her practice. She'd read it many times – a Shakespeare quote, and didn't he have the wisdom of the ages? 'I wasted time, and now doth time waste me.'

FORTY-TWO

For the first time since meeting Val, Carson wasn't glad to hear her voice on the phone. She called at lunchtime Friday, when the three movers were lounging with him in his kitchen, eating pizza he'd ordered. He went out onto the broad balcony to talk, stepping into hazy sunshine that made him squint. The sound gleamed more blue than gray, and was dotted with boats helmed by people reveling in the Seattle springtime – something he too would like to be doing, but his enthusiasm for spring, for Val, for moving to Malibu was as boxed away as his belongings.

'It's all over,' Val said, and Carson forgot for a split second that she would mean the Bali surfing competition. 'I edged her out! You should *see* the water – I didn't know if I could hang on, but I did!'

He forced himself to sound more enthused than he felt. 'Hey, that's great, congratulations!'

'Yeah, thanks. Wish you were here ... Oh, hell! I gotta go for now – I told this guy from ESPN I'd give him three minutes before the awards, and he's coming

337

this way. How's the packing going? And here comes the ABC chick – sorry for the rush! Call ya later!'

Later. Later would have to be better; she wouldn't be quite so wound up. Would he be more in the mood to talk to her even then? Everything in his world was dimmed by Meg's bad news, and the longer he lived with it, the worse he felt.

What must she be going through? Had she told Hamilton? He'd spent some time on the Internet, reading about ALS – and just thinking about it horrified him. She'd sounded so calm ... Too calm. Too accepting. Why didn't she fight it? He needed to talk to her again, encourage her to *do* something. She was a doctor, for God's sake – she'd have to know of something more than what he'd been able to unearth. Some experimental cure, or if not a cure, something that could bring a remission. Losing her to Hamilton had been bad, but that paled next to the black hole he saw opening in his life if he were to lose her to *this*. He had to see her.

He stepped back inside. 'Listen, guys,' he said to the movers, 'something's come up. I need you to take the rest of the day off.'

They looked at each other, seemed to shrug as one unit, and then Ernesto, the lead, said, 'You're gonna need to reschedule with the office, for us to finish. We got stuff lined up all next week.'

'Yeah, okay,' Carson said, boxing up the remaining pizza for them to take. From his fridge he took the last four beers and handed them over, hurrying the guys out. 'Don't drink and drive, now.'

As soon as they'd gone, he moved some boxes aside and sat down on his sofa, rubbing his mouth with one hand. He had no choice – he called his real estate agent and told her to delay the closing, even if it meant the buyers decided to take their offer off the table. 'Tell them I had a family emergency.'

That wasn't exactly a lie – Meg was like a distant . . . sister? *Oh, right*, he thought, *a sister*. She was more than a distant relative of any kind, certainly more than a sister, but what she was to him was not as easy to name as what she was not. She was not his girlfriend, fiancée, wife. She was not even his friend anymore. He thought of *soul mate* but shied away from the cliché – then thought about it further: his soul's mate . . . Was there such a thing? He wasn't sure. His *heart's* mate, though, he was sure she was that. Which didn't mean he didn't love Val. The feelings were completely different. Meg owned a piece of him Val would never see or reach or even comprehend. He should have fought for Meg, should have pushed through the pain of his wounded pride and showed her how wrong she was . . . Ah, the genius of hindsight.

He called his travel agent. When a seat on an evening flight was arranged, he called his parents. His mom answered.

'Hey, Ma, you know how when I left the other day you said you wished you could see more of me? I apologize for the short notice and all, but if one of you can stand staying up a little late tonight, I'll join you for a nightcap.'

Silence. Then, 'Carson, does this have anything to

339

do with Meg? Because if it does, let me remind you how conveniently she left you for Brian Hamilton when he was the one with all the money.'

'It's not like that, Ma.'

'Oh no? Wasn't she calling to tell you she's getting divorced?'

He closed his eyes. If only. He repeated what Meg had told him, then said, 'I don't know what I can do for her, if anything. I just . . . I just need to be there.'

He waited while his mom processed the news. She said, 'Okay, I can understand that. What about Val? Does she know?'

'I'll talk to her tomorrow. This . . . it doesn't have to be a problem. She's very understanding. We can keep things on schedule.'

'Oh, honey,' she said. 'I'm so sorry about Meg. How awful for all of them . . . Just give us a call after you land, so we'll know about when to expect you.'

'Thanks, Mom,' he said, relieved to have her support. And then he decided. 'You know, it's gonna be late – I don't want to disturb you guys. I can bunk in the shed.'

'Honey . . . I understand how you're feeling, but you haven't slept there in forever; I'm not sure the AC unit even works anymore. Use the guest room like always. If it makes you feel better, we won't wait up.'

'I . . . I'll feel better if I stay in the shed. If that's okay.'

'You know we'll just be glad to have you here,' she said.

FORTY-THREE

On Friday in the school's small cafeteria, Savannah sat with her usual lunchmates: Rachel and Miriam, a slight, stunning girl whose father once played baseball for the Minnesota Twins. Talk was of whether they should go downtown to the Cinco de Mayo festival later, but Savannah's mind refused to stay engaged. She kept drifting to the things Kyle said to her the night before, when she'd again lain in her bed talking to him late into the night. Sweet, intimate promises of what they'd do when he got back in town tonight.

With Kyle so much on her mind all week, she'd scored 72 on her trigonometry exam and 81 on her world history quiz, and fallen asleep during the movie they'd watched in art yesterday afternoon – but she was keeping it together. Only Aunt Beth seemed to notice she was making herself scarce at home; last night after she and her dad had gotten back from Dairy Queen, Beth had come up to her room and sat on the bed for a minute. 'You're like a mouse in a houseful of cats,' Beth said, smiling. 'It's a boy, right?'

Savannah was glad to admit she was seeing someone. She said, 'Mom doesn't know, though – the nerve thing has made her really distracted and all, so, you know, I didn't tell her.' Beth's face clouded at this. It *was* a lame excuse . . .

Beth said, 'She does have a lot on her mind – but I think she'd be glad to hear your news.'

'It's no big deal,' Savannah said. 'You can tell her if you want.'

But Beth said no, she'd leave that to her. 'Don't be afraid to share stuff with your mom; you're at the top of her list, you know.'

Savannah thought of this again. It sounded good, but as far as she could tell, the top of her mom's list right now was Grandpa Spencer – which she had to admit made sense. His surgery went well, but he was in a lot of pain, and that made him cranky and demanding. Aunt Jules had remarked, 'And he wonders why I was *so* ready to get out of the house at the first possible chance!'

She understood Aunt Jules perfectly. Not that her parents were so awful, but they were hardly around, and they hardly noticed when *she* was around. They had so little to do with the *truth* of her life, and she definitely didn't feel central to theirs. If anything, she felt like a chore, always having to be taxied to and from school or practice or games or lessons . . . she could not *wait* to get her car.

Tonight Kyle was staying again at what she now

thought of as 'their' hotel. She wanted to take him out for dinner and then see a movie. 'Great plan,' he'd said, 'if I can, like, keep my hands off you long enough.' He said he couldn't wait to taste her again.

'Sa-*vannah*. Where *are* you?' Rachel waved a tuna sandwich in front of her face.

She pushed Rachel's hand away. 'No place. What?'

'Are you coming downtown with us or not?'

A few weeks ago she would've joined them at whatever, without question – and any girl who declined to hang with her friends because of a guy would've earned her derision. Before Kyle, she didn't understand why a girl would choose a guy over her friends. Now she got it, though: some guys were worth it. None of the ones her friends had gone for, but that was the difference between her and them – she had higher standards.

'No, I can't go; I have a date.'

Rachel whispered in her ear, 'I told you I can't cover for you again.' Her family was leaving first thing tomorrow for a wedding in Australia.

'I know. It's cool. I'm not staying over.'

Miriam tossed a piece of bread crust at them, hitting Savannah's shoulder. 'No secrets,' she said.

'Yeah, Rachel,' Savannah said loudly. She told Miriam, 'She was confessing how she prefers Michael Jackson's body over Ashton Kutcher's – so there, the secret is out.'

She laughed as Miriam squealed her disgust, and then she ducked Rachel's mock punch.

Rachel said, 'You think *I'm* bad – Savannah's hot for *Marilyn Manson.*'

'Oh, baby!' Savannah said with faked passion, thinking that they had no idea what the real thing felt like – but she did.

FORTY-FOUR

Anna Powell's very last diary entry, made on the night before she died, came early in the twelfth notebook. Meg knew it was there and had avoided reading it, resisting the finality of her mother's last words. For all that she hadn't wanted to become ensnared in the past and the pain it could bring, the more she read, the more she didn't want her visit with her mother to end. What she'd discovered, though, in creating her own journal, was that the end wasn't final, not for the reader; she could go back to the first entry and visit her mother all over again.

And so on Friday night after her sisters' tearful exits, with Savannah gone to the movies and Brian out to dinner with a client, she treated herself to Chinese takeout and white wine. Then, when she thought she could stand it, she braved the last entry.

September 10, 2005
   Low: 64°; high: 89°. Clear, breezy, and hot.
   I have a headache tonight that just won't quit.

Must be the humidity, or maybe a storm's brewing and I'm feeling the drop in barometric pressure.

Spencer was gone to that orchid show today, so I made plans to have lunch with Meggie, just the two of us. Call me crazy, but I've had the oddest feeling, like there's been an angel on my shoulder bugging me to talk with my oldest, get things off my chest. For what good I don't know, but I decided to just do it so that angel'd be happy.

Meggie picked me up, and I noticed how she drove slowly past the McKays'. 'Word is that they've got a bumper grapefruit crop coming this winter,' I said, just making conversation. From the road, you can see gobs of ripening fruit, which is not always the case. Some years aren't so favorable. Anyhow, she speeds up then, like I've caught her doing something bad.

So I start in with the little speech I'd been thinking up, even though I meant to wait till we were done eating. All I wanted her to know was how worried I am about her, how I just don't feel right about the way we encouraged her to marry Brian. Oh, he's a fine son-in-law, caring and polite and supportive and all, but he's not the kind of man to make her happy. Something's missing in him. I've given it a lot of thought, and if I had to pin down just what the thing is, I would call it passion. He's got energy and dedication and ambition to spare, and some would say that's what passion is, but no, I'm talking about the sort of energy that connects a person to the power of nature and life. Like Spencer has, and Savannah. Like Meggie used to when she was little. And Kara, bless her, with those four boys and all those ideas!

Spencer isn't always sensible, it's true. But in all my 64 years, for all the hardships I've endured because of his crazy ideas or wrong assessments or my own shortsightedness or what have you, I've always been glad to be his wife. Meggie and Brian, they live so well, but I know – we all know – something's missing there. Brian stifles her, drains her. I think that whole way of life, fine as it looks, has disconnected her from everything she loved as a girl.

I started to tell her my worries – that she will turn out a depressed and lonely empty-nester if this all keeps up – but as soon as I said, 'Honey, I'm a little worried about you these days,' she starts talking about how well Savannah's doing in school and how they're going to buy her a new car for her birthday next spring! Off track I went like a duck after a bug, putting in my two cents about all these kids getting everything given to them these days. Not accusing her and Brian, mind you – I do have one or two diplomatic bones in my body – but giving my opinion that a child who never has to work for anything is being deprived of important life lessons. Meggie didn't disagree.

At the restaurant, I try to launch my little speech again, only I try to be more subtle. 'Only a couple more years until you and Brian are on your own,' I say, 'and won't that be a change? You getting pregnant right away didn't give you much time to just be a couple.' She agreed, which I thought meant we were making progress, but then she starts telling me about a fifteen-year-old patient of hers who's pregnant, and married too! And I can't seem to steer the subject back to her and Brian . . . So I gave up. I figure maybe I have mistaken what the angel wants.

We had a nice time together, Meggie and me, which is worth a lot. I can't think of the last time we spent an afternoon just talking, no real agenda (that she knew of, anyway). I suppose either I should mind my own business and let her mind hers, or wait for a time when she's open to talking about her troubles.

If she ever is – with me anyway. Could be she blames Spencer and me for them, and I can't fault her if she does. I need to work up the nerve to just ask her outright and tell her I'm sorry. But Mother Above, you know I don't enjoy stirring pots! Right now, though, I'm going to see if I don't still have some of those extra-strong pain pills from when Spencer had his double root canal. I need to be rid of this headache or I'll never sleep, and heaven knows a good night's rest would do me a world of good.

A long sigh shuddered through Meg.

She did blame her mother in part; it would have been good for her to do some pot-stirring; Meg would've said yes, Mom, you were wrong to encourage my marriage and so was Dad. And she would've said, but I understand, and it's my fault too, and Brian's. With the blame spread all around, neither she nor her mother would have had to feel so burdened by it. If only she hadn't been so determined to avoid talking about her marriage, if only her mother hadn't given up so easily . . .

If only.

Were there sadder words than those?

FORTY-FIVE

Savannah waved as Kyle pulled up to the curb in front of the movie theater, where her dad had dropped her off minutes before.

'Sweet Savannah,' Kyle sang from the window of his car, a late-nineties Pontiac. The seats were gray cloth, threadbare and stained – he'd left the windows down in the rain too many times – but she hardly cared.

'Aren't you gonna park?'

He grinned his dimpled grin. 'How 'bout we skip the movie? I been waiting sooo long to see you and, you know, there's just no way I can keep my attention on the screen.'

How could she refuse him when he smiled like that? She got in, and they left the theater, Kyle lighting up a joint as soon as they were on the road. 'Here you go,' he said, passing it.

'I'm good,' she said. 'You can go ahead, though.'

He held the joint in front of her. 'C'mon – you can't get addicted. You had fun last week, right?'

To protest would make her a hypocrite, after joining

him the last time. And she didn't want him thinking she was judging him, or that she was acting her *age*. 'Yeah, okay, I guess I'll have a toke.'

Handing it back to him after, she said, 'Now I have something for you.' She took a fat envelope from her purse and set it on his lap. 'To help with summer class tuition. Did you register yet?'

'Babe! That's so generous. How much is it?'

She leaned close and whispered against his ear, 'A thousand.'

'No shit!' His excitement thrilled her, and she bit his ear playfully. He said, 'But hey, can you *really* afford that?'

'Yeah, it's from my savings, like before. I told you, I don't need it for anything. Might as well use it for something worthwhile.' Like making him happy – and maybe grateful to her too. Make him think of her as a partner. By the time she was out of high school he'd be done with his undergrad work at Florida State, and they could get some really great apartment together in Tallahassee. Then she'd go to State too, while he worked on his master's. Her parents might even help pay his way – they'd love him by that time, once they got past the age difference. And if not, oh well.

She and Kyle passed the joint back and forth as they crossed town, and by the time they arrived at the hotel she felt like she might have flown there. Kyle checked them in while she waited in the car, singing along to a No Doubt song and rifling through his glove box. Instead of the song lyrics, she sang, 'Pen-cil, registra-tion, tire gauge, tiny flashlight, tiny, flashlight, tiny flash-light . . . French fries, condoms!' At the bottom of the compartment were three condoms, packaged together in a crusty strip.

'Found the stash,' Kyle said when he got back to the car, startling her. Hadn't he just gone inside? Time behaved so *oddly* when you were stoned.

She held up the strip. 'You must be a Boy Scout or something – always prepared!' Except that last week he hadn't bothered with condoms, saying it was just as fun to find alternate places to finish the deed. Well, either way, as long as she didn't get pregnant, it was all good.

In the room, he set his canvas knapsack on the bed and dropped down next to it. 'Like every good Boy Scout, I have one of these – got it in Miami.' He took out a digital camera. She started to sit down next to him, but he held up a hand like a stop sign. 'Wait – photo op.' He turned on the power, focused on her, and took a picture.

She was glad she'd dressed up in a new lime green skirt and white cotton blouse; it was trendier than what she usually wore, but the aunts, who'd been just about to leave for the airport, had all approved. Her mom managed to come far enough out of her funk to say she looked 'really great' in her new clothes, which made her feel guilty and deceptive. Aunt Beth was probably right – she should tell her mom she *liked* a guy, if only to start warming her to the idea that she was seeing someone.

'Unbutton your shirt,' Kyle said. 'Be my model.'

She started to undo the buttons. 'Wait. These are just for you, right?'

'Just for me,' he said, aiming the camera at her.

From there, it was easy to shed the shirt and show off the lacy white bra, also a recent purchase – with the skirt and top and a few other lacy things – charged to her mom's credit card. She'd cleared the shopping ahead of time, and even had a plan for excusing the airline and hotel charges when they showed up: she'd speculate that whatever looked wrong to her mom was the result of identity theft. Simple.

'Now the skirt.'

Kyle took out a small vial of pills while she undid the skirt's hook and wiggled it down over her hips. Feeling bold, she struck a pose for him. 'You like?'

He stood up and grabbed her hand, pulled her to the bed. 'Feel how much I like,' he said, moving her hand to his crotch. He liked it a lot.

Holding up a tiny yellow pill, he said, 'I got these great 'ludes, which you can try if you want, but don't, like, think I'm pushing 'em on you, right? They extend the trip is all.' He popped the pill into his mouth, swallowed without water. 'But it's cool; you might not be ready for this stuff.'

She tried to assess the offer sensibly. He'd just taken one, so how bad could they be? She *was* ready – to prove it, she grabbed the vial and shook out a pill herself, popped it into her mouth just like he'd done. Such a tiny pill couldn't do any harm.

But then the drug took hold, and she would only remember, later, hard-edged flashes of what happened in the time afterward: Posing in her underwear. Posing without. Sex toys from Kyle's bag. A knock on the door while she lay with hands and feet bound loosely in playful bonds – 'A friend,' Kyle said, going to the door. Then Kyle inside her in every way possible. Was the friend still there? She couldn't remember seeing anyone, and no one else was there when the drug began wearing off.

Time slowed to a catchable speed, and Savannah looked at the bedside clock.

'Oh my god,' she said. 'I am so busted!' It was almost one AM.

She dressed fast, then found her cell phone and saw missed calls from both of her parents' phones and Rachel's too. Panic rose in her like a flash flood. What could she tell her parents? 'You need to take me home.'

Kyle, still naked, went to her. 'Oh, babe, hey, I'm sorry. I – we – overdid it. Whew! What a ride, though!' He ran his hands over her breasts and then down, reaching under her skirt. In her ear he said, 'You are the hottest little thing I have ever seen.'

The heat of his mouth tickled her ear, and his words pleased her – but she felt ashamed too. How could she have done all those things willingly? Was she *that* kind of girl? 'Hey . . . those pictures—'

'Are my treasure.' He pushed her hair back and kissed her neck.

Unsure of what was real and what she might have conjured up, she wanted to ask if someone really had been there watching them. Had Kyle only *talked* about how sexy it would be if somebody watched them? But she didn't ask. Best to let it go for now, think about it later when she felt more balanced, more sober.

Kyle drew her hand down to his erection. Again? Every part of her was sore, used.

'I really need to go home,' she whispered, tears rimming her eyes.

'Five minutes,' he said, pushing her onto her knees. She didn't know how to tell him no.

FORTY-SIX

Meg was awash with relief when she heard Savannah come home. She stood up from the living-room sofa, pushing off with her good arm.

'Where in God's name have you been?' Her relief drained away instantly and she was filled just as quickly with anger, now that she knew her child was safe.

Savannah looked past her, to where a trio of potted palms framed a corner of the room, and said, 'With friends.'

Brian, who'd been waiting up too, said, 'Not with Rachel.'

'I didn't *say* "with Rachel".' Savannah's face was thick with stress, and she looked like she'd been crying.

'Are you hurt?' Meg asked, going to her. Savannah wouldn't meet her eyes, but everything in her posture spoke of defeat. 'Do you want to talk to me alone?'

'I'm fine – okay? I'm fine. I'm just really tired.'

'You're just really *grounded*,' Brian said, going to the kitchen and turning off the lights. 'Don't even think about making plans for the rest of the weekend.'

'Fine!' Savannah yelled, still standing at the edge of the Chinese wool rug as though the rug defined a force field she couldn't enter – or didn't want to enter, Meg thought. As though inside the field would be questions, challenges, perhaps consequences even worse than what Brian had just doled out.

'Honey?' Meg asked, crossing the rug and taking Savannah's hand; her anger was gone now too, replaced by concern. She'd seen women who'd been abused, who'd been sexually assaulted – they looked a lot like her daughter did right now. Shifty eyes, slumped shoulders, an air of trauma that you could smell on them like skunk.

'I'm going to bed,' Savannah said, pulling away. 'I'm *fine*,' she said again, and Meg wondered who she was trying to persuade most. *Something* had happened, for sure, how many times had Savannah said *fine* in a minute's time? Her vocabulary was much broader than that. Although at one-forty-five AM, who was their most coherent? Maybe she was just exhausted – maybe she'd argued with a friend, or a guy. Maybe she'd done something *responsible*, like refusing to ride with a friend who was drunk, and decided to walk home. Meg tried to believe that her own suspicions were the biggest problem, that Savannah was, as she said, fine.

Watching Savannah escape down the hall, Meg waited until she heard the slam of the bedroom door before telling Brian what she thought might be going on.

'I've seen the markers on other women – she

could've been assaulted or bullied or . . . or . . . or something like that.' Saying it aloud scared her, made her ache for her daughter. Where had Savannah been, really?

Brian came and sat on the arm of the sofa. 'Or maybe she's trying to look pitiful so she won't get in as much trouble.'

'You can't be serious.'

'I'm saying it's possible. I mean, you heard her – she was surly. Probably figured we'd be busy with your sisters and never even notice she didn't get home on time.'

'She knew they were leaving this evening,' Meg said, shaking her head. 'This is so unlike her.' She looked down the hallway. The three-part gold-leaf crown molding along the ceiling caught her attention; it had cost three times what she'd paid for a semester's college tuition. So much money, and for what?

Brian said, 'Let's deal with her in the morning. I need a break from all the stress – and you must too,' he added. Was he alluding to the ALS, in addition to her father's kidney surgery, her sisters' visit, their daughter's first curfew violation? If so, it was his first foray into that neighborhood since their talk Wednesday morning. They needed to discuss what it meant to all their lives, get into the heavy details – not now, of course, but soon.

'You go ahead,' she said. 'I think I'm going to sit up for a little while longer, until I feel calmed down. I'm not sleepy.'

'I'll stay up if you want, but I'm supposed to tee off at eight.'

'No, you go ahead. Set your alarm.'

He stood, started for the bedroom, then paused as if he was going to say something – but apparently thought better of it and went on.

Meg took a glass, a bottle of gin, a pen, and her journal out to the screened porch. Savannah needed time to calm down – and she did, too. She sat in her favorite chair, breathing the humid night air deep into her lungs, trying not to think of them weakening the way her arms and leg were doing.

She wrote:

> *Savannah, I'm torn right now, wanting to go to your room and find out what happened to you tonight, yet remembering myself at your age and the ways I protected my own privacy. Would you welcome my concern or shun it? Although I'm worried that you've been harmed in some way, I realize I'm probably overreacting. It's so hard to let you be the pre-adult you've become . . .*
>
> *With your aunts here, I haven't had any time to write. The need to make this something substantial for you weighs on me; the sand in my hourglass seems to run faster every day, and yet I've said so little of what matters. I need my whole lifetime to guide you – that's how it feels. When I was sixteen, though, I was sure I didn't need my mother at all, and the idea that she might want to guide me even in my adult years would've seemed ridiculous. I would've wondered*

why she wouldn't let go, would've told her to
pick the most salient bits of wisdom and leave
the rest for me to discover on my own. I
wouldn't have thought of how she was still
learning lessons herself.

Meg used her left hand to pour the gin, saving her right for the work of the journal. The little inconveniences of the encroaching disease were adding up, but she was keeping her frustration in check, knowing that what would come, if she held out very long, was much worse – and if she couldn't handle the little things, how could she hope to manage the bigger ones?

She sipped the drink, felt its heat move from throat to belly like a long wick set afire. The warmth settled in her stomach and she savored the feeling, thinking of when it too would move to the list of lost pleasures. 'Stop it,' she told herself. She needed to stay focused on her daughter, and her task.

She continued:

It took Grandma a long time to see some of
the errors of her earlier judgments – and I never
knew, not until I read her diaries. She'd tried to
tell me one of her biggest mistakes, as she
thought of it, but I wasn't ready to hear her. You
might not be ready to hear some of my conclu-
sions either; I know that. But try, Savannah.
And get help when you're confused or upset,
when you can't understand why in the world I
did what I plan to do. My efforts to explain

*might need to be . . . supplemented. Aunt Kara
remembers a lot of what I do about my childhood, about how it was for us, growing up.
Manisha is a good resource for questions about
my career and my disease – and you know she
loves you like her own child. Dad should also be
able to help – although he'll be hurting too.*

For a little while anyway, she thought. And then
he'd do his damndest to move onward and upward,
as he liked to say, shrugging off the weighty albatross
of her disease and suicide.

'Suicide,' she said aloud. Why did it have to have
such a negative, desperate connotation? Most doctors
believed in it, even if not all of them would say so
publicly. Brian's circle, though, was likely to see it as
an act of madness. Would *he*?

Maybe it *was* madness. She *might* be one of those
patients Bolin had talked about whose ALS defied
conventional wisdom. Hope rose in her, but only for
a moment; the disease was a wildfire in her now – but
God, she hated to accept it! Why couldn't she be one
of the lucky ones?

When her wave of self-pity subsided, she regained
her pragmatism and thought how if she couldn't be
lucky, she could at least remain in charge. A small
comfort, but she'd take it.

*Some people will question how I handled my
illness and my death, and you might too. Your
friends might not understand. People might say*

I was selfish, or that I'll have committed the ultimate sin. Let me tell you up front: I don't believe in the Christian hell – hell is here on Earth, in the mistakes we make, in the ways people suffer, in the bloodshed and famine and wars – in the insistence of our culture that a dying person can't lawfully be aided in a merciful death. When you understand how ALS acts as an inescapable prison, how it can degrade a person, strip them of their humanity, their pride, their ability to be and do the things that define 'living', maybe you'll understand why I chose not to put me, or you, through that.

Now I'll get off my soapbox.

She stretched her hand, rubbed the weakened muscles, and frowned at how sloppy her handwriting had become. Her ability to hold and use a pen wouldn't last a lot longer; well, she'd just switch to writing left-handed if she had to. Whatever it took to make sure she'd covered as much as she could. This would be all Savannah had of her.

Thinking of what to say next, she thought about Carson and their history. Should she encourage Savannah to get answers from him, too? She wished she knew how far to go with that subject. Savannah knew little about her relationship with him. But how important was it for Savannah to see that picture clearly anyway? Only if Carson was her father was it in any way essential. Right now Meg wasn't sure there was any value in opening a box as fraught with harm as

Pandora's. Yet ... in addition to the terrible things Pandora unleashed when she opened *her* box, she'd also found *hope*, waiting at the bottom. It wasn't too much to ask that hope also be at the bottom of *this* box, if not for her, then for Savannah.

After seeing Carson last Friday, Meg was convinced that even if he wasn't Savannah's father, he could be a good influence on her. *If* he wanted anything to do with a teenage girl he wasn't otherwise obliged to know. She took a long drink of the gin, wishing it could help her untangle the matter, burn through the knots in her mind, in her heart. Didn't Carson have a right to know he had a child – if he did? Didn't Savannah have a right to know he was her father, if he was? Wasn't it only right that Brian know Savannah wasn't his child, if, in fact, that was the case? The risk of trauma to all three of them was high if Savannah was Carson's – and yet, she couldn't rightfully take her mystery with her to the grave.

But how to discover the truth? She'd need to get a comparative DNA test on Savannah and Brian, which she could do without Savannah knowing. A routine blood draw would provide the sample. Brian would have to be told – would have to consent – unless ... unless she could get some kind of sample from him without his knowledge. Blood was ideal, but other things would do. Semen, for example. Which she could get without having to tell him a thing ...

Was she capable of that kind of ruse? Was it any worse than the reason for the ruse in the first place? Probably she should feel ashamed of this willingness

363

to deceive him – yet had her first deception done him any harm? He lived exactly the life he wanted. If she got the DNA comparison, secretly, and found that he was in fact Savannah's father, he would never even know there'd been a question. If the test showed otherwise? He would be livid, there was no way around that; the way she'd obtained the sample would be the least of it. So really, there was no reason to let him into the loop until and unless she had to.

Which didn't mean that getting the sample for this purpose would be a pleasant thing to do. Her heart wouldn't be in it, now more than ever.

Leaving her things on the porch, she limped through the house to see if Savannah had gone to sleep. When she reached the bedroom door, she listened carefully, even though no light showed around it. She heard the soft strains of guitar music – Savannah playing – and reached up to knock. But she hesitated: should she just give her daughter the time and space to handle whatever had happened herself? With so little time remaining for them, she didn't want to create a hostile rift. Before she could decide, she heard a metallic melody – Savannah's phone. She pressed her ear to the crack where the door met the doorframe.

'Hey . . . no, I'm sorry for overreacting . . . I know you didn't mean . . '. yeah, I think it was a little too much . . . just tired . . . yeah? . . . Of course I love you too . . .'

Meg's eyes widened. Who? Who did Savannah love?

'No, you keep it. I want to help . . . grounded . . . birthday party next Saturday . . .'

Then she couldn't make out anything; Savannah must've hung up or gone into her bathroom or closet. Meg stood there, stunned. Savannah had a *boyfriend*. A *serious* one. And she hadn't even guessed ... How far removed she was from her own daughter's emotional life! This truth sickened her.

Savannah had a boyfriend, and he was part of whatever went on earlier – and Savannah still loved him. They must've had a fight. *What* was 'a little too much'? Had Savannah been drinking? That would explain the red eyes, the aura of guilt. Thank God it wasn't as bad as she'd feared; thank God Savannah got home safely.

Meg left the doorway, deciding to wait for a better time to confront Savannah about all this. Tomorrow, perhaps, or within the next few days – there was no point doing it when they were both tired and moody. They'd have to talk about birth control too, as she'd meant to do last week.

Incredible. Savannah was in *love*.

Meg went back to the porch and took up the journal again.

> There's a story I want to tell you about when I was a teenage girl and fell in love. I thought I'd been in love before – in seventh grade it was a Cuban boy named Rico; then there was this really funny guy, Neil, when I was in eighth ... I went out with a few others too, but none of them were very good fits. Then, just before I turned sixteen, I finally recognized what had been right

before my eyes all along. My real love was my truest and best friend – Carson McKay.

At the time, I swore I breathed for Carson's benefit, and I couldn't see a future that wasn't filled with his laughter, his affection, with endless, perfect days of togetherness. He wasn't thinking of a music career then, and I figured there was no use in considering any kind of medical career – but that was fine. We thought we'd partner with our parents in running the farms. Back then, I had no doubt at all that my vision of our future would come to pass.

Does learning this upset you? For me, the memory is like a beautiful fantasy, a dream I had once, a long time ago – but to you it probably feels as if a small bomb has exploded. How could I have loved Carson that way and never told you? Why would I raise you on his music and yet keep the truth hidden away? Maybe you're wondering if Dad knows. Rest assured, he does. Rest assured, too, that when I married Dad I put my past away. Only now is it emerging with such strength that I can't hold it back.

Never be mistaken in this one thing: some truths will not bear being suppressed forever. It has occurred to me that the ALS could be some cosmic penalty for the choices I made so many years ago.

It was all wrong, all wrong.

Meg closed the pen inside the journal, her eyes

bleary, her hand too weak to continue. As much as she wanted to keep writing, to resist sleep – there wasn't time enough for sleep when the hours were trickling away like blood from a mortal wound – she knew her stubbornness was futile. Pulling her sweater around her shoulders, she lay down on the chaise and closed her eyes.

FORTY-SEVEN

Carson drove his rental car up his parents' driveway and parked. The engine ticked, cooling, while he sat in the darkness looking out at the pale form of the shed. Here was his refuge, finally. What he would do next – tomorrow, the days following, he didn't know. In theory, he would finish whatever it was and then board another flight next Friday, for St Martin. In theory, this . . . this thing with Meg wouldn't affect his wedding plans or his bride-to-be in any detrimental way. Most likely, he'd see Meg once, offer his – what? Support? What else did he have to offer, other than his need for her to find a way out of her prognosis? She didn't need his money, he had no miraculous treatment in a black valise, he wasn't even especially effective at prayer. He just wanted her to know he was there, that he still . . . cared. He wanted to insist that she not try to handle everything herself.

But of course, she had a husband to assure her, to aid her. She had her in-laws, her dad, her sisters, her child. He pushed his hands through his hair and wondered what in God's name he was doing here.

Inside the shed, the air was cooler than he expected; someone had been in and gotten the AC working. He left the lights off and climbed to the loft. It was better to be here in the dark, where the sharp edges of the truth were muted, blended into the shadows. Here in the dark he could imagine, as he'd done that night before her wedding, that hope was not gone. That a part of Meg was still his, that she wouldn't leave him forever.

It had taken until he was seventeen, Meg almost sixteen, for her to come around . . . Not counting their tentative childhood explorations, their relationship was limited to friendship. Close friendship – the closest – but not romantic love. Then, as if because he'd willed it, everything changed.

For a year he'd watched her take an interest in someone, then lose interest and consider someone else; she'd even claimed to be in love a couple of times. She'd tell him about her feelings for those other guys, her eyes moony, her head cocked as if listening for the bell her mother rang to call her home – only she was listening for something else. Cosmic confirmation, maybe, that her whim matched what the universe wanted for her. He'd already heard the truth whispering through the glossy leaves of the groves and knew that if he was patient, she'd see what was already plain to him: that the two of them were meant to be together.

And then she did.

It was May. They were in her backyard, which doubled as the chicken's range, sitting on the stoop having popsicles. Meg wore a striped T-shirt and short terry-cloth shorts. Her hair was pulled up in a pony-tail that fell onto her back like a pale copper rope. He wanted to cut the elastic and watch her hair fall onto her shoulders. He wanted to feel it against his skin, imagined how it would hide his face like a waterfall if he were to lay on his back with her above him. He wanted her to want the same thing.

Julianne, who was seven, had the sprinkler on for Beth and her to play in. Meg watched the girls chase the chickens through the wet grass, shaking her head.

'Look at that – Jules outgrew that swimsuit a year ago.' Julianne's butt was exposed by the high-cutting legs, and the shoulder straps stretched far down front and back, showing her bony shoulder blades and chest.

'I can fix that,' he said. 'Hold this.' He handed Meg his ice pop – a grape bullet, half gone – then took out the buck knife Spencer had given him for his thir-teenth birthday. Not minding the sprinkler, he went over to Julianne.

She saw the knife and her eyes grew round.

'Just hold still,' he said, and with a few quick tugs at the tight pink fabric, he cut through the middle, creating a two-piece suit, albeit with ragged edges and a bottom half that only just clung to Julianne's little-girl hips. 'There. That should feel better.'

Julianne looked down at her bared tummy, then back up at him, and grinned. 'Hey, Beth, look, *I* got a bikini!' she yelled.

Carson, water running off his hair and nose and jaw, walked back to Meg. She watched him with her head cocked.

He took his ice pop, noticed that she'd let it drip purple down her hand, and smiled.

'That's ingenuity, what you did. She's so excited,' Meg said, looking at him closely. 'Me, I was just going to make her strip. I like the way you think.'

'I like how your eyes change colors, depending on what you wear.'

She smiled shyly. 'Oh yeah? Well, I like how yours turn forest green when . . . when you look at me like you are now.'

Without thinking, he kissed her, her mouth sweet and sticky with orange ice pop. Their first true kiss. When he pulled back, she opened her eyes and nodded.

If only it had all remained like that . . .

Sitting here in the love seat, he stretched his legs out in front of him and listened for the opening and closing of his door, for two telltale creaks on the stairs. He waited like this until the sun eased over the window sill, and then he put his face in his hands and wept.

The sound of knocking pulled him from a dream where he and Meg had been digging for pirate treasure along the edge of the lake, as they'd done thirty years before. He'd pressed a shovel into her hands. '*Keep digging!*' and she'd laughed at him. '*Silly, there's no gold here.*' Her hair, long and tangled and wild, shone like spun copper. She grinned and stripped off her blue sundress, its crocheted lace trim ripped and dangling at the back, then ran, naked and laughing, into the water. He watched her swim and wanted to follow, but someone was calling his name, holding him back. He came awake then, disappointed that the voice came from his mother outside at his door.

She knocked again. 'Wake up, Car. I've got sausage and eggs hot on the stove.'

'Coming,' he yelled, then unfolded himself from the love seat, where he'd nodded off maybe an hour earlier. His shoulder popped as he stretched.

Shep, the mutt, trotted alongside as Carson went to the house. His parents were seated in their usual spots, his mom to the right of his dad at the square table. They'd changed many things in the house over the years – countertops, flooring, even the size of the house itself, adding a small wing to the traditional two-story structure – but the table was the same one they'd eaten at for his entire childhood, the fourth seat oftentimes claimed by Meg.

Val sat there most recently. Today, Shep took it, hopping up and waiting politely for whatever dona-tions they would offer. This was a change, a dog at the table; in earlier years his dad would not have tolerated it. This morning, his dad was the first to feed Shep, handing over a bit of sausage in a manner that told Carson this was nothing new. They'd mellowed, his folks, and it brought him comfort and pleasure to see them this way, still together, still content – more content, even, than when he was a kid. In September they'd mark their forty-third year together. He admired them, and envied them; assuming he and Val got married a week from now, the odds of *them* reaching forty-three years of marital harmony were pretty slim. None of the men in his family were blessed with longevity, all of them dead before eighty. He knew, though, that the number of years you lived was no measure of how good your life had been. The measure was in *how* you'd lived. And what you left behind.

'So, you got anything in the works right now?' his dad asked when he sat down with them.

His mom said, 'What, you mean besides a wedding and honeymoon?'

'I mean his music. When are you going on tour again?'

Carson dunked a corner of toast into an egg yolk, took a small bite. 'Gene's working on that. My label's been talking about a new release of my own hand-picked favorites for late this year – live recordings, probably. I s'pose I'll have to promote that, if it comes together.'

His dad asked, 'Writing anything new? Anything for Val?'

'Leave him alone,' his mom chided.

'What'd I say?'

'No,' Carson said pointedly, eyeing his parents. They'd obviously spent some time talking about the Meg situation and his unexpected return home because of her. 'But I've been pretty busy – maybe you noticed that?'

'Of course we did,' his mom said, feeding Shep a whole piece of toast, which Shep took to his bowl near the door. 'Just let us know if there're things we can help you take care of this week. I've already got the flower order under control, and Dad's getting the tuxes on Wednesday.'

'So,' his dad said, 'what's the plan for today?'

Carson stood and took his plate over to Shep. He had no real appetite. 'I don't know, Dad. I'm figuring it out as I go.'

The first thing he had to figure was what to tell Val. She called late in the morning, when he was back at the shed after a long walking tour of the groves. As had always been true, his dad was doing a good job of keeping the farm maintained – the fields mowed, the trees groomed, the lakes free of gators. Shep helped with that job, as did a group of college student volunteers who came out periodically to comb the grounds and 'rescue' any dangerous wildlife. The increasing development all over the state made the gators bolder and more desperate for access to water. They'd been found in people's swimming pools. Unfortunate as the outcomes were, a recent spate of attacks on humans made sense, given that it was mating season. As it was, theoretically, for him and Val.

He dialed her cell and she answered, 'Hey, handsome, how's it going? Did you get everything crated?'

'Not quite,' he said, sitting down on the stairs. 'But . . . they should get it finished up soon. How'd things go yesterday, after you called?'

'I tried to call you later – didn't you get my voice mail? We all went to this luau sort of thing. Wade won the limbo contest. I guess that's no shocker!'

Wade, whose limber, muscular body was the anatomical ideal. He and Val could be twins. 'Sounds like fun.'

'I miss you, though. Am I gonna see you before Friday night?' They'd left their plans for this week unfixed, dependent on his tying things up in Seattle.

'No . . . Actually,' he said, peeling off his socks, 'I decided to come back to Ocala.'

'Ocala? Why?'

'A friend – you remember Meg Pow— I mean, Hamilton?'

'The one from the concert. And the tailor, right?' Her voice had a cautious tone.

He tried to tread carefully. 'Right. Well, I just found out that she's . . .' – he stopped and cleared his throat – 'she has Lou Gehrig's disease.' That wasn't a complete explanation for his sudden change of plans, but he hoped it would suffice.

'That's *awful*,' Val said. 'But . . . but what's that got to do with you? I mean, I don't want to sound, you know, callous or whatever . . . Are you visiting her in the hospital or something?'

He rubbed his chin. There was only one justification for his drop-everything trip, and he didn't want to give it, but he also didn't want to lie. 'No,' he sighed, 'it's not like that.'

'What is it like?'

'It's . . . the thing is, well, Meg and I used to be best friends, you know? Growing up?'

'But you said you hadn't seen her for like twenty years. So you couldn't exactly be close *now*.'

'Well . . . right, that's true. We aren't. But before that, well – look.' He stood and began pacing from kitchen to living room. 'We were going to get married. I mean, we hadn't set a date, hadn't, you know, planned it all out yet – I didn't give her a ring,' he added, hoping that would diffuse the story's impact on Val.

'And what happened?'

'It didn't work out.'

'Obviously.'

'Obviously.' He stopped at the table, pressed his hand to it. 'She found someone else. But, when I heard she was . . . was dying, I just felt like I should come see her. So here I am.'

'Okay . . .' Val said. 'Okay. So there you are. Okay.' She seemed to be pulling the details together. 'Wow,' she said, 'that's such a bummer for her . . . It's really thoughtful of you to go see her.'

'I guess,' he said. He wanted to tell her how miserable he felt, and how helpless. He wanted to feel like he could unburden himself and know that she would bear it gladly. But that wasn't the nature of their relationship. She was all upbeat energy, a woman whose struggles had been only physical: girl versus surf. A bad day was a calm sea or a better competitor or her mother pestering her about how she planned to wear her hair for the wedding. This fresh, undamaged quality was much of what had attracted him, but he knew as he stood there with his cell phone pressed to his ear that this was also why he had no business asking her to committ to him.

'Val?'

'Yeah?'

'What would you say if I told you I want to stay here, in Ocala – or someplace close by?'

'What, all week?'

'No. All the time. *Live* here.'

'Be serious, Car,' she laughed. 'It's *inland*. Why would you want that? Not because of this Meg – I mean, it's not that, right? I mean, she's like, dying . . . pretty soon.'

His stomach balled up tight. 'Right. No, not because of Meg. My folks—'

'They could move to Malibu.'

'I . . . I just need to be *home*,' he said, not knowing until the words were out how true they were. Once, he'd run away from here, but now he was running back, praying it wasn't too late to reclaim . . . what? Not Meg, no; of course he couldn't have her. His history, then. *Their* history. It was something.

'Carson, what's going on?' Val asked, sounding rightfully irritated.

He reached into his pocket and took out Meg's gold chain, laid it in a circle on the table. 'I owe you an apology,' he said, tracing with the tip of his finger the delicate ring it made. 'I should've told you – about Meg. I should've told you it was never really over.'

FORTY-EIGHT

Meg decided to go through with her DNA quest
Tuesday night.

After packing up her office earlier in the day, she'd
taken a detour to see the land. Her farm, and Carson's.
The past. Before she couldn't get in her car and drive
herself there, or anywhere, again. Cruising past his
driveway, she saw a blue sedan coming from the other
direction, its signal on to turn. As the car passed, she
glanced at the other driver and was startled to see
Carson. Why was he back? She had to pick up Savannah
and so she kept going, but the encounter stayed with
her the rest of the day. Knowing Carson was nearby
lent her the courage to get the answers she knew needed
to be had.

At bedtime, Brian climbed into bed beside her. She
wore a satin nightshirt, not too suggestive, but a change
from her usual soft yellow cotton. Brian, as was his habit,
wore his plaid drawstring pants – a safe indication that
sex wasn't on his mind. When he was interested, he
came to bed naked, saving a step.

He slid under the sheets and propped himself on his elbow. 'So . . . you got everything done at the office today?' His tense tone belied his casual words.

She nodded. 'I did. All sorted and boxed – I'm leaving the furnishings. Did I tell you Manisha has two candidates for joining the practice? So things will work out okay there.'

'Good,' he said, a little too heartily.

The topic was awkward for her too, if only because it was so difficult for him. And while talking about the end of her career didn't seem like the best route toward romance – or sex, anyway – she thought she might ease his mind some by showing him that she had things under control, that she wouldn't be a burden.

She said, 'You know ALS debilitates people completely, but I thought you should know you won't have to do anything for me. You probably won't even have to see me in that condition.' She was still determined to create her own exit, though she hadn't been able to resolve, yet, how and when.

Brian dropped back onto the pillows. 'Meg, I can't talk about this.'

'What do you mean, "can't"? We *have* to talk about it. It's not going away until I do.'

He looked shocked. 'How can you *do* that?'

'What? Talk about it matter-of-factly? I don't know . . . I just know I have to. *We* have to. Listen, I know it's weird – but sooner or later in life you face this kind of stuff. We just thought it'd be later.'

'Men are supposed to die before their wives,' he said, his voice straining. 'I . . . I don't – it's not right.' He turned away, facing the closet's double doors. The closet, which was a bigger space than the room she'd shared with Kara, with custom shelving and drawers for every conceivable purpose. Would he empty it right away when she was gone? Maybe she would empty it herself ahead of time, saving certain things for her sisters and Savannah. And for Carson, whose John Deere T-shirt lay neatly folded beneath a stack of silky pajamas.

She touched Brian's shoulder. 'Hey – it's going to be okay. I'll make it as easy on you as possible.'

'Don't be stupid. It can't be any kind of "easy", don't you know that?' When he looked back at her, his eyes were wet.

'Come here,' she said, reaching for him.

Their joining was as simple as that. Far simpler than she'd expected, and more genuine too. She didn't think about Carson, not for more than a moment when she acknowledged how differently she felt toward Brian. Protective. Sympathetic. Not passionate in the least. There had been a time, earlier in their marriage, when she'd made an effort to be an enthusiastic partner; her body had longed for the intensity she'd had with Carson. Brian, though, was uninspiring in bed. If she was attractive, clean, and willing to have straight-forward sex, that was all he needed. Tonight was not so different from past nights, except that she knew – and maybe he did too – that it would be their last.

After Brian was asleep, she sat on the edge of the marble tub using a swab and slide to prepare the DNA sample for the lab. Surprisingly, she felt much better about everything now. She hadn't gone to Brian with a scheming spirit; she'd gone to him as a good friend saying good-bye. The DNA test, too, felt like a right move, a step taken toward the truth, whatever it might be. Finally.

The following afternoon, Meg tucked Brian's sample in her purse, then had Savannah drive them to the clinic for Savannah's supposedly routine checkup. From there, they went on to the lab.

'Why do I have to have blood work?' Savannah asked on the way. 'I just had a checkup. I'm not sick.'

'For the drug test, obviously,' Meg said, straight-faced.

Savannah jumped as if she'd been jabbed. 'What? That's – I'm not—'

'No? Good. Make sure that you don't.' She smiled a little, to herself. It was good to shake up your kid every now and then. 'Now, about Friday night . . .'

With Savannah captive in the car, this was the best chance she'd had so far this week to bring up the subject of what had happened the other night. They went back and forth with the 'nothing' versus 'something' argument, and then Meg said, 'Honey, I'm not as clueless as you might imagine. I'm not asking because I want to admonish you; I'm asking because I'm concerned. If you'll stop pretending that I'm crazy, I'll try to treat you like the young adult you're trying to be. Oh – turn left up here.'

After she turned, Savannah said, 'Okay, fine. I'll tell you. I have a boyfriend, and we had a fight.'

Progress, at last. 'A boyfriend?' Meg tried to sound surprised. 'Anyone I know?'

'No.'

'Where does he go to school?'

'You know what, Mom? I *want* to tell you, but I know you'll be mad. You and Dad are just so . . . *conservative*. You're all, like, so concerned about the right school, the right neighborhood, the right parents . . .'

Meg frowned. *Her?* 'No, that's not true. I don't care about that stuff, as long as the boy is, you know, a decent human being. He could be purple and from Saturn—'

'Nothing can live on Saturn,' Savannah said, instantly becoming, in Meg's eyes, nine years old again. If only.

Meg blinked away the thought. 'You get my meaning,' she said

'Well, *Dad's* like that. So even if you *were* cool with, with the guy, Dad would never be, and I just . . . I don't know. I was *going* to tell you . . . eventually.'

But eventually might be too late. Meg said, 'Okay, well, I'm glad of that. I want – no, I *need* – you to know that I'm . . . that there's more to me than it might seem, just like you. I'm not just a doctor and a mom and a wife. I've been busy being those things for as long as you can remember, I'm sure, but I'm as complex a human being as you – as anyone. You can *talk* to me, okay?'

Savanna shrugged.

'There's the place,' Meg pointed with her left arm. The right, cradled today in a sling, she saved for the important tasks. It was weak all the time now, and, fearing worse was coming soon, she'd journaled a lot about her early life and the history of Powell's Breeding and Boarding, the orchid effort before that, even a summary of what she remembered being told of her parents' courtship. She'd also written Kara and Beth and Julianne's phone numbers, addresses, birth dates, and the particulars of their husbands and kids, wondering when Beth would find the right man. It saddened Meg to see her alone, though Beth insisted she was content being single at thirty. Yesterday Beth had called to say she was moving to Ocala in six weeks, ready to keep tabs on their father, ready to do for Meg whatever needed done. Meg thought of Lana Mathews's sister, Penny. She vowed to herself that, even though she'd done plenty of diaper-changing for Beth three decades ago, she would not under any circumstances permit Beth to return the favor. She would make her exit before it came to that, no matter what.

They pulled into the lab's parking lot. Inside the squat gray brick building, some anonymous man or woman would draw from Savannah's arm the answer to a sixteen-year-old question, and another would mail it to Meg's office after five business days. What would the test show? Right now, Savannah was likely thinking about whether to reveal *her* secrets, but the most substantial revelation the two of them might share would be much more dramatic than where Savannah's boyfriend went to high school. Meg wished she could tell her so, as if to say, *Whatever you're worried about is nothing by comparison to my secrets, so how about you just tell?*

Savannah shut off the car. 'So *why* am I doing this? You don't need to check for drugs, Mom, I swear.'

Maybe Savannah had something to hide, but Meg knew she also just hated needles; when Savannah was nine and cut her knee open, skateboarding with her friend Jonathan, Meg and two ER nurses had to restrain her just so the doctor could get her prepped with anesthetic. Last year, when Savannah went for her tetanus booster, she'd come out of the exam room in tears.

'Routine stuff. Anemia, the health of your blood cells, the function of certain glands. Just remember not to look, and it'll be over before you know it.'

'His name is Kyle.' Savannah opened the door.

'Hold on.' Meg reached for her shirt, caught the hem. 'What did you fight about?'

Savannah paused. 'Stupid stuff. Let's just get this over with, okay?'

For the moment, Meg let her go. But she watched how Savannah moved, walking inside; her posture hadn't changed much since Friday night despite the apologetic resolution Meg had overheard. Yes, it might be needle dread, but she guessed it was more. The 'stupid stuff' Savannah and this Kyle had supposedly fought over still weighed Savannah down.

They signed in. Almost right away, the phlebotomist called Savannah back. Meg stayed behind long enough to drop off Brian's sample, then followed.

She sat across from Savannah and watched the dark

blood fill the first of three vials, two of them intended for the tests she'd described to Savannah, the other bound for the more crucial purpose. Meg imagined she could see the twisting strands of DNA thick in the vial, eager to show that her last hours with Carson had resulted in the marvelous creation now seated in front of her. She might as well admit she wanted Savannah to be Carson's – selfishly wanted this, it was true. Such a desire had little regard for what Savannah might feel when she learned such a truth, little regard for the confusion, anger, hurt, loss she would surely suffer. Savannah idolized Carson, but she didn't know him as a man, let alone think of him as anyone's dad. Brian, for good or bad, was her father de facto; no DNA test would dissolve the experience of their sixteen years of cohabitation.

The wish was selfish, but grounded in the love Meg still had for Carson, love she hoped she could show Savannah, share with her somehow.

Still . . . the risk of hurting Savannah made her nervous, protective. So okay, if Carson proved to be the one, she didn't *have* to tell Savannah, or Carson, or Brian.

Or maybe, like her daughter sitting here with her eyes squeezed shut, she was afraid to face what really wasn't such an awful thing. Savannah might well *benefit* from the knowledge.

Funny, Meg thought, how she could look into the abyss of mortality without fear but trembled at the prospect of harming her daughter. Watching Savannah, she reassured herself that the decisions she'd been making these past many days were, ultimately, for Savannah's own good.

The technician laid aside the third vial and pressed a gauze square to Savannah's arm. 'There you go,' the woman said. 'You can open your eyes.'

FORTY-NINE

Feeling like a stalker, Carson sat parked behind a blooming gardenia hedge, waiting for Meg and Savannah to emerge from the medical lab. He hoped their presence there, and at the clinic before that, meant Meg was pursuing some kind of treatment. He hoped she'd told her family about her illness and had been persuaded to try whatever there was to try. As long as the treatment wasn't worse than the disease, that is – he couldn't bear the thought of Meg suffering.

Every day since his arrival he'd tailed her, as if by knowing her movements around the area he would be able to decide how – or even if – he should approach her. Since his conversation with Val on Saturday, he'd been swinging wildly from one emotional extreme to the other, a trapeze artist in a two-ring circus. Val was wounded but willing to stand by him while he worked through this thing with Meg – that's what he'd called it, 'this thing with Meg'. He felt bound to honor his commitment to Val, couldn't see any *logical* reason not to. Then he'd swing the other way, toward what he thought of as his dark side, the place where Meg still held him captive and he was convinced that she always would.

He was honor-bound to marry Val, and yet honor-bound not to.

And so he drove around Ocala in his rental, a car that was too small and underpowered for his taste, feeling incapable even of turning the damn thing in for something better. He kept thinking he'd go see Meg, then return the car and get back to Seattle and finish packing up. But here it was, Wednesday afternoon, and he was no closer to a decision than when he'd arrived Friday night.

She hadn't been looking for him yesterday, he knew that much; she'd only been . . . looking. As he was now, as she and Savannah emerged from the gray building and walked, Meg limping and with her arm in a sling, toward what looked like a brand-new SUV. She'd come a long way since the days of having to share her parents' old Ford wagon. And now she was facing the end of the path, the destination they were all bound for – regardless of what sort of car was in the garage – but which everyone studiously ignored. Death was for other people, always; wasn't that the way of it?

Impulsively, he got out of the car and waved. 'Meg!' he called, loudly enough for them to hear him across the parking lot.

As one, she and Savannah turned and spotted him there. He waved again and jogged over. 'Hi. I thought that was you,' he said.

Savannah, looking far more startled than Meg, said, 'Hey, hi! Is some evil doctor forcing you to give up your blood, too?' She unfolded her arm, and he saw gauze taped inside her elbow. He felt deflated; so it wasn't a visit on Meg's behalf.

He said, 'No, I'm – I just had to stop in to, um . . .' An excuse failed him. 'That is, well, I got sort of turned around – it's been a long time since I drove through this side of town. I was just about to go in there,' he pointed to the oil-change shop at the other end of the lot, where he'd parked, 'and ask for directions.' That sounded slightly plausible. From the way Meg looked at him, he could see she hadn't bought it.

Savannah apparently had. She said, 'Where are you going? I pretty much know my way around now that I've been driving for a while. With my permit, I mean. I can't get my license until Saturday.'

'Monday,' Meg corrected, 'when the testing center's open. But Carson doesn't need to hear every detail.' She looked amused. That was good; at least her sense of humor wasn't lost already. To him she said, 'She's just relieved to have lived through the blood draw.'

'Of course,' he nodded, looking at Savannah, so pretty, so much like her mom. 'Doctors *are* evil. You're lucky to still be alive.'

The words were out before he realized how incredibly insensitive they sounded.

'She is,' Meg said quickly, glossing over his gaffe. 'Most of the time we have our henchmen just drain the person dry.'

They all laughed, and then no one seemed to know

what to say next. He groped for a topic, found a clue in Savannah's comment about her license. 'So Saturday – you must be turning sixteen.'

'Yeah, we're having a party at the house . . .' Her tone suggested she wasn't looking forward to it, and he wondered why not. She went on, 'Hey, if you wanted, I bet it would be okay for you to come.'

Obviously he had to thank her and decline. He knew this, and yet he wished desperately for it to be otherwise. He wanted to be a part of Meg's life, spend a few hours in her company, just be where she was. But even if he could be there, he couldn't imagine that Brian Hamilton would be too thrilled to have him around. He imagined the introduction Hamilton might make. *Hey Preston, old boy, let me introduce Meg's old flame, a guy who was* Punk'd *on MTV back in January . . .* Of course, Hamilton wouldn't have had time to watch MTV when they were teens; he'd have been too busy reading the *Wall Street Journal*. He'd know about *Punk'd* only from channel-surfing during commericals on the Golf Channel.

But more than the social and cultural differences separating Hamilton and himself, there would be the knowledge that Meg was once *his*, and that Brian had basically extorted her commitment. Men didn't forget these things. Ordinarily, he wouldn't even consider putting himself in the same space with Hamilton; too much temptation to maim the guy. Ordinarily, though, Meg wouldn't be terminally ill.

He said, 'You know, I really appreciate your invitation, but I gotta pass. Other obligations.'

'Oh, sure ... that's cool,' Savannah said, looking disappointed.

'Carson's wedding is Saturday,' Meg said.

'You're getting married on my *birthday*? Oh my God, that's so great!'

'I'll expect you to remember to send anniversary cards,' he joked, though his heart was hardly in it.

'Yeah, absolutely,' Savannah said, smiling.

Meg, whose eyes were deep pools of thoughts he could only begin to guess at, said, 'But maybe we'll see you again before you head out of town.'

An invitation. He felt it more than heard it. 'Sure,' he nodded. 'I'm not leaving until Friday.' Less than forty-eight hours from now, but he'd happily give all the remaining hours to Meg. Would Val begrudge him stepping out of their relationship that way – if such a thing could even happen? He would never tell her. She was giving him a lot of emotional leeway as it was. It couldn't happen, though. Meg had a daughter to tend, a party to plan. She might give him a platonic hour or two, at best.

He'd take it.

'Well, we're off to find a birthday outfit,' Meg said. 'But here – Savannah, grab the notebook from my purse.'

Savannah gave her the notebook and Meg held it so she could write with her slinged hand. 'Here's a map of how to get back on the main routes from here.' She wrote for a minute, then ripped the page off and handed it to him.

In addition to the roughly drawn map was, in place

of a street name she knew full well he was familiar with, a phone number and *10 PM*. He looked up at her. 'This is terrific, you've rescued me.' The look in her eyes – the relief that must match the look in his own – made his knees weak. He swallowed hard, conscious of Savannah's presence, and added, 'You know how guys are about directions. I would've been going in circles all evening.'

They said their good-byes and then, when he was seated again in the little rental car, he stored the number in his cell phone and began to count the minutes until he could use it.

FIFTY

Meg's phone rang at a minute before ten. She was in the den, alone with the shadows that stretched across the waxed parquet, holding but not reading an article titled 'How and Why to Live with ALS'. She'd read it before, more than once, in fact; it was only wise to do what she'd counseled an unfortunate few of her patients to do, when facing the sobering facts of their own incurable disease: make sure you know what you're doing when you choose to ride it out, or not.

She answered the phone, elated to see the name on the display. 'Carson. I'm so glad you called. Sorry for the subterfuge earlier.'

'No, I – of course.'

'You must think I'm a crazy person.'

'No crazier than a guy who supposedly got lost in the town he grew up in and visits periodically.'

So she was right in suspecting that his appearance outside the lab was no coincidence. She wasn't foolish enough, though, to imagine his motivation was anything more than concern for a dear old friend. Hopefully it wasn't simply pity.

'Where are you now?' she asked.

'Home. At my folks', that is. Usually I stay at the house, but I've reclaimed the shed for the week,' he said, his voice soft with memories. 'Are you at home?'

'In the den.' She thought of him there in the shed, surrounded by the details of their youthful dreams: the blue cupboards, the vines she'd stenciled over every downstairs window, the colorful rag rugs Beth and Julianne had braided one summer under Kara's guidance – they'd all wanted to be involved in their big sister's romantic future. She wished she was there again, in the innocent past.

He said, 'Can you talk?'

'Nobody's around.' Savannah was in her room on the phone. Brian was in Jacksonville for the night, due back tomorrow evening. 'I was wondering, though, if you wanted to . . . that is, if you felt like coming by.'

'Get reacquainted with you and Brian?' he said with a humorless laugh.

'No, Carson, of course not. He's out of town. And Savannah wouldn't even know you're here; she never comes out of her room this late. But if you'd rather not . . .'

'I'm on my way – oh, directions would be good.'

While she waited for him to arrive, Meg looked over the 'How and Why' article once more. To the credit of its author, it didn't sugarcoat the reality of ALS, and it didn't use religion as an antisuicide stick. Under the 'Why' column were 'family events and milestones' and 'opportunity to help advance research'. Nowhere did it say 'because a cure is on the horizon'. Even the most optimistic medical advice wouldn't make that claim. In essence, the pamphlet reminded the patient of things they might wish to experience, or witness, while waiting for the end. 'Remember,' it said, 'you have the right to live out whatever ambitions you feel you can accomplish.'

Which was all she was doing by inviting Carson over. And what a relief it was that he wanted to see her, that he didn't hate her after all. She was glad he hadn't asked what she hoped to accomplish with this meeting, because she had no answer for that. With the path ahead shrouded in fog, instinct was her only guide.

She checked on Savannah, whose door was closed but who was now singing softly and playing her guitar. For her birthday, Meg would give her a collection of Joni Mitchell CDs. The car was a wonderful gift, no question, but hardly personal. Brian hadn't even let Savannah choose the color. He insisted they go with white, for its superior visibility. He wanted her to be as safe on the road as possible, which Meg couldn't fault; if only he also gave that kind of attention to the things Savannah cared most about. When had he seen her play ball last? When had he listened to her sing, except by accident?

For that matter, when had *she*?

Thank God Beth was moving to Ocala soon; Savannah would have someone with far fewer distractions to tend her these next two years, and hopefully beyond. As Meg knew well, a girl didn't stop needing to be guided just because she *thought* she did.

She went to the foyer where, with the lights off, she could see out to the road. Soon she saw headlights, the slow approach of a dark-colored car. As she headed outside to the driveway, her breath seized in her throat; now that Carson was here, she wasn't sure what she would do, what she would say. Her invitation had been an impulse that she wasn't sure, now, how to handle.

Too late to turn back, though. She looked down at her clothes, suddenly self-conscious. The outfit – silk-blend capris the color of a canyon sunset and a hand-embroidered white silk tee – was what she would have once called 'rich bitch' clothes. At least she'd left her shoes off; being barefoot brought her a little closer to the young woman she'd been – plus, she walked more steadily without shoes, even her flattest sandals.

There was no disguising the sling she now wore; although he'd seen it earlier, she slipped it off and dropped it next to a camellia shrub.

Carson shut off the car and got out. She saw him gaze up at the house's expertly lit stone exterior, saw him scan the copper light fixtures and gutters, the tiled roof, the patterned cobblestone driveway; when he looked at her, she expected him to make some comment about how upscale her life had become, how she'd done so well for herself. She was ready with a response about how he likely lived as well or better himself – but instead of saying anything, he walked over to her, put his hands on her shoulders, and pulled her into his arms.

She closed her eyes, pressed her cheek against his shoulder, so solid and warm beneath his shirt. His smell, his shape, the lean taper of his waist where her hands held onto him were a homecoming for her senses. He tightened his arms around her and buried his face in her hair, murmured something low and reassuring. That she couldn't make out the words over the thump of his heart in her ear mattered not at all.

He released her slowly, until they stood apart again. 'Well, that's better,' he said.

'Definitely.' Her voice was husky. She cleared her throat. 'Come on inside. I'll buy you a drink.'

They went to the den and settled onto opposite ends of the velvet sofa, glasses of Amaretto in hand as props to bridge their awkwardness. Never would either of them have predicted that some day they'd sit together in a room like this, on brushed velvet, with damask-covered armchairs nearby, four layers of drapery covering the windows. A room with six expensive liqueurs in antique crystal decanters. They were people who belonged someplace with thin cotton curtains and secondhand furniture – and by *secondhand*, she didn't mean antique. They belonged in a room with plain pine floors, where barn cats wrapped around their ankles and the smell of orange blossoms drifted in through metal screens; a place with blue cabinets and rag rugs. This room felt like someone else's life; she felt disoriented here, as if she'd taken a wrong turn somewhere around 1987 and kept going, missing the danger signs all along the way until now.

'Those decanters were Brian's grandmother's,' Meg

said, to make conversation. She held up the cut-crystal highball glass in her left hand. 'These, too. I tried to give them to my mom, but she wouldn't take them. "Too fancy for our place," that's what she said. They're too fancy for me, too, but how can you not use something so beautiful? I'm going to give them to Beth when she gets here.'

'She's coming to visit?'

'Moving back. To help with Dad – and me, though I hope to not need much help.'

Carson's gaze slid away and he took a drink. 'Good stuff,' he said.

She would let him avoid the subject, for now. 'I got this rum on St Bart's, but I'm sure you can find it in St Martin too, if you look. Rum's like water in the islands.'

'That's no exaggeration,' he said. 'I had my share when we were there recently – though I do try to keep it reasonable these days.'

She recalled the newspaper feature about him leading the wild life, and her mother's attempt to discuss it. 'I'm glad to know that.'

This was a little better, not so awkward. He looked like he was relaxing some too, though he rubbed his chin the same way he'd done at the tailor shop. Even so, what a relief it was to know she hadn't lost him entirely, that even in this surreal place she had access to him, for a little while anyway.

He said, '*I'm* glad Beth's coming back. I don't know quite how to ask this, but . . . I was reading about, about the ALS stuff, after you called me last week, and I saw that some people do pretty well for a long time.'

'Some do,' she said, glad to get on the subject rather than leave it like an unmentioned elephant in the room. 'Though it's subjective, the definition of "well".'

'You seem to be doing all right,' he said cautiously.

'I'm functional. My right hand and arm are the worst. My left is weakening, but still okay. I can dress, I can drive, I can eat – and drink.' She took a sip. 'I'm doing my damnedest to get a journal written for Savannah. My father gave me some notebook diaries my mom kept, and I can't tell you how much they mean to me.' She didn't tell him that she'd begun to notice her speech was being affected – only an occasional mumbled word or dropped sound, but enough to show that things had taken a serious turn for the worse. She might accommodate the disease, she might even forget it for a few blissful minutes, but it was now certain that she wouldn't be one of the 'lucky' ALS patients.

Carson said, 'Ah, Meg, I feel so awful about this . . .' His voice broke. 'It just . . . it doesn't seem real. Or fair. It's not *fair*.'

She sighed. 'What is? Nobody guaranteed us "fair". The way I see it, I'm just glad to have had my daughter,' *or ours*, she thought. 'And my career. And . . . and the farm and groves and the lakes . . . And you,' she added softly. 'You know I'd do it all differently if I could do it over again – but I can't. So . . .'

'So I'm glad you let me come spend a little time with you. I hope . . . well, it would help me a lot if you'll let me see you now and then. If you want me to, that is.'

She didn't answer right away, sure that he was anticipating a future where she remained mildly incapacitated for a long stretch of time, where he – and Val? – could come by to visit. How to tell him otherwise, when he was looking at her with so much hope in his eyes? Of course she wanted to see him, but he had to understand how she felt.

She said, 'Carson . . . here's the thing: I'm not the kind of person who's willing to endure everything ALS dishes out just so I can live until my last *possible* breath. I'm not willing to be a prisoner left motionless inside my own body. My nerve sensation's not going to go away. *Clear thought* won't go away. I'll feel, see, and hear everything but be completely unable to respond. I can't do it, Car. I can't . . . *be* that way.'

'No . . . no, I can see why.' He put a hand to his mouth for a second. 'But there must be treatments you can try.'

'Other than for symptom management, nothing's been shown to have more than the smallest effect, not on the full-blown cases like mine.'

'What about experimental stuff? Other countries, or . . . ?'

She shook her head. 'It's hard to believe, right? As advanced as medicine is – we expect to at least get a fighting chance. But the truth is, doctors are powerless in more areas than you want to know.'

'It's so . . .' He sighed loudly. 'Jesus. What will you do?'

400

She shrugged and turned her glass so that it caught the light and refracted it onto her lap, tiny slices of rainbow on her dark sienna pants. 'I haven't decided. But you know, I'm a doctor; I can put my hands on just about anything I need, if that's the route I go.'

'What other—?'

'Possibilities? Methods? Nothing violent, I know that. No guns, no razor blades, nothing messy. I'm not crazy about blood.'

He laughed, in spite of the somber topic. 'That figures. Me, I'm not crazy about flying, and I think I spend half my life on planes. That's probably *why* I'm not crazy about it.'

'You've seen so much of the world, though, right? One thing I'm glad for is the traveling I've done. Not all of it was for pleasure, but I've been to Europe and Mexico and Canada – Banff is astonishing. Have you been there?'

'I haven't. I always mean to go; it isn't that far from Seattle, comparatively. But I'm always going somewhere else, you know?' He drained his glass, got up to refill it. 'More?'

'No,' she said, concerned that her speech would get messy after more than one drink. Neither did she want to get sleepy while he was here. It was such a pleasure just to share space, to reacquaint herself with his motions, with the deep tenor of his voice, refined, now, from his years of performing. She wanted to appreciate every single sense of him, undulled even slightly.

Carson looked down at his hands, picked at a callus on one finger; she could tell he was thinking about how to ask the next obvious – but difficult – question. She waited, letting him take as much time as he needed, though she knew her answer wouldn't satisfy him. Finally he said, 'When? I mean, how will you know when you're . . . ready?'

'I'm not sure. I suppose it'll be when I feel like I've done what needs doing. I haven't even told Savannah the whole truth yet. She thinks what I have is just a nuisance disease – that's what I've led her to believe. I can't put something so heavy on her so close to her birthday.'

'God, Meg. I don't know how you're keeping it together. I'd be a basket case.'

'Habit,' she said.

Until a few weeks ago, so much of what she did, how she lived, even what she *thought* was habit. It was easier to let routine take the place of conscious living – because she'd been afraid of what might happen if she looked too closely at herself, her life. A person could go too far, though, in trying to avoid facing the mistakes in her past. She could be so determined to clear an alternate path that she failed to see she was cutting a trail to nowhere.

Odd though it sounded, having ALS was beginning to feel like a free pass to ditch routine and do what she wanted. This attitude, she saw now, was what her father was trying to encourage in her; it was what her sisters were expecting when they waited for her answer to what she was going to *do*. They all imagined that she would be more self-centered with the end so near, that a little selfishness would be reasonable and right.

In the past, she would've called that attitude irresponsible; tonight, she understood.

'But I guess Brian's been supportive,' Carson said, his tone saying he suspected otherwise.

'He's baffled. This disease doesn't fit his game plan. But I can't be too hard on him, you know? He's always had good luck. His strategies have always worked, but this time there *is* no winning strategy.'

'Hard for me to feel too sorry for *him*. He set you up, Meg – way back when, I mean.'

She nodded. 'He needed an edge over you. Otherwise, why would I choose him? I'm not saying I approve, or that I'm happy about it, but I understand; he used the tools he had.'

'Wish he'd used them on somebody else.'

They sat silently for a long moment. 'Africa,' Carson said suddenly. 'Did you get to Africa yet?'

'No,' she said, smiling to think of him on the tire swing that long-ago day, 'but I remember your promise – which I won't hold you to. What about you? Have you been to Thailand?'

'A few years ago,' he said. 'My last world tour included Bangkok.'

'Oh, that's right, you said something about it at the show in Orlando.'

He nodded. 'But it wasn't . . . the experience wasn't what I wanted it to be.'

'You didn't like the lemongrass shrimp?'

He looked into her eyes. 'You weren't with me.'

He had never let go, just like her.

'I'm so sorry, Car,' she whispered.

The moment wrapped around them, timeless and forgiving, and then Carson stood up and reached into the pocket of his jeans. 'I brought you something.'

In his hand was her gold chain.

'Oh,' she breathed, overcome to see he'd kept it.

He sat down close to her and hooked the chain around her neck, smoothing it over the ridge of her collar bones just like the first time. 'There,' he said. 'That looks right.'

Meg wiped her eyes on the edge of her shirt, not caring that mascara would stain the silk. As she did, a sound in the hall made her look up. Savannah, in a long loose T-shirt, came in the room, saying, 'Hey, Mom—' then stopped dead. She looked at Meg, plainly astonished to see Carson there.

'Savannah! Hi, honey! I'm sorry, I should've told you Carson was coming by . . .'

Carson scooted over a little and Savannah pulled down the hem of her shirt to cover her thighs. 'Hi, Carson. Um, Mom, I was just gonna ask you if Rachel can stay over after my party. Her mom says she can.'

'Okay, sure. I don't see why not.'

Savannah continued to stare. 'So . . . what are you guys doing?'

'Well, Carson had to—'

'I found something of your mom's and thought I should return it before it got lost again.' He stood up as if to prove nothing inappropriate was going on.

'Wow, that's really nice of you. What'd you lose?' she asked Meg.

'This necklace,' Meg said, touching it.

Carson said, 'I found it a long time ago, but it's taken a while to get it back to her. Looks good, don't you think?'

'Yeah, it does. She never wears any necklaces – she's pretty boring that way.'

Meg, surprised that Savannah paid any attention to what she wore or didn't wear, just shrugged, but Carson smiled, and she knew by the sad curve of his lips that he understood what Savannah did not: she left her neck bare deliberately.

'It's getting pretty late; you need to get to bed,' she said, and Savannah frowned her disappointment. 'Besides, you're not exactly dressed for company.'

'Mmm, guess I can't argue with that,' Savannah said. She told them good night and backed out of the room. Meg went to the hall, listening until she heard the bedroom door shut.

Back in the den, Carson was sitting down again, on the edge of the sofa. 'That didn't look too good.'

'I suppose . . . but I'm not too worried. She's going to know the truth about my history before long anyway – that I had a life before Brian, and particularly that you were an important part of it.' She sat down next to him, hip to hip, and marveled at how good it felt to do exactly what she felt like doing.

Touching the necklace again, she said, 'Thank you for bringing this.'

'Meg . . . ?'

'Hmmm?'

'I . . . listen, I've been thinking about what you said before – that you aren't going to wait until, well, you know, you don't want to become completely . . . and I want to . . .' He pushed his hands through his hair, its waviness made more obvious by the disarray. 'I want to . . . I'm going to postpone the wedding.'

She turned in alarm. 'Car, *no*. That's – you need to keep that on track. I'm not going to be responsible for any interruption of your plans. That's not . . . that's not what this is about.'

'*You're* not doing anything, Meg. I'm doing it. It's not just you – I've had some doubts for a while.'

'She adores you.'

He nodded. 'I know. She deserves better, though. She deserves someone who returns her feelings a hundred percent. I've tried, honest to God, but the best I've been able to do is about seventy-five.'

'But – your wedding's *Saturday*. You can't call it off now. You're just having cold feet.'

'And who wants to get into bed with a guy whose feet are icy, huh? No . . . I'm going to put it on hold.' He stood and paced the room. 'No – no, hell, I'm just calling it off. Completely. I won't string her along.'

Meg stared at him. He sounded very sure of his decision, and he looked . . . relieved. Even so, she feared he was making an emotional choice that, no matter how much it buoyed her – and to be sure, it made her so buoyant she felt lightheaded – it might be a serious mistake for him.

'Carson, I don't have a future, you know that. You're feeling sorry for me, but that's going to pass. I'll be gone, and you'll have practically another lifetime ahead of you. Don't . . . don't jeopardize your happiness.'

He sat again, hands on his knees, head down. 'There *is* no happiness for me if I'm not giving my all. Do you understand, Meg?' He looked at her. 'It's you I want. For five minutes, five hours, five days – whatever it is, I'll take it and be glad. Please. Let me.'

His words were an unexpected oasis. She looked into his eyes, so fond, so familiar – so much like Savannah's – and smiled so broadly that she broke into laughter.

'Okay,' she said.

FIFTY-ONE

Two hundred colorful balloons seemed about to lift away the party tent under which twenty teenagers were eating gourmet pizza Saturday evening. Pepperoni, of course, but also many other kinds with names Savannah didn't bother to know, covered with toppings like avocado garlic and pesto, baby corn and cilantro. And there were salads: potato, both red and mustard; Italian, with mushrooms and olives and pimento and fresh Asiago cheese; mixed greens with mandarin oranges and strawberries. Plus a chest freezer full of ice cream treats and five big galvanized tubs with every teen-friendly drink the caterers could think of. A three-tiered chocolate birthday cake swagged with lacy frosting – a neat trick – sat amidst the rest of the food like an overdressed girl without a date.

In the yard next to the tent was her glossy white Honda, a beacon of excess. There were balloons strung from both side mirrors and a huge red bow sitting on the hood. Savannah, standing at the edge of a group of chattering girls, thought the bow was cheesy, and wished the car was lime green or something vivid, but she couldn't say she wasn't glad to finally have it. Now she could make her own rules, more or less. Caitlin, who'd arrived with a tiny brown dog peeking out of her shoulder bag, had actually admired the car, saying her Mini was great but she felt a little like a circus clown driving around in it. She was planning to trade for a BMW X3.

Savannah eyed the crowd – her dad's cronies and their kids, mostly. In spite of the party being in her honor, in spite of the food and the cake and the presents and the attention, she wished she could be someplace else. Interesting to learn that even Caitlin, who seemed to have everything, wasn't as content with life as she ought to be, and why was that? Why wasn't enough *enough*? Savannah found this troubling – not just about Caitlin, but more about herself. Her life was as good as anybody's – better than most, she suspected – and yet here she was, at her sweet sixteen, feeling disconnected from the whole scene.

All these kids in their expensive brand-name clothes, all of them guaranteed a good shot at achieving as much as their parents had – *if* their parents didn't turn on them the way Kyle's had. They had everything handed to them. They never seemed to get caught breaking the rules or the law . . . and she was just as bad. Well, she, at least, was trying to help others – Kyle for one, and the manatee population for another – and meant to make over her life in her own terms as soon as she could. The next twenty-four months would definitely be the slowest ones of her life.

Rachel, dressed in a peasant skirt and ruffled top she'd bought in Australia, brought Savannah a soda and interrupted her mulling. 'Here you go, Birthday Girl. Did he call yet?'

All day, Savannah had been both expecting Kyle's call and dreading it. Yes, they'd made up about the way he'd coerced her to stay even longer last Friday, but she still felt pretty weird about that whole scene. He had pictures of her *naked, posing*, doing she didn't know *what* all because she was too embarrassed and scared to ask him. He hadn't called or chatted online with her in three days, and even before, she wasn't so excited to hear from him. She wasn't so sure about things just now. The drugs, the sex – none of that was what she wanted, or not in that way . . . but she didn't know how to refuse without offending him. Yet she missed him, couldn't wait to see him again; it *hurt* that he hadn't called today.

'Nope,' she told Rachel. 'But his cell phone's not working, so . . .'

'Jonathan was asking me about you – you know, like, are you going out with anybody right now. I told him to ask you himself.'

Savannah looked across the tables to where Jonathan stood talking in a group with the five other guys there. They seemed to be a sort of skittish unit, unsure of how to mingle with the girls, some of whom they'd known forever. She noticed how mature Jonathan was looking all of a sudden, really tall, and more muscular than he'd been just a few months earlier. She liked his hair, which was sandy blond and straight except where it curled a little around his face. Did he really want to go out with her? Like, date? The idea sort of appealed – and made her feel immediately guilty. She loved Kyle. The stuff that happened wasn't all his fault. They were stoned. She'd gone along willingly.

Miriam, who was standing next to Savannah, said, 'Jonathan is so cute. And look, you two match.'

Savannah laughed. They did match, both of them wearing green shirts and khaki bottoms – shorts in his case, a skirt in hers.

'Fate,' said Lydia Patel. 'My mom would say it's a sign.'

Rachel said, 'She *has* a boyfriend.'

'Who no one has ever seen,' Miriam reminded them.

Lydia nodded. 'What's up with that, Savannah? Why isn't he here?'

She couldn't tell them, not about his true age and not about how . . . *wrong* he'd be in her dad's eyes, and not about her ambivalence over her uncharacteristic behaviour and Kyle's encouragement of it. What must he think of her? Was he feeling weird about it all, too? Worrying about how he'd behaved, too?

She told her friends, 'He had to work until closing.' Or she thought maybe he did; he'd said his manager at Home Depot was loading him with extra hours since he'd missed so much while in Miami.

'He couldn't take off for your *birthday*?' Caitlin said. 'Sorry, but if it was me, I'd ditch a guy who couldn't plan ahead and all. Did he give you a present at least?'

'Not yet,' Savannah said. 'He's going to, though.' She

assumed he was. He hadn't said so, but she was hoping that that just meant he wanted to surprise her.

'Speaking of presents,' Rachel said, pulling her by the arm toward the table where a colorful pile of gorgeously wrapped boxes and elaborate gift bags waited, 'why don't you open some? I heard this was a *birthday* party.'

It was when the kids were all crowded around the table watching her unwrap colorful crystal earrings, four Vera Bradley bags of various colors and sizes, iPod accessories for her car, Broadway tickets for *The Lion King* – from Rachel, who knew the movie was one of her all-time favorites – that she got the biggest surprise of the party, announced by Jonathan.

'Hey, check it out! That's Carson McKay!'

Everyone turned at once to look where Jonathan pointed, past the pool to the portico. It *was* Carson – in shorts and a Hawaiian shirt, looking a little nervous but smiling that famous friendly smile.

Her mom, who'd been standing with the grandparents and a few other adults, waved her welcome. 'I'm glad you could make it,' she said, making it obvious that she knew he might show. But what about his wedding? What about Val? Savannah wanted to ask but held off, in case the answer was something he didn't want to advertise to everyone. It wasn't lost on her, though, that he'd been in the den with her mom late Wednesday night, and now he was here on what was supposed to have been his wedding day. Whatever was up, she hardly cared – he was here! Unbelievable. *This* was a privilege she wouldn't want to have missed.

412

Carson carried a white envelope. When he got to where she stood, he put it on the table and gave her a quick kiss on the cheek, making her the envy of all the females in an instant. 'Happy birthday,' he said. 'Sorry I'm late.'

'Are you kidding? It's so awesome you're here!'

Her mom made the general introductions. 'As some of you already know, and as Jonathan pointed out, this is Carson McKay. Carson, who's been a good friend of mine since elementary school, had a change of plans for this weekend, so I thought he might like to come by.'

Carson bowed slightly, then stepped back with the adults to watch Savannah finish opening gifts. She saved his envelope for last. Inside was a card, and on the front, a painting of a field of waving grass and wildflowers beneath a broad blue sky. She opened the card; he'd copied down a poem, which she read silently:

> *To make a prairie it takes a clover and one bee,*
> *One clover, and a bee,*
> *And revery.*
> *The revery alone will do,*
> *If bees are few.*
>
> *Emily Dickinson, 1896*

She considered it for a few moments, then thought, *exactly*. Beneath the poem was *'Happy 16th Birthday!! Please join me and the band for a jam session (to be arranged); you choose the tunes. With affection, Carson.'*

She read that part aloud, unable to keep the thrill out

413

of her voice. 'Wow! Thank you so much! I'd love to – but you'll have to promise not to notice how bad I am.'

The rest of the evening passed in a happier blur of Carson-centered activity. He was a huge hit, answering questions and signing napkins, plates, shirts, whatever people brought to him. Using Savannah's guitar, he played 'Happy Birthday' as the caterer lit the candles on her cake, and even persuaded her to sing a short duet with him poolside later, when the party was just about done. Only her dad's barely disguised scowl and her wounded thoughts about Kyle intruded – and only a little bit.

After she said good-bye to her guests and plopped down on the bonus room sofa with Rachel, her mind returned to Kyle like the poem's bee to clover. Why hadn't he even called?

And then as if bidden by her worries, her phone rang, beginning what would be one of the most troubling nights of her life.

'It's him,' she said, looking at Rachel.

'So answer it.'

'Yeah, okay . . .' She stood and went to the book-shelf, her back to Rachel. 'Hello?'

'Hey, how's it going?'

'Fine,' she said coolly, waiting to see if he'd forgotten what day it was.

'I was gonna call you earlier, but, like, I was working on this plan, right? A kind of birthday surprise.' He hummed the beginning of 'Happy Birthday', then said, 'but I didn't have the details worked out, you know, till now.'

'Oh, well, that's okay . . . I had a good surprise already – Carson McKay showed up at my party.'

'Dude's trying to move in on my territory,' he said. 'Not cool.'

'He's my *mom's* friend,' she laughed.

'I bet your mom's hot.'

'*What?*'

'McKay's woman's hot, right, and *you're* hot – so I'm saying every chick in his life is probably hot. His mom, too, whattya want to bet?'

She lowered her voice and asked, 'Are you high?'

'On life, babe, on life. 'Cause dig this: I have a birthday proposition for you! Could I say "proposition" if I was stoned? No. Now here's my surprise: I propose that you and me get together permanently.'

'What do you mean, permanently?' He couldn't mean *marriage*.

'I mean, you pack your stuff and we get out of town – like, get our own place where we can be together twenty-four/seven.'

'Oh . . . wow.' Funny how relieved she was that he didn't say marriage. She wasn't ready for that. Was she even ready for *this*?

'I don't know,' she said, holding up a finger to show Rachel she'd be back, then going into her room to talk in private. 'Is it legal? I'm *six*teen, not eighteen, remember?'

'Babe, I remember. No, here's the thing. Legal doesn't matter; I have a plan to make it so we can do whatever we want, right? I just love you so much, Savannah – I hated that you were, like, mad at me. I can't stand waiting two whole years to have you all to myself. Don't you want to be together full time?'

Her heart swelled. 'Of course,' she said, going into her bathroom and closing the door. 'Are you really saying I should *run away*?'

'Heh, *now* she's getting it. Yeah. Come on, run away with me.'

This was something she'd never thought of, leaving home to be with Kyle *now* ... But why not? Her Grandpa Spencer left his family when he was fifteen to go work with his cousin, mucking stables at a big Ocala horse farm. In some places, girls her age were long married and already raising kids. She imagined living with Kyle, the two of them doing whatever they wanted to do whenever they wanted to do it. No judgmental fathers or preoccupied mothers to worry about. No curfews to pressure her and Kyle. No heavy parental expectations.

Still, it was such a big step, and she had *plans*. 'I don't know ... I mean, where would I finish school?'

'You can get an equivalency diploma.'

'That won't get me into college.'

'Maybe not Princeton but, you know, the state schools will take anybody. You don't need all that elitist crap anyhow, right?'

'Right, but ... let me think about it, okay?'

'What is there to think about? I love you. You *say* you love me—'

'I do!'

'Okay then. Decision made. Pack up and come on – oh, hey, you still have your savings account, right?

You're gonna want to withdraw what you got, 'cause you being underage means we'll need to skip out of the country for a while.'

'Hold on – leave the country? How would we do that?'

'We – I mean *I*, have it all figured out, babe. I'll tell you when I see you, okay? 'Cause you never know who can hear cell phone calls.'

Watching herself in the mirror, she was sure she looked older than sixteen, and no question she *felt* old enough to be on her own. What she wasn't so sure about was Kyle. If he was willing to ditch the drugs . . . then *maybe*. But how was she going to talk him into that when so far she hadn't been able to even resist them herself?

She said, 'Can you hold on a sec?'

'Sure.'

She pressed MUTE and set her phone on the counter. The girl in the mirror stared at her with worry plain on her face. 'I know, it's crazy . . . but suppose I say no and he ditches me?' She'd be back to her irritating, uninspiring routine.

Kyle was funny, he was adventurous – and except for that crazy night, he made her feel smart and pretty and talented and worthy of regard. Her mom always said she was those things, but it was different coming from Kyle. From Kyle it felt real and true. Her mom was her *mom*; she had to say stuff like that.

Yet she wasn't certain she could safely tie her fate to Kyle's.

In the mirror her eyes were as dark as she'd ever

seen them, a serious stranger's eyes. 'I'm just not sure I can say yes. I need more time.' Time to see whether he'd change. Time to see if they could get on the right track and stay there. And then maybe she wouldn't feel so anxious about leaving this place behind in favor of having a *real* life.

Now all she had to do was persuade Kyle to go straight.

Turning from the mirror, she took her phone and un-muted it. 'I'm back.'

'So we're all set, right?' he asked. 'Come over and we'll get, you know, organized. Did your dad come through with the car?'

'Yeah, it's pretty nice.' Nice of her parents to give her this gift of freedom, this reward for being almost always responsible and well behaved. 'But listen—'

'Great,' he said, not listening. 'Get here as soon as you can – I'll give you directions. I'm just outside Summerfield, off 301.'

Maybe the thing to do was talk about her worries in person, face to face. Then she could judge whether they really had a shot at making this work. If he was truly willing to go straight she'd see it in his eyes. She said, 'Can you come get me? 'Cause, you know, I won't have my license till Monday.'

He laughed. 'And your point is what?'

'I – never mind. Fine, okay.' She was as good a driver today as she'd be on Monday so what difference, as long as she was careful? This way she was sure to get back home before her parents could even know she'd been gone. She could feel a vein pulsing in her neck as she copied down directions. 'I'll meet you there as soon as I can.'

Back in the bonus room she found Rachel hanging backwards off the sofa and talking on the phone.

'Hold on,' Rachel told whoever was on the line. She looked at Savannah expectantly.

'He wants to see me tonight,' Savannah said. 'To give me my present in private.'

Rachel said into the phone, 'Call you later,' and hung up, then turned herself upright. 'Ooh, very romantic. Did he say what it is?'

'No – that would kind of spoil the surprise, don't you think?'

'I bet it's lingerie. Do you think? Or jewelry! God, I wish a guy would give *me* jewelry.'

As far off the mark as Rachel was, Savannah felt more assured seeing her envious grin. 'Anyway,' she said, 'I need your help.'

'Name it.'

'Will you stay here and hang out in my room? Keep the door closed, and if anyone comes looking, just say I'm in the bathroom. They won't, though – they never come back here once they've said goodnight. And I'll be back before morning.'

Rachel said, 'Got it. Now whatever you do, don't, like, go over the speed limit or get in a wreck.'

'You are the best,' Savannah said, hugging her.

Rachel pretended to scowl. 'God, I *hate* you, you are so lucky! Promise you'll introduce me to one of his brothers or something.'

'I promise. Now I gotta go.'

As she hurried out, her parents' voices carried from their bedroom, raised in debate over who knew what. She didn't bother to try to make out their words, and refused to let herself worry about what they'd think or do if they discovered she was gone.

Driving down the dark street, she focused on making a plan. The first thing she had to do after she got to Kyle's was make sure not to get off track by smoking dope or taking pills. With so much at stake she was sure she could succeed this time.

And it would be great if they could have sex – no, *make love*, with nothing but love and desire fogging up their brains. That would be the nicest birthday gift. *If* his roommate wasn't home. Maybe they could go someplace else if he was . . . But absolutely no drugs, nothing to alter the experience or make her feel . . . skanky. Everything was still good between them; obviously he was as in love with her as ever – she just needed to get them on the right track. Then everything would be *amazing*.

If he wouldn't give up the drugs and all, though . . . well, he'd just *have* to. He loved her, he wanted her to be happy with him – he'd understand, or she prayed he would. He was so sweet, so well-meaning; he'd definitely give up the stuff she didn't like once he realized how strongly she felt about it. That's the kind of thing you did for love.

FIFTY-TWO

Meg closed the bedroom door so their raised voices wouldn't reach Savannah and Rachel. 'I'm sorry,' she said, turning back to Brian. 'But I don't see anything wrong with inviting Carson. Savannah was thrilled – you saw that.'

'What about me, Meg? I wasn't thrilled. You didn't even tell me you were doing it!'

'Because I knew you'd react like this!'

'How would you like it if I invited one of *my* ex-lovers to our daughter's birthday party? What if Lisa Hathaway had shown up and *you* had to be polite and act like it didn't bug the shit out of you?'

'It's hardly the same thing,' Meg said. 'She's a local news anchor, not an international star that Savannah idolizes.' Her lips had trouble with the words, and she made herself slow down. 'Besides, as far as I know, you and Lisa don't have any sort of current relationship.'

Brian pointed at her. 'This is what I'm saying – since when do you have a relationship with McKay? You're not telling me anything, Meg. Jesus!'

She turned toward the window, looking out onto the still-lighted pool. He didn't know the half of it. Not only hadn't she told him Carson might come by today, she also hadn't told him she'd seen Carson Wednesday, nor that she'd called him before that – she hadn't even mentioned seeing Carson, James, and Val at the tailor's. She hadn't told him about her visit to Lana Mathews's home or about her mother's diaries or the journal she was writing for Savannah.

For all that they'd shared a bed, a room, a home for almost half her life, he wasn't someone she wanted to share her innermost thoughts with. She knew now that this had always been true, that it explained, in some measure, the arm's-length intimacy of their family life. If Brian had ever wanted more from her, she would not have been able to marry him, to live together in relative harmony for so long. How strange it was that now, when she was pulling further away, he wanted to pull her closer. Could he be feeling jealous, competitive, even knowing that she was dying? It was flattering to think he cared that much, but sad too, especially because he was not the one she had chosen to turn to – would not have chosen, even without Carson back in her life.

Turning to look at him, she said quietly, 'All right, Brian. You want to know what's going on? First, I'm committed to finding some way to end my life before I become fully incapacitated.'

'What are you talking about? You're going to – are you talking about *suicide*?'

She nodded. 'So that no one has to see me suffering, and so that I don't have to suffer.'

422

'But . . . ALS is painless. I read it in that booklet you got.'

'It's painless, but that doesn't mean people don't suffer with it.' She thought of Lana. 'They suffer dependency, paralysis, indignity . . . Once all your limbs stop working, once you can no longer talk or chew or swallow, it becomes, in my opinion, an excruciatingly slow death you just lie there waiting for. *That* is suffering. And can you imagine Savannah seeing me like that, day in and day out?'

He looked agitated. 'You can't just . . . I mean, okay, yes, I can see how . . . but I mean, how am I supposed to . . . Come on, Meg. Think about the stigma – and your life insurance won't pay out.'

She forced herself not to react. He was upset, he was grasping at straws. Even without the insurance, Brian wouldn't ever hurt for money, and she'd leave Savannah well provided for; her lawyer was working on that. Even if the DNA results showed that Brian wasn't Savannah's father and Savannah lost her trust funds, she'd be able to get through college and into adulthood without financial strain.

'You know the money isn't a problem,' she said calmly, 'and as for the stigma, it couldn't be any worse than the stigma of having her mother lying in a hospital bed in a diaper, needing full-time care.'

'It's *suicide*, Meg.' He stared at her as if she'd lost her mind. 'And if you think I'm going to help you, forget it.'

She hadn't expected his support, but his unwillingness to even consider helping her if she asked, if she needed him, saddened her just the same.

She drew a deep breath, then said, 'The second thing you should be clear about is that while I'm still around, Carson wants to be involved in my life in whatever ways he can. And I want him to.'

'Christ.' He sat on the edge of the bed and rubbed his forehead. 'Anything else you want to dump on me while you're at it?'

'I'm sorry to sound so abrupt ... but there's just no point in wasting time and energy dancing around the subject. I ... well, I'm going to live my last days honestly, and I hope you'll be able to respect that.'

Brian looked up. 'Honestly, huh? How about *responsibly*? How about thinking of Savannah instead of yourself?'

Her temper flared. 'How about you make a list of what *you've* done for her in sixteen years, then make a list of *my* efforts – except you can't, because you don't even *know* what all it's taken for me to manage her life and yours and my own all this time. Don't you dare try to tell me I'm not thinking of Savannah. There's not a time when I'm not balancing her needs against my own, even now.'

'You're the one who wanted a kid, Meg – you did that all by yourself.'

'Didn't I,' she agreed.

They glared at each other, and then Brian looked away. 'I don't want to do this.'

'Then don't. Savannah already knows that Carson and I are old friends. If you'll handle things maturely, that will help a lot.'

'What, I'm supposed to welcome him into my house

– give up my wife and my bed, too?' He stood and gestured as if offering the bed to Carson. 'Should I bunk in a guest room until, what, you slit your wrists or OD?'

'Give me a little credit, Brian. All I'm asking is for you to be . . . understanding. I've done my best by you; you know I have. But things are different now.'

Brian left for the bar at the club, saying he needed some space to think. Meg didn't mind; she had no energy left for *his* emotions. It was hard enough to manage her own.

She poured some milk and took a short stack of chocolate-chip cookies to the den. In between bites of soggy cookie, she wrote in the journal:

May 14, 2006
    Your sixteenth birthday today, and the party
was better than I feared, since Carson showed
up. Take him up on the offer to play with the
band – you have such great potential, such a
pretty voice, such a feel for music.
    I hope I'll be able to know how you're doing
after I'm gone, that whatever comes after this life
will let me peek, from time to time, into yours.
Maybe I'll see you onstage one day, singing and
playing your songs. Maybe one day you'll host an
awards show where Carson gets a lifetime
achievement award. Or maybe music will only
ever be a hobby, which is fine too. Do everything
you can to be whatever – and whoever – you

most want to be. Don't let your dad or your friends or any man in your life distract you from the truth of your heart. There is nothing worse than looking back on your life and wishing you'd done it all differently, that you'd resisted the pressures, that you'd followed that truth faithfully. As the saying goes, I'm here to tell you not to make the same mistakes I made.

But you, my wonderful daughter, you are the one thing I would never change about my past.

I watched you today, surrounded by other teens, all of you so grown-up looking. I remembered one weekend morning when you were maybe eight, and Jonathan had spent the night; the two of you were droopy with exhaustion, having succeeded in an 'experiment' of staying up all night. I was exhausted too, having been unwilling to sleep while the two of you were up – this was before Jonathan could swim, and I worried that you'd decide to take a three AM dip in the pool. But also, I wanted to witness your delight in doing something so exciting and 'grown-up' as canceling bedtime. When the sun came up, I made waffles and the three of us ate them with our fingers, remember? And no plates – we poured on the syrup, then sat on the floor to eat, catching drips on our knees.

Jonathan said, 'Wait till I tell my mom we broke all the rules!'

'Who makes up the rules anyway?' you asked.

Jonathan said, 'God, right?'

I said, 'Well, some are just to make parents' lives easier, but some rules are nothing but old habits that people are afraid to change.'

So here's my advice: Follow the rules that make your life work best, Savannah, and discard all the rest.

Meg put the pen in her mouth, rubbing her hand and thinking what write next, and then the phone rang. When Savannah didn't answer it, she stood, stumbling a little before regaining her balance, and hurried to the desk to answer.

'Hello?'

Static, rustling, heavy breathing. Meg was about to hang up, then she heard 'Mom?'

She braced herself against the desk for better balance. 'Savannah? Honey, is that you?' Why would Savannah be *calling* her?

'Mom, I—' More static. Savannah was talking fast, but Meg could only make out the words *Kyle* and *car* and *get me?* and *Summerfield, please hurry.*

The boyfriend. Another fight? She couldn't tell if Savannah heard her when she said, 'I'm on my way.'

FIFTY-THREE

Savannah crouched in the dark underbrush as something crawled over her neck. She didn't dare move again, or Kyle and his horrid friend would hear her, find her, take her back to their nasty excuse for a house – or just rape her – kill her? – out here in the woods. Her breath came in rapid, shallow gasps and she prayed silently for her mom to get there fast.

Maybe she should've called 911. She thought of her phone, lost in her panicked run . . . Too late now. Maybe her mom would call the police – but probably not; their connection was so poor that Savannah didn't know if her mom could even *hear* her, let alone understand that she needed help *now*. God, she was stupid. Stupid not to call the cops, stupid to come out here in the first place, stupid, *stupid* to have believed in Kyle . . .

Everything had begun pretty well. Except for the house being a very rural, very small, unpleasant-smelling pigsty, she was glad to be there with Kyle, to feel his arms around her and hear him whisper, 'Happy, happy birthday,' in her ear. She accepted his offer of a Coke and tried not to wrinkle her nose at the sight of food-encrusted countertops and overflowing garbage pail.

'Hey, come have a seat,' he'd said, leading her past sloppy piles of junk mail and magazines to a worn, gold-colored sofa in a dingy front room. Thrashy rock music blasked from a cheap stereo. He turned it down a little. 'You hungry? My roommate – you know, Aaron – he's bringing in some pizza.'

She brushed crumbs off of a seat cushion and sat down. 'Actually, I'm good. We had pizza. And lots of cake.'

'Yeah, of course.' Kyle sat down next to her, leaned back and put his feet up on an old milk crate. 'So, the big one-six. Now you're legal for relationship purposes, heh.'

She smiled. 'Yep, as if it mattered.'

'And, now we're free.'

She sipped the Coke and nodded, reluctant to jump immediately into the discussion she'd tried to script in her head during the drive. She wanted to wait for the right moment – maybe he'd suggest they get high, which would be the natural time to say why she thought neither of them should do it anymore.

For now she asked, 'How would it work? You know, getting out of the country and all?'

Kyle sat up, eager to explain. 'It's a masterful plan,' he said. 'Me and Aaron, we've worked it all out.'

Alarmed, she said, 'Aaron helped?'

'Aaron is, like, the key. He has all the connections. He's, you know, my source.'

His *source*. For drugs. Which, from the look of the

place, was where they spent all their money. And hers too?

This was as good an opening as any. She said, 'You know, I want to talk to you about that, about the drug stuff.'

'Aaron's great,' Kyle continued, as if she hadn't spoken. 'He knows the *ways*. He gets the *goods*. Fake ID, passports, tickets – oh, did you get that money out?'

'No, not yet. I—'

'We figure our first stop will be Mexico, right, 'cause it's easy to get through the border, and Aaron, he knows a guy there.'

Savannah had just opened her mouth to protest that she didn't have any interest in traveling with some drug dealer when Aaron came in with three cardboard pizza boxes balanced on his upturned hand.

His hair was dirty-blond, and he was so pale his skin appeared almost translucent. His eyes were hidden behind dark sunglasses. 'Hey!' he said, looking at her. 'If it isn't my favorite six-pixel chick!' He continued into the kitchen, dropping the pizza boxes on top of the junk mail.

'Six –?' she began. What was he talking about? And then it dawned on her: he was talking about the pictures, Kyle's photos of her from the night at the hotel. Her stomach tightened into a ball, and she whispered, 'You didn't *show* him—?'

Kyle shrugged. 'He was *there*.'

The Coke she'd just swallowed threatened to come back up. How could he be so casual about something so painfully personal?

From the kitchen, Aaron was saying, 'So are we all set with the car?'

Kyle said, 'Uh, no – haven't had a chance to get to it yet, man.'

'Then it's dinner conversation,' Aaron said, lighting a joint. 'Come on, let's eat.'

Kyle jumped up. 'I'm starved.' He left Savannah there on the sofa, mortified.

She watched while Kyle shared the joint and loaded a paper plate with sausage pizza, panic spreading through her chest like hot lead. This wasn't working at all the way she'd planned; she needed to get out of there, go home and think things through. Kyle was not the guy she thought he was, not at all. The truth ricocheted in her mind as the sweet scent of marijuana drifted her way.

She stood up, conscious of her short skirt, her bare legs and shoulders, the shape of her nipples visible beneath her tank top. 'I gotta go. My parents—'

The men looked at her in surprise, then Aaron said, 'What's up with her? I thought you said she was on board.'

'She is. Right, babe?'

'Actually,' she began, but Aaron's eyes narrowed and he jumped up, getting her bag off the floor.

'Hey!' She went to grab it away from him but Kyle stood up, stopping her.

'Hey yourself,' Aaron smirked, pocketing her keys. 'I got a buyer for the Honda – good money. We can't back out on the deal now.'

Kyle smoothed her hair back from her face. 'Come

on, babe, we aren't even gonna need a car. Let Aaron take care of it, he knows what he's doing.'

The dread that had pricked her conscience from the first mention of Aaron's name now jabbed her as she looked into Kyle's eyes. She knew now for certain that she had no ally in him. Just as quickly she knew that if she hoped to get her keys and get out of there, she had to start by playing along.

'Fine,' she sighed, dredging up a nervous half-smile.

Aaron pushed a chair out with his foot. 'Here you go, Six-Pix, have a seat.'

Kyle waited until she was sitting, then he sat down too.

'Now,' Aaron said, 'let's discuss the *pièce de résistance* of our plan – something I just came up with a little while ago. It's brilliant, Six, I'm telling you. You're gonna love it.'

She smiled as though in agreement already. 'Can you call me "Savannah"?'

Aaron laughed. 'Now, soon as we get into Mexico, here's what I'm gonna do . . .' He went on to outline a plan to extort money from her parents by offering to destroy the photos of her in return for as much as they could get. 'Couple hundred grand minimum, I'd say, considering the kind of assets Daddy's got.'

'Wait. You can't . . . I mean, this is a joke, right?' She looked around the tiny room, a space hardly larger than her bathroom at home, as if she might be on a hidden camera. 'This isn't serious?' The last thing she wanted was for her parents to get wind of any of this, but especially not of the pictures.

Aaron said, 'It's not like they need the money.'

'How would you know?'

He pointed a slice of pizza at himself. '*I* know *everything*. Real estate values, company holdings – it's all on the web, Six.'

Kyle said, 'You have *trust funds*, babe, so there must be lots of money to go round. Anyway, we won't get caught. And can you think of a better way to get the cash we need?'

'I don't know – by working, maybe?'

He snorted. 'For seven bucks an hour, right? You see where that's, like, got me so far.'

She tried to keep the desperation out of her voice. 'C'mon, Kyle – we can make it all work some other way. I'm not doing it.'

'Don't, like, get all self-*righteous*,' he said amiably.

'Well, I can't believe you'd blackmail my parents – and that you're willing to *use me*—'

'Yeah, okay, we get it,' Aaron sneered. 'Sixteen, bro – not old enough, I told you. Look, Six, we don't need your approval; we got the photos uploaded, so all we need to do is call Daddy.'

Kyle glanced at Aaron and Savannah caught his look, an expression that said *Let me handle this*. Then to her he said, 'Listen, don't sweat it, right? It's just an idea.' He frowned at Aaron for Savannah's benefit and said, 'Give it a rest for now, man.'

She smiled gratefully, letting Kyle think he'd fooled her. He *had* given her a reprieve, but for how long?

Savannah pushed her chair back and said, 'I need to use the bathroom.' What she needed was a minute alone, to get her thoughts together and come up with a plan. Somehow she had to get Aaron to give her back her keys, and somehow she had to get Kyle to ditch the blackmail idea. She added, 'And then I guess I'll join you guys for a slice,' to make it look like she was loosening up. When she reached for her bag, hoping to at least protect her cash and her bank card, neither man stopped her.

'The door at the end of the hall,' Kyle said as she stood, then he and Aaron turned their attention to which day to leave and which airline to use.

The hallway to the bathroom was short and narrow. As she passed a dark bedroom, a bright bit of light inside the room caught her eye. She paused, looked back toward the kitchen, then stepped into the bedroom and around the end of the bed, where she could see better. In the corner was a folding card table where a laptop computer sat, a camera tethered to it.

And where the pictures of her now scrolled across the screen.

She stared, cringing – they were ... revolting. Nauseating. Kyle, Aaron, they saw her like *this*.

It took her less than a minute to decide what to do.

Now, after climbing out through the bedroom window with Kyle's camera and computer stuffed into her bag, she was crouched, trembling, in the woods.

Aaron's voice carried from somewhere behind her and to her right. 'That sneaky little bitch – I told you to get someone older.'

'She said she was twenty.'

'And then she said she was fifteen and you fucked her again anyway! Use your *brain*, Jesus!' They were coming closer. 'I can't believe we don't have a fucking flashlight!'

Savannah said a prayer of thanks.

'When I find you,' Aaron yelled, 'I'm gonna teach you a lesson, little girl! You'll be screaming for help, I promise you that! You won't walk for a week!'

Kyle again. 'Chill, man, you'll freak her out.'

Too late.

Her whole body shook. She clutched at the damp ground to help keep herself balanced and still. How long since she'd called her mom? How long before someone showed up and rescued her? What if Aaron found her first? A sob rose in her throat and she clenched her jaw to stifle it.

The bug – spider? – crawled from her neck down onto her back, and she started to cry.

FIFTY-FOUR

Meg tried calling Savannah back twice but got no answer. Worried, she hobbled toward the kitchen to find her purse. Then, remembering that Rachel was supposed to be staying over, she yelled for her in the off chance she was still here.

Rachel appeared in the hall with her cell phone to her ear. 'Yeah?'

'Is that Savannah?'

'Uh, no – she's, um, she's in the bathroom.'

Meg was confused. 'Are you sure? Because she just called and said she needs me to go get her – but her phone cut out, and now I can't reach her.'

Rachel hung up her phone. 'Ohmigod, did she wreck her car?'

'Wreck her—? So she's *not* in the bathroom?'

Rachel shook her head. 'Is she okay? I *told* her to be careful.'

Meg waved Rachel into the kitchen. 'Talk,' she said.

Rachel told Meg what time Kyle had called and what

little she knew about him, based on what Savannah had told her.

'She met him online and—'

'Wait. Online, like, from the Internet?'

'Yeah – from her webpage.'

'She has her own webpage?'

Rachel gave her a funny look. 'Um, we all do. I can show you.'

'No – I mean, thank you, but I'll look into that later.' They all had their own webpages? What else did they 'all' have? Diaphragms? VD? And how had she missed this apparently essential element of her daughter's life? Why hadn't Savannah told her, or showed her? What other secrets did she have?

She asked Rachel, 'What else?'

'Well . . . she said he's nineteen, and I guess he lives near Summerfield.'

Now things were adding up. 'Right, okay – but where? *Where* near Summerfield?'

Rachel looked as if she might cry. 'If she's hurt – oh God, I'm so sorry! I never should've gone along with her plan. I never asked her exactly where he lives, 'cause, you know, she was coming back tonight – she's not hurt is she? I never thought—'

'Of course you didn't,' Meg said, then pressed her hand to her mouth. That was the problem: *none* of them ever thought things might not work out the way they planned. They were all too smart, too lucky, too deserving, too well intentioned.

In truth, they were too naïve.

She told Rachel, 'I don't know if Savannah's okay.'

Saying the words sharpened the reality, and Meg had the urge to *run* to Summerfield . . . as if she could.

She tried Savannah again. The phone rang several times, then went to voice mail. Meg left a brief message saying that she was on her way, trying to sound calm and assured. Next, she tried to reach Brian – who also didn't answer. Out of pettiness, probably. She left a message saying that Savannah was in trouble and he needed to call back *now*.

With a frightened Rachel watching her, Meg called the police, though she suspected, rightly, that they wouldn't see the situation as urgently as she. They'd 'send a patrol round out Summerfield way', the dispatcher said, and give her a call if anything turned up. 'Don't worry, ma'am – teens, they just get wild hairs now and then. Almost always turns out okay.'

Almost always.

She told Rachel, 'Have your sister pick you up, all right? I have to go.'

Meg's plan was to drive down 301 and, like the police, look for Savannah's car. Hopefully she'd be able to get through to Savannah when she was closer – or Savannah would get through to her, either way, and then she'd know exactly where to find her. It wasn't a terrific plan, but it was better than waiting at home.

She managed to get the Lexus started and out onto the street. Her weakening left arm was tasked with the gearshift, the turn signal, the steering wheel. As she drove down the block, her right leg seemed to be failing, growing feebler by the moment. Five blocks from the house, a rabbit darted into the road; Meg swerved and tried to brake, but her reflexes were too slow, her foot too weak. She felt the sickening bump and, horrified, realized that the poor rabbit she'd just hit *could* have been a child. In a cold sweat, she pulled to the road-side and parked.

As determined as she was to find Savannah, there was no way she could make it to Summerfield safely.

Choking back her frustration, she called Savannah's cell again. Then Brian's, where she left another message. Then she tried Savannah yet again; still no answer.

Meg pressed her forehead to the steering wheel and looked at her useless arm in the glow of the dashboard lights. Dismay and anger flared in her belly. Her daughter *needed* her, and she was sitting here half-paralyzed in an SUV that cost more than her parents' first house. Ludicrous! 'God *damn* this disease!' she yelled, then sobbed. 'God damn it!'

There was no time to lose, though. Her daughter, her baby, was waiting, somewhere. *Please, God, tell me she's okay* ... She wiped her eyes and her nose and then, because she knew she could count on him, she called Carson.

A few minutes later, when she was back home waiting for him to pick her up, she suddenly knew how they might locate Savannah: the Honda had a GPS transmitter. So not only could Savannah find her way to and from anyplace on the continent, she could also be *found* – or the car could. Brian had explained it all back in March when he'd ordered the car. At the time Meg had only half listened as he listed its features, seeing the GPS as just another of his gadget-geek interests. Now she blessed him for his foresight and went to his desk to find the receiver he'd also bought – the device that would get her closer to her daughter, where she should've been all along.

Fifteen minutes after she'd called him, Carson was there helping her into the passenger side of the Lexus, getting her seatbelt buckled, listening to her directions. She was glad he didn't ask questions, didn't speculate about Savannah's behavior or accuse Meg of being a neglectful mother – though she certainly felt like one. She felt *criminal* in her lax attention to how Savannah was spending her time. The only thing that helped was that Carson simply drove them toward the Honda's location, fast.

Once off 301, the blackness of the night surrounded them. The roads were poorly marked. Each wrong or missed turn put another knot in her gut, made her heart rise a little higher in her throat. Each passing minute added a new brick to the load of guilt she was shouldering – about Savannah and everything else.

She looked at Carson, tempted, suddenly, to offload some of the weight by confessing the possibility that Savannah was his.

As they bumped along rough, patched pavement, Meg crafted her confession silently: *Carson, remember the morning of my wedding? Well, there's something I think you should know* . . . Her heart thudded, wishing, hoping – yet she couldn't tell him now, not like this. Maybe not at all. To lighten her burden would only create a burden for him, and she wasn't willing to do that.

Finally they found the right road and rolled to a stop, fifty feet from where Savannah's Honda sat, ghostly in the darkness of the ramshackle street. The car, its wheels off the edge of crumbling macadam, was parked in front of a mailbox missing both door and flag.

Meg stared at the tiny house sitting back in an overgrown lot and wondered why, if Savannah made it here, she'd called so soon wanting to be picked up.

'Maybe she's not here,' she said. 'She could've been carjacked.'

Carson nodded. 'Could be, but if this Kyle guy lives out this way—'

'Yeah, too much of a coincidence. So she must be here.' And something must be wrong.

The sand driveway was thick with weeds and hosted a Pontiac with badly sagging rear suspension. No wonder Savannah hadn't wanted to say where Kyle went to school, didn't want to talk about a guy who came from such meager beginnings. For a moment Meg was embarrassed by how far she, and by extension Savannah, had traveled from her own inelegant beginnings, so far that Savannah had felt unable to tell her anything specific about Kyle.

She'd been surprised, when she and Brian were dating, that he had seen past her family's poverty, that he'd selected her when he might have picked someone much more like himself. She asked him why, once – years later, when they'd been to a party of his peers and were more than tipsy on hundred-dollar-a-bottle wine, and he'd looked at her and grinned. 'Opportunity,' he'd said. 'You had great growth potential.' As if she were an investment fund. Even then, she wasn't sure how much of a compliment it was.

Maybe Savannah looked at Kyle that way, like a promising opportunity that would grow ever better under her care. Maybe she was Brian's daughter, through and through.

Carson turned the car off. 'Let me go first.'

'Wait – I'll try calling her again.' She peered at the house while she called; only one thin line of light was visible, through a gap in the living room curtains. 'Still no answer.'

'How long since she called you?'

'Almost an hour,' she said, her throat constricting. 'Let's try the house.'

'Meg—'

'I'm not going to just sit here.'

With Carson following, she limped through the damp weeds to the front door. Breath held, she knocked.

The sound of footsteps was followed by the sudden glare of a bare-bulb porch light, and the door was opened by a young man in ragged khaki shorts and a dirt-smudged T-shirt. 'Yeah?'

'I'm looking for Savannah.'

'Don't know who you're talking about.' He started to close the door.

'Wait!' she yelled, trying to see around him. 'Are you Kyle?' He was very good looking, but definitely not a high school student.

He hesitated to answer, but his face gave him away. Finally he said, 'Maybe.'

She moved the strap of her sling where it pulled against her neck. 'Let's not play games, all right? I tracked her car by GPS. The police are on their way here.' Or they *should* be – *would* be with one quick call, if needed. She hoped. Then hoped not to need to call. 'Where is she?'

Kyle sighed and opened the door. 'Why don't you come in? You'll get eaten up by mosquitoes out there, right?'

Meg looked at Carson. He shrugged as if to say, *What choice is there?*

Inside, the smell assaulted her, stale, pungent, like old grease and sour milk and something else, a sweet, smoky odor – marijuana? She looked, first, toward the darkened kitchen doorway, and then to her right, to a dirty gold sofa. The floor, chipped Formica tile circa 1965, was stained and grimy with spills that had collected dirt, giving the grayish floor a haphazard pattern of moldy-looking amoebas. She didn't want to even guess at what all the spills might have been.

Meg's patience was wearing out. 'Where's my daughter?'

Kyle scratched his jaw. 'Wish I knew.'

Just then Carson tapped her shoulder. She turned and saw that he was pointing outside – at the Honda. From here they could see what they hadn't noticed walking up to the house: the headlights were smashed out and the front bumper and hood dented as if someone had taken a baseball bat to it. Meg opened her mouth but no words came, just a small, animal-like noise.

Carson stepped past her and gripped Kyle's arm. 'Answers,' he said. 'Now.'

FIFTY-FIVE

'*Savannah Metallic*,' Savannah whispered. Her throat felt tight, but the ache in her chest was easing now that she saw her mom's SUV a hundred yards away, through the trees.

She'd crept northeast – she was pretty sure it was northeast – further into the woods and away from the sounds of Aaron bashing her car. An owl had flapped past her head, also in retreat. Aaron's voice spit the cool night air as he yelled, 'It's too risky' – *slam* – 'to sell it now' – *slam* 'so I hope your little bitch' – *slam* – 'is happy!' When the bashing stopped, she stopped, waiting. A minute later she'd heard the rumble of Aaron's Camaro as he tore down the road, and she knew the worst was over.

Her legs, scratched and cut by underbrush, hurt everywhere, and God only knew how she must look. Dried mud crusted her fingernails and felt stiff on her face where she'd wiped at her tears. Still, she was here, mostly uninjured, glad to be alive. Alive and ready to confess her stupidity and go home.

Thinking *home* made the tears well again.

Before she could go home, though, she had some crucial things to do. She lifted the strap of her bag up over her head then laid the bag down, drew the laptop out, and dropped it facedown onto the ground. Then she dug into her bag, feeling around for her penlight and for the miniature Swiss army knife attached to it.

In the dim light and with careful deliberation, Savannah unscrewed the computer's hard-drive access cover. That done, she pulled out the drive and unscrewed *its* cover, squinting to see the tiny screws. She took the cover off; how best to destroy the data that could so easily destroy her future? First, she gripped the knife and stabbed it into the green panel. She scraped the blade across the tiny copper pathways again and again. Then she wedged the blade under the board's edge and pried it up until it snapped off on one corner. A small round disk – the actual memory? – was easy to pop out. With the blade, she dug into the ground, making a narrow but deep hole in which to bury the disk. No one would find it here, and even if someday someone did, it would be rusted and unidentifiable. Nothing but metal junk. Same for the green board, which she broke off its case and went to bury thirty yards away.

Now the camera: within three minutes, all the pictures were deleted, the memory card removed and pried apart. She heaved the camera off one way, then threw the laptop carcass as far as she could in the opposite direction.

There. Now no one else would ever know.

She headed toward the house, gearing up for whatever she was about to face. Angry parents, for sure. And if Kyle was still there . . . ? What would he be telling them? He was slick, for sure. Charming.

'Bastard,' she said.

Had she ever been anything more to him than a body and a bank?

No one waited in the Lexus, so she moved on to the house. Maybe she'd get away with giving them a simple story about an argument over . . . drug use. Sure. She could say Kyle and his friend wanted her to join them, but she refused, and because they were stoned, they got kind of crazy and she got scared – yeah, that might work. Whatever Kyle might've told her parents, she'd give them her version and they'd believe *her*. Not some jerk who lied to their daughter and was now lying to them.

She felt confident she could pull off the scene – right up until the moment she stood inside Kyle's doorway and saw his rueful face.

'Savannah!' said her mom, Kyle, and Carson – *Carson*, not her dad – all at once.

Savannah burst into tears. 'You are such a fricking *liar*,' she yelled at Kyle as if she hadn't heard anyone. She hardly had. 'You were just using me! How could you?'

'Wait, babe,' Kyle began.

Her mom, who was sitting on the sofa, stood up. 'Honey – dear God, look at you! Are you all right?'

Savannah glanced down. Her legs were a mess of

bloody, dirty scratches, her arms too. 'I'm okay,' she said, wiping her nose. She pointed at Kyle, who was sitting cross-legged on the floor near the kitchen. 'What did he tell you?' Without waiting for an answer, she walked over to Kyle and said, 'I *loved* you, and all you were in it for was . . . was, like, *money*,' and sex, of course, but she couldn't spit that out in public. 'So that you and that asshole could get your jollies off the rich girl!'

Kyle stood. 'No! I mean, okay, maybe at first, but—'

'Go to hell!' she said, the tears still streaking her dirty face. 'But first I want my keys.'

'Aaron – he was pissed so he took 'em with him.'

'And you let him,' she said, and he must have sensed the violence she was feeling, because he didn't argue.

'Babe,' was all he said, his eyes wide and sad.

'I hope I never see you again.' She choked back a sob and turned for the front door. In half a dozen steps, she was folded into her mom's waiting arms.

The tension of unasked questions filled the Lexus as Savannah, her mom, and Carson left Kyle's. Now that she was a little calmer, she wondered what Kyle had told them, and she was sure they wanted to know more about why she was there in the first place. For a while, though, they just rode in silence, as if the increasing distance from Kyle's house might put everything right.

If only it could, she thought, pressing her cheek against the cool glass of the backseat window. If only being apart from him, knowing the truth about who he was and how he did things could undo how rotten she felt inside. He hadn't wanted her at all; he'd wanted someone to subsidize his habit and spread her legs and not ask questions – all of which she'd done. Good God, where were her brains? Was this what 'love' did to you? Could it be this easy to fool yourself – and be fooled?

But maybe Kyle *did* feel something for her . . . she wanted to believe he did . . . but even *if*, that obviously hadn't been enough for him to be decent.

He'd *invited* Aaron to come to the hotel that night, wanted the pictures taken. So, okay, maybe at first she'd led him to believe she was the sort of girl who'd do all that sort of stuff – but not after their fight. And then he *still* loaded those pictures onto his computer and used them for his screen saver and let Aaron call her Six-Pixel Chick. And *then* thought blackmailing her parents was a fine idea, went along with every part of Aaron's supposedly new plan – she was starting to doubt how 'new' it was – never once thinking it wasn't *right*, and that she might not agree with it.

Her mom turned toward the backseat and said, 'How are you doing?'

Savannah shrugged. 'Feeling stupid.'

'He said you stormed out after fighting with his roommate about lending him some money. But that's not all, is it?'

'Do we have to talk about this *now*? I'm . . . I'm just really tired.'

'No, okay.'

Her mom's kindness made her feel like crying, again. She looked away. 'I'm gonna catch a nap, okay?'

She dozed the rest of the way, the murmur of her mom's voice and Carson's a pleasant lullaby she wished could last forever.

FIFTY-SIX

With Savannah showered and tucked into bed, Meg joined Carson and Brian in the den.

Brian was saying, 'I tried calling Meg several times – but the reception's so poor out there.'

'Sure,' Carson said. 'They need more cell towers down that way.' Meg sat on the sofa near Carson, while Brian was in the wing chair. He said, 'I would've left the club right away.' She knew he was chafing at Carson being her hero; she could see it in the way he kept clenching and unclenching his hands.

She said, 'Well, Savannah's clean again, and the worst of her cuts is bandaged up. She's still not saying much, though.'

'We're going to have to discuss what to do with her,' Brian said. Plainly he meant *after Carson left*. Poor Savannah . . . Before she'd gotten into bed, she'd insisted that she hadn't been harmed tonight, beyond the visible wounds. Meg knew there were emotional wounds, though; it was obvious that Savannah felt betrayed by Kyle, that she'd gotten her heart broken at the very least.

'I'm gonna head home,' Carson said, taking Brian's unsubtle cue. He stood.

Meg stood too, bracing herself against the sofa's arm. Her leg felt rubbery, but she tried not to let it show. 'Come on, I'll walk you out.'

Carson glanced at Brian, but *she* didn't. Whatever Brian thought, about this choice or anything else related to Carson, she didn't care to know right now.

When they were outside on the driveway, crickets chirping in competition with the cicadas in the trees, Carson pulled her to him. How good it felt, how right. She fit in his arms just as she always had.

He stepped back, leaning against the car but keeping his arms looped around her waist. 'You were very impressive tonight.'

'What did I do?'

'It's what you *didn't* do – you didn't berate her or force her to tell you everything.'

'God, I feel so awful for her … She needs a little time to sort things out – what good would pressuring her do?'

'I agree,' he said, 'but it's got to be hard not to do it. You showed remarkable restraint.'

'Thanks.' She choked up, hid her face against his shoulder until the feeling eased. 'She's so inexperienced – well, *was*. God knows what all's been going on that I've been completely blind to.'

They stood together, quiet and thoughtful. The insects hummed around them, oblivious to the pettiness of human life. How simple, how lovely to be a bug, Meg thought, your life's path determined by absolutes: find food, mate, reproduce, die. No existential dramas, no guilt – no emotions at all. She couldn't help thinking what a blessing that would sometimes be.

Carson said, 'When can I see you again? I have to go to Seattle on Monday, get things resolved with my condo. I could come back by the weekend, though, for a few days. Then I'm off to Hawaii – a Memorial Day gig. I can't get out of it.'

'You don't have to come back here in between,' she said, remembering that he didn't like to fly. Savannah would be taking most of her attention anyway; who knew what the effects of her misadventures would be? 'That's a lot of air travel. I can wait to see you after.'

'That's okay,' he said, kissing her on her forehead. 'Don't you know you're worth it?'

FIFTY-SEVEN

The first thing Savannah did after she woke up at eleven-thirty Sunday morning was haul herself into the shower again, using the hottest water she could stand. If only she could wash out her brain and her heart, rid herself of every trace of Kyle and his nasty friend. She leaned down to scrub between her toes and saw the one bright ray in her life: watery blood streaming down the inside of her thigh.

When she finished showering, she felt a little more human, but still mostly like a whipped dog. How idiotic she'd been! If anyone, *anyone* found out about how she'd even considered running away with such a loser, she'd be a pariah. Brainy Savannah – yeah, right.

She could hardly face herself in the steamy mirror. How was she going to face her dad? She wouldn't blame him if he took back the car. She wished someone could take back her whole life. Or the last couple of months of it, anyway. Erase everything that had happened since the minute she got into the webpage stuff, with all her big ideas of finding a boyfriend who was more mature than the guys she knew.

Kyle was more mature, all right. Thinking of him made her head hurt, made her heart hurt, and she understood how some girls turned to heavy drinking or drugs or thought about suicide after being dumped – or totally betrayed – by a guy they loved. She understood the temptation of those sanctuaries, false though she knew they were.

After she was dry and dressed, she did what she could to cut Kyle out of her life: deleted him from her cell phone and from her buddy list, blocked his e-mail address and any messages from him to her webpage. She saw a message from Rachel waiting – *CALL ME!!!!!* – and sent her a short note: *Am fine. It's all good! CU later.* Damage control.

She found her parents at the kitchen bar – both of them, on a Sunday! In her honor, obviously. She hadn't seen her dad before five PM on a Sunday ever, she was pretty sure. It could only mean they were going to double-team her on this disaster; she ducked her head and waited.

'Good shower?' her mom asked, a little too cheerfully.

'Uh-huh.' She went to the pantry and took out cereal, more for the activity of it than because she was hungry.

'Dad and I have been talking, and we think it might be good for you and me to take a little vacation.'

Vacation? She got a bowl and spoon, got out the milk, all without yet meeting their eyes. Her mom sounded so pleasant – surely there were going to be angry words, some kind of lecture, some punishment. The 'vacation' was probably a trip to see potential boarding schools.

'Where?' she asked, sitting next to her mom and pouring the cereal.

'I was thinking Hawaii. We've never been . . . and, with my, um, condition, it's going to be harder for me to travel in the future.'

Savannah looked up. Her mom's expression was so sincere, her eyes so kind. Instead of lecturing her, they were offering a *trip*.

God, what a lousy kid she was.

Her voice wavered as she said, 'That sounds great. When were you thinking?'

'In a week or so.'

Their generosity made her throat close with tears. She swallowed hard. 'That's – I mean, yeah, okay. Thanks.'

So far her dad hadn't spoken, and she wondered, suddenly, if this plan was really cool with him or if he was silent because he disagreed. She hesitated to look at him; it was so embarrassing, them knowing how she'd been taken in by Kyle. Embarrassing and degrading; he must think she was a fool, no smarter than some bimbo. *He'd* never put himself in a position of disadvantage.

'So . . . I'll miss school?' Not that she minded.

Her dad said, 'Mom's thinking she'll arrange for you to make up exams after you get back.'

She ventured a quick glance at him. His face was neutral – which was better than she expected. 'Oh, okay. I can do that.'

She ate, eyes on her Frosted Flakes, aware that her parents were watching her. What were they *looking* at? After her third bite she said, 'Could you guys please stop watching me?'

A stool scraped back. 'You're going to talk to her?' her dad said.

'Yes – go ahead. We'll go at four.'

Savannah watched him go. 'What's at four?'

'We have to go get your car.'

'Can't I just stay here?'

Her mom frowned. 'Even if I could drive it home myself, the answer would be no.'

Well, she had *that* coming. And the discussion that followed too, which was, more or less, the one her mom had been intending to have with her for weeks.

First, the practical stuff: If she and Kyle were having sex, had she used any kind of barrier birth control?

'Yes,' Savannah said, tracing silvery flecks in the granite counter with her fingertip, 'and also no.'

How many times unprotected? 'Three, maybe more.' She'd lost track. She added, 'But those times he always, you know, stopped before . . .' Or she was pretty sure he had.

Her mom looked grave. 'Do you realize you put yourself at risk for HIV, hepatitis, chlamydia, herpes, syphilis, and gonorrhea, in *addition* to pregnancy?'

'I'm sorry!' she cried. 'He seemed so great! He said he loved the same stuff I do . . . Anyway, I'm *not* pregnant.'

'No? You got your period? Well, that's a relief. And in six months or so, if several HIV and hepatitis and herpes test results are negative, you can cross those off your list of worries too.'

Savannah shrunk under the pressure of those worries. 'So . . . all those things – I won't know if I have them right away?'

'I wish I could tell you otherwise. Syphilis, chlamydia, and gonorrhea show up fairly soon – within a few weeks. Tomorrow I'll get you some preventative antibiotics for what's curable. The rest, only time will tell.'

'God.' She hung her head. 'I'm sorry. I'm *so* sorry.'

Her mom touched her arm. 'Oh, sweetheart . . .'

They talked a little about her webpage, and her mom said she'd have to surrender her computer temporarily, 'while we figure out how to protect you from yourself'.

She had that coming, too.

'Now listen, I have to ask you another hard question. Are you listening?'

'What?' Savannah said.

'The things you did – you consented to all that, right?'

'Yes,' she said, taking full responsibility for all the things her mom never need know had happened.

'And obviously you lied about where you were spending your time, so that you could see him.' The pain in her mom's voice was just what she had expected she'd hear.

'Mom . . .' She shrugged. 'Look, I know I did it wrong, but come on, you never would've let me date him and . . . you know, I loved him. He made me feel like I was special and . . . and important.' Or he *had*. She wiped hot tears off her cheeks.

Her mom put her hand to her mouth and nodded. 'All right,' she finally said. 'All right. It's not that I approve of how you've handled things but I understand. And I'm . . . I'm sorry that Dad and I somehow let you down. You are *very* special, and *very* important. Nothing is more important. I mean it, and I'm sorry.'

Savannah wiped off more tears. 'It's okay,' she said.

'No, it's not. I'm going to do better, I promise.'

'Yeah,' she whispered, 'me too.'

Her mom hugged her close and stroked her hair. 'Okay.'

Savannah went back to her room and flopped on the bed. Hawaii sounded good – maybe they'd reset things there. Maybe she'd be able to explain, for herself and her mom, how she already missed what she'd *thought* she had with Kyle.

Love . . . it was so tricky and messy and misleading. How did anyone survive it? How did anyone know when it was true? She put on her headphones and played her favorite ballads as if the music would explain everything, emerging from her room only when it was time to go get her car.

It wasn't until later, when she saw her mom set a vase of irises on the mantel next to Grandma Anna's photo, that she remembered today was Mother's Day.

FIFTY-EIGHT

While Savannah napped on an inflatable lounger in the pool Monday afternoon, Meg paged through her mother's diaries, keeping one eye on her daughter from the kitchen as though keeping her in sight equated to protection, the way it once had. Even when she'd seen Savannah these past months, she clearly hadn't *seen* her. Blindness was not part of ALS, so she could blame only herself.

In the unused pages of the last diary – blank space that represented time her mother didn't get, a bit of ripped newsprint caught her eye. It was her mother's obituary.

Ocala Star-Banner, Monday, September 12, 2005

POWELL, ANNA LOUISE, 64. *Mrs Anna Louise Powell, formerly Jansen, passed away Saturday night in her sleep, victim of a sudden heart attack. Born July 27, 1941, in Clemson, South Carolina, to William and Alice Jansen, the former Anna Jansen*

460

moved to Marion County with her family at the age of 15. She married Spencer Powell, originally of Pittsburgh, PA, in 1963. Mr and Mrs Powell had owned and operated Powell's Breeding and Boarding since 1972. A member of the Marion County Ladies' Committee for the Betterment of Rural Living, the Cover-to-Cover Book Lover's Club, the Central Florida Breeder's Association, and volunteer to several Ocala-area senior citizens' aid services, Mrs Powell was a beloved and generous person who will be sadly missed. Mrs Powell is survived by her husband Spencer; daughters Dr Meghan Hamilton of Ocala, Kara Linford of Sacramento, CA, Elizabeth Powell of Berkeley, CA, and Julianne Portman of Quebec, Canada, and their husbands; and eight grandchildren. Visitation is 7 PM tonight at Montecito Funeral Home. Graveside service Tuesday, September 13, 11:00 AM, at Our Lady of Tender Mercies Estates.

Of course she'd seen a copy before, but the presence of one *here* was proof that her father had known what the notebooks were, that his act of giving them to her was deliberate . . . So that she could know her mother better – and know him better, too, guided by her mother's devoted yet honest words.

He might not have anticipated the other side effect – that she would come to know herself better as well – but she thanked him for that benefit just the same.

These positive results reassured Meg in an important way; she believed, now, that good intentions *could* lead to good outcomes, and sometimes did. Fate could reward as well as punish. She looked again at Savannah, drifting on the calm blue water, and thought, *She needs this lesson too.*

'Thanks, Dad,' she murmured.

PART IV

There is no remedy for love but to love more.
– Henry David Thoreau

FIFTY-NINE

In the week before they left for Hawaii, Meg began constructing opportunities to talk to Savannah. Trips to the grocery store, meal preparation, closet cleaning . . . keeping Savannah out of school and off the phone and computer gave them one-on-one time they hadn't had for years.

She didn't focus on the trouble Savannah had been through – Savannah met with a counselor to work through that without her parents present, as the counselor suggested. And Meg also didn't bring up ALS, though she knew that talk was coming soon. Her symptoms continued to worsen in small ways almost by the day, and she knew Savannah was uneasily aware that she pressed more of the physical tasks on her. All the driving, all the cutting, measuring, stirring, all the button-pressing of remote controls and ATM machines and phone calls. Savannah watched her closely, much the way Meg watched her father. One morning when they were getting ready to go to the market, Meg asked Savannah to pull her hair back for her, a strangely intimate role reversal. Savannah did it, asking, 'Mom, can't they *do* anything about your arm and stuff?' It would have been a good time to confess, but Meg couldn't make the words travel from her brain to her lips.

Otherwise she let their conversations go where they would. Boys, college, politics, ecology, music. When they were in the airport waiting to begin the first leg of their trip to Hawaii, Savannah brought up Carson.

'We'll see him there, right? I mean, besides at the concert?'

'Yes, some – he's going to be pretty busy.'

'So tell me what happened with him and Val,' Savannah said, feet propped on her carry-on bag. Jets roared onto the runway out the window in front of them, to the delight of a pair of small boys who had their faces pressed to the glass.

Meg said, 'Well, mostly he realized that they weren't a good enough fit. He thought she deserved someone who would be completely devoted to her.'

'And why wasn't he? I mean, she seems great.'

Meg gave her the answer her own mother might have given. 'She does, but you know, love has its own ideas. We can't force it, and we can't fight it – not very successfully, anyway.' As well she knew.

She checked the time. 'We should be boarding soon; give me a hand getting the passes out, would you?'

'Do you love Carson?' Savannah asked, stopping Meg cold.

'What? Why would you ask that?'

'You can't answer a question with a question – that's

cheating.' Savannah took the boarding passes out of Meg's bag.

'I just wondered why you – well, the answer is, of course I do. I've known him forever. He was like a member of my family, and—'

'Mom,' Savannah said, looking at her plainly, '*I* try to be straight with *you* about everything. Besides, I'm not a baby. I know you and Dad aren't exactly hot for each other. You can tell me.'

Meg looked at her daughter, at the genuine care and love on her face, and realized that this moment was a wish granted. 'Okay,' she said, 'you're right. But before I get into how I feel about Carson, let me tell you how it was.' And she began the story she'd wanted to tell Savannah for so long.

The pleasure of Hawaii had little to do with Hawaii itself and almost everything to do with the removal of mother and daughter from their previous lives. Because everything, Meg thought, watching Savannah body-surf at Hauula Beach, everything that came before this precise moment was gone, done – figments of the past that mattered not at all to the roll of the surf or the caress of the Pacific breeze on their bronzed skin. The past was gone, the future not yet arrived, and so they lived in each moment, whether that moment was a sunset seen from the Coast Guard station at Kaena Point or a view of Saturn from one of the Mauna Kea Observatories – where the resident astronomers were pleased to give Carson and his close friends a tour of the night sky – or the moment when Meg sat on the sand alongside her daughter early one morning, Diamond Head rising stoically behind them, and told her she had ALS.

Had she ever done a harder thing in her life? Even leaving Carson that long-ago day had not been anything like this.

There was no easy way to broach the subject, so as they'd watched seabirds skittling across the foamy sand, pinkened waves breaking gently along the shoreline, Meg said, 'Savannah, I need to confess something. What I told you was wrong with my arm and leg was a lie.'

'Well . . . so, what *is* wrong?'

Meg pursed her lips, then forged ahead. 'I have something known as Lou Gehrig's disease.' She described it as simply as she could.

Savannah's eyes grew wide in disbelief and horror. Then her face crumpled and she put her hands to her mouth. 'No, Mommy . . .' She shook her head. 'No – you can't . . . Oh God, oh God! I've been – oh my God, I've been such a terrible daughter!' Tears streamed down her face. Meg's chest tightened as if squeezed in a vise, and she tried hard to keep from sobbing herself. But in the end she couldn't help it. She wrapped Savannah in her arms and rocked her.

'No, no,' she said, her mouth against Savannah's wavy hair. 'No, you are the best daughter ever.'

They cried together until both of them were red-eyed and blotchy and empty of tears. And then, when neither of them knew what to do next, they looked at each other and actually smiled at their bad luck, at the absurd paths life took. There was nothing else for it.

They walked the beach, holding hands, and then Savannah stopped suddenly and said, 'Will it be horrible? Will there be a lot of pain?' And Meg assured her that no, when her time came, it would be exactly the opposite. This small grace made them both feel a little bit better.

Meg knew Savannah's acceptance was temporary, a gift of this suspended time, but she was grateful for both of them to have it. The blessing of youth was the ability to forget – or if not forget, to continue. Savannah began to do what she, Meg, was doing: valuing their long days together without thinking too much about the raised axe above Meg's head.

They had more long conversations. Savannah revealed that her last fight with Kyle and his roommate had to do with lewd photos and extortion; she confessed to misusing the credit card; she apologized for sliding into behaviors she was thoroughly opposed to – 'I lied, I snuck around, I rationalized everything! I'm really, really sorry.' Meg forgave it all – of course she did, because hadn't Savannah been punished enough?

They shopped, they swam – or Savannah did; Meg stayed, now, where the sand remained safely underfoot. They boated, they ate – poi and pineapple and fish that had been swimming only minutes before appearing on their plates. And sometimes, Carson joined them. But not too often. He was protective of the bubble of time surrounding her and Savannah. Her time with him would come afterward, after she delivered Savannah to Beth for a week of seeing the Berkeley campus and helping Beth get packed.

She'd thought it impossible that two weeks in Hawaii could make a dent in her regret for time lost with Savannah, but she'd been wrong. Sitting here on the beach, seeing Savannah in the glowing evening surf getting instruction from a girl she'd met there, Meg was content. The sun was on her back, her skin smelled of coconut; the world – *her* world, at least – was in order. What she did or didn't do with her daughter twelve years ago, eight years ago, two years ago, last month, made no difference to the joy of now. Life could be reinvented continuously. The past wasn't *gone*; it was simply diminished, put in its place so that *now* could be appreciated, in the fullest sense of the word.

As for the future? Her body hadn't let her forget what lay ahead, but at this moment that path was nebulous, irrelevant. It didn't need to be trod while she was *here*. That was the pleasure of Hawaii.

SIXTY

Savannah was asleep in Beth's guest bedroom upstairs while Meg sat at the kitchen table, her mind as full as a river after torrential rains.

As ever, time had proved relentless; even Hawaiian trips couldn't go on indefinitely. Here again was her future, only now it had become her present: a foggy night in a cottage on Panoramic Hill, minutes from the UC Berkeley campus, where her sister poured warm milk into a pair of brown stoneware mugs.

'I know she got a little off-track,' Beth was saying as she set a mug in front of Meg, 'but you've raised a great kid. You really don't have to worry about her, you know.'

'Maybe not . . . but there are still plenty of things even a great kid can't control.' There were a lot of things beyond anyone's control, in fact, but she didn't want to focus on those. The conversation she'd asked Beth to stay up for was about controlling one of the few things she could.

She circled the mug with her hands and said, 'I'm

hugely grateful to have you coming back to Ocala. Dad's looking forward to having you around.'

'*You're* my priority, you know.'

Meg looked down at the mug. 'Thanks, but it's Savannah's welfare I'm most concerned with. Which is what I wanted to talk to you about.' She met Beth's eyes again. 'I plan to name you as her guardian in my will, and I want to make sure you're okay with that.'

Beth put her hands around Meg's and pulled them away from the mug, grasping them across the tabletop. 'I'm honored.'

'It's not just an honor,' Meg said.

'No, I know that.' Beth squeezed, then let go. 'But she's sixteen already; odds are fairly good that both you and Brian will be around to see her through to eighteen.'

The truth about what Meg intended for her not-quite-so-rosy future slid right to the very tip of her tongue before she bit it back. Instead she said, 'I'm not much for playing the odds, okay, so I need to know for sure: will you take care of Savannah in my place? No matter when that might be?'

'Meg, I'd give you my soul if you asked for it.' Beth's eyes were so round, so sad and earnest. 'I hate that you have to think about any of this . . . but I want you to know, I really respect how proactive you are, taking care of all this stuff way ahead of time. You've always been the sensible one.'

Not always.

There was no time, though, to dwell on what could not be helped by warm milk and a sister's promise.

* * *

Meg's father met her in the parking lot when she came to see him after her return. Blue passionflower bloomed along the lamppost behind him, the flowers hand-sized harbingers of summer. He waved as she climbed out of the taxi, and walked over to give her his arm.

'Good trip?' he asked. She'd just gotten home from Beth's late the night before.

'Marvelous. Beth and Savannah send their love.'

'When's Beth getting here?'

'Next Thursday. I'll write it down for you.'

They went slowly up the sidewalk to the building, her limp more pronounced than ever, and instead of getting impatient with herself, she took the time to notice the new pots of striped purple and white petunias outside one resident's door, another's long planter filled with red, white, and blue flowers – done for Memorial Day, she guessed, or in early anticipation of the Fourth of July. Another had put out a pair of copper-roofed bird feeders that gleamed in the sunset. Even here, where all the residents were in their own sunsets, so to speak, many of them made the effort to appreciate nature, to beautify their surroundings – to *live*, as long as they were living. She liked this about the place, and hoped it translated to the people cultivating friendships and taking care of each other a little, too.

'That leg's getting to be a real problem,' her father said.

Everything was, in fact. 'I'm seeing a physical therapist tomorrow.'

'Shoulda seen one yesterday,' he joked, and squeezed her a little to make sure she knew his teasing was

473

affectionate. He never had been good at showing his feelings – not his caring ones, at any rate.

When they were inside and cooling off at the dining table with her father's new favorite drink, the mint, lime, and rum Mojito, she said, 'I need to thank you, Dad, for paying Bruce and for giving me Mom's diaries.'

He looked surprised and a little embarrassed by her directness. 'Well, sure.'

'You made her happy. Not just because you did those things – though if she's watching, I'm sure she's glad. But I mean, always. Did you read them, the note-books?'

'I mighta looked at 'em a little,' he said.

'Then you know. She loved you despite everything. And I do too.' She gazed at him steadily, so that he'd feel the weight and truth of her words. 'None of us knew how wrong things would go – it all looked really good, in the beginning. Anyway . . . I was angry with you for a long time, but I'm not anymore.'

'Aw, now Meggie . . .' He looked at his drink as though it had become the most fascinating thing in the room. 'You've been too good to me all along – just like your mother. Crazy coot that I am. She's waiting for you, you know,' he added, looking up at her.

She smiled. 'Yeah, I think maybe she is.' It was a good thought, welcome and comforting.

'Yep,' he said, nodding. 'I saw her the other night – you won't believe me, but I'm telling you I did. Woke up at four or so – damn bladder. I think I might want them stones back if it means I don't hafta pee every five minutes – anyway, I woke up and there she was, sitting on the bed, holding on to that blanket you used to carry with you everywhere.'

'What blanket?' Meg said.

'Don't you remember? That blue-and-yellow flannel thing, with the little pink roses. I guess your Aunt Brenda sent it as a baby gift. You carried it around till it was nothin' more'n a scrap. But it was new when I saw it the other night,' he added, scratching his head. 'And I asked her, "That Meggie's?" And she said it was, and I said, "Guess you'll be waiting for her." And she said she would.'

Meg had only the vaguest memory of the baby blanket, recalling the sensation of smooth, soft flannel against her face more than the fact of the thing itself. As for her father's vision, she wouldn't presume to doubt him. He looked convinced, and so although her logical doctor's mind told her it was only a pretty fantasy, or perhaps a dream, she was glad to allow that it *might* be real. In fact, she was finding herself growing more and more curious about what she *would* find when her time came.

'Do you want me to give her any message when I see her?' she asked.

'Oh, nah. I see her regular enough.' He stood up and went to stand behind Meg's chair. 'I hope you'll stop in now and then too,' he said, and kissed the top of her head. 'I like all the attention. I'll be back in a sec.' He walked toward the bathroom, then stopped and turned back toward her. 'That reminds me, when's Beth gonna get here?'

The newspaper lay on the kitchen counter, open to the obituaries. Meg was puzzled at first – what kind of macabre message did Brian mean by this? Then she saw it: 'Silver Springs Mother of Four Succumbs to Lou Gehrig's.'

The headline must've caught his eye. It was a long obit, lovingly crafted by Lana's family, no doubt, detailing every accomplishment of her too-short lifetime. Brownies and Girl Scouts, Spanish Club, gymnast, candy striper, Sunday School nursery teacher, wife, mother, widow, brave victim of a disease about which too little is known. Brian must have thought she'd be interested, particularly in the part that said Lana had 'died peacefully surrounded by her children, sister, father, and in-laws'. No suicide for her. No stigma.

Well, that was the exact right choice for Lana – presumably, it was. If Penny was to be believed, Lana had lived and died on her own terms. Just as Meg herself intended to do; better late than never.

She thought about Penny and about Lana's girls, so dedicated to Lana. What would happen to all of them now? They were left to make do with so little, while she, Meg, had far more than anyone needed. She went to the phone.

'Hi, Penny? It's Meg Hamilton.'

'Oh, hey there! I didn't expect to hear from you again.' *Ever*, Meg thought. Penny said, 'Maybe you saw the paper?'

'I did. I'm very sorry for your loss.'

'Oh, thanks, hon. She died real peaceful-like. Lungs just up and quit, you know?'

Meg knew.

'How are the girls?' she asked.

'Nicole is right depressed just now, but that'll pass. Colleen wrote a poem, read it at the funeral. Should I get her to say it for you?'

'No.' She didn't think she could bear that just now.

'No, but I was wondering, are you keeping the girls, or—?'

Penny sighed. 'I am. It's crazy, ain't it? How I think I'm gonna manage them and hold a job and get Lee back I purely don't know. God willing, it'll all work out.'

God willing. 'I'd like to help out a little, if you'll let me.'

'You?' Lana said, surprised. 'Hon, that's real kind of you, but you got a heavy load of your own. You need to just take care of you.'

'I can't drive anymore. My arm – well, you know. So I'm going to sign over my car to you. There's room for all the girls.'

'Now, Meg—'

'Please, let me do this for them, and for you. It . . . it'll ease my mind.'

'Well, thank you, then. Heavens. Far be it from me to refuse a gift,' Penny said. 'Now tell me, hon, how can I help you?'

'You already did.'

Brian left work early and was home to see Meg before she left for Carson's.

'I could drive you,' he said.

'No, but thanks.' This – waiting for a cab there in the foyer, with her packed bag sitting by the door – this was already awkward enough.

Brian sat on the settee next to her. 'You think I hate you, but I don't.'

'I don't think that. You have a right to be . . . unhappy about all this. That makes perfect sense. I wish, well, I wish things had turned out better for you.'

He bowed his head. 'Me?' He laughed ruefully. 'Me, I'll manage. It's you who deserves a wish.'

'I'm getting it,' she said. She knew he had been referring to her disease, but she was trying to tell him how much joy there was in having just spent such wonderful time with Savannah. She was saying how glad she was that he could offer to drive her to Carson's. She was getting so much of what she wanted, and she was grateful that was what she wanted him to see.

'So . . .' he said, 'you'll let me know when to expect you home?'

She nodded.

'It'll be quiet around here this week . . . again.'

'You won't notice; you'll be gone most of the time.'

'I'll notice.'

A horn sounded outside. Meg grabbed her cane and pushed herself up. 'If you'll take my bag, that would be great.'

He did, helping her outside and down the front steps as well.

They stood at the door of the cab. She leaned toward him and kissed him, pressing her lips to his cheek with fondness and regret. If she had only loved him better. If he had only loved someone else.

SIXTY-ONE

'Welcome back,' Carson told Meg, nervous as he held open the door of the shed. She didn't go in right away but stood on the step looking into the main room, leaning on her cane. The cane was new since Hawaii. He could tell she hated it, but without it she was too unsteady to walk more than a few steps, and that was worse.

'It looks just the same,' she said. 'If only I did too.'

'You look even better,' he said truthfully. Except for the cane and sling – things that looked like aids for recovering from an injury, say – she appeared fine. He could hardly believe she was dying; such a thing made no sense. He said, 'You're more beautiful than ever, in fact.'

She held up the cane. 'It must be my accessories.'

'Here,' he said, scooping her up. 'Let's do this right.'

He carried her inside, just as he'd once imagined doing after their wedding. If only they had long years of togetherness awaiting them – but who ever really knew whether that was what they would get? He read in yesterday's paper a sad story of a newly wed soldier struck and killed by a truck while crossing Route A1A in Pompano Beach. If anything, the bride would've been worrying over the soldier's upcoming assignment to Iraq, not his jog across the road to a convenience store for grapefruit juice. Like Meg had said, life gave no guarantees.

He set her down in the kitchen. 'I took the liberty of anticipating your every desire,' he said, opening the fridge. It was filled with all the things he remembered she liked – orange soda, pineapple juice, chocolate milk, Hostess Ho Hos – and whatever else he'd seen at the store that he thought might appeal. Wine, beer, soda, key lime pie, deli meats and salads; the idea was that they wouldn't need to leave the place at all the entire week.

'I don't know,' she said, peering inside. 'Not *every* desire's in there.' She turned and put her arm around his waist. 'But I'll start with an orange soda.'

'Let's start with this,' he said, and he kissed her. As on the day he'd kissed her on her back stoop so many years ago, her lips were both foreign and familiar – but a sweeter, more longed-for kiss he had never known.

They spent the evening outside, lounging in new chairs he'd bought for their stay. The cypress tree, some 125 years old, made a cool, intimate canopy for watching birds flit back and forth to orange trees now heavy with late-season fruit. Convincing his father to take a week's vacation – to Paris, where his mom had wanted to go since forever – had hinged on the oranges being just shy of ready. 'Call it an early anniversary trip,' he'd told them, to sweeten the deal. It was important that Meg not feel like his folks were watching over them while she was there. When he dropped his mom and dad at the Orlando airport, his mom hugged him and said, 'I'm proud of you, you know.' His dad had nodded. 'Yep. The right thing's usually the hard thing.'

It wasn't hard, though, to see Meg here next to him in the evening shade, her body relaxed and languid and brown from her weeks in the Pacific sun. It wasn't hard at all to think of how in a few minutes he would take her inside, upstairs, and show her how desirable she still was. The hard thing, right now, was waiting. He wanted to meld them back into a single being, one pulse, one love – wanted his love to save her, foolish hope though it was. He wanted to give her timelessness if nothing else, and he believed their lovemaking would at least do that.

'Do you remember when we met?' Meg asked.

'On the school bus. First day of first grade.'

'Kindergarten, for me.'

'You were showing everyone a picture of your baby sister.'

She laughed. 'Kara. I was as proud as if she were my own.'

'I remember asking Mom and Dad later why we hadn't met your family yet – of course it was just us kids who hadn't met.'

'Imagine them not putting our social lives at the top of their agendas!'

'I made up for lost time, though. God, I must've

lived at your house every summer after that year,' he said. 'It was so much more *fun* than being alone here at home.'

'So that's all I was to you, huh? A good time. A diversion from boredom.'

'Absolutely.' He kissed her palm, the inside of her wrist, and then leaned over and nipped her neck. 'What did you think it was about?'

'I think you ruined me for all other men,' she said softly.

God, he adored her. 'All part of my diabolical plan.'

A flock of monk parakeets flew toward them and landed in the branches above, a bright green-and-gray swarm of cheerful chatter. Meg studied them, or seemed to. Then she said, 'What do you think comes after this?'

'Oh, something I think you're going to like a lot,' he said, leering.

'Incorrigible man. No, I mean, after *life*. Or life as we know it, anyway.'

'Ah. Well . . . I'm all for reincarnation. I like to think there's some kind of holding pen for souls, and when it's time – however that's determined – you get to be born again.'

'As a human? Or could you be any living thing?'

'Human. I think there's a sort of predetermined electrical structure for everything – you took chemistry, right?'

'Um, yeah.' She smiled. 'Lots of chemistry.'

'Right, so I figure we're all about electrons and protons and neutrons and stuff – preformulated and unchangeable, except maybe by cosmic accident. You know, like, if there's a sunstorm or something when you're in the pen, you might end up as a carp or – I don't know, an earthworm.'

She laughed. 'Not very reassuring.'

'What do *you* think comes next?'

'Peace – if you've done right in your life. If not, I think there's some kind of accountability. Not hell, but maybe a kind of purgatory – maybe that's what ghosts are all about. People can see them and take them as a warning.'

'Have you ever seen a ghost?'

'No . . . but I've never seen radio waves or satellite signals, either, and that doesn't make them fictional.'

She had a point. 'So maybe we're both right.'

'Maybe we are.'

Above the orange trees, in the darkening sky, he spotted the night's first star. He pointed at it. 'Make a wish.'

She stared up at the star and then said, 'Okay. Did you make one?'

'Yep, but I can't tell you, or it won't come true.'

'Of course.'

'I can show you, though,' he said.

'I wish you would.'

SIXTY-TWO

He'd thought of everything. Fresh, cool sheets, candle-light, even Miles Davis on the stereo, which he said was a bit of a cliché but he hoped she wouldn't mind.

She didn't.

She also didn't mind the vine tattoo that wound from his left forearm up over his shoulder, across his back and down to his waist. She didn't mind the calloused pads of his fingers moving over her eager skin, or the way he lifted her hair off her neck to kiss her there, or the urgency of his hands, his hips, when it came to that. It was just as it had always been and just as it had never been – so much *more*, in some ways; they weren't kids anymore, in the flush of discovery. Now they knew their bodies, knew their preferences, knew where the bound-aries of pleasure had once been – and found out how to cross them. It was a reunion of spirit as much as flesh, and Meg savored every sensation.

They made love like it was an art, Carson pressing into her as if his life, *their* lives, depended on it. As if he could secure eternity.

And maybe he had. She would find out before very much longer, she thought, lying beside him later, when the candles burned lower in their votives and the moon shone in through the window. The answer she'd been looking for, the *how*, came to her in the lazy, happy aftermath of their lovemaking. Came unbidden, as if she'd needed only to be sated, physically and emotionally, in order to recognize it. She thought about it while she watched the moon rise higher and disappear above the cypress branches, deciding also *when*. And then she slept.

Idyllic days followed, reminding her of those summers when they were children, in the years before she knew how poor her family was, before Beth was born, before she got yoked with more responsibility than a girl that age ought to handle. She and Carson read and talked and ate and napped, and made love often. They went to their tree, where the swing still hung, and told every story of their days there that either of them could recall.

'Remember when the rope snapped with Jules on the swing, and she fell and broke her wrist?'

'Remember that time we caught the baby coral snake, and then you took it to school for show-and-tell?'

'Remember the striped horse blanket?' Carson asked, and then he produced it from behind the tree and made love to her there on the shady ground.

They talked about his idea to build a house on the far side of the groves, as if she would be there to see it, to share it, a harmless fantasy she didn't mind indulging. She practically lived in her pajamas – the John Deere T-shirt and a pair of light cotton drawstring pants. No shoes. No jewelry, save for her chain. No interruptions from pagers, no phone calls except from Savannah.

On Wednesday morning, their seventh day, Meg sat out behind the shed, the journal in her lap, the letter from the lab tucked inside. Next to her, Carson was reading *Moby-Dick*, which he said he'd always meant to read, having been given to understand that he and Ahab shared some personality traits. 'Intensity of purpose, obsession with the past – Gene told me to read it,' he said.

'You're not Ahab,' she told him, smiling at how intellectual he looked in his reading glasses. 'You know when to quit.' He said no, he never quit things, he just changed tactics. 'Okay, then,' she cautioned, 'just make sure you never end up in the whale's mouth.'

He smiled. 'Don't spoil the ending – and don't worry about me.'

'It's my privilege.'

She hadn't mentioned the letter to him, the tests, and she hadn't opened the envelope yet either. It had come while she and Savannah were away; when she'd found it in the pile of mail Manisha dropped off for her, she'd eyed the envelope as if it was a basket holding a cobra. What if the analysis said Brian was, in fact, Savannah's father? Each day, when she wrote in the journal, she thought about opening the letter, and each day she held off. She looked at it now, a white envelope, nothing at all extraordinary about it, and then, making sure that Carson was involved in his book, she slowly wrote across the back:

My love,

That day of my wedding, I deceived you and Brian both. I wanted your child if I could have it, a souvenir of the love I still had for you but thought was otherwise lost to me forever. Please forgive my selfishness. Inside this envelope are the results of a DNA comparison showing whether or not Brian is Savannah's father. I thought I had to know, but now I can't bear to look – I want so badly for you to be the one that I'd rather not know if you aren't.

If you decide to open this, know that neither of them is aware of the test; if she's your daughter, you can reveal the results or not – I trust your judgment. I know she loves you anyway.

Yours always . . .
Meg

She tucked the envelope back inside the journal. Later, she'd put it with the other letter she'd written to him, along with notes she wanted him to give to her sisters, to Manisha, to her father, notes she'd been crafting little by little these past several weeks. In the early mornings this week, she'd finished up Carson's letter while he slept. Better that *he* not know too much ahead of time, either; she couldn't bear for him to worry over it or, out of love, try to stop her.

She opened the journal to a fresh page and wrote to Savannah. The effort it cost her arm and hand was like that of trying to push a boulder across a field, but she wouldn't let herself get frustrated. There was time, yet.

At one AM the moon, not quite full but just as bright as if it were, was edging into the western sky. Meg slid out from under Carson's arm, trying not to wake him. He murmured, 'Hmmm? Where you going?'

'Bathroom,' she whispered. 'Go back to sleep.'

He drew her back down to him and kissed her sleepily. 'Love you.'

'I love you, too.'

He let go, and she stood, steadying herself with the bedpost, while he bunched his pillow and settled back into it, eyes closed. His lips were curved in the sweet smile she'd known almost all her life. He looked purely content.

Making her way down the stairs, she concentrated on not falling. She went into the kitchen, keeping the lights off. The journal, the letters, all were waiting for her in a drawer, and she put them out on the counter, next to the coffeepot. Thinking better of it, she moved them to the table; he wouldn't bother with coffee.

The door squeaked when she opened it, and she paused, then pulled it almost closed, stopping before the squeak could voice again. To make sure Carson wasn't following, she sat on a chaise and waited. A chorus of frogs and crickets and cicadas made the night surprisingly loud; an owl hooted repeatedly in the distance. Moonlight trickled between the cypress branches, making spiky shadows all around her. A truly beautiful night.

Relying heavily on her cane, she made her way through the grove. James McKay's careful upkeep made the walk easier than it might have been, the pathways kept trimmed and clear of fallen fruit and branches. Startled fruit bats winged past her now and then, surprising her at first. As she neared the lake, the frogs' song grew louder. Carolyn's dog, Shep, came trotting over when he saw her come out of the grove.

'Good dog,' she said, patting him. He sniffed at her bare legs and then sat when she stopped at the water's edge, as if to join her in admiring the glossy black surface, the reflection of the moon lighting the middle of the seven-acre lake.

Shep was the latest in a line of dogs trained to help James keep the lake free of alligators; the McKays still swam there occasionally, and had offered it for use to the two adolescent boys whose family bought her farm next door. Even so, she'd looped a powerful flashlight over her wrist before leaving the shed, and took it off now, shining it slowly across the water's surface in search of telltale pairs of shining eyes.

No gators. She sat down on the sandy bank, then lay back and looked upward into the clear night sky.

For eons, humans had done just as she was doing now, had compared the brightest stars to the dim ones, had noticed patterns and pictures, had wondered what it meant to be *here* instead of *there*. Uncountable stars, uncountable people . . . She was no different, in essence, from a woman of ten thousand years ago, a hundred thousand. All of them had the same chemistry she did, the same two hands, two legs, two eyes, two ears, the same capacity for hoping that death would bring a magnificent knowledge. Enlightenment. Completion.

How lovely that the sky, so black and vast, wasn't fearsome; it was surprisingly welcoming, in fact. The blackness wasn't real – the telescope on Mauna Kea had proven that to her. All the apparent black space was filled with ever more points of light. Endlessly, astonishingly filled; the blackness was an illusion, a limitation of human sight.

Somewhere out there, unseen, the energy of souls collected. Or maybe that energy was everywhere, like light.

She stood up – an awkward process even without her arm bound by the sling – and waded into the lake. It was warm in the shallows, like bathwater, but cooled a little as she moved farther out. Shep paddled in after her. When the water got deep for him, he turned back, but she kept on, walking slowly until the bottom dropped away beneath her. She lay on her back and pushed out to the middle, her left arm and leg doing most all the work, their counterparts little more than rudders. Finally she floated there, her hair streaming out around her head – halolike, she imagined, thinking how she would look from above.

When the idea of coming out here had first occurred to her, she'd thought of how babies, before their births, lived like amphibians in their underwater enclaves. Right up until their removal from the womb, babies were cushioned and caressed in a liquid nest. Their exit was a shock; they wailed, they sputtered, but soon they were soothed and quiet, ready to go on with whatever came next. It was reasonable to guess, then, that the process might work very well in reverse.

Tonight, the lake would be her mother.

After a few minutes, even her good arm struggled to do its part in keeping her afloat and her legs were begging for rest. She treaded water weakly for a minute more; then, when she couldn't keep her chin above the surface, she allowed her body to sink with relief.

Eyes open, breath held, she fixed the watery moon in her sights. The Holy Mother's nightlight, her mother had told her sisters and her, when they were young.

When her lungs, too, begged for relief, she gave up her air in a sudden, instinctive gulp, a weak, ineffectual thrash. Better this, she thought, calming herself, better this than months of slow-motion drowning in full, helpless view of the ones she loved.

The ones she loved . . .

She kept her eyes on the moon's reassuring light, and before long, sooner even than she expected, her body and mind relaxed. She wished only that she could tell Savannah and Carson, her father, her sisters, even Brian, how easy this was for her now, how right. Cradled and soothed, she lay still in the deep water and watched in fascination as the light grew closer, wider, welcoming, pure.

PART V

I hold it true, whate'er befall;
I feel it, when I sorrow most;
'Tis better to have loved and lost
Than never to have loved at all.
*   – Alfred, Lord Tennyson*

SIXTY-THREE

From her note on the kitchen table, Carson knew that wherever he found Meg, it would be long past too late to call 911. He did call, though, after Shep led him out to the lake and he saw her there. He called them first, then swam out to find her cool and lifeless but open-eyed and with a soft smile on her face. 'God, Meg,' he whispered. His body shook as if a fault line had collapsed inside him.

He pulled her to shore. He should have suspected she would do something like this. In her entire life, had she ever inconvenienced anyone on her own behalf? *She* was the caregiver; she was the one making sure things got done right. What she had done here was fitting – heroic, really. Like her note said, this way her wishes could not be mistaken or ignored. Even by him. Because God knew – and so did Meg – that if he'd been given a choice, he would not have been able to let her go. Not yet.

He dropped to his knees and held her there, sobbing, inconsolable, until the paramedics arrived.

'There now,' a uniformed young woman said

soothingly, unclasping Carson's arms. 'There, let us give you a hand.' A quick confirmation of what he'd said – that it was surely too late to save her – and a few questions followed; then they laid Meg on a stretcher as carefully as if she could break and carried her solemnly toward the house.

An hour or so later, after the Emergency Medical Service and police confirmed Meg's 'accidental' drowning, he watched in silence while a pair of kind men from the funeral home took her away. The morning – was it only eight-fifteen? – was blindingly empty as he went back to the shed to make the other calls.

She'd left careful instructions for him, including the details she thought might go into her obit, and an essay she'd written a month earlier on the fundamental human right to control one's own death – and a physician's obligation to enable that right. Her letter said she thought the local paper might want to run it, but he would do better, get it into the national media if he could.

Along with all of that, bound by a rubber band beneath which she'd tucked the photos they'd taken at the concert, was the journal she was making for Savannah. He studied the photos, then turned them over. *For Carson,* she'd written. *To remember.*

With trembling hands he dialed Spencer, then Kara, whom Meg had specified as second on the list. He hardly knew what he said to them, working on autopilot, guided by Meg's instructions. As predicted, Kara tearfully volunteered to call Brian, Julianne, Beth – and Savannah – and so now he sat, face in his hands, the envelope from the lab sitting in his lap.

His trepidation in opening it was at least as great as Meg's must have been. Was Savannah his daughter? What a terrifying, amazing possibility. He'd wondered about it sixteen years back, when his mother told him she'd seen the birth announcement in the paper. Wondered – and wished – only for a few days, deciding that Meg had done exactly the opposite of what she did: he figured she had made sure *not* to get pregnant by him, so that she would have a child who was unequiv-ocally Hamilton's heir. She had fooled him, had been as careful not to reveal her plan that day as she'd been this week. Fooled him for his own good. Protected him – protected *all* of them, more like. In the end, though, she had made sure he could know the whole truth, both times. In the end, she'd done it all for love.

He set the letter aside and spent the day on the chaise, ice tea at hand, reading the journal. Meg's letter gave him permission to read it if he liked, asking only that he make sure it got to Savannah directly, not through Brian or even Beth. That she'd thought of all these details, that she'd trusted him so well, made him cry, made him ache with longing to have her back. To say, *You amaze me.* To say, *Thank you.*

Her last entry to Savannah, which he came to late in the afternoon, was difficult to read. The writing was pinched and wobbly; it had obviously cost both heart and hand a lot of effort. It read:

> *Dearest daughter,*
> *This will be my good-bye.*
> *I suppose this entire journal sounds like a*

commencement speech combined with a wedding toast – I'm sorry about that. That's my job, though, to impart the wisdom of my years to you as you move, now, into this next major phase of your life: the time after Mom. God willing, it will be a long and wonder-filled time for you.

When you were very small, you used to ask me questions about everything that caught your attention. Why are toads bumpy? What makes flamingos' knees bend backward? Why don't my shoes grow when I water them? Always you wanted the answers, and I tried to give them. The best part of my day was my time with you, even if that time was a few minutes of sleepy questions before you fell asleep.

Once, you asked why, if scientists could tell from ninety-three million miles away what the sun was made of and how hot it burned, they couldn't figure out for sure what happens after we die. I didn't have a good answer for that. Death seems so simple, doesn't it? It is, after all, tied with birth for the most regularly occurring experience we living things have. I quoted Peter Pan to you: 'To die would be my greatest adventure.' You said that maybe scientists actually had figured it out – but hadn't figured out, yet, how to come back and tell everybody what they learned.

You'll ask, now, why I didn't stick around as long as my disease would allow; I'm a doctor, after all, sworn to uphold life – my own included, you might argue. Already you've read in here my views about becoming a prisoner of my disease, and how I couldn't stand to put you through the torture of watching me decline. Though my choice to stop here might feel premature to you, I absolutely believe it's the most merciful option. I can't imagine anything worse than the shared helplessness we all would feel as I died a slow death before your eyes.

This is a terrible thing that has happened to us, no question. When my disease was diagnosed, I thought of how awful my options were. How should I choose to die? It reminded me of those unfortunate people stranded in the World Trade Center on September 11, 2001, making the choice whether to die by fire or by fall. Terrible situations, horrifying choices – and yet there is a strange sort of freedom, a strange sort of honor, in choosing.

Last point: for most of my life, I kept my best memories, my truest feelings, locked up so they couldn't knock down the façade I'd built. A very pretty façade, a respectable one, but a façade just the same. Almost too late I learned that happiness exists only in what's real and true. I recovered those parts of my life these past months, and have been happier than ever before. So now it's time to go.

Go forward, and keep my words close to your heart, for no matter where I am when you read this, you will always be close to mine.

All my love,
Mom

Carson closed the journal and took off his glasses, fresh tears blurring his vision. The grove ahead of him was a wash of green spotted with orange, but he stood, put the letter from the lab in his back pocket, and walked to the lake once again.

He saw Meg everywhere: last night, limping along the path in the dark; at age six, hanging like a monkey from a tree branch; at fourteen, running ahead of him to the lake, barefoot and laughing, winning the race before he was halfway across. He would bring Savannah out here – no matter what the letter said – *if* he read it – and fill in the parts of the past Meg hadn't had time to tell.

With his heart in his throat, he stood at the lake's edge and carefully slit the end of the envelope with his buck knife. It wasn't too late, he thought as he drew out two pages, to drop them into the water, and no one, including him, the wiser. That would be the easiest thing, guaranteeing him a future with the fewest complications, expectations, obligations.

'—ations,' he said, hearing a thread of melody beginning to form in his head.

The paper seemed imbued with a power all its own, willing him to read. He took his reading glasses from his pocket and put them on. His hands trembled as he unfolded the report and scanned its business-like introductory paragraphs. Technical speak, explaining statistical probability, acceptable ranges. What did it add up to, though?

Shep came by and nosed him. Carson patted him distractedly, forehead furrowed – and then, he smiled.

They are not long, the days of wine and roses:
Out of a misty dream
Our path emerges for awhile, then closes
Within a dream.
                                        – Ernest Dowson

EPILOGUE

New Year's Eve

Johnny Simmons stood onstage, his arm around Carson's shoulders, a capacity crowd of nearly a thousand eager fans watching them. Savannah stood just offstage, braiding and unbraiding a length of hair. It was hard for her to breathe.

'. . . liked it so well here, he thought he'd stick around and hassle us on a regular basis,' Johnny was saying. 'Think we can stand to have him here a few times a year?'

The crowd roared their approval.

'Have it your way,' Johnny said, then he backed out of the spotlight and joined Savannah in the wings.

Carson, casual as always in blue jeans, had added a black vest over a tee-shirt for the occasion. He took the microphone from the stand and said, 'Thanks for being here to usher in the New Year with us! You know, I couldn't think of a better way to celebrate either!'

Whistles and cheers.

'I managed to convince the band that central

Florida's not such an awful place to winter, so we've been soaking up some rays and working on some new stuff for you all. Even Gene, our manager, hasn't heard it yet,' he said, shading his eyes so he could look down into the front row. Gene gave him a thumbs-up.

Johnny put his arm around Savannah. 'Ready?' he said in her ear.

She didn't trust her voice, so she just nodded.

'You'll be great, no sweat!' he said.

Carson was going on, introducing each of the band members. She was at the end of his list; her stomach tightened, and she was glad she hadn't been able to eat earlier.

'. . . a very special welcome to a guest of ours tonight, Miss Savannah Rae!'

She froze in place, and Johnny gave her a little push. There was no choice, the spotlight had her in its beam, and so she went to center stage, to Carson's welcoming hug. She kept her eyes on Rachel and Jonathan and her Aunt Beth, who shared Gene's table. Her practiced smile felt glued on her face. She *looked* good, at least, wearing jeans like Carson, and a lime green shirt that had a smiley face done in silver glitter.

When the crowd quieted again, Carson said, 'Tonight's Savannah's first public performance, but she's been playing guitar and writing songs for a good while now. The first number we're gonna do for you is a song she and I wrote together in honor of her mom, a very close friend of mine whom we lost back in June.'

He looked at her and nodded. 'All set?' he whispered.

504

'No,' she squeaked, but she smiled and went to take her spot to the left of the piano while he settled onto the bench. She slung her guitar strap over her shoulder, waited for Carson to cue the band, and then listened to the soft piano intro, her hands poised to join.

Carson told the audience, 'There's something about the New Year that both brings back the past and sets us on a forward path, don't you think? This song,' he said, 'is called "Salutation".'

The distraction that planning for this concert had brought Savannah, these past six months, was sometimes all that seemed to be tethering her to the planet. She hadn't been ready to lose her mom, and she was angry for weeks – until Carson finally persuaded her to read the journal. He said, 'I know you didn't want this to happen, but let her explain, Savannah.' He'd been so patient with her, biding his time while she hid out at Beth's because her dad was gone to Atlanta and London and DC and Boston.

And so she read the journal, read it three times over, and found her heart opening up again, like a morning glory in the rising sun. Being angry seemed selfish, when she put herself in her mom's shoes. Some people might think *suicide* was selfish – and sometimes it was, if you were ending a life that could be healed, could be fixed. If not – well, she could see how a person could at least keep their dignity by choosing their terms.

She was proud of her mom and forgave her for not saying a final good-bye in person; that good-bye would've been purely impossible.

505

There was Savannah's cue: She joined Carson for the next stanza, just the two of them playing and singing this part together.

Take just what you need, nothing more;
The road is long, and your shoulders are only so
*   wide.*
Take just what you need and close the door;
Every day you'll find fresh roses and wine.

The song was their way of passing on her mom's wisdom. When they were working on the lyrics, Carson said, 'It's like she gave us this song, don't you think? She wrote about how, if you lock away the past, you're denying or losing things that are worth keeping. But if you drag *too much* of your past with you, it just weighs you down.' Savannah couldn't see it so easily at first, but after a while things began to make sense. Even though she'd forgiven her mom, she still needed to make peace with her loss, not dwell on the past and let it sink her. She had to take charge of her own life again – she had to *live* it.

Carson had been so easy to work with – who understood her loss better than he did? And last month, when he came to see her at Aunt Beth's – where she had her own room done in the pale colors of the seaside – and sat her down and held her hands and told her what her mom had really been up to that day he saw them outside the lab, she was almost ready for his news.

'You know what a love triangle is, right?' he'd asked.

'Are you talking about you and Mom and Dad?'

He nodded. 'Only in our case, what we really have going on is a love *square*.'

'I don't follow,' she said. Did he mean including Val, whom he said had been hurt but gracious about their breakup?

'It's your mom, your dad, me – and you.' He showed her a letter from the lab, and what her mom had written on the envelope.

'A love square,' she echoed, taking it all in. She liked the image, all sides even.

Her dad – Brian – he was always going to be her dad; there was no changing her history – took the announcement pretty well, in public anyway. He didn't seem to be all that surprised. She was still figuring out how to rearrange her own thinking, how to fit Carson in alongside her dad. She found herself staring at Carson all the time, looking for herself in his features and the ways he did things. It helped a lot that she *liked* him. He was a great person – moody sometimes, but then so was she. There, that was another thing they had in common.

They came to the chorus again, and she looked out past the stage lights to the adoring faces of Carson's fans. She felt a lump in her throat, like pride; they liked her, they liked the song – she knew Carson wouldn't let her go astray, but still, the crowd's reception was reassuring. They were hearing the music and the words she'd helped to write, *hearing* it, responding, under-standing.

The song was coming to a close, moving from its

powerful middle strains to a duet of their voices and instruments once more. She leaned into the microphone, tears leaking from the corners of her eyes as she watched Carson, whose eyes looked bright with tears too, and thought of her mom. As she and Carson sang the last refrain, as she moved her fingers to the final notes of the song, she closed her eyes. The crowd erupted into cheers and applause, and she was sure that she felt her mom's warm hands on her shoulders.

'For you,' she whispered.

ACKNOWLEDGMENTS

What you have in your hands is my first published work ever. And so my first acknowledgment is to you, my dear reader, whose interest in reading this book and others is the reason *Souvenir* found its way into print. Thank you!

Aspiring authors are known to draft their acknowledgments pages well ahead of time, like movie people do acceptance speeches for the Oscars. When we finally succeed we are grateful to *everyone* – the grocery store clerks who rang up the wine we needed after a lousy writing day, the neighbor who didn't laugh when she saw us getting our mail while still wearing pajamas at 3 PM, the power company employees whose daily jobs keep the electricity going to our computers . . . Those people, however, won't be looking for their names here, and good thing, since I don't know most of them.

I do know, however, that I am *particularly* grateful to the following wonderful people:

My husband Andrew and our four boys – Ben, Daniel, Tom, and Nick, for never doubting I would get here and celebrating with me when I did. My mother, Sally Campbell, whom we lost way too soon but whose faith in me still warms my heart. My grandmother, Cele Heuman, along with Earl, Mary, Jerry, Bryan, Steve, Traci, and Susan Fowler, who never said 'if' but just waited for 'when'. Art and Adele Dellava, too. Faithful cohorts Pam Litchfield, Robert Egler, Mike Legeros, Peggy Houser, and Pat and Bernie Clarke. First photographer Larry Lubliner, and his brilliant assistant, Jean Lubliner. The members of NC's Best Writers (modest as you are): Sharon Kurtzman and Janet Silber, my so-called beta readers, then also Marjorie McNamara, Maureen Sherbondy, Louisa Jones, Lisa Morgan, Becky Gee, and Kathleen Laughlin – who gets a particular nod for suffering through grad school by my side. Thanks also to the creative writing graduate faculty at North Carolina State University: John Kessel, Wilton Barnhardt, Angela-Davis Gardner, Elaine Orr, John Balaban, and Tom Lisk.

My most humble thanks to the astonishing professionals without whom *Souvenir* might yet be a pile of marked-up pages in a box on my shelf: my agent, Wendy Sherman; my foreign-rights agent, Jenny Meyer; my editors, Linda Marrow, Maxine Hitchcock, and Charlotte Herscher; and wonder woman Keshini Naidoo, whom I suspect is an expert puzzle-solver.

In Conversation with Therese Fowler

What inspired you to write *Souvenir*?

Well, I was feeling pretty low, because I'd written a novel that was getting lots of praise but no offers of publication. I needed to be realistic: did I really have a future as a novelist? My part-time job as an editorial assistant was being converted to a faculty job in six months, so I needed to make some choices about my future.

At the core of that unsold novel was my fascination with the things people will do in the name of love. I thought, what if I use that fascination in a *love* story? The idea excited me enough to rationalize that I could wait until I was actually out of work to job hunt. I kicked around my ideas, then set about writing – and finished just before I was officially out of work!

When I knew the sort of story I wanted to tell, I took inspiration from my own life: the untimely loss of my mother, my wish that she had left some of her own words behind, my own struggles to fill all the roles girls and women are tasked with, and my belief that there is such a thing as true love. I'm an odd mixture of optimist, skeptic, realist, and romantic – which may explain what inspired me to take on the issues you'll find in *Souvenir*.

What research did you do writing *Souvenir*?

Medical facts, mostly, regarding Meg's career as an obstetrician and then her experience with ALS. I needed to understand the disease and all its manifestations, as well as the ways it's diagnosed, in order to know how Meg's story would go.

I was in my car one day and, just by chance, came across a radio program about ALS. It was very upbeat and featured a woman who had the disease. She said she was putting her faith in the possibility that some miracle treatment would allow her to beat the progression of her disease. I listened and, like anyone would be, I was impressed by the woman's optimism. But by this time I knew that the snail's pace of progress did not justify this level of hope – that so many others who'd begun with the same faith and optimism had inevitably succumbed to the disease just the same.

I thought, why don't we ever hear about the *other* kinds of heroes? People who, upon recognizing they face a losing battle, bravely choose to die on their own terms? There are so many more of them – *they* are surely the truer face of ALS, as well as other incurable, fatal diseases, and their stories too often go untold.

One of my early-draft readers took issue with Meg's decision to go 'before she had to'. It seemed selfish, she said. And so I made sure to show that Meg had a very narrow window of opportunity in which to carry out her own wishes. Her ability to do so made her a heroine in my eyes. She'd made a life of putting everyone's needs ahead of her own, so I thought it only right that, facing such an awful decline, she be allowed to put her own wishes first.

How do you write? Do you have a routine?

I write with my eyes closed and both hands behind my back, of course, like everyone else!

No, seriously, I wrote *Souvenir* while also working part-time, so there was some juggling involved. What I did then is what I do now – I simply steal what time isn't being used by something more pressing. Most of my work gets done while my sons are in school; I get my tea and my laptop and either work at home in our sunroom, or, occasionally, at a book store or café.

The writing gods blessed me with efficiency; once I know the general direction of a scene or chapter, I'm able to write it out pretty quickly. Which doesn't mean it's any *good*, of course; I revise continually.

Do you draw upon your own experiences with family and friends as you create characters and plots?

All writers do; it's our experiences and observations that fuel our ideas. My characters are never people I know, however. Rather, I start with an idea that's centered on *situation*, and the characters seem to grow out of it. The characters in turn determine what the plot becomes.

Before I committed to my writing dream, I earned a BA in sociology, with cultural anthropology as my sub-field. From that you can see I find people and society inherently interesting. A lot of what shows up in my stories is my subconscious dredging up bits of things I've studied, read, or observed, or done myself.

Usually it's *after* the writing is on the page that I can identify where something originated. The scene with Meg and her sisters rummaging through the box of photos, for example, was born of a similar event with my brothers and me, sorting out our mother's belongings shortly after she died.

How did it feel to place yourself in Meg's shoes?

Oh, wow. It was so tough, but so rewarding.

When I'm writing, I imagine myself as each of my characters, then try to experience the events through their perspectives. Being Meg meant I was living with regret and ambivalence and loss for *months*. But that gave way to a feeling of pride on her behalf.

I have such sympathy for Meg's struggle to do right, when there *is* no absolute 'right' to be done.

Which character do you feel most connected to and why?

All three main characters are very dear to me. I identify most with Meg as a mother and a wife and a daughter and a professional who's pulled in so many directions and is trying to do it all well. But I adore

Carson – maybe because he's a middle-aged, sensitive, slightly rough-at-the-edges creative soul like me! And as for Savannah, I can't help but remember how hard it was to be sixteen and how badly I wanted my life to be *mine* . . .

This question is too hard. Give me a different one!

Souvenir is a real tearjerker. What was the last thing to make you cry?

A repeat viewing of *Brokeback Mountain* recently did me in. My teenage sons don't quite understand this yet, but love is love! Oh, and that amazing scene in *Steel Magnolias*, where Sally Field's character M'Lynn breaks down at the cemetery – I saw it on TV not long ago, and it gets me every time.

At the risk of being accused of egregious self-promotion, I'll also admit that re-reading *Souvenir* made me cry, at least until it got to the copy-editing stage (when I'd seen enough of it for a while!). I told my husband, 'It's so sad – Meg wasn't cured *this* time, either!'

Who are your literary influences?

It wasn't so long ago when I was impressed by anyone and everyone who'd managed to get a book into print! Authors whose work impresses me in my pursuit of the art, though, fall into two categories: the 'masters', meaning they turn up on college reading lists everywhere, and contemporary authors whose work resonates with me.

First, I am a terrific admirer of Nabokov. He was a word-crafter and story-crafter of the first degree. I love Melville, especially *Benito Cereno* – like Nabokov, he understood so well the passions that motivate us, for good and ill. And Jane Austen, who was so clear-thinking and artful, and really knew how to write a page-turner using the affairs of the heart.

My contemporary influences are primarily the group of women I think of as the A-list: Anita Shreve, Ann Patchett, and Anna Quindlen. They write beautiful, moving, thoughtful stories a person can become immersed in – my favourite kind of fiction.

What are you working on next?

My new novel is a drama about a woman whose life has gone awry, though not quite so drastically as Meg's, lucky for her! In the midst of trying to get her feet underneath her again, she becomes emotionally trapped between her feelings for an old flame and his grown son. They all have secrets, skeletons in the closets, hidden agendas – it's great fun to work on!

Points for Discussion on *SOUVENIR*

'Do for love what you would not do.' What does this mean for all of the characters? Love is shown as bearing a great responsibility. Where does love stop and duty begin for each of the characters? Can love and duty be separated? Should Meg have tried?

Consider the mother–daughter relationships within *Souvenir*. Are they satisfactory and/or troubling?

Compare and contrast the different families within *Souvenir* – the Hamiltons, the Powells, the McKays. Are any of them traditional or dysfunctional? What do you understand by those terms? What are their values, concerns, and priorities?

'Memories are like spinning blades: dangerous at close range.' In what way is memory explored in the book? Are there false memories at work here?

Truths are revealed and documented in Anna's notebooks and Meg's journal. Meg is determined that she only writes the truth in her journal, even if she is unable to tell the truth in real life. How is the written word liberating and restrictive? What purposes do the note-books and journal serve for their authors and readers? Are Carson's lyrics his form of journal, a means of catharsis?

Was Brian wrong to 'buy' Meg's love? Why doesn't Meg leave him when she is free to?

Despite having everything money can buy, Savannah complains that 'most of the time she felt invisible'. In what way is her upbringing as challenged as Meg's?

Examine Meg's role as a doctor. Is it a help or a hindrance when she suspects she is ill and receives the diagnosis? Is there a terrible irony at work that her job is to help bring new life into the world while she is being robbed of hers?

'It was as if she, Meg Powell, would cease to exist at the end of the wedding ceremony, becoming some unfamiliar woman called Mrs Brian Hamilton.' Examine the issue of identity within *Souvenir*. In what ways does family help construct or destroy identity?

Meg and Carson's love endures despite the years apart and their very different life experiences. Is Therese Fowler saying that true love never dies or that people and their emotions never really change? How far do you think this may be correct?

Despite being a straight-A student, Savannah quickly becomes embroiled in Kyle's dangerous games. Is this mere teenage rebellion or a cry for help? Has modern technology – the internet, etc. – helped facilitate her behaviour?

What is Meg's attraction to Clay? What does he represent to her?

Every character has something to hide. What and why? What are the repercussions of their respective secrets?

Enjoyed *Souvenir*? Read more drama,
passion and tragedy in . . .

The Days of Summer

Jill Barnett

1957, Los Angeles, two speeding cars.

**A tragic accident, destined to change the future
of two families forever . . .**

Power . . . The Bannings are a privileged dynasty headed up by
ruthless oil magnate Victor. His grandsons, Jud and Cale, are being
groomed to take over his vast empire, and to acquire more wealth
– at any cost.

Passion . . . The Peytons are presided over by Kathryn, widow of
rock star Jimmy. Her daughter - the beautiful, feisty Laurel - has
been her obsession since Jimmy's death. But now Laurel's 17 and
there's one unexpected danger Kathryn hasn't planned upon: love.

Fate . . . Decades later, the two families cross paths again in the
most shocking way and the consequences are unimaginable....

Discover how it all ends in Jill Barnett's sizzling tale of feuding
Californian families.

'Drama, passion and romance collide in this perfect read for long,
lazy summer days.' Tasmina Perry, author of *DADDY'S GIRLS*

ISBN: 978-1-84756-002-5